D1288593

LIBRARY
North Central Michigan College
1515 Howard St.
Petoskey, MI 49770

There Is No End
to This Slope

a novel

RICHARD FULCO

F
F956

Copyright ©2014 Richard Fulco

All rights reserved. Worldwide paperback edition published in the United States of America by Wampus Multimedia, Winchester, Virginia. Copyright ©2014 Wampus Multimedia.

This is a work of fiction. Names, characters, places, and incidents are either the product of the author's imagination or are used fictitiously, and any resemblance to actual persons, living or dead, business establishments, events, or locales is entirely coincidental.

Jacket design by Wampus Multimedia (www.wampus.com). Author photo by Colleen Dougherty.

ISBN-13: 978-0-9797471-7-5
ISBN-10: 0-9797471-7-1
Library of Congress Control Number: 2014931621

Wampus Multimedia Catalog Number: WM-090

www.richardfulco.com

07/2014
Amazon
$16.19

"You Haven't Done Nothin'"
Words and Music by Stevie Wonder
©1974 (Renewed 2002) Jobete Music Co., Inc. and Black Bull Music
c/o EMI April Music Inc.
All Rights Reserved. International Copyright Secured. Used by Permission.
Reprinted by Permission of Hal Leonard Corporation.

"Papa Was A Rollin' Stone"
Words and Music by Norman Whitfield and Barrett Strong
©1972 (Renewed 2000) Stone Diamond Music Corp.
All Rights Controlled and Administered by EMI Blackwood Music Inc.
All Rights Reserved. International Copyright Secured. Used by Permission.
Reprinted by Permission of Hal Leonard Corporation.

"Nobody's Fault But Mine"
Words and Music by Otis Redding
©1968 Irving Music, Inc.
Copyright Renewed
All Rights Reserved. Used by Permission.
Reprinted by Permission of Hal Leonard Corporation.

"Rocket Man (I Think It's Gonna Be A Long, Long Time)"
Words and Music by Elton John and Bernie Taupin
©1972 Universal/Dick James Music Ltd.
Copyright Renewed
All Rights in the United States and Canada Controlled and Administered by Universal –
Songs of Polygram International, Inc.
All Rights Reserved. Used by Permission.
Reprinted by Permission of Hal Leonard Corporation.

"Da Ya Think I'm Sexy"
Words and Music by Rod Stewart, Carmine Appice and Duane Hitchings
©1978 Music of UNICEF, WB Music Corp., EMI Full Keel Music and Nite Stalk Music
All Rights for Music of UNICEF Controlled and Administered by EMI April Music Inc.
All Rights for EMI Full Keel Music and Nite Stalk Music Controlled and Administered by
WB Music Corp.
All Rights Reserved. International Copyright Secured. Used by Permission.
Reprinted by Permission of Hal Leonard Corporation and Alfred Publishing Company, Inc.

"Get Up (I Feel Like Being a Sex Machine)"
Words and Music by James Brown, Bobby Byrd, and Ronald R. Lenhoff
©1970 (Renewed) Dynatone Publishing Company
All Rights Administered by Unichappell Music Inc.
All Rights Reserved.
Reprinted by Permission of Alfred Publishing Company, Inc.

ACKNOWLEDGMENTS

As much as I'd like to think that I wrote *There Is No End to This Slope* solely on my own, I had plenty of assistance in various stages of the writing process. I'm grateful to those who willingly gave their time to read my book in its nascent stage as I was floundering in my apprenticeship, particularly Richard Roundy, Eugene Lim, Maria Hernandez-Ojeda and Helene Golay. Thank you.

Once I figured out how to write the novel, I needed to become better acquainted with my cast of characters and discover the story I wanted to tell. I can't thank Peter Melman and my editor Anne Horowitz enough for teaching me so many things about my book.

I'm forever indebted to Dr. Alden Brown who helped me deconstruct the novel at a time when it so desperately needed it. Thank you for your generosity, time and brutally honest critique.

In the seven years that it has taken me to complete *There Is No End to This Slope*, pieces of it have been written everywhere: bathrooms, subways, park benches, airplanes, concert venues, Hunter College High School and several coffee shops and the like, most notably the Tea Lounge, Southside Coffee, Brooklyn Commune, Le Petite Parisien, Montclair Library and the Cullman Center. Thanks for the tea, coffee and comfortable chairs.

So many people assisted me along the way. Many thanks to Mary Gannett and Henry Zook at BookCourt, Richard Nash, Elford Alley, Calvin Williams, Robin Cerwonka, Jack Perry, Linda East Brady, Roger Trott, Jeff Strickland, Lois Refkin, Desiree Jacobs, Jason Warburg and the Dougherty family.

Much love to my Mom and Dad for your undying faith in me.

A heap of thanks to Larry Papini and Jim Pace for your years of friendship and putting up with a heap of my shit.

I am grateful for Mark Doyon's friendship, integrity and wisdom. Thanks for your pithy replies to my neurotic emails. When I discovered that you and I share an appreciation for many of the same bands and songwriters, I knew everything was going to be all right.

Most of all I'd like to thank my biggest advocate, my partner, my best friend, my wife, Colleen Dougherty. You had enough determination and fortitude for the both of us. Without you, I don't think I could have persevered. You freely gave your time, support and love without any strings attached and that's more than I could ever offer in return. I love you, C.

September, 2013
Brooklyn, New York

For Chloe and Connor

I have dreamed of you so much that you are no longer real . . . I have dreamed of you so much, have walked so much, talked so much, slept so much with your phantom that perhaps the only thing left for me is to become a phantom among phantoms, a shadow a hundred times more shadow than the shadow that moves and goes on moving, brightly, over the sundial of your life.

—Robert Desnos

There is never any ending to Paris and the memory of each person who has lived in it differs from that of any other.

—Ernest Hemingway

THINGS

I was sitting at a colossal oak table in the center of the English department at Cobble Hill High School, watching a mouse that was stuck in a glue trap cling desperately to life. It had been struggling ever since my arrival, and when I could no longer bear to watch it suffer, I took hold of a metal trash can and crushed the life out of the poor thing. When I was sure that it was dead, I kicked the corpse into the can, swept a pile of droppings that looked like chocolate sprinkles on top of the remains and returned the can to its rightful place underneath the chairperson's desk by the windows.

Outside the vast, oval windows, across the East River, a stunning view of downtown Manhattan awaited my wandering eye. It was a year after the September 11 attacks, to the day, and the skyline was nothing short of impressive, even without the Twin Towers—although when I looked quickly at the spot where they had once dominated the horizon, I could swear that they were still there.

The summer had exhausted itself. There's nothing more debilitating than the "dog days" of August in New York City. The humidity is sheer harassment. For some New Yorkers, September offers a chance at renewal, and for a moment I wondered if I was in store for a rebirth; then I closed the window shade and returned to my wobbly chair.

While I was opening the boxes of grammar textbooks I had set down next to the haphazard piles of *The Great Gatsby*, *The Scarlet Letter*, *Of Mice and Men* and *The Adventures of Huckleberry Finn*, Emma Rue sauntered into the office, pulled a bunch of papers from her mailbox and, without even a glance, tossed them into the trash with the dead mouse. Her white off-the-shoulder summer dress offered a fairly good view of her tan, one that she had obviously been cultivating all summer long. The heels of her white leather shoes added at least four inches to her petite frame. The clacking was obtrusive; her sweet scent was distracting; her entire outfit, I thought, was fairly aggressive for a high school teacher. But I was really hot for her anyway. We'd met last spring, though I wasn't sure if she remembered me.

She flashed me a friendly smile, then located her friend, Pamela Flaherty, sitting at a nondescript corner desk where the tenured staff were situated, examining the hefty textbook that I had just sold to the chairperson. It was my first sale of the school year, and I thought it might be a sign that good things were heading my way. Maybe I could even parlay my newfound optimism into a date with Ms. Rue, so I pretended to be leafing through a catalogue, jotting down figures, titles and ISBN numbers, while I eavesdropped on her conversation, hoping that she would say something about me.

—Studying up on the comma, Pam?

—The friggin' queen wants us to teach a unit of grammar. Do you believe this shit?

—I don't know a thing about grammar.

—It's going to be drudgery trying to motivate these kids.

—The kids? Who's going to motivate me?

—I could care less about transitive verbs.

—Well, I won't waste my time with grammar. She'll never know.

—You better be careful. The queen is hot on your trail.

—You forgot. I have tenure now.

—That's right, Emma. Should I congratulate you?

—All I know is that the queen can't touch me.

The English faculty secretly referred to Dr. Elizabeth Hicks, the chairperson for more than twenty-five years, as the queen. Last spring, I had seen her and Emma Rue spar over the English Regents. Dr. Hicks had insisted that all eleventh grade students take several practice tests while Ms. Rue had argued that by simply completing the required reading and writing assignments throughout the year, her students would be sufficiently prepared to take the exam in June. I concluded that Emma's refusal to teach to a test had to do with the fact that she was more interested in exploring ideas and fostering critical thinking. When she referred to herself as "a *teacher*, and not an *instructor*" and told Dr. Hicks that "rules and regulations were meant to be broken; that's when the real learning takes place," I did everything in my power to refrain from shouting, "Atta girl, Emma!" I anticipated that my grammar textbooks would cause another clash between the two women.

I continued to eavesdrop, waiting to see if Emma would say anything about me, but she was busy amusing Pamela with stories of her summer vacation in Andalusia, Spain, where "the sparrows fly randomly around the Cathedral of Saint Mary in Toledo, Córdoba is heavenly white, Ronda's paradoxical canyons are both frightening and stunning and the narrow streets of Sevilla's Jewish Quarter are some of the most charming in the world."

—You should be writing for a travel magazine, Emma.

—Pam, I swear this year I'm going to finish my essay on the Aran Islands.

—I don't know how you pay for all of these excursions on a teacher's salary.

—"For everything else, there's MasterCard."

—You better be careful or you'll be like me: thirty-eight and still paying off school loans.

—I'll keep that in mind, Mom.

—Hey, I'm just looking out for you, babe.

—I know. You care about me. You really care. So who's the tall guy?

—He's the bastard who sold us these bloody textbooks. You should have seen him before, making a big stink about a mouse in a glue trap.

—Ooh, I can't stand those traps. They're inhumane.

—He repeatedly slammed the rodent with a garbage can. It splattered all over the floor.

—He was only euthanizing the poor thing, Pam.

—You don't understand. It wasn't as if he was trying to put it out of its misery, it was like he was trying to erase it from ever having existed. It was kind of freaky.

—Oh, whatever, Pam. Sometimes a little overkill is necessary. He's kind of cute.

—You think? Too thin for my taste.

—He has a great nose.

—What's up with his hair?

With Pamela Flaherty's rhetorical question, Emma Rue sauntered over toward me. I dropped my pen, turned away from the paperwork, and rubbed my fingers through my hair, which was longer than I usually kept it. I guess Pamela didn't care for it. Whenever I'm approached by a beautiful woman I can't help but whisper something like "Holy shit" or "Sweet Jesus" or "You've got to be kidding me." With Emma heading straight for me, I think I mumbled all three and something like "This has got to be my lucky day" for good measure. She chuckled, so she must have been flattered. My eyes worked their way up, and when I settled on Emma's face, I stared directly into her pale blue eyes, practically through her, my stare was so deep. My mouth was probably hanging wide open, another poor habit of mine.

—Hey there. Have you read any good books lately?

—Well, I, uh, sell a lot of good books. What are you interested in?

—That depends. What are you selling?

—I have whatever it is you're looking for.

—I'll take anything you have, a tragedy or a melodrama, just don't offer me a grammar textbook.

 —Too late. Dr. Hicks just ordered ninety copies of *Grammar the Easy Way*. Hi, I'm John Lenza.

 —Emma Rue. How come I've never seen you around here before, John Lenza?

 —You have, actually. Dr. Hicks introduced us last spring.

 —I'm sorry. I was so out of my mind last year. I've blocked everything out.

 —I admired the way you stood up to her.

 —We've had our fair share of bouts.

 —You must be a dancer.

 —Yes . . . well . . . uh . . . I dance. Well, I used to before I started teaching.

 —It's your posture.

 —It's your nose.

 —What?

 —It's epic. It turns to the left.

 —I suppose it does.

 —It's Roman.

 —*Roman* is really just a euphemism for *enormous*.

 —It represents strength.

 —Would you like to get a cup of coffee later?

 —I'd like that. I know this wonderful little place on Smith Street.

 —Which do you prefer, cappuccino or espresso?

 —Cappuccino. Espresso is too overwhelming.

 —Whipped cream or cinnamon?

 —Neither.

 —Funny, I thought you'd be a whipped cream kind of a girl.

 —Ooh, you're very naughty, Mr. Lenza. I like that.

I had Emma pinned against the elevator wall and wrapped her bronzed thigh around my waist. Her dress slid back onto her hip. The car shook. We lost our balance and fell into the fire alarm button. Bells rang while my hand groped her ass. Her arm was also around my waist; her fingers roamed the interior of my waistband. Bells continued to ring, but we didn't care. Eight flights of ecstasy. When the elevator door opened, we stepped off, still embracing, without missing a thrust of the tongue, and inched our way toward Emma's apartment door. In the hallway, a few inquisitive neighbors got a satisfying glimpse of our uninhibited lust. With the poise of ballroom dancers doing the tango, we drifted past the gawking spectators, twirled into the apartment, glided through the sparsely furnished living room and into the cramped and stuffy bedroom. We left the front door open. A lecherous old man lingered.

Emma pulled off my tie and shirt. After I kicked off my shoes, she unbuckled my belt and tugged my pants and boxers down to my ankles. I stood there in my white undershirt and black socks that were pulled up just below my knees, sporting a full-blown erection, looking completely unsexy, I'm sure. Before I could unzip the back of her dress, she pulled away, preventing me from further exploration. Emma, in a furtive manner, without the assistance of her hands, wriggled out of her white dress, keeping her heels on. She pulled me down on top of her and drew the shade with a perfunctory yank of the chain as if she had been through this routine a million times before. The bedroom was completely covered in darkness, so I couldn't see her breasts, her hips, her thighs, anything. I was really turned on by the unexpectedness of it all, but a little disappointed that I couldn't see her body. Lucky for me I had an active imagination to keep me going. I'm something of a voyeur. In fact, the previous spring when Dr. Hicks had introduced us, I had observed Emma's perky breasts underneath her tight, black, low-cut sweater. And there I was, five months later, resting comfortably between her legs with her perky breasts tucked inside my sweaty palms.

We stayed in bed for a while, under a silk sheet that was cool to my skin. While I was pretty content with the silence between us, Emma was determined that we make some kind of connection.

—I am so fond of you, John.

—Well, that doesn't sound half bad.

—You're adorable. You really are.

—You think I'm adorable? I like to think of myself as debonair.

—You're something. You know that?

—You're something too.

—I am really fond of you.

—Now *fond* is a word you don't hear every day. It's very nineteenth century, don't you think?

—What's wrong with the word *fond*?

—Oh, I don't know. I was hoping that you'd say you're addicted to me. Something like that.

—How's *I'm crazy about you*?

—That's slightly better.

—John, I have a confession to make.

—Only one? I have several, but you go first.

—What just happened—you know—between us—

—Something happened between us?

—Stop kidding around. You know—the intimacy.

—It was great.

—It was. It was also the first time I've ever made love.

—Wait. What?

—I'm not a virgin or anything, but I've never *made love* before.

—You mean, to a man?

—I've had *sex* plenty of times, but this was the first time it actually felt like *love*.

Was she trying to say that she was in love with me? She couldn't be. Could she? I didn't know how to respond, so I didn't say anything.

—I was with my ex, Josh, for a long time, but it never felt like that.

—I was that good?

—We were both that good. Together. Don't you think so?

—No, no, no, we were great together. It's just that I don't have much to compare it to.

—Do you mean you've never had sex?

—Hell, no, I've had plenty of sex. I just haven't been in love. Well, what I mean to say is that I was in love with a girl—still am—who is no longer—

I had been in love with only one person, my best friend, my childhood friend and next-door neighbor, Stephanie. She died just before our high school graduation, never having sex with a stranger—at least, I don't think she did—never experiencing the ambivalence of such an escapade, the rush of possibility, which I myself had just experienced for the first time. I'd had a handful of meaningless relationships since Stephanie died, but there was something about Emma that made me think that this time around things might be a little different.

—Don't tell me you're married.

—No, no, no, I'm not. I've never been. Have you?

—I lived with Josh for seven years, but we never tied the knot.

—And you guys broke up.

—Last week.

—Just last week?

—Things just didn't work out. I can't say I didn't try.

—So then you can't really be in love with me. I'm just a rebound.

—Who said anything about being in love? I'm just saying that it felt more like love than sex. Wait a minute. You were confessing something to me. It's your turn.

—Right. I was saying—I can't believe I'm going to say this—I'm in love with someone who passed away.

—Recently? And the wounds are still fresh. That sort of thing?

—No, a long time ago, actually, and I can't get over her. I know it's crazy but she's all that I know, all I've ever known, about love. I'm afraid to let her go.

—When did she die?

—1985.

—Wow! That's a long time to hold on to someone.

—You're telling me, but what can I do? I've tried to get over her but I can't seem to—

—I could no longer deal with Mr. Get-In-and-Get-Out—that's what I called Josh because he only cared about his sexual needs—so I asked him to leave. Haven't heard from him since.

—It's only been a week. He might come back, you know.

—Maybe whereas your ex never left. She's still here.

—That's kind of true, but we were never really together.

—Oh, an unrequited kind of thing.

—Yeah, something like that.

—Sounds to me like there might be some lingering guilt.

—That's kind of true too. Are you sure you're not a psychologist masquerading as an English teacher?

—Nope, just somebody who has read a lot of novels.

—Stephanie loved to read.

—Okay, enough about the Ghost of Christmas Past. What do you say we give this thing a shot?

—What thing?

—You and me.

—You don't think I'm a deranged lunatic for being in love with a dead girl?

—No, I think you're a deranged lunatic for killing that mouse.

—You don't understand. It was dying. I just helped it along.

—Forget about that. I think it's kind of sweet.

—Kind of sweet that I killed a mouse?

—No, that you're still in love with your dead friend . . . What's her name?

—Stephanie.

—Right, Stephanie. It's a little deranged, I'll admit, but maybe I can help you get over her.

We stayed in bed all night. I stroked Emma's long brown hair and stared into the darkness while she burrowed into my underarm, sleeping off the unpredictability of the afternoon, probably sick of hearing me ramble on about my obsession with a girl who died in 1985. Who could blame her? It had been a promising day, and I didn't feel like sleeping. If I went to sleep, the day would end. With all that talk of Stephanie, I started thinking about her, something I was wont to do whenever I was feeling content.

Stephanie spent countless hours in the public library, clasping a book in both hands, inches from her dark brown eyes that you couldn't clearly detect underneath her long, jet-black bangs. She was the only person I knew who actually read all of the books that were assigned to us in high school, including the three books we had to read every summer. Stephanie absolutely hated *Madame Bovary*—it wasn't so much Flaubert's writing but

7

the novel's superficial protagonist, Emma Bovary, who caused Stephanie so much grief. While our twelfth grade class discussed the esteemed nineteenth-century novel, it was clearly apparent to all of us, including our teacher, Mrs. Simmons, how much Stephanie despised everything about the tragic heroine who is disillusioned by the realities of life, ambivalent about her own desires, and eventually retreats into a fantasy world. Whenever Stephanie started to snicker, we knew we were in for one of her tirades.

—What's on your mind, Steph?

—What's wrong with this chick, Mrs. Simmons?

—What do you think is wrong with her?

—She's not content with anything. Nothing. Absolutely nothing satisfies this infuriating woman.

—I guess that's what makes her a tragic figure.

—I get that, Mrs. Simmons, but she's so pathetic.

—We must look at Emma Bovary through an appropriate cultural lens. The time period she lived in—

—She didn't have many options. Am I right, Mrs. Simmons? That's why she married Charles Bovary in the first place.

—That's right, John. A woman's options were limited.

—Yeah, but she wasn't happy with Léon Dupuis either. Or the other guy. Nobody made her happy. Nothing made her happy.

—Perhaps, Stephanie, that's because Emma doesn't appreciate the little things life has to offer.

—That's because she's a self-loathing, entitled little bitch.

—Mind your language, Stephanie, but you've got a point. Perhaps you can write about Emma's sense of entitlement in your next paper.

—She doesn't know what she wants. How could she not have the faintest idea? I don't get it. I want to be a painter. It wasn't hard for me to figure that out. That's what I do. That's what I love to do. Emma just loves to pity herself.

—I think you're being too hard on Emma Bovary.

—I'm sorry, Mrs. Simmons, but I don't have sympathy for a shallow woman with a sense of superiority who takes her own life because she doesn't know what she wants.

—Wow, you should talk, Steph. You talk about suicide all the time.

—John, that's enough.

—That might be so, John, but it's a curiosity of mine. That's all. I'm not half as serious about it as you are.

—Okay, enough, you two. Stephanie, you have certainly displayed more passion for Mrs. Bovary than she ever did for herself.

Stephanie's insights and intense rants kept us all awake during first period. She was the smartest kid in the class, if not the entire school, and the only teenager I knew who really cared about literature and art. I admired the fearless way she offered her opinions.

In contrast, Emma had an obscure way of communicating, as I was to learn later on. She often said one thing but meant something else entirely. Saying she was "fond" of me was probably her roundabout way of conveying that she could really fall for me if she only allowed herself to. Calling me "adorable" most likely meant that I was average looking, not debonair. And my nose wasn't Roman; it was just big.

MORE THINGS

I was five years old when my father moved my mother, sister and me from Bay Ridge to Staten Island, but I moved back to Brooklyn, much to my family's dismay, when I enrolled at Brooklyn College right after high school, and I stayed there when I dropped out after one disastrous semester. "We left Brooklyn to give you a better life. Why would you wanna go back to that shithole?" I'd lived in New York my entire life. It was what I knew, and that familiarity had a way of making me both comfortable and restless.

My family was only fourteen miles away, just south of the Verrazano Bridge, but they may as well have been in South America. They never hopped in the Cadillac to visit me, which was okay because it sort of exonerated me from having to join them for Sunday afternoon dinners, at which I would be obligated to stuff myself on antipasto, lasagna, meatballs and braciole.

When I moved into Emma's one-bedroom apartment in the East Village after just two weeks of dating, I thought my mother was going to throw herself off the Verrazano. My father told me that I was making a "colossal mistake," and looking back he was probably right, but at the time it was exciting to be with someone like Emma and kind of good to be out of Brooklyn. We were moving quickly, but that was the way Emma operated: swiftly, impulsively and often recklessly. Aside from breaking up with her boyfriend of seven years, giving up dancing to teach high school English, and her distaste for Sunday evenings because of her dread of the workweek, I really didn't know much about Emma Rue. What did that say about me? Was I also impulsive and reckless?

During our first three months together, our lives were set on autopilot. From Monday to Friday, we woke up at seven, showered, made coffee, and rode the F train to work. The book distributor I worked for, EverCover, was near Cobble Hill High School, so occasionally we met up after work and rode back home together. We'd take a walk along the FDR Drive and eat around eight. After dinner, we drank red wine while I caught up on some paperwork and she graded papers. We watched a little television and eventually fell asleep by eleven. We got up around nine on Saturdays; had breakfast at our favorite diner on First Avenue; walked through the East Village; stopped in a few trendy boutiques, used bookstores and record shops; sat in Tompkins Square Park with a turkey sandwich and iced coffee; went to a movie or play; had dinner at ten; drank red wine, made love and fell asleep around one. We stayed in bed until noon on Sundays; Emma read *The New York Times* while I read a novel or play. Around one, while Emma stayed in bed, I went to the bagel shop for onion bagels, lox and a couple of cappuccinos. Later, I watched some kind of sporting event on television while she wrote in her journal. We ate dinner at seven, drank red wine, watched a movie (no action films or chick flicks, as agreed), complained about our jobs and fell asleep around eleven. Everything. Together. Press play and watch us go through the motions. The routine provided us with structure, which we perceived to be happiness, when all we really were was distracted.

I was determined to make some kind of connection with the woman I was living with, so one Sunday night, after we drank a couple of bottles of Merlot as we complained about our jobs, just before Emma fell asleep, I asked her a bunch of questions.

—John, it's not a big deal. I don't like jazz. So what? You don't like dance music.

—Please tell me you're joking, Emma. Dance music?

—I love Madonna, especially her earlier stuff. Kill me.

—I have a couple of questions I need to ask you.

—John, please don't make a big thing out of this. These are healthy differences. We'll teach each other new things and learn from each other.

—Elvis or the Beatles?

—I don't want to take your silly quiz.

—Just answer the question, Emma. Indulge me.

—I don't want to contribute to your neuroses.

—Please, it's important to me. Elvis or the Beatles?

—Mariah Carey.

—What? What? What? Okay, I'll try to keep an open mind. Iggy or David?

—Never heard of them.

—Oh, man. Indian or Chinese food?

—I thought we were talking about music.

—Just answer the question, please. Indian or Chinese?

—Neither.

—New York or Paris?

—Madrid.

—Faulkner or Hemingway?

—Woolf.

—Boots or sneakers?

—Stupid question. Heels, of course.

—Jeans or skirts?

—Skirts. Short and tight. I am from Long Island.

—Theater or film?

—Dance.

—This could be colossal, Emma.

—Don't make a big deal about such trivial things, John.

—In the long run, our differences could make a difference. That's all I'm saying.

—You're putting too much credence in this ridiculous quiz of yours.

—I consider it a game.

—Whatever it is.

—I hope you're right, Emma.

—I know I am.

The next morning, Emma was quick to point out that I had been arrogant. Sure, I could be somewhat pretentious at times, but I was entitled to my opinions, wasn't I? I just failed to understand how an intelligent woman could have such shitty taste in music. Dance music? Really?

I should have taken her love for Madonna as a sign; there were countless blood-red flashing signals and titanic billboards, but I was pretty adept at being completely blind to them.

When I was a boy, I wrote and performed my plays in my backyard. They were more like skits, Abbott and Costello routines that contained more than a fair share of Chaplinesque pratfalls. Stephanie helped me produce them: she decorated the sets, coordinated the costumes and organized the props. She also designed the flyers that we posted on telephone poles and tucked inside the newspapers I delivered after school. We stood in front of the corner deli, handing out flyers to the neighborhood kids. Admission was a quarter. My mother sat in the back with her friends, smoking and chatting about the meat they were defrosting for dinner. Meanwhile Stephanie's mother, whose husband recently shacked up with his secretary, sat by herself. The younger kids, licking snow cones and fudge pops, fidgeted in the front row. Stephanie sat among them, feeding me the lines I forgot, cheering me on and laughing at every joke. She had a kind of gruff snort (for a girl) that infected the other children. No matter the size of the audience, Stephanie's laugh made me feel like I was performing on a Broadway stage.

Aside from writing and performing my plays, I loved baseball. After splitting the box office with Stephanie, I spent every cent from my shows and paper route on baseball cards. I had always been a diehard Mets fan, supporting them through some very lean years. The Yankees bought their teams while the Mets (I liked to think) represented the blue-collar ethos of my Italian American heritage. Pack after pack, searching for my favorite Mets: Bud Harrelson, John Stearns, Ed Kranepool, Dave Kingman and my favorite player, Lee Mazzilli. Mazzilli, or simply Maz, as New Yorkers affectionately called him, was from a working-class Sheepshead Bay neighborhood. He wasn't extraordinary by any means. He was no Joe DiMaggio, never hit more than sixteen home runs or had more than seventy-nine runs batted in, but he played hard and gave it all he had. Mediocre ball players like Lee Mazzilli influenced me more than anyone else when I was a kid.

Despite having written plays as a boy, it wasn't until senior year of high school, when Stephanie turned me on to Samuel Beckett and Harold Pinter that I first fell under the spell of a playwright. My family didn't understand my desire to write and perform. They understood things like defrosting meat and baseball. Fortunately, I was fast and could play the field, so they forgave my peculiar obsession with theater. Baseball and theater. Both need an audience. And people desire drama. Having always been a frustrated performer, I too desired drama, and that's why I was drawn to Emma Rue. As long as she sat in the front row during my show, fed me lines, cheered me on and laughed at all my jokes, I would go along for the wild ride, no matter how treacherous the road ahead was going to be.

One frigid Sunday evening in January, I tried again to connect with Emma. The day began routinely enough. We slept late, read in bed for a while and enjoyed onion bagels, lox and cappuccinos under a thick comforter that made me sweat like a pig. Later, I took in a football game while she wrote in her journal. We ate dinner around seven, drank red wine, watched a movie, and while we were complaining about our jobs, I told Emma to put down her glass, so I could make another confession.

—My real name is Gianni.

—Yeah sure, John, Johnny.

—Not Johnny. Gianni. G-i-a-n-n-i.

—So, you've got Italian roots.

—Yeah, but nobody calls me Gianni, except my mother. Stephanie did too. It's John. Always John.

—Do you think you're the only person in the world who has issues with his roots? Join the club.

—It's a big thing. Don't you think?

—It's only as big as you enable it to be, Gianni.

—Don't call me that, Emma. I told you I don't like it.

—This is pussy shit, Gianni. Get over it.

—I'd really like to.

—You've got bigger issues, like holding on to that dead girl. It was a long time ago. You had nothing to do with her death.

—Actually, that's the thing.

—Don't tell me. You killed her?

—This is not a joke, Emma.

—Okay, what happened, John? Tell me. Maybe I can help you.

—We used to play a dangerous game. I made it up. And one day it got out of hand . . . You know, I don't think I'm ready to tell you just yet.

—Have you been bottling this up all this time?

—I tried to tell a priest once.

—A priest? What the fuck do priests know? Tell me, John. Go ahead. I'm listening.

—Some other time, Emma. I appreciate it. I'm just not ready to go there.

—Okay, I understand. When you're ready, I'm here. Can I at least call you Gianni? I really like it.

—I prefer that you don't.

—Wow. I don't know what to say.

—You're pissed.

—Hurt. I'm hurt, John. That's all.

Later that night, I was sitting on the bedroom floor, dreading my Monday morning commute to EverCover Books. Emma was wrapped in the thick comforter on an unmade bed, sleeping off her drunkenness, something that I had discovered she was prone to do on Sunday evenings. I had placed a trash can just below her head for fear that she might suffocate on her own vomit. Too much self-pity. Too much life. Too much Merlot. Too many "things." I feared that I had gotten on the Cyclone at Coney Island and I couldn't get off. I tried to commemorate the moment with a poem, but my emotions overwhelmed my pen. "Watching Emma Break" never moved beyond the title. An idea that failed to give rise to expression. That was nothing new for me. I hadn't written a thing since the plays I'd performed in my backyard. I tore up the sentimental drivel and threw it in the trash can underneath Emma's head.

While Emma slept, grinding her teeth, I stopped struggling with the poem, opened a bottle of Pinot Noir that I had been saving for a special occasion, and played my favorite Beatles album, *Revolver*. I listened to Jazz whenever I was feeling pensive; classical indicated that I was feeling creative; Motown conveyed my happiness. The Beatles were usually in heavy rotation whenever I was feeling hollow. Only the lads from Liverpool—John and Paul's catchy melodies, their competent harmonies, George's tasteful guitar solos and Ringo's reliable drumbeats—could haul me out of the doldrums. They failed miserably that night.

Despite the millions of blood-red flags that had been waving before me, I asked Emma to marry me—or maybe she asked me, I don't remember. Either way, Emma thought it would be "great fun." She was sick of calling me her boyfriend. A gentleman my age required something more sophisticated: *husband*. I hoped that our marriage would prove to my family that I had finally become a grown-up, capable of holding down a full-time job and fending not only for myself but for my wife, too. My plan, unfortunately, backfired: the Lenza family was convinced that I was behaving like a child and spiting them by marrying the wrong girl. Emma wasn't Italian; she didn't cook or clean; her parents were divorced; her father was a drunk; she didn't want children; she spent money like a drunken sailor; hell, she *was* a drunken sailor. In the end, if I were to disregard my family's wishes and marry her, they demanded at least to have their fifteen minutes of fame at some gaudy affair in a cheesy catering hall.

My older sister, Gina, as matron of honor, aspired to walk down the aisle alone, propose a toast to the bride and groom, maybe even catch the bouquet and hand it off to an unwed girl.

My mother desired to shine in her vital role as mother of the groom: the grandiose sequined gown, the glittery, overpriced shoes, the expensive haircut, makeup painted on so thick she'd be the envy of every tacky lady behind every Clinique counter in the world. There would be the critical slow dance with her son to some third-rate song, maybe Bette Midler's "Wind Beneath My Wings," while hundreds of guests looked on, uncomfortable in their formal attire, the men in cheap suits and hideous ties, the women in ostentatious dresses and cumbersome heels, an amalgam of offensive cologne and sweet perfume, pinky rings and gold necklaces, hair gel and lipstick. The bridesmaids wearing chintzy, frilly gowns they'd never wear again, the incessant toasts, the ornate cocktail hour, the hackneyed wedding band, the smoke machines, the cutting the cake, tossing the bouquet, clinking of wineglasses, the ridiculous line dances, the entire tasteless extravaganza.

My old man was more concerned with matters of restitution. He believed that his attendance at countless weddings over the years—nearly all obligatory business affairs with brides and bridegrooms he didn't know—had entitled his children to a gift of their own, preferably a handsome check.

I would have liked a simple ceremony and modest reception with just our immediate family and friends, but Emma thought that it would be more romantic if we eloped. I knew that our elopement would further devastate my family, but I didn't want to disappoint Emma, so I went along with her demands, which included writing our own vows and tying the knot at city hall.

Even in the dead of winter, Emma tanned herself at the salon and wore the white off-the-shoulder summer dress she had been wearing the day we met. Her four-inch heels restricted her from taking normal strides in the snow and ice, so we were compelled to take baby steps all the way to the courthouse. I was thoroughly wrinkled in the black pinstripe suit I kept in the back of the closet. My narrow red tie fell just above my abdomen. Emma pleaded with me to cut my hair and shave my beard off. I compromised with her, trimming them both for the occasion. Emma pinned a slightly wilted white carnation to my lapel, and I presented her with an average bouquet of red and pink carnations.

The sterility of the New York City courts, the complete antithesis of elegance, failed to spark anything remotely passionate in either of us, so Emma suggested that we scrap the vows and get the proceedings over with as quickly as possible. I had slaved over those vows! It was the first piece of writing I had completed since my childhood plays, and I pleaded with her to let me recite them. Eventually, we struck another compromise: they'd be read later that evening at the bed-and-breakfast in Cold Spring where we'd reserved a room for the night.

The frail judge threw on a wrinkled powder-blue gown that must have been hanging in her chamber since 1972, ran a brush through her frizzy gray hair, stepped onto a wobbly podium and went through the motions. "By the power vested in me by the State of New York, I now pronounce you husband and wife." When it was over, we shuffled off to Grand Central Station and hopped on the Metro-North. As the train made its way around a sharp bend, I viewed the frozen Hudson River through a grimy window, thinking about the mistake we had just made. When I turned to Emma for reassurance, she was busy writing in her journal and, without looking up, told me to take a nap.

After an overpriced, mediocre seafood dinner that left us hungry later on, we nearly froze on our walk back to the bed-and-breakfast. Emma drank too much Merlot and fell asleep early, while I, basking in the glow of the fake fireplace, took off my wedding ring, which was too big, put aside the want ads—I was under the illusion that I was going to quit EverCover Books—and wrote a letter to Stephanie. Since I'd met Emma, I had been thinking about Stephanie more than ever, but I'd never actually sat down and written her a letter. It just seemed kind of natural to me.

February 5, 2003

Dear Stephanie,

I got married today. It wasn't anything spectacular. We went to City Hall and five minutes later we were man and wife—that's not politically correct nowadays, is it? When we played house, way back when, we were "man and wife." You would have been proud of me. I wrote my vows. Emma—that's my wife—promised that we'd read them when we got to the bed and breakfast, but she drank too much and fell asleep. She doesn't love me the way you love me. I have to go now. It's getting late and we're leaving early tomorrow morning.

Love,
Gianni

She doesn't love me the way you love me. I thought about that sentence or a long time that night. Actually, I've never stopped thinking about it. I tore the letter into a million pieces and tossed it in the trash can underneath the desk. No need to cause Emma any unnecessary pain. She already knew how deranged my attachment to Stephanie was.

When Emma and I returned home, everyone greeted us with downright contempt, as I had expected. Emma's parents reluctantly acquiesced to our marriage—"At least she finally settled down"—whereas my entire family took it as a personal affront. I didn't think they would ever speak to me again. My father was deeply insulted that Emma hadn't taken my surname or at least a hyphenated form—Rue-Lenza: "What kind of a girl doesn't take her husband's name? It's what you're supposed to do." Meanwhile, my mother suffered post-traumatic stress disorder: "Italian girls make the best wives. Your grandfather married an Italian girl. Your father married one. You're supposed to marry your own kind. It makes life easier. There is an understanding. Even your sister, who dated Colin all those years, eventually came to her senses, dumped the drunken Irishman and married one of her own before it was too late. You'll come to your senses one day."

Emma's brother, Thomas Rue, held his thirtieth birthday party at a fashionable restaurant in Union Square. The entire Rue clan was in attendance, including Emma's parents, who put aside their differences for one evening and drove in from Valley Stream together. It was the first time Emma and I had stepped out as a married couple. Emma had been drinking her new favorite cocktail, a cosmopolitan. After one cocktail, her inhibitions faded and she was the most charming person on the planet. Four cocktails later, she could become volatile and unpredictable. I had nothing better to do, so I kept count. One before cocktail hour. Two during cocktail hour. One during her indiscreet family story, just prior to dinner. Thomas might have been the guest of honor, but Emma seized the spotlight from her younger brother early in the evening. She had her hand on the chest of a tall, tan man in a beige double-breasted suit who had his arm around her waist when she launched into her toast.

—My little brother, the little darling, is all grown up now. Thirty years old. You're a man, darling, but I'll always remember you as that geeky little kid who played with his microscope all day long. He was always looking at things: worms, moths, leaves, hair. It was a tragic day for him when his microscope broke. For all of us. Dad, who had one too many, was yelling at me for some insane reason. I think I was at Tony's house after curfew or something like that. He was so pissed off that he came looking for me. He dragged me home and went through his typical misogynistic bullshit, telling me that a seventeen-year-old girl should not be out late at night. That a girl should be home with her family, where she belongs. He slapped me, called me a slut and flung me into my room. Tommy, the little darling, came to my defense. He took a swing at him. Can you imagine? Dad just laughed and told him that he was lucky he had missed. But that didn't stop little Tommy from taking another swing at Dad. This time Dad retaliated. He didn't lay a hand on the darling boy on account of Tommy's epilepsy. Instead, he grabbed Tommy's microscope, brought it to his workbench, took hold of a hammer and smashed it into a million pieces. Do you remember that day, Tommy? And now my little brother is thirty years old. He's still throwing punches, though. Aren't you, Thomas? My father? Well, let's just say he hasn't changed very much. No hard feelings, Dad. Happy birthday, Tommy.

Her monologue, however alienating, was most impressive from a performance standpoint. It was a cross between Mercutio and Richard Pryor, a kind of Shakespearean stand-up comedy routine. Her forced chuckle—which was insufferable and my second clue that she was smashed—failed to settle the stunned crowd. A few of the older women escaped to the buffet table. Emma grabbed the hand of the tall, tan man in the beige double-breasted suit and draped his arm over her shoulder. Just looking at them together like that, I bet people thought they were married, that he was John Lenza.

When Emma broke into tears, the tall, tan man gave her a tender hug. At that point, those folks who had been lingering finally dispersed. I watched Emma cry on the tall, tan man's shoulder. My third clue that she was drunk. He put both of his arms around her waist and kissed her head. She took a long cigarette from his gold case, and he lit it for her. And that was my fourth clue.

We hadn't eaten yet and she was already out of control. I feared the worst was yet to come. I had to do something before she embarrassed herself (and me) any further, so I put on my compassionate, concerned husband face, picked up a couple of plates from the buffet table and made my way across the dance floor to where Emma was still hanging on the arm of the tall, tan man, chuckling, slurring her words and calling everyone *darling*.

—Hi, Emma. The food is out. What do you say we hit the buffet table?
—I'm not hungry. But thanks anyway, darling.
Before the tall, tan man could fully extend his hand to greet me, Emma

had stepped between us and planted a big, wet kiss on my cheek. I tried to pull back, but I was too slow. I hated sloppy, wet kisses, and she liked giving them, especially when she was sloppy drunk. She gave the tall, tan man a sloppy kiss on his forehead, and he wiped it off with the back of his hand.

—You'd better eat now before all the good stuff is gone.

—I just said that I wasn't hungry, John.

—I think you should have something to eat . . . you've already had four drinks. I don't want you getting sick—

—Have you been counting my cocktails again?

—You know how you get when you've had too much to drink.

—I already have a father, John. I don't need another one, that's for sure.

Without a wave, a wink or a nod, the tall, tan man made a quick getaway. Maybe he knew what was coming. Emma called out to him, but he didn't turn around, strolling into the crowd and disappearing from view. When Emma turned to spar with me some more, she spilled her cocktail all over my wrinkled black pinstripe suit.

—Who was that?

—What is your problem, John? This is a party. I'm trying to have a good time.

—Is he an old boyfriend?

—What is your problem?

—You know how you get when you've been drinking, Emma.

—No, I don't know how I get. How do I get? Tell me, Gianni.

—Don't call me that. You know I hate it.

—Oh, right. That name is reserved for your dead girlfriend. You've got bigger issues to deal with than my drinking, John. Believe me.

It was terribly wrong of me to have thought that I could control Emma's drinking, but having an acute messiah complex, I never stopped making an effort. Her drunkenness had a way of pushing all of my buttons. I think I was really trying to save my own life rather than hers.

As if we hadn't already been a spectacle, she began shouting that I was a control freak. Emma's mother stormed into the bathroom while Mr. Rue strolled over to the bar. I put Emma's plate down and grabbed hold of her arm before she could race off after him. When I tugged her by the elbow, a struggle ensued, and I dropped my plate. It shattered across the dance floor. I thought about cleaning the mess, but I felt it would be best that we leave before there was any further damage, so I dragged her toward the door. I think I saw the tall, tan man and Thomas raise their glasses, toasting our performance. Maybe they had been in my situation before, having lugged a totally ripped Emma home from a bar on Long Island, watching her puke her guts up all over her bed. We made it to the door, just past her grandparents, who were waltzing in front of the deejay, when Emma dropped to her knees.

—You're fucking hurting me. Let go of my arm.

—Will you get up? Everyone's looking at us.

—Why must you ruin my good time?

—You've ruined it for yourself.

—No. No. You. You have ruined it. Everything.

—What are you talking about?

—You have ruined us.

—You don't know what you're saying. You're drunk.

—I know what I'm saying, John.

—Come on. Get up.

—You've destroyed us.

—You drink too much, Emma.

—And you don't love me the way you love your dead friend.

It stung like hell, but she was right, though I wouldn't tell her as much. We bolted out of the restaurant and walked off in separate directions, but then I turned back and pursued her down a deserted Sixteenth Street, where she came to a sudden stop, stumbled backward into a parked car, collapsed into the gutter and vomited. I helped her up. She wiped her mouth on her sleeve, gave me a sheepish look and started to cry.

—I don't know what's wrong with me, John.

—There's nothing wrong with you.

—I broke my heel. These are brand new.

—We'll bring them to the shoe guy.

—Will you help me?

—Sure, I'll take them there myself.

—I need your help with the drinking, John.

—I'm not sure what I can do, Emma.

—What the fuck, John? You're my husband.

—And your husband is telling you that you need real help, more than I can offer.

—Help me, John. I've been trying to help you get over your dead girlfriend. Help me with one of my things.

I couldn't really help her; she needed to help herself, and as much as I distrusted therapists, I firmly believed that she was in dire need of professional help. I'll admit I needed help too. I wasn't prepared for what was happening to us. I hadn't signed up for all of the dysfunction. We'd both gotten ourselves into this mess, and we'd have to do the hard work to get ourselves out, but I wasn't sure either of us was up to the task. I gave Emma the number of my old therapist, Dr. Miller, whom I'd consulted after I dropped out of college, when my life was spinning out of control and I nearly died, but Emma never called her. Despite what Emma might have believed, I did not abandon her. I could have taken off, but I stayed right there with her, though I knew that I couldn't save her or our marriage. I liked to think of myself as a savior, but I really wasn't. I was having trouble just keeping afloat.

By the spring of 2003, still in my first year of marriage, I was doing little more than watching *Law & Order* reruns and whining about my dead-end job. I'm a fairly intelligent guy, perhaps too intelligent ever to amount to anything. I had been a textbook salesman for seventeen years. I loved books, just not textbooks, and I especially hated selling them, but I couldn't bear to leave my job while my marriage was falling apart. Too many things were breaking down around me. I was worried that my center could not hold and I'd have a replay of 1985. I feared that the life I was living couldn't present me with the necessary things to sustain me. What it came down to, I think, was that I was a third-rate man, dreaming of a first-rate life. A prisoner of my own dysfunctional philosophy.

Was I destined for tragedy like Stephanie?

I suggested to Emma that we take another trip, having already traveled to Prague during the holiday break and Florence over the winter break, but Emma said that she needed all of spring break to find a new job. Teaching had become oppressive, Emma said, so much so that she was willing to give up her tenure. She was sick and tired of planning lessons for apathetic teenagers, re-reading the same ten novels that she had been teaching for the past five years and grading the same paper on Hamlet's existential crisis. Pamela Flaherty phoned some of her contacts, and just like that Emma secured a position as assistant director of education at a not-for-profit arts organization. It was an office gig, a nine-to-five grind, but she found solace in the fact that she was helping to fund cultural projects for inner-city schools. I have to hand it to Emma, she was not afraid of making life-altering decisions in the time it takes to toast a slice of bread.

Right after Emma started her new job, she suggested that we move to Brooklyn, hoping that a change of scenery, a fresh start somewhere new, somewhere different, might resurrect our marriage. Brooklyn would be new for her, maybe, but not for me. I was going backward. I'd felt at home with the fashionistas, hipsters and trust fund babies in the East Village. But I went along with Emma's idea anyway, doubtful that any last-ditch effort would fix things between us.

We signed a one-year lease on the only apartment we looked at, a one-bedroom in a two-story brownstone in Park Slope. The landlord, Pete Marzo, who lived on the first floor, had been recently widowed. He carried on and on about how well his wife, Clara, had taken care of him. "It's a woman's obligation to take care of her husband. And let me tell you something, my wife fulfilled her duty to the utmost degree." We pitied the old guy, but he sold us on the second floor apartment and its beautiful hardwood floors. After we moved in, Pete asked Emma if she was Jewish and then told her that it would be okay as long as she kept the apartment clean and didn't scuff the refurbished floors. Pete loved his floors. Emma hated Pete.

Inspired by the temerity with which Emma was forging her new career, I took my thirty-sixth birthday off from EverCover Books in order to start writing the play I had been talking about writing forever, but I ended up spending the entire day in bed, making lists about my life: the failures, letdowns, regrets, disappointments and dreams I'd had. I was stretched across the bed with Colette and Dante, two cats we'd recently taken in. I'd found Colette, hiding underneath a pickup truck in front of the apartment, and Emma had seen Dante scrounging for food across the street in C-Town's dumpster. I was now underneath the thick comforter, sweating my ass off as usual, while John Coltrane's *Blue Train* played. Crumpled pieces of yellow paper lay scattered about me.

For a change, Emma left work at five so we could spend some time together. I heard her come in but stayed right where I was. She called out to me, but I pretended that I couldn't hear her. I wanted her to come to me. Emma traipsed into the bedroom, surprised to see that I was still in bed. She unfolded a paper ball and read aloud, "Wish I had continued making music."

—I didn't know you were a musician. You were in a band?

—My guitar is in the closet, behind your journals.

—Oh, that's a guitar?

—Well, it's not a machine gun.

—Why don't you play anymore?

—It's a long story. Hey, where are the silk sheets?

—I threw them away.

—You threw them away? Why?

—They were old.

—You threw them away because they were old? Was anything wrong with them?

—Yeah, I just told you, they were old. Is this how you spent your birthday? In bed? Feeling sorry for yourself?

She hit me in the head with a paper ball then turned down the music. She picked up another paper ball and read it to herself, then rolled it up and tossed it at me, again nailing me in the head. She had terrific aim. The Mets could have used her.

—You said that you were going to do some writing today.

—I have been writing.

—Yeah, writing about Stephanie, I see. This is an unhealthy obsession, John.

—I was thinking about the accident—

—That was a long time ago. It wasn't your fault.

—I wish I could believe that.

—Why do you blame yourself?

—She died just before her birthday.

—What happened? Tell me about the stupid game you guys played.

—I don't want to go into it on my birthday.

Emma ordered food. We ate chicken pad thai in bed, but the food didn't agree with me. I had developed chronic abdominal pain. My grandfather died of colon cancer, and my father had an operation on his colon.

—Why are we eating in bed? It's really unsanitary.

—I think I might have colon cancer, Emma.

—Aren't you being prematurely morbid? You haven't been to the doctor yet.

—I just have a bad feeling, that's all.

—Anyway . . . the wine is nice.

—I thought you only drank Merlot.

—I try new things, John. You should know that about me.

—There's so much that we don't know about each other.

—What do you want to know?

—Did you write your wedding vows?

—Of course. Did you?

—I worked my ass off on them. Can I read yours?

—Sure thing, but first open your birthday presents.

—Presents? Plural? I like the sound of that.

—I hope you like them.

—I like anything that's plural.

—Gluttony does not become you, John.

Emma placed a torn C-Town plastic bag into my callused hands. The gifts had been meticulously wrapped in the *New York Times'* Travel section, each package decorated with a colorful bow: India in indigo. Germany in gray. Russia in red. I figured that Emma was making an effort to be with me again, but I couldn't have been more wrong.

I opened the packages one by one, only to discover jar after jar of salad dressing: french, bleu cheese, italian, creamy italian, ranch, balsamic vinaigrette, raspberry vinaigrette, russian, thousand island, catalina, lemon poppyseed, caesar. You name the dressing, and it was in the plastic bag, tormenting me. When I was finished, engulfed in a sea of bottles, I tried to hold back the sadness and the pent-up rage.

—You're not laughing.

—No, it's really funny. Ha. Ha. Ha.

—What? What's wrong?

—It's funny, see, because I don't even like salads. I get it now. Thanks.

—I was trying to make you laugh.

—It's funny. It's just that we're not, Emma. Nothing about us is funny. Nothing ever was.

—I thought we could use some laughter in our lives.

—We could use something, anything, but this . . . this is just downright depressing.

—Well, at least I remembered your birthday.

—I said I was sorry about that a hundred times.

—I just thought I'd make you laugh for a change. You're so unhappy with me.

—It's not time to laugh, Emma. Laughter doesn't feel right.

—I never heard you say that before. You were always one to joke.

—Well, at least your gift isn't as bad as the one I got on my twelfth birthday.

—Why? What did you get?

I told Emma all about the pool party with my friends and family.

My father barbecued hamburgers and hot dogs while my mother made sure everyone had enough beer and soda. Gina organized a game of pin the tail on the donkey with the younger kids while a few of us did belly flops in the pool. Rod Stewart's raspy voice struggled to be heard over the hiss of static on AM radio: *If you want my body and you think I'm sexy, come on sugar let me know.* I couldn't wait to open my presents. My grandmother had given me a stereo for Christmas, and my parents had promised to buy the Cars record that I had been begging for.

—How about Frank Sinatra?

—That's your music, Mom.

—The Carpenters?

—Who are they?

—There's this new singer, Christopher Cross.

—I never heard of him. I want the Cars. The first record and the newest one, *Candy-O.*

—Who the hell are the Cars? What a ridiculous name for a group.

—They're a new wave band. They have this song "Let's Go."

—New wave band? I don't like the sound of them. How about Chicago?

—Mom, I want the Cars album. Please.

—You don't really want such trash.

—They're my favorite band, Mom. Why won't you get me something I want? You didn't buy me Intellivision for Christmas like I asked for.

—Okay. Whatever you want, Gianni. It's your birthday and your wish is my command. You're practically a teenager. My little boy is becoming a man.

—Please stop saying I'm becoming a man. I'm only twelve.

It was finally time to sing "Happy Birthday." I was sitting at the head of the table, bursting with excitement, sopping wet and shivering. I made a wish—*I hope to play for the Mets one day*—blew out the candles, cut the first slice of cake and tore into the boxes and envelopes: a Mets tee shirt, a pair of shorts, *Batman* comics, Monopoly, baseball cards, money. These gifts were okay, but where were the Cars records? My mother waited until Stephanie, the last guest, left before she reached into her pocketbook and pulled out one unwrapped cassette tape. "Oh, I nearly forgot, Gianni. Happy birthday." She placed a Barry Manilow cassette in my pruned hands. Barry Manilow? This was my worst nightmare. It contained all of his nauseating hits. I despised each and every one. My mother didn't even have the courtesy to remove the large yellow price tag—SUPER SAVER—that was plastered over Barry's beak.

I did my lame impersonation of Barry Manilow singing "Mandy." Emma laughed. Then we laughed, together. And then we never laughed together again.

One night shortly after the salad dressing fiasco, Emma called to say that she'd be working late again. Her lateness had become a pattern, and I was growing suspicious. With nothing else to do, I turned on the Mets game, opened a can of lentil soup and buttered a loaf of stale Italian bread. Only the first inning and the Mets were already getting trampled. I spread *The New York Times* want ads across the coffee table and circled random advertisements with a red pen so Emma would think that I'd spent my day off doing something productive, looking for a new job instead of listening to my old Beatles records, watching ESPN and napping on the couch with Dante and Colette. By the fourth inning, the Mets had surrendered, but I couldn't pry myself off the couch. Part of me was hoping good ole Emma would come home, sneak up behind and slam me over the head with an anvil, euthanizing me the way I had that poor, dying mouse in Cobble Hill High School.

The longer I stayed on the couch, the further my mind wandered. I was beginning to think that Emma wasn't really working late, that she was sleeping with her new colleague, the guy she couldn't stop talking about, Zack, a happening dude who'd recently moved from Iowa to Williamsburg. Emma thought I was jealous of him because he had published a book of poems. The more I thought about the two of them together, the more enraged I got. I tossed both cats from my lap and flung a few pillows across the room; one struck the table lamp, sending it crashing to the floor. The cats darted underneath Emma's desk. I busted my knuckles on the bathroom door, and while I was bandaging my hand, I heard Pete Marzo at the top of the stairs, knocking on the door. He must have been worrying about his sacred floors, so I thought it would be best to ignore him.

He rammed his cane five more times against the door, shouted something and hobbled away, but not before he rammed his cane one final time. Meanwhile, I was sitting on the edge of the bathtub, examining the paint that was flaking from the ceiling and floating into the tub. The showerhead never stopped dripping. I turned all three handles until my hand was red, but I couldn't stop the drip. Drip. Drip. Drip.

I walked into the kitchen, which also needed a fresh coat of paint, and poured a glass of Pinot Noir. Across the alley that separated my building from the one next door, my blonde neighbor with the fake tan and fake tits had one leg on the kitchen countertop. She was moving back and forth, up and down, bending and stretching. I imagined that she was bending and stretching for me, trying to turn me on, trying to entice me, so I pushed back my chair, took off my bathrobe and pulled down my boxers. From the moment we'd moved into this apartment, I had relied on my hot neighbor to arouse my libido. She'd never let me down. I really wanted Emma to bend and stretch and look at me with the hungry eyes she'd had when we first got together, but my neighbor would have to do.

I was still fantasizing, poised to shoot my load, when I realized that Emma was standing behind me. I was too mortified to turn around.

—You disgust me. You fucking disgust me. You're a degenerate. You know that?

—Emma. I can explain. Shit.

—Is this what you call looking for a job?

—I was pounding the pavement all day.

—Do you like exploiting women, John?

—Is that what I was doing?

—What were you doing? What the fuck was going on in here? The lamp is shattered. The apartment looks like Hiroshima. The cats have taken cover underneath the desk. What the hell happened to your hand?

—There was an accident.

—Pete cornered me on my way in. He said that you were making a racket up here. He said that you were pounding on the floors.

—Piazza hit a home run. I got excited and hurt my hand. That's all.

She told me that I repulsed her a hundred more times, and she was right—I was a degenerate, but I wasn't exploiting women. We hadn't had sex in a long time. I didn't take a vow of celibacy when we got married. Emma gave me the same sheepish look she had given me the night of her brother's birthday when she asked for help.

—Don't I do it for you anymore, John?

—Yes, of course you do, but we haven't done it in a long time.

—Don't you find me attractive anymore?

—Yes. Very. But you're always coming home late. You haven't made any time for us.

—I'm working.

—Who are you with?

—My colleagues, John. I told you, I'm working on this big project.

—You're always calling to say you're going to be late then you don't come home for hours. Sometimes you don't even call at all.

—I'm sorry. I get caught up in the work and forget to call sometimes.

—What about that time you stayed out all night?

—Pam kept me out. I got really drunk and lost track of time.

—Tell me who you're sleeping with. The tall, tan guy at your brother's party?

—Tony? He's a childhood friend.

—Is it the new guy, then? Zack?

—I'm not sleeping with anyone, John. Including you.

—You don't have to rub it in, Emma.

—I'm sorry. I didn't mean it that way. I'm sorry.

Throwing tantrums had always been one of my things, and they infuriated Emma, so I threw one that was worthy of an Academy Award that night, scattering papers, kicking a table over, throwing a wine glass against the wall, hurling curses and threats and storming into the bedroom. Emma pursued me. I tried to slam the door in her face, but she blocked it with her foot.

—Why do you always walk away?

—I have nothing more to say to you.

—I don't know what happened to us, John.

—What did happen to us?

—I'm scared.

—I'm scared, too.

—I don't know what to say.

—Tell me how you feel.

—I feel like shit. We're falling apart.

—We had a good run.

—A good run?

—Maybe a trip would help clear our heads.

—Staying put feels like the right thing to do now.

So we stayed put.

THE FREEWHEELIN' GIANNI LENZA

In 1979, me and Stephanie were freewheelin' twelve year olds, racing our bicycles downhill to the beach, blazing trails through the phragmites on our quest to find the murky water of Great Kills Harbor. One day, we stumbled on a closed area of the beach and climbed into a lifeguard's chair that was wide enough for both of us. Since medical waste was being dumped just offshore, outrageous things got washed up on the beach, and it wasn't safe to sit in the sand, which was really just dirt.

We ate peanut butter and jelly sandwiches: crunchy for me, creamy for her, strawberry jelly for me, grape for her. Stephanie had made brownies. I'd brought cans of Yoo-hoo. We were set. We stuffed the flyers that she had designed for my latest play inside the newspapers I would deliver later that day. I spilled Yoo-hoo on a bunch of the flyers, smearing the picture of a monarch butterfly underneath the title of the play—*Pulling Wings off Butterflies*—but I slipped them in anyway. I was beginning to feel playful, so I sat on Stephanie and tickled her legs. She cackled and snorted so hard that snot gushed out of her nose, which made me cackle and snort so hard that snot gushed out of my nose, too.

—This is a great day, Gianni, don't you think?

—It's no different from any other day.

—Yeah, but we're lucky that we get to do stupid stuff like this all the time. Some kids aren't so lucky.

—You really think we're lucky?

—Yeah, I think we are.

—If you say so. It's just another Tuesday to me.

—It's a great day, Gianni. You'll see when you get older. These are the days you'll look back on.

—Really?

—Really.

THERE IS NO END TO THIS SLOPE

I was beginning to feel weird, sitting on top of her, kind of the way I'd felt the night before my twelfth birthday party. I'd searched all over the house for the Cars albums I thought my parents got me. While I was sifting through the junk in the back of my father's closet, I stumbled across his *Playboy* collection stacked underneath his bowling ball. It was the first time I had ever seen a woman's naked body. The Playmate's spread made me wonder what Stephanie might have looked like naked. Thereafter, whenever I started thinking about Stephanie in that way, I'd go to my father's closet and sift through his *Playboy* collection.

After we finished lunch at the beach, we found a bunch of flat rocks near the bulkhead for a skimming competition. I was averaging five or six skips whereas Stephanie struggled and her stones sank to the bottom. When our arms grew tired, we cleaned up our new hangout and built an obstacle course from the debris on the beach. Discarded car tires were a crucial part of the course that also included a Tarzan swing made from a frayed piece of rope and a balance beam constructed from empty plastic buckets. Stephanie found an old fishing pole, tied a red bandana to it and stuck it in the sand. We declared the beach ours: "S & G's Paradise."

—Hey, Steph. I wonder what's on the other side of the ocean.

—Straight ahead of us? If we were to sail that way . . . I think it's Europe.

—I thought it was China.

—Let's build a raft and sail out to sea, like Balboa and Magellan.

—Can I be Columbus? I don't know who those other guys are.

—When we get older, you and me, after high school, we'll travel the world.

—I don't want to leave Staten Island.

—For a year, Gianni. Maybe two. Who knows? Maybe forever.

—My mother's not going to let me go.

—My mother could care less what I do.

—That's not true. She's just going through a rough patch.

—My father is a crud. She's better off without him.

—Don't talk that way about your dad, Steph.

—We'll hop trains and hitchhike. We won't need that much money. We'll pack lots of peanut butter and jelly sandwiches.

—It sounds kind of scary.

—Where's your sense of adventure? You've got to take risks, Gianni. That's what life is about.

—That's like six years from now. A lot can happen in six years, Steph.

—Well, I'm going with or without you.

It was getting late and I had to deliver my newspapers before dinner, so we tossed them in my delivery bag and rode our bikes back to the neighborhood. We put our heads down and zoomed past the old lady with the glass eye who was always standing in the front window. I was glad that she wasn't on my route.

When we approached Mr. Marino's dilapidated house on the corner, I started complaining about the considerable amount of money he owed me.

—He owes you thirty-seven weeks? How is that even possible? Don't you collect every Wednesday night?

—Yep. I don't know what to do about it.

—Have you asked him for the money?

—Yep, and he keeps telling me to come back next week.

—This is completely unfair. I can't believe that you still deliver his newspaper.

—What can I do?

—He owes you—let's see. Do you have a pen?

I think Stephanie was more annoyed at my passivity than at Mr. Marino's cheapness. She was so startled by the figure that she calculated another hundred times to make sure that she had the correct amount. Same figure. Same irate Stephanie. As it turned out, Mr. Marino owed me $46.25. Stephanie said that the time had come to put an end to Mr. Marino's bullshit. I begged her to let me handle it, but she had already banged on his front door with both fists.

—You do know whose house this is.

—I don't care if the Son of Sam lives here. This is not right, Gianni. That's your money.

—Alfonse Marino is the biggest bully around.

—Like father, like son.

—Somebody's coming down. What are you going to do?

—I'll take care of this. Don't you worry.

—Are you going to break his legs? What are you going to do?

—I'm going to reason with him.

—I wish you'd let me handle this.

—If you had handled this in the first place, I wouldn't be standing here.

Mr. Marino was all smiles when he opened the door. He was holding a meatball hero in one hand and a can of Budweiser in the other. When he took a humungous bite of his hero, a meatball dropped onto his white boat shoes. He shrugged, wiped his mouth on his bare forearm then spoke with his mouth full.

—Oh, you've brought me my afternoon paper. A little late, ain't we, John?

—Mr. Marino, I believe you owe my friend some money.

—Who are you?

—Never mind who I am. You owe John a lot of money, mister.

—Is that right, John?

—Yes, Mr. Marino.

—Geez. I didn't know. This is the first I'm hearing of it.

—The first you're hearing of it? I don't think so, Mr. Marino.

—Don't you think you're being rude, Miss? Miss . . . what's your name?

—I think that speaking with your mouth full of meatball is rude, Mr. Marino. So we're even.

—Tough broad.

Mr. Marino put his beer can on the ground, stuck the meatball hero in his mouth and fiddled around in the front and back pockets of his tennis shorts. He patted his thighs, extended both arms forward, empty palms up, and offered me an apologetic look.

—Nothing. It looks like you'll have to come back next week. I'll take care of you then.

—I'm sorry, but that won't do, Mr. Marino.

—Who is this bitch, John?

—How dare you call me that!

—Whatever. Hand over my paper, kid.

—You're not getting this paper until you fork over $46.25.

—$46.25? Are you out of your mind? That's highway robbery.

—You owe thirty-seven weeks, Mr. Marino.

—That's impossible. I couldn't possibly owe that much.

—You do and you'll give it to us now.

—John, tell your little girlfriend here that I've been a loyal customer for years. I'm good for it.

—She's not my girlfriend.

—Whoever she is, tell her to give me my fucking newspaper. Now!

—She's just my friend.

—Let's go, Gianni. I've heard enough.

—Wait! You can't hijack my newspaper like that. It's mine. I need it!

—We've cut you off, Mr. Marino. And we're going to report you to Gianni's boss at the *Staten Island Advance*.

—But I need the want ads. I'm out of work.

—I'll tell you what. You give us, say, ten bucks, and we'll give you today's paper. If you want tomorrow's paper, it will cost you another ten.

—You drive a hard bargain, kid.

—Think of it as a layaway plan.

Mr. Marino reached into the pocket of his white undershirt, pulled out a crisp ten-dollar bill and handed it to me. Stephanie shoved the newspaper into his hands. He called us "little shits," then slammed the door in our face. We were so thrilled Stephanie had slain the mighty Goliath that we stashed my bag of newspapers behind the shrubs in front of Mr. Marino's house and dashed off to the candy store in town where we bought ten dollars' worth of baseball cards, Pop Rocks and Coca-Cola. We rode our bikes to the elementary school playground, which was just down the block from our house, sat on the big slide and tore into my baseball cards, while Mr. Marino's exemplary son, Alfonse, was spray-painting his tag on a school wall.

—Look what Alfonse is up to.

—Who cares about him? He's a jerk.

—He scares the hell out of me. He's thirteen and he already has a full beard.

By the time Alfonse Marino was ten years old, his future had been mapped out for him: he would either be a drug dealer or a hit man for the Mob. His picture would be hanging in the post office one day. The rumor was that he got the scar on his left cheek from a knife fight he had in the sixth grade. One time he busted Anthony DiMarco's nose because he said that DiMarco was "breathing too close to him." For kicks, he shot stray cats with his pellet gun. He was a heckuva nice kid.

—Gianni, what was all that business with Mr. Marino?

—What do you mean? Give me a hand opening these packs. Don't let Alfonse see or he'll take them.

—"She's not my girlfriend; she's my friend."

—I don't know. Do you want the gum? It's stale.

—Why would I want stale gum?

—'Cause you like it.

—You're as blind as a bat, Gianni Lenza.

—What? You don't want the gum?

—You're a lost cause. You know that?

—Okay, I'll eat the gum. Geez.

I tore open the bag of Pop Rocks with my teeth, then poured half of them into Stephanie's mouth, but she had to spit some out because I had poured too many in. I opened the can of Coke, cutting my finger on the tab. I stuck my bloody thumb in my mouth while I tipped the can in Stephanie's mouth. She kept her mouth open so I could watch the Pop Rocks pop away. We waited impatiently for Stephanie to explode, but nothing happened, so she spit the Pop Rocks out, took another gulp of Coke and contemplated our next move.

—Maybe we should try milk. They say that milk really works.

—I don't know why you want to explode in the first place.

—It's an experiment, Gianni.

—A stupid one, if you ask me.

—Who's asking you? Come on, let's go home and get some milk.

—I don't want you to explode, Steph.

—Then you try it.

—There's no way I'm going to do that.

—Chicken.

—I'm not a chicken.

—You're afraid of your own shadow, Gianni Lenza.

That's when Alfonse Marino snuck up from behind, put me in a headlock and wrestled me to the ground.

—Why are you always writing plays, Lenza?

—I don't know. Because I can.

—You're a faggot. That's why. Say it: "I'm a faggot."

—Your secret is safe with me, Alfonse.

—You think you're better than me, Lenza? Don't ya?

—I didn't say that. You did.

—Only queers write plays. Say it: "I'm a queer."

—You're just jealous 'cause you can't even write your own name.

—Listen to this kid. He's got a death wish. What are you laughing at, Stephanie?

Stephanie, who found great pleasure at my wisecracks, was snorting really loud, and this irritated Alfonse. So he loosened his grip around my neck, gave her a long, menacing stare and threatened her. "Just keep your mouth closed, or you'll be next." But Stephanie didn't back down.

—You're a real jerk, Alfonse. Get off him.

I wasn't prepared to concede victory since Stephanie thought I was afraid of my own shadow, so I flicked his nose. "Did you forget about me, Alfonse? We were in the middle of something."

—You're right, Lenza, we were. You were saying that you're a little homo who writes gay plays.

Alfonse pinned my arms down with his knees and sat on my chest. I was worried about my face, particularly my mouth. I had just gotten my braces off, and my father would have killed me if anything happened to my new teeth. Stephanie picked up a couple of cans of Coke, and just when my nose started to bleed, she smashed Alfonse in the head with both cans as if she were playing the cymbals. While Alfonse reached for his head, I pushed him and squirmed free. We grabbed our stuff, hopped on our bikes and flew to Stephanie's house where she snatched a gallon of milk and some brownies, slipped out the side door without her mother noticing and joined me behind the pool in my backyard. Stephanie handed me a wad of tissue that I stuffed up my bloody nose.

—Thanks for helping me out with Alfonse. And his dad.

—Don't mention it. You didn't need my help. You handled it well on your own.

—Really?

—Of course, you needed my help. But at least you stood up to Alfonse. That takes guts.

—I guess I'm not a chicken after all.

I wanted to prove to Stephanie that I wasn't afraid of my own shadow, so I poured Pop Rocks into my mouth and chugged some milk. We waited a long time, but I never exploded. My father whistled for me. It was time for dinner, so I said goodbye, but Stephanie wouldn't let me leave until she had described every detail of the next experiment she wanted to try, involving my father's bottle of scotch and a blowtorch.

—This one is really gonna knock your socks off.

BLACKOUT

In the summer of 2003, the blackout gave rise to a bona fide celebration in all five boroughs. When the computers were down, cell phones disrupted and fluorescent lighting dead in work cubicles, New Yorkers stepped down from their spinning wheels, clipped the locks on their cages and fled for their lives. And then something surprising took place: they became more sociable, composed, seemingly agreeable and nearly sedate. Was Con Edison conducting a social experiment? Bars on the Upper West Side poured free draught beer to beleaguered travelers; bodega owners on the Lower East Side distributed lemon ices; some downtown restaurants offered an elaborate array of hors d'oeuvres. Stranded commuters sipped cocktails on their six-hour trudge across the Brooklyn Bridge. All of New York was partying while I was trapped in my apartment, sparring with the only other party pooper, Emma Rue.

We were separated by twenty feet of parquet floor, but we might as well have been on separate continents. It had been a long time since we'd discussed our marriage, which was in such decline we hardly spoke, rarely engaging in chitchat on trivial subjects such as the weather or the apartment's attractive parquet floors. It was obvious that we both concluded that our brief experiment with matrimony had been an utter failure, and it was only a matter of time before we officially resigned from our positions as husband and wife.

Emma was drinking Merlot, reading Kate Chopin's *The Awakening* (for the millionth time) by candlelight in the study, while I was reclining on the couch with Colette in my lap and Dante on my chest in complete darkness. I was pulling lint from my beard and watching Emma from behind my shaggy bangs. I kept my hair long just to spite her.

I hadn't eaten all day, and the delicious scent coming from Pete Marzo's apartment was making me ravenous. Except for a pitcher of water, half a stick of butter, a box of baking soda and eight million bottles of salad dressing, our refrigerator was bare. On such a stifling evening, Pete was cooking the gravy he'd been making for the past fifty years without the help of Clara. Pete had been kind enough to offer us a pot of rigatoni and meatballs, but Emma had declined, informing the old guy that we had already eaten. Emma never cooked, never attempted Pete's recipe for gravy, never even toasted a slice of bread, and she never cleaned either. I was always picking up fur balls from the corners of the apartment, wiping spills on the kitchen linoleum, changing sheets. Emma didn't want anyone to know that she didn't like to cook or clean, including my mother, a gourmet cook in her own right. So there I was, silently decomposing on the couch, while Emma was so engrossed in her book and well on her way to getting bombed that I figured it would be a hundred years before she noticed my fetid, rotting corpse.

I had been beating myself up all summer long, picturing Emma with Zack the Poet. Nobody was going to tell me that my suspicion was, in fact, fiction. Every Saturday morning they took kundalini yoga together; he escorted her to modern dance recitals since I refused. I was miserable, and the thought of Emma having fun with someone else intensified my misery. I wanted her to be as depressed as I was.

I tried to lift my spirits by playing a scenario, one that had swarmed in my head that summer: a tanned Emma, in her white off-the-shoulder dress and four-inch heels, sat on a plush red velvet couch in the back of a dimly lit wine bar in Williamsburg, brushing up against Zack, who was fairly good-looking (for a poet), tall and virile, his blond hair gracing the collar of his beige corduroy blazer, which was clinging to his chest. He rubbed her bronzed thigh, gazing over his vintage eyeglasses into her pale blue eyes. Emma shifted in her seat, noticeably aroused by his touch. I watched them from the bar, then hopped off my stool and strode into the back room like Clint Eastwood before a gunfight. They were flirting and didn't see me standing before them until I said something nonchalant, such as, "Howdy, folks," and while Emma responded with, "It's not what you think," I seized Zack by the scruff of the neck, lifted him off the couch and smashed his skull with an empty wine bottle until his face was a bloody pulp. While he was at my feet, writhing in pain, I uttered the cliché "I took it easy on you this time. Next time I won't be so charitable." I spit a hunk of tobacco, narrowly missing his bloodstained head, guzzled his glass of wine, gave Emma a wink and swaggered away into the night. It was a strange fantasy for somebody who had only won one fight in his entire life.

Emma was sitting at her desk, tilting backward on a chair with two unstable legs, while both of her feet were perched on the windowsill. Chopin's novella and her journal were carefully positioned on her legs and a third book—Charlotte Perkins Gilman's *The Yellow Wallpaper*—was within arm's reach on her cluttered desk. She was reading both books simultaneously, picking one up, then the other, underlining, circling, highlighting and scribbling things in her journal. The swiftness and ease with which she read astounded me. She stood up, and I thought she was coming my way, but she walked to the closet and pulled out another journal from a large plastic bin that contained hundreds of spiral notebooks. In the year or so we had been together, I'd never read a single word of Emma's writing. For all I knew, the vows she had written—if she had written them at all—were sandwiched between poems about Zack the Poet and the unfinished travel essay on the Aran Islands.

The Awakening would inevitably bring Emma to tears, yet it somehow managed to console her. I think she felt most comfortable when she was forlorn. I heard her whimpering; she was most likely crying over her favorite passage, one that she liked to read from time to time: *An indescribable oppression, which seemed to generate in some unfamiliar part of her consciousness, filled her whole being with a vague anguish. It was like a shadow, like a mist passing across her soul's summer day. It was strange and unfamiliar; it was a mood. She did not sit there inwardly upbraiding her husband, lamenting at Fate, which had directed her footsteps to the path which they had taken. She was just having a good cry all to herself.*

Meanwhile, the couch was feeling more like a coffin than my favorite spot in the apartment. I was bored and needed to do something, so I took off my bathrobe and undershirt, pulled my boxers up over my navel, my black socks just below my knees, and danced around the living room, biting my lower lip, sticking out my gut, herky-jerky movements, arms and legs flailing, the antithesis of anything remotely cool or sexy. My spasmodic movements mesmerized the cats whereas Emma ignored my stupidity until I started singing James Brown's "Sex Machine." *Shake your arm. Then use your form. Stay on the scene like a sex machine. You got to have the feeling sure as you're born.*

—John! John! John!

—Check this out, Emma.

—Do you mind?

—Hey Emma, come here. Dance with me.

—I'm reading.

—Take a break. Come and dance with me. Let's see your stuff. You're a dancer.

—I'm busy, John. I thought you were looking through the want ads.

—Never mind. Your loss. The Godfather of Soul's got nothing on John Lenza.

Emma rejoined Edna Pontellier and her quest for an identity aside from that as wife and mother. I stumbled into her study like a nerdy, self-conscious teenager who was about to ask the hottest girl in his class a simple question about last night's homework. I snuck up behind Emma, cupped her breasts and whispered *Dracula* style, "Good evening, my dear. I've come to suck your blood." Before I could sink my teeth into the nape of her neck, a gust of wind blew out the candle, the chair slipped out from underneath her, and she crashed down. I extended my hand, but she refused my help.

—Thanks, John. You nearly killed me.
—You're sexy when you're so involved in a book.
—John, please, not now.
—Your shorts are killing me.
—I wear these all the time.
—I think it's time we take a break.
—You've been taking a break all day.
—I'm tired. Work has been extremely stressful lately.
—I want to be left alone with my books. Okay?
—But I'm feeling . . . you know . . . kind of sexy.
—You look ridiculous. Have you seen what you look like?
—They say laughter is the best aphrodisiac.
—Do you see me laughing?
—Why don't you find me attractive anymore?
—Don't be ridiculous. I can't find the matches.
—It's true. You're not attracted to me anymore.
—I can't see a goddamn thing in here. Do you see the damn matches?
—Let's step into the bedroom. Or we can do it right here.
—Not now, John!

My old girlfriends thought I was pretty funny. There was a time when Emma had thought my corny jokes, self-deprecating remarks and silly dances were funny, too. Most guys thought my attention seeking was downright pathetic; actually, so did I. Even though I was approaching middle age, the need to be needed was as intense as ever.

Emma thanked me again for "nearly killing her," gathered her pens, highlighters, books and wineglass and made her way to the front stoop, where she read under the orange glow of the full moon. At first, I considered retreating to the couch, back to my coffin and shroud of silence, but I resisted the impulse; the battle had just begun. I wasn't ready to put down my rifle and raise the white flag, so I followed her outside.

The orange moon dangled just above the five-story apartment building that was under construction across the street. Even though the realtor sign on the building's front lawn classified it as a "boutique," it was a shoddy structure, a colossal eyesore whose ugliness had been taunting me all summer long. Every morning, when Emma left for work, the builders, led by their fat foreman, whistled and made lewd comments. I wanted to take a hammer to the fat foreman's bald head but didn't think my chances of landing a single blow were very good. So instead of taking any action whatsoever, I just whined incessantly. "I hate those guys. They're doing such shitty work. And I wish they'd stop with their catcalls." Emma had the nerve to defend the workers. "They think they're complimenting me. They're trying to be nice." I was amazed that she interpreted such lewd behavior to be flattery. My wimpy, whining routine always sent Emma to either the bedroom or the stoop.

Emma was curled up on the top step of the stoop, sipping Merlot. Her books were closed, resting on her lap. She had been trapped by Pete, who was rambling on about how unbearably loud our street had been in the sixties, when automobiles rode up and down the cobblestones. Pete tapped me on the shoulder with a long silver flashlight and asked about the racket I had made the other night and if the floors had been damaged. I was smiling, but I really wanted to smash him in the face with his flashlight for prying. Pete read my crooked smile correctly and, thankfully, changed the subject.

—Ain't this something, John? Clara would of enjoyed this.

—It's something, all right.

—I ain't seen nothing like this. Not since 1977.

—I remember hearing about the looting in Bushwick.

—Those savages are always trying to find ways of getting something for nothing. They don't have no decency. I bet Bed-Stuy is a war zone right now.

Pete was capable of spewing all kinds of racist bile. He had a way of making me cringe and wish death upon him. In spite of that, I tried my best to remain neutral: "Really?" "I didn't know that." "Okay, sure." "That's interesting." "Cool." I never wanted to encourage his tirades, just steer clear of them. Emma, on the other hand, took Pete head on.

—Savages? You mean the people who—

—That's interesting, Pete. The city was really struggling in '77.

—New York was a cesspool in the seventies.

—That was a different time. The Koch administration.

—I remember the garbage strike of '75. President Ford told us to drop dead. Imagine that?

—It's a different city now.

—It's a wealthy city.

—Where did all the New Yorkers go?

—New Jersey. Florida. Arizona. Colorado. Places like that. Who can afford to live here? People used to come to New York to make money, and then they'd leave, but now they stay. Giuliani cleaned up the city too good if you ask me. He should of done something about the Puerto Ricans, though.

—If you detest people of color so much, then why did you stay?

—It's my home, Emma.

"White flight" had taken place in the late sixties; scores of Brooklynites—Italians and Irish, mostly—had made their pilgrimage to the most accessible, obvious and unimaginative alternatives like Staten Island, New Jersey and Long Island, searching for a higher quality of life, but all they'd found were a few more trees and a parking space. While the Lenza family had relocated to the suburbs, stalwarts like Pete Marzo had stayed behind. The irony of all ironies was that Pete had watched the price of his one-hundred-year-old brownstone skyrocket during the reversal of the trend and the gentrification in the early nineties under the Giuliani administration, when droves of white folk, mostly from such sedentary places as Iowa, Ohio and Kansas, moved to Brooklyn, but only after it had become an accessible, obvious and unimaginative destination.

Like me, Pete was a native New Yorker, a type threatened with extinction in Park Slope. The city's gentrification was one of his favorite topics of discussion. I considered myself somewhat of a New York historian, so the both of us, exchanging roles as teacher and student, had spent countless hours sharing personal stories and intimate knowledge of the Big Apple, but whenever he complained about the fringe benefits minorities received, while white people had to work hard for everything they got, I'd give him a lame excuse like "Emma's expecting me"—even though she wasn't home for most of that summer—and leave him ruminating alone on the state of our beloved city.

Meanwhile, there was a block party in full swing, looking as if it had the potential to descend into chaos. Down the block, a group of parents were drinking some kind of booze in clear plastic cups while their children rode skateboards and scooters past our stoop. Packs of teenage boys, drinking beer from brown paper bags, wandered the streets. Up the block, a group of younger boys played stickball in C-Town's parking lot, while a clique of girls looked on. Across the street, Donna Summer's "Love to Love You Baby" was pumping from a double- parked silver Hummer with tinted windows and a "Jesus Christ is my Savior" bumper sticker. It kind of felt like the blackout of '77. The only folks missing from the party were Ed Koch, Mario Cuomo, Reggie Jackson, Billy Martin, Jimmy Breslin and the Son of Sam. Emma tried to sip her wine by the orange glow of the moon, but ultimately she succumbed to the lure of the evening.

—I'm going for a walk. Would you mind taking my books upstairs, John?

—I'd like to talk to you for a minute, Emma.

—I'll be back. Don't wait up.

—It's dangerous out there, Emma. All of those rapists and drug dealers from Fourth Avenue are probably on the prowl.

—I have news for you, Pete: not every black man is a rapist or a drug dealer.

—Why are you ignoring me, Emma?

—I'm going for a walk, John. We'll talk tomorrow.

—I want you to stay right here.

—You're not my keeper, Gianni.

—You know I hate when you call me that.

—You better let John escort you, Emma. I'd never let Clara walk the streets alone at this hour.

—Get your head out of the fifties, Pete.

—Emma, come back here.

We watched her prance down the steps, twirl past the skateboarders, drift into the darkness and disappear into the bedlam of the evening. Some local kids hanging out in front of the corner deli were shooting off their mouths along with fireworks. Bottle rockets. Blockbusters. I had always despised such pointless noisemakers, preferring colorful explosions that distinguished themselves from a glowing distance—the blossoming of kaleidoscopic flowers, the sprinkling of crawling spiders, the *ahhhs* from the crowd.

—You should go after her, John. She needs the protection of a man.

—I'll get my shoes.

—Make it snappy. Those savages are running loose. I'm sure of it.

I brought Emma's things upstairs, but I didn't get my shoes. Instead, I put on my robe, poured a glass of wine and leaped onto the couch. Maybe Emma would never come home. Maybe she'd just keep walking all the way to Zack the Poet's boutique apartment in Williamsburg. Maybe I'd never see or hear from her again.

Colette stretched out across my chest, and Dante nuzzled inside my underarm. I rubbed her belly and scratched his head. Their purring pacified my need for unconditional love. I opened Emma's journal and searched for the vows she claimed to have written, but I didn't get very far. I was distracted by the high-pitched bark of a little black and white Shih Tzu in front of the apartment. The dog belonged to my neighbor with the fake tan and tits. The pooch was running in circles, barking at the fireworks, while my neighbor chatted with Pete, who handed her two juicy red tomatoes from his garden. She pressed them to her fake breasts, which were busting out of her yellow belly shirt. I thought about joining them, but I was so defeated with hunger that the thought of descending the stairs again overwhelmed me, so I went to sleep on the couch.

Emma's return several hours later coincided with the electricity. The slamming of the front door woke me, the fluorescent lighting blinded me and when I heard Emma coming up the stairs, I pretended to be asleep. She stood over me. I felt her stare, scrutinizing me. She hadn't looked at me in a long time. I was hoping she'd pet me instead of Dante. Maybe she was afraid that by touching me she would feel something she didn't want to feel.

When I opened my eyes, Emma was kneeling beside me, pulling strands of hair from my eyes. Blood from her wrist trickled onto my chin.

—What happened to you?

—A dog bit me.

—Who? What dog?

—Your girlfriend next door—the one with the fake tan and tits—her dog bit me. I must have startled her. What is my journal doing over here?

—That little Shih Tzu? Are you okay? Come back here.

—It's a little nick.

—Do you need stitches?

—Fortunately, Buffy has had all of her shots. Were you reading my journal?

—Let me wrap your wrist.

—I'll take care of it.

—You're bleeding all over the floor. Come here.

—I'll clean it up.

—Let me help you.

—I'll take care of it. I hope you weren't looking at my journal.

—Put some of that orange stuff on it.

—Because there is some personal shit in there.

I wanted to kiss her bloody wrist and tell her everything would be all right, but she walked into the bathroom, clutching her journal close to her chest. She closed the door behind her. I stared at the hole I had put in the door, wiped my mouth on my bathrobe sleeve and thought about the things she might have written about me in her journal. Had she written any poems for Zack the Poet? Had she really written her wedding vows? The travel essay on the Aran Islands? What would she write tonight?

Colette sniffed the trail of blood Emma left behind. When she moved toward it, tongue splayed, I nudged her away. I thought about cleaning the floor, but the rags and cleanser were too far away, underneath the kitchen sink. I fell asleep and didn't wake up until the following afternoon.

The next day, Emma surprised me by suggesting that we attend couple's therapy. I thought it was too late for us, but I went along with it anyway.

Pamela Flaherty had recommended the therapist she and her ex-husband had met with, a young guy, younger than the both of us. He wore a cowboy shirt, black Levi's and black cowboy boots. He had a tattoo of a rattlesnake on his forearm. A copy of Deepak Chopra's *The Path to Love* was prominently displayed on his desk, and he held a thick black binder in both hands, a pencil behind his ear. The first thing he asked was if we had insurance.

—Shouldn't we be getting to know each other?

—Yes, sure, John, but I thought we'd get the insurance stuff out of the way.

—I'll make it easy on you. We don't have any insurance.

—Okay, so would you like me to put you on a payment plan?

—Can we get on with this and talk about matters of restitution later?

—Sure, I'm sorry, John. Let's begin. Who would like to start?

—Shouldn't you begin the session? You are the therapist.

—Would you like me to begin things?

—What do you think?

—What do I think?

—Are you going to answer all my questions with a question?

—John, behave yourself.

—I've been polite so far, Emma.

We sat there in silence for a while, smiling, fidgeting, looking at each other, looking away, looking at our shoes. Then Emma broke the ice.

—My husband is in love with a girl who died in 1985. It's perverse, really. He blames himself for her death, and he can't move past the tragedy. Do you think he's a necrophiliac?

—Now I'm a necrophiliac? You used to think it was sweet.

—I was lying. It's perverse.

—Thanks for sharing, Emma.

—Yeah, thanks for sharing. Is this forty-five-minute session going to be all about me, Doc?

—Remember, John, I'm not a doctor.

—Right, Jake. Sorry, Jake.

—I'm sorry, John, but I had to get that information out there.

—You said you'd help me get over her, Emma.

—I tried. I really did.

—I was foolish to think that our marriage would help me get over her.

—You have a deep-seated psychosis.

—Oh, do I? What do you think, Jake? Do you think I have a deep-seated psychosis?

—Well, do you think you have a deep-seated psychosis, John?

—I thought we were here to talk about our marriage. Why are we discussing Stephanie?

—Would you like to discuss Emma, then?

—Yes.

—Okay.

—Emma is my first "real relationship."

—I knew it.

—You knew nothing.

—You're unavailable, John. You're a great date, but the day-to-day stuff? Not so great.

—Why has this become all about me? Let's talk about your drinking,

Emma. And your boyfriend.

—Would you like to discuss Emma's drinking and boyfriend, John?

—Would I like to discuss them? That's why I brought them up.

—What would you like to say?

—My wife is an alcoholic and she has a boyfriend.

—We both drink, John.

—Your father's an alcoholic. It's hereditary. Isn't that right, Jake?

—Is that what you think, John?

—When are you going to stop answering my question with a question?

—I'd like for you to come to your own conclusions, John.

—Oh, is that what you'd like? I thought you were just being lazy.

—Behave yourself, John.

—What do you mean when you say Emma is your first "real relationship"? Didn't you have a relationship with Beverly?

—Beverly? Who the hell is Beverly?

—The dead chick's name is Stephanie.

—Why are we back on me?

—Why do you think it came back to you?

—Stop it. Stop it now.

—Answer the question, John.

—Okay, Emma, I will. I had a couple of meaningless relationships after Stephanie's death.

—Meaningless? Why do you call them meaningless?

—It wasn't a sex thing. They were meaningless because I never met their families.

—So family is important to you?

—What kind of drugs are you taking, Jake? 'Cause I want some. Of course family is important to me. Isn't it important to everyone?

—We're family, John.

—We don't feel like family, Emma.

After the first session, I told Emma that I was never going back to that imbecile.

—Come on, Emma. We both know more than that moron. What kind of name is *Jake* for a psychotherapist, anyway?

—Let's give him another try.

—These sessions cost a lot of money.

—So saving money is more important than saving our marriage?

—I didn't say that. But I mean, shit, our debt has really piled up this year.

—I'm not ready to give up, John. Sounds to me like you are.

—I'm not giving up. I just think that you need to work on yourself first.

—What's wrong with me?

—I don't want to go down this road again, Emma.

—No, go ahead. Tell me. What do I need to work on?

—Well, you drink too much, for starters.

—Am I the only one who drinks in this relationship?

—We both do, but you get out of hand. You have to admit that.

—So, I'll go to AA.

—Okay.

—Anything else you want to get off your chest?

—There's the little thing between you and Zack.

—How many times do I have to tell you? I am not sleeping with Zack! He's just a friend.

—I wish I could believe you.

—There's something wrong with you, John. Why don't you trust me?

—I don't really trust anyone.

—What about Stephanie? Did you trust her?

—She was the only person I ever trusted.

—How do you think that makes me feel?

—I didn't mean to hurt you, Emma.

—I can't get inside you, John. You won't let me in.

—I'll try to let you in, but I'm not going back to that money-grubbing pretty boy.

—Did you think he was good-looking?

—In a dimwitted sort of way, but that's not the point, Emma.

—Well, I thought he was pretty good, actually.

—For God's sake, Emma, he graduated from Brooklyn College.

—So?

—So, I'm not going to trust my life with somebody who went to the same school I did.

—But you never graduated.

And with that pronouncement, our healing together had terminated. It was too late for us. Emma had stopped sitting in the front row of my show, feeding me lines, cheering me on and laughing at all my jokes. I didn't mind that she had stopped listening to me complain about my dead-end job and babble on about my idea for the play I was never going to write, but once I figured out that our marriage only escalated my abnormal obsession with Stephanie, I knew that I needed to find a new audience.

—I'm tired of listening to you talk about your sick, neurotic attachment to a dead girl.

—You resent my feelings for her.

—I'm sorry that you lost the love of your life, John, but how do you think that makes me feel? You never made room for me. You just don't love me the way you love her.

Emma was straightforward, truthful and positively right. I never took hold of her because I never let go of Stephanie.

FIREWORKS

We limped into 2004. I made my customary New Year's resolution: stay at home and watch the incomparable Dick Clark. I really wanted to be alone, so I had been urging Emma to shack up with Pamela, who had offered her a place to stay until her new apartment was ready, but for some reason she lingered in our place until the insufferable end. At least I tried my best to make the most of our last night together by making dinner and renting our favorite movie, *When Harry Met Sally*. That's more than I could say about my soon-to-be-ex-wife, who spent the entire evening packing and getting ready to move out the next morning. It was only fitting that our marriage should dissolve on such a trivial holiday, one that we both despised.

New Year's Eve is just an excuse to get drunk, stay up all night, do regrettable things, and blame the lure of the evening for any bad behavior. I had spent every New Year's Eve in New York, thirty-six of them to be exact, but never considered, not even for a second, going to Times Square to watch the ball drop with thousands of screaming, intoxicated tourists. I had also refused to pay an outrageous sum for some below-average prix fixe dinner at a trendy café that felt justified in ripping off its customers because it offered a complimentary glass of cheap champagne.

So there I was, greeting the New Year, bidding the old one good riddance, anticipating my independent life while standing at the threshold of something new and unknown, and that prospect thrilled, overwhelmed and terrified me.

Emma was moving back to the East Village and there wouldn't be enough room in her studio apartment for her desk and bookcase, so she'd have to leave them behind. I'd already listed them on Craigslist, but there hadn't been any potential buyers yet. Her knickknacks and books were boxed away. Her clothes were packed (twenty Hefty bags) and stacked next to the plastic bin of journals by the front door; whatever clothes had fallen out of fashion (ten Hefty bags) had already been sent to Goodwill. Her candles and incense, though, were still scattered throughout the apartment. She would pack them last.

I had tucked some of my favorite photographs in my nightstand, thinking Emma wouldn't miss them: a picture of us at Yaffa Cafe on St. Mark's Place, one of me in Old Town Square in Prague, the two of us at an outdoor concert, sitting on a blanket in Prospect Park, and one of Emma on our trip to Florence last February.

We'd strolled across Ponte Vecchio, dodging a horde of tourists negotiating the price of gold, and then we walked along the arid River Arno to the Uffizi Gallery. The street vendors and local merchants sold kitschy Tuscany items such as I'VE BEEN TO THE TOP OF THE DUOMO tee shirts, posters of the great Italian writer Dante preventing the Leaning Tower of Pisa from falling over and (tourist favorite) neon-green pistachio gelato. It was our last day in Florence, and I was worried that the Accademia di Belle Arti, which housed Michelangelo's *David,* would be closed before we arrived. Deaf to my objections, Emma was determined to have her portrait painted.

The rogue artist, with a beret pushed back on his greasy, curly head and a cigar pinched in the side of his mouth, highlighted her long eyelashes. He exaggerated her high cheekbones, made her smile deeper and wider and her pale blue eyes brighter, even more elliptical. I wondered if we were looking at the same woman. To me, she looked hideous. A group of spectators gathered to watch the artist's depiction of the American ingénue. People were pointing, smiling and snapping pictures. Emma was sitting center stage, distracted by all of the attention she was receiving, looking out of place and awkward, while I stood behind the artist. I got a kick out of watching her squirm with embarrassment, so I took a picture. Of course, we missed *David.*

Emma packed the portrait in the plastic bin with her journals, then asked for the photograph I had taken, but when I handed it to her, she took one look at it, grimaced, gave it back to me and began sifting through my drawer like a detective, searching for damning evidence or a clue to our troubled past. She pulled my wedding ring out of the drawer and sighed. "I spent a lot of money on a ring that never fit you. Why didn't you have it fixed?" Then she grabbed the picture she had taken of me in Prague last December, before we were married, and held it up to the light in order to get a good look. It was a favorite of mine.

—I always loved this picture.

—Me, too.

—Can I have it?

—You'll just end up burning it.

—That's not true, John. I like it.

—Yeah, go ahead. Take it.

We had strolled through the Old Town, stopping underneath that overrated Astronomical clock when a light snow began to fall. I stepped away from Emma and walked into the middle of the square next to the Jan Hus statue, lifting my face toward the sky and opening my mouth. "We better hurry if we're going to make it to the castle." I didn't say anything, just continued catching snowflakes on my tongue while tourists snapped pictures of the statue and that damn clock. Emma took my hand, inviting herself into my private world, lifting her face toward the sky and opening her mouth. The two of us, relishing an Eastern European moment. The ridiculous clock rang. Again. People cheered and applauded, pointed fingers, snapped photographs. The snowfall was steady now.

John and Emma in an isolated snapshot. Our hands, tightly clasped. Our faces tilted toward the sky as we stood underneath the gaping clouds, snowflakes melting on our eyelashes and tongues. Emma stepped back and snapped a photograph of me alone in my little world.

We made our way to the castle. On the walk up the hill, I tossed a snowball at Emma, missing her but thumping an elderly woman in the back of the head. The woman looked up, thinking it had fallen from a building. We laughed and scampered away before she discovered the culprit.

The castle was closed for renovations, so we made a pilgrimage to the John Lennon mural, where we paid our respects to one of my heroes. We sang the first verse to "All You Need Is Love." Another couple chimed in on the chorus. Then we followed a narrow dirt path to the Charles Bridge. A thick fog drifted in. The song, the walk, the snow, the fog, the bridge—all of it made me a little horny, so I pulled Emma close to me and kissed her neck. She kissed my forehead, then broke free of my embrace and walked down to the Vltava River, where she lifted her arms above her head, spreading them wide as if she were blessing the frozen water. I pelted her in the back of the head with a snowball, but she didn't turn around. I threw another snowball but missed. Only when she was good and ready did she turn around to face me.

—I don't want to lose my freedom, John.

I had absolutely no idea what she was talking about, but she had killed my mood, so I tossed another snowball at her, this time pegging her in the forehead.

—Stop it, John.

—Snowball fight!

—It's easier for men.

—Sure, we have better arms.

—I'm talking about relationships.

—You need a good arm to be in a relationship.

—Women have to give things up.

—Jesus, Emma, do you think I want to give up *my* freedom?

—It's just easier for men. That's all I'm saying.

A year later, we'd each have more freedom than we knew what to do with. Little did I know that my newfound freedom would weigh me down just as my marriage had.

Emma sat yoga style on her pink mat in the middle of the living room floor, sipping wine and dividing our photographs. In fact, she divided all of our possessions—dinnerware, furniture, books, CDs, credit card bills—into two carefully stacked piles. Even the cats were divided! Colette stayed with me because I had found her; Emma held on to Dante, who was presently in Pamela's custody. Emma's pile and John's pile. Two neat piles. Neat.

Tired of waiting for Emma to join me at the table, I ate penne and smoked salmon without her. I had asked her to pick up a bottle of Pinot Gris, but she'd bought—and I think it was out of spite—a white Zinfandel instead. I turned on *When Harry Met Sally*, the quintessential romantic comedy—funny, witty and not terribly histrionic. *You did not have great sex with Sheldon. . . . A Sheldon can do your taxes. If you need a root canal, Sheldon is your man, but humping and pumping is not Sheldon's strong suit.* We'd watched it together last New Year's Eve, and I hoped it would generate some chemistry on this particular New Year's. Despite the awkward silences and strained conversation, I was still hoping to get Emma into bed one last time.

At midnight, fireworks erupted over Grand Army Plaza. We stood in the front window, watching the symmetry of reds, whites, blues, greens and purples swirl, explode and pop in the purple sky. With every burst, Pete cheered from the sidewalk just below our window, pounding on a pot with his cane. I thought I saw Emma smile, so I put my arm around her waist, thinking we were sharing a moment. The sudden shift in her stance caused my arm to drop. I stuffed my hands into the front pockets of my bathrobe and stared down at the parquet floor while Emma stood on her tiptoes, moved left to right, and twirled with the grace of an intoxicated Martha Graham. Emma pirouetted into the living room then informed me that she'd be leaving in a few minutes to go dancing with Pamela. I moved closer to the window to get a better view of the fireworks. "Ahhhh!" Pete cheered and banged steadily on his pot with his cane.

During the lackluster finale, Emma continued her obnoxious pirouettes by the bookcase, then pulled out a copy of *The Yellow Wallpaper*.

—I need to take this. Is that okay?

—Of course. It's yours. I never liked that book anyway.

—Joan Didion. *The Canterbury Tales. Tess of the d'Urbervilles.* These too.

—*Tess* belongs to me.

—It's mine. Don't you remember I bought it in that little bookshop in Cold Spring?

—Go ahead. Take it.

—It's mine, John.

—I guess it is.

—Listen to Pete. He's such a fool.

—Sounds like he's having fun.

—Fireworks represent war, John, and I don't think there's anything "fun" about war.

—So they represent the bursting of bombs. They're still beautiful.

—War is not beautiful, John. *And the rockets' red glare, the bombs bursting in air, gave proof through the night that our flag was still there.*

I rushed to the couch and buried my head underneath a pillow, but peeked out at the television when Harry and Sally were becoming friends. *Great. A woman friend. You know, you may be the first attractive woman I've not wanted to sleep with in my entire life.* Retrieving my plate from the table, I stabbed a piece of salmon, but it fell off my fork and onto the floor, where Colette was quick to pounce. I put the plate next to her so she could eat the entire fish. Emma called to me.

—*Angela's Ashes. Madame Bovary. Anna Karenina.* I'm going to take these to my place. Is that okay?

—Actually, *Madame Bovary* is mine. It was Stephanie's copy.

—I'm afraid not, John. It's one of my favorite books. Of course, it's mine.

—Forget it. You can have it. She hated that book anyway.

—Well, it's mine, John. These Toni Morrison novels are mine, too.

—Take them all, Emma. They're all yours. You can have everything.

I was tired of talking, tired of fighting, tired of Emma. All I wanted was good food and wine, maybe even a little sex and a long, restful sleep that I wouldn't wake up from until Emma was gone for good.

I really missed sex, and my window of opportunity for one final roll in the hay with my soon-to-be-ex-wife was rapidly closing. I turned off the movie. Emma was crying. Her tears had a way of veering both of us off course and onto treacherous terrain: I could become sympathetic. She could become remorseful. The truth lurked somewhere between my apologies, her despondency and the failure of our marriage. There is a great deal of truth in failure.

—I'm sorry about tonight, Emma. I should have made more of an effort.

—No, it's my fault. I've always been too demanding.

—There's still some penne left.

—At first, I was thinking our separation would bring us together. You know what I mean? I wanted you to work on yourself, find some inner happiness, self-reliance, while I worked out my own things.

—I'm afraid that was never going to work, Emma.

—You're right. But this feels so . . . final.

—That's because it is. What's this pile over here?

—Those are the damaged books.

—What do you want me to do with them?

—I don't know. Leave them on the curb?

—Is there something here worth saving?

—I don't know. I don't know.

—I'll take a look.

Emma appeared so vulnerable, so defenseless. I confess . . . it really turned me on. And then I did something that was completely out of line: I kissed her, not affectionately either. I was trying to get down her pants. She smacked me so hard I saw stars; then I grabbed her arms and shook her with such force that I frightened the hell out of both of us.

Emma turned and sauntered into the study, poured a glass of white Zinfandel, opened *Madame Bovary* and withdrew into Flaubert's world. How could she read after what just happened? How could she read after four glasses of wine? I followed her lead and tied the belt on my bathrobe, took a seat on the couch and started flipping through the channels. Colette purred while I watched Dick Clark, who had to be a million years old by then, feign jubilation. He struggled to steady the microphone, which was shaking furiously in both of his hands. It looked as though at any minute he was going to drop the damn thing, keel over and croak on national television before millions of viewers. It would have been Dick's shining moment, his grand finale. But he didn't kick the bucket that night, and while he was introducing yet another boy band, I grabbed my plate and drifted into the kitchen.

Across the alley, my neighbor with the fake tan and tits was on the phone, dressed for bed, neatly tucked inside her pink bathrobe, her blonde hair pulled back into a long ponytail. Buffy was in her lap. When she lifted her head, I could see that she was crying. I considered opening the window and calling out to her, wishing her a happy New Year and all, but I didn't want to intrude, so I turned out the light and leered at her, hoping that she'd take off her robe and start stretching her hamstrings. At some point, I closed my eyes and dreamed about New Year's Eve 1984, the only time I made out with Stephanie.

Despite the bitter cold, I was at a keg party on Great Kills Beach. While me and Anthony DiMarco were doing kamikaze shots and singing "My Generation," Joey Santone was making out with Stephanie. Joey was the lead guitarist in my band, which wasn't really a band at all; it was just me, Joey and two cheap electric guitars. DiMarco suggested that I do something, but when I pulled the couple apart, Joey thought that I was horsing around. When I called him a "dimwit," he just scratched his head, laughed and pushed me away in jest. With DiMarco's prodding, I continued to step between them. After fifteen minutes of this pathetic routine, Stephanie told me to "cut the shit." Joey figured out that I wasn't joking and gave me a couple of precise punches to the chin. I got lucky when I flinched, accidentally lifting my knee into Joey's balls. While he was bent over in agony, I hit him with a decisive uppercut to the jaw, sending him crashing into the keg of Budweiser. I grabbed Stephanie's hand and ushered her past drunken stares and snide remarks to our favorite spot, the lifeguard's chair in the secluded part of the beach we'd discovered in our freewheeling days of S & G's Paradise.

—You embarrassed me in front of all our friends.

—It wasn't the first time I embarrassed you. Probably won't be the last, either.

—This isn't funny, Gianni. I was having fun.

—You had your tongue down Santone's throat.

—What's going on, John?

—I wish you had some more self-respect.

—Self-respect? You're talking to the wrong girl. I was having fun. I like Joey.

—He just wants to get down your pants.

—I think you got him all wrong.

—No, I think I got him just right. He's a burnout.

—So what? That doesn't make him a bad guy.

—It doesn't make him a good guy.

—Is that the way you talk about your friend behind his back? I can only imagine what you must say about me.

—I'd never say anything bad about you, Steph.

—You want to know what I think? You think you're better than everyone else.

—Don't be ridiculous.

—Yeah, you do. You're so judgmental.

—I have a right to my opinions.

—Yeah, but you're so critical of everyone. You should look at yourself in the mirror once in a while.

—What's that supposed to mean?

—You hide from yourself.

—What kind of bullshit thing is that to say?

—It's the truth. Everybody else has problems but you. Joey's a burnout. I don't have any self-respect. You got a lot of things to work on, Gianni. Despite what you might think, you're not perfect.

The Atlantic Ocean reflected the bright, white moon above us. It started to snow, so I wrapped my arms around Stephanie and apologized. She rested her head on my shoulder and said she was sorry, too. With mascara running down her face, she looked at me with her big brown eyes, put her thin arm around my waist, and the next thing I knew, we were making out. Stephanie had more experience than I had. Her tongue was a tiny spear, and its thrusts were long and deep. She put her hand on my thigh. I was too busy dwelling on my erection to reciprocate with anything even remotely sensual. I didn't know what to do with my tongue. And I was absolutely clueless as to what to do with my dick. I pulled away from Stephanie and told her I wasn't feeling well. We headed home.

Like most teenage boys, I believed in the ridiculous philosophy that it was impossible to be friends with your girlfriend. You had your friends for things like playing stickball, jamming and doing kamikaze shots; a girlfriend was for going to the movies and fooling around with. My friendship with Stephanie was all mixed up. I loved her, but she was my best friend, and I didn't know what to do about my feelings. I was afraid if I told her how I really felt about her, our friendship would end.

I had walked Stephanie home many times, once when she'd had too many screwdrivers at a sweet sixteen party. (Seemingly every weekend, one of the neighborhood girls was guest of honor at some extravagant affair. I'm not sure if it was a Staten Island thing, an Italian American thing, or both, but in those days, if I wasn't spending money on baseball cards and record albums, I was spending it on birthday gifts for girls I hardly knew.) I held Stephanie's hand while she vomited into the gutter, and afterward she'd thanked me for being such a good friend. Now, on the beach, Stephanie wasn't drunk, wasn't sick and didn't need my help. I knew I wasn't being a good friend to either Joey or Stephanie that night.

At home I couldn't sleep, so I picked up my guitar and strummed the chords to a song Joey and I had been working on. My father woke the entire house, shouting from his bedroom, "If you don't put that damn thing away, I'm gonna come and do it for you. And trust me, I won't put it away in one piece." I put down my guitar and started tossing tennis balls at Stephanie's bedroom window. Our homes were only separated by a little patch of grass that my father had ripped out (along with my favorite maple tree) and covered it with concrete. He said that he was too old to rake leaves and mow the lawn. Eventually, Stephanie came to her window. Her black hair was pulled back into a long ponytail, and her Cure tee shirt was twisted around her skinny body. She was rubbing her eyes like a little kid, looking as cute as hell.

—Hey.
—Hey.
—Whatcha doing?
—I was sleeping, Gianni.
—I can't sleep.
—Have you tried counting sheep?

—I've tried everything.

—I got to get up early tomorrow morning. We're going to see my grandparents.

—I'm sorry that I woke you. I thought that you'd still be up.

—What's wrong? Are you okay?

—Was your mother mad that you got home late?

—She didn't even notice. What's up, John?

—What's up?

—You called me. Remember?

—Yeah, right.

My feeble attempt to communicate confused her more than anything. Rather than telling her how I really felt, I did idiotic things like pull her off Joey Santone's lap and wake her in the middle of the night to say "hi." I didn't know how to tell her that I loved her. She tolerated my cowardice and, I think, indulged her own cowardice by telling herself that boys should make the first move. Unfortunately, I didn't have any moves. Never did. I dreamed about having the right moves—like Elvis, like Bowie, like Jagger—beautiful, bold and determined. No such luck. I was stuck inside this scrawny, awkward frame with two left feet.

—Is there something you want to tell me, Gianni?

—Is there something I want to tell you?

—Are you going to repeat everything I say?

—No. I'm sorry.

—That's good, John. Well? What can I do for you?

—Hi, Steph.

—You woke me up to say hello?

—How are you?

—I'm good. What's going on?

—Nothing. I was just thinking, you know?

—Is there something wrong?

—No. I just wanted to see you.

—You see me every day.

—Did you see *Beverly Hills Cop* yet?

—Not yet.

—Oh, it's really great. You should go see it.

—Thanks. I'll be sure to.

—You'll love it.

—Good night, John.

—Good night, Stephanie. I'll see you tomorrow. Well, not tomorrow, but soon.

—Happy New Year, Gianni.

—Happy New Year, Steph. I'm sorry about tonight.

—Joey's not a bad guy.

—I know he's not. Neither am I.

—Now, that's debatable.

—What do you mean by that?

—Just pulling your chain, Gianni.

I never did tell Stephanie that I loved her, and four months later she was dead. I know she wanted me to say it. I wish that I had been brave enough to say it, for her sake and mine. And I wish that I had taken her to see *Beverly Hills Cop*.

The slamming of a door woke me up, and I was no longer in Staten Island with Stephanie; I was in Brooklyn with my soon-to-be-ex-wife. At least I thought I was. When I called out to Emma, there was no answer. The TV was on, and Dick Clark was introducing his next guest, Nelly, who was going to sing his number one hit, "Hot in Herre." I looked around for a note but found nothing. Good ole Emma left without saying goodbye, so I blew out her candles and incense, tossed them in the trash can underneath the kitchen sink and went to bed.

IN SEATTLE

I had steamrolled through my marriage. Emma was back in the East Village; her boyfriend, Zack the Poet, had probably moved in by now. I stayed behind in Brooklyn, unsure of how I was going to pay the rent on my measly salary. Emma went to the Manhattan courts and paid for the divorce, charging $350 to her MasterCard. She sent me a bill for half the amount, which I tore into pieces and chucked into the trash can under the kitchen sink.

I couldn't remember the last time I had phoned my mother. She had no idea what was going on with me, but I didn't want to hear her say, "I told you so," even though she wouldn't have said those exact words. Instead, she'd have said something like, "You never could take care of yourself, Gianni. That's why I'm here. Come home."

The day after I received Emma's bill I decided that I'd commemorate my divorce by getting out of bed. I needed to do something, see something, go somewhere that matched my mood. Somewhere gray. So I uprooted myself and spent the two weeks my job grudgingly conceded (eighteen years of service yielded ten meager days of vacation) in Seattle. While I was there, I dreamed of staying for good and leaving my failed marriage and sales gig behind, dreamed of beginning a new life in a place where nobody knew me, dreamed of pretending to be someone else, a writer for instance. One of my fantasies was to have my play produced at a theater in London's West End. I imagined this would be the ultimate reward for having endured such a ragged life as textbook salesman. It was a strange fantasy for somebody who had only thought about writing a play, never fully committing to the hard work involved. Since leaving childhood behind—when I *had* written and performed plays in my parents' backyard—I had struggled to write an imaginative word. I had never even completed a haiku, but I had managed to write my wedding vows and, from time to time, letters to Stephanie.

I scoured independent bookstores in Seattle's University District, buying a ton of dusty books, even reading a few. *A Moveable Feast* nurtured my other "writer fantasy": the disillusioned American expatriate sitting in a café on the Boulevard Saint-Germain, smoking cigarettes and drinking absinthe while writing the great American play. The innocent yet ambitious waiter Dítě in *I Served the King of England* made me laugh for the first time since Emma and I had split up.

By some Seattle miracle, as I sat in a little café in Fremont drinking warm tap beer, my longing to be someone else coaxed these words from my pen:

watching emma break

in the setting sun
a fading woman
searches for
her former self

how could one so fearful
travel so far
from her home
your wife is broken

all
you want is
to share this evening
with anyone

who will laugh at your
corny jokes rub your
cheeks kiss the back
of your clammy neck

A lanky, pasty waitress with a yellow apron hanging well below her supple hips, who was curious to see what I had been working on, read the poem from over shoulder.

—You should send it to a magazine or something.
—I'm still working on it.
—It feels done to me.
—Trust me, it's not ready yet.
—Are you a poet?
—Me? No. So what do you do when you're not waiting tables?
—I go to school.

—And what do you want to be when you grow up?

—A massage therapist.

—So, you must be good with your hands.

—So, you must be obnoxious.

—No. Yes. I guess I am.

—Are you the guy in the poem?

—No. Yes. I guess I am.

—My boyfriend dumped me yesterday.

—Look at us. Two peas in a pod.

—I get off in a half hour.

—I'll be sure to stick around.

—Great. Try the chicken Pad Thai.

—I was thinking about having the personal pizza.

—I'd steer clear of that. That is, unless you like the taste of cardboard.

—You know, there's a lot of protein in paper.

—Stick to poetry. You're just not that funny.

The waitress's apartment reeked of sweet perfume, incense and cigarette smoke. A bare bulb hung in the center of the living room; a tattered red Chinese shade cradled the long, rusty chain. When the waitress tugged the chain, rust flaked off onto her hand. She rubbed it on her thigh, lit several candles and incense, which were strategically placed around the apartment, then slipped off her sandals, floated into the next room and turned on the stereo.

—How about some Marvin Gaye?

—Does that mean you want to *get it on?*

—You're not very original.

—I never said I broke the mold.

—Some wine?

—Sure, but don't think you're going to get me drunk and take advantage of me.

—Are you ever serious?

—I like what you've done with your place.

—Is that another joke?

—No, it's cozy.

—It's a dump.

—You want to see a dump? You should see my apartment. Although the floors are pretty nice.

—I'd like to move to New York someday.

—I'd like to move to Seattle someday.

—I want to get lost in a big city. Try something new. Be somebody else.

—What's your rent?

—What kind of question is that?

—It's a standard New York question. We're always comparing rents.

—How about that massage now?

—You just want to get me naked, don't you?

—Here's a towel. I have to get my oils.

—Ooh, I like the sound of that.

I slipped off my Converse, shed my tee shirt and jeans. I wasn't sure what to do with my boxers and socks, so I took them off too, wrapped the pink towel the waitress had given me around my waist, sprawled on the table and stared at the water stain on the living room ceiling. The waitress pulled her straight red hair into a ponytail, poured oil into her hands, said, "Turn over, Don Rickles" and seized my scrawny shoulders. After the initial jolt from her strong hands and hot oil, it didn't take long for me to settle in.

—How does that feel?

—Incredible.

—Just relax. Listen to your breathing and don't think about a thing.

—I think I might have colon cancer.

—Oh, I'm sorry to hear that. Hopefully this will take your mind off things.

I hadn't been feeling well—my stomach was killing me. The shit with Emma had exacerbated it. Before I'd left for Seattle, I'd visited a gastroenterologist.

Dr. Ford had had at least three fingers on his right hand, which was wrapped in yellow latex, up my ass when he'd started asking personal questions.

—What is it that you do for a living, again?

—I sell textbooks.

—So you have to deal with teachers all day long.

—Administrators. They're even worse.

—I always wanted to be a teacher. Such a noble profession.

—Wealthy people like you always say condescending things like that.

—Wealthy? Me? You must be confusing me with some hotshot cardiologist.

—You make a lot more money than teachers do.

—If I were to do it all over again, I would teach literature. Who wrote, *I celebrate myself, and sing myself, and what I assume you shall assume, for every atom belonging to me as good belongs to you*? Hey, not bad for a simple doctor.

—That's Walt Whitman.

—I had to memorize that poem in high school. I think I still remember the whole goddamn thing.

—You memorized the entire poem?

—I had to recite it in front of my tenth grade English class.

—That's impressive. It's a really long poem.

I was still bent over. Dr. Ford's fingers were firmly entrenched, exploring my inner terrain, when he started reciting Robert Frost's "Mending Wall":

—*Something there is that doesn't love a wall* / *That spends* [slip] *sends frozen gr… gr… gr…* [stutter] *ground well under it* / *And* [hesitation] *and spills the upper boulders* [pause] *in the sun* / *And makes gape* [slip] *gaps even though two can pass ab… ab… ab…* [stutter] *abreast* / *He is all* [hesitation] *all pine and I am [long pause] apple orchard.* Wait a minute. I think I skipped a line or two. It's been a while.

—You're mixing up two poems.

—I think you're mistaken, John.

—Dr. Ford, I know a little bit about American poetry.

—Whitman's not American. He's English, for God's sake.

—He's the quintessential American poet.

—Are you sure William Whitman's American?

—Yes, he was from Brooklyn, as a matter of fact, and his name was Walt.

—Eh, Walt, William . . . close enough. I must be thinking of William Carlson Williams.

—Carlos. His middle name was Carlos. And he's American, too.

—Geez, what a stickler. Are you this hard on those teachers you sell your textbooks to?

His fingers still inside me, good ole Dr. Ford continued to butcher William Whitman's "Mending Wall." I couldn't take much more.

—Dr. Ford? Dr. Ford?

—Great poem even though I don't have it all down. *Good fences make good neighbors.*

—Will it be much longer?

—What? You don't like my recitation? Too monotone? It's been a while.

—Your delivery is fine. It's just that I need to get back to work.

—Well, you're going to have to relax, young man. You can't go anywhere with my hand up your ass.

Dr. Ford advised me to abstain from broccoli and beans and to make an appointment for a colonoscopy. "I felt something, but it's probably nothing." With the men in my family being prone to colon cancer, I was terrified.

When I opened my eyes, the waitress was leaning over me. Her face was about an inch from mine, and she was tugging on my beard.

—Are you awake?

—Emma?

—I was worried for a minute there. You were so still you looked dead.

—I was dreaming about you.

—You've got bedroom eyes. You know that?

—My eyes aren't my best feature, if you know what I mean.

—And your nose.

—It's Roman. I know.

—It turns to the left.

—I was told it's epic.

—Epic? That's a good one.

—See? I knew it was big.

—So, did you like the massage?

—What massage?

—Are you ever serious?

The waitress tried to kiss me while she was laughing, so her teeth collided with mine. I pretended to be kissing Emma and puckered my lips tightly. The waitress pried my mouth open with her tongue and slid it between my teeth, sending it on a routine expedition in search of mine. I stopped fantasizing about Emma and became conscious of the waitress's tongue. A mouth isn't massive by any means, really, but mine may as well have been the Grand Canyon because she couldn't find my tongue anywhere.

—What's the matter?

—I'm not sure.

—Is it the woman in the poem?

—I feel so guilty.

—Breakups take time. You'll sort things out.

—I forced her to leave.

—You'll figure it out. Things will get better. You'll see.

—I shouldn't have told her about Stephanie.

—Look, I didn't invite you here to talk about your girlfriend.

—My wife. She died.

—I'm sorry. I see that you're still wearing the ring.

—It was my fault. Why did I make up that dangerous game?

—I'm not your shrink, John.

—I'm sorry. I thought I could talk to you.

—You don't even know me.

When I got up from the table, the towel dropped to the floor, and I stood there completely flaccid. You'd think a man who hadn't been laid in a while would have been turned on but not me. I started to cry uncontrollably. The waitress sighed, turned on the light, turned off Marvin Gaye, blew out the candles and incense and poured my glass of Pinot Noir down the drain. Then she downed her glass, lit a cigarette and began folding up her table.

—I'm sorry. Where were we?

—You don't have to apologize, John.

—You want to try that again?

—It's okay, really. Put some clothes on.

—I don't feel like myself.

—Give it time. You will.

—I'm sorry. You're a beautiful woman.

—Please don't flatter me. My heart's broken too, you know.

—Let me give you something, for the massage.

—I don't want your money.

—Please take something.

I dropped a crumpled up twenty on the kitchen counter. The waitress made it into a ball and threw it at me, pegging me off the top of my head. I picked it up and left.

I walked in common time along Lake Union, singing George Harrison's "Something." I often sang when I walked—the Beatles, Bob Dylan, the Rolling Stones, stuff like that. Simple melodies. If I could only write something that simple, that melodic, something that could make me weep, make others weep.

I took a few photographs of the Aurora, a modest drawbridge with a light blue façade. It didn't compare to the majestic Brooklyn Bridge or the sweeping span of the Verrazano; still, it was a thing of beauty. It was simple. It was melodic. It made me weep. It had probably made others weep, too. An old guy in a rickety rowboat struggled with his oars. When he got a handle on them and found his stride, he rowed straight for the Aurora. I took a picture just as his boat sailed underneath the bridge. Then I picked up the flattest rock I could find and tossed it, but once it hit the surface it lost momentum and sank to the bottom.

Fremont was an eccentric neighborhood with more than a few contentious statues: the populist sculpture *Waiting for the Interurban,* the gigantic statue of Vladimir Lenin that adorns the square, and the *Fremont Troll,* an eighteen-foot sculpture with a hubcap for an eye, situated under the Aurora Bridge. Despite the faint scent of urine, I perched on the troll's hand. It was my favorite time of day (sunset) and my favorite day of the week (Saturday), but I was miserable. The torment that had been steadily rising inside my gut from the time I'd set foot in Seattle now overwhelmed me. I wasn't really sitting under a bridge in Fremont. I was in Staten Island with Stephanie, so I did what I had been doing more frequently in those days: I wrote her a letter.

WEIGHT OF NOTHING

Seattle didn't lift my spirits, it only demonstrated how unprepared I was for the emptiness that followed Emma's departure, how crushed I was by the weight of loneliness, the heaviness of sorrow, the burden of grief. Emma might have been out of my life, but I was carrying her sizable ghost on my back, which was buckling under the pressure. I'd thought that once Emma was gone I would feel light and free—nothing on my back and nothing in my heart. Nothing but the weight of nothing. I was trying to survive, even though I was thinking a lot about dying, convinced that it would take great courage to end a cowardly existence, never considering that it might take even greater courage to endure a ragged life such as mine.

As much as I hated to admit it, I desperately needed professional help. Despite having very little money and no health insurance and being skeptical of therapists, I made an appointment with good ole Dr. Miller, whom I hadn't seen since I dropped out of college and nearly did myself in. To be honest, I needed a team of shrinks working nonstop around the clock. I needed Dr. Freud himself. I needed all of Vienna, but Dr. Miller would have to do for now. On the way to my first appointment, I took about a twenty-minute stroll through Park Slope to Southside Coffee, where I had become a regular. For the price of a cappuccino, I made the claustrophobic, dark establishment with dilapidated couches and frayed Persian rugs my home away from home.

I was sitting on a lumpy couch near the front window as dust fell from the ceiling fans that spun in colorful unison, landing on my head and shoulders. On the couch next to me, two mothers were breastfeeding their infants while their older sons played leapfrog on the couch behind me. It was sing-along time, and I was surrounded by a thousand baby strollers. In their attempt to drown out "The Wheels on the Bus," the baristas played the Grateful Dead at an ear-splitting volume. Jerry Garcia's guitar solos disrupted my lame attempt to complete the poem I had started in Seattle, "Watching Emma Break." Nothing was coming of it and rather than do the hard work, I convinced myself that I needed more distance before I could fully express my loneliness. I didn't want to admit that I was more devoted to the idea of being a writer than to actually being a writer; fantasizing didn't require any work, whereas writing required tons.

The other so-called writers in the coffeehouse were sipping expensive coffee, staring blankly at their laptop screens and inspecting the clientele as it came and went. One young writer, in conversation with another, was comparing his style to that of David Foster Wallace while another young writer was telling an older gentleman about the story she was going to write once she found the time. There wasn't a Hemingway among us. Hemingway, who was most likely hung over, actually sat his ass down at his desk and bled.

The pale, bulky, bald-headed man I'd come to recognize as a Southside regular was sitting next to me, reading a novel. He was always reading a classic work of literature. I wondered if he had a job or if he was, like me, avoiding it. He and I were no more than casual acquaintances. We'd never ventured beyond a "hello" or a "nice day," but on this particular afternoon, he had already given me more information than I cared to know.

He was close to three hundred pounds, but he went by the name Teeny, he'd told me, a nickname he'd earned back in Cuyahoga Falls, Ohio, where he'd been the first male cheerleader at his high school. He'd taken great pride in cheering for his school's football team. Teeny Duncan had also been his town's first openly gay person. He'd founded the high school's straight-gay alliance club and gained legendary status when he attended the Halloween dance with his boyfriend, a black boy from the other side of town. Eventually Teeny had dropped out of high school, run away to New York and nearly died of alcohol poisoning. But then he'd gotten his life together, committed to AA and had been sober for more than twenty years.

Teeny wore white carpenter pants that were covered in blotches of paint; his work boots were off and several of his toes were poking through the holes in his white socks. He made occasional slurping sounds, disturbing chewing noises, and with each turn of the page, he exhaled as if he were hiking up Mount Everest. He may have been slovenly, but he had impeccable taste in literature. He was tackling *The Great Gatsby*, which he said he read every April to commemorate its publication.

—That Daisy Buchanan is one entitled rich bitch.

—What does Gatsby see in her, anyway?

—The old sport should have hooked up with Nick. He might have lived longer.

—That would have made for a very different novel.

—James Baldwin would have had the balls to bring them together.

Bored with Teeny's gay theory, I started to eavesdrop on the conversations around me. The group in the back were now singing "Old MacDonald Had a Farm." The breastfeeding mothers were now sipping Guinness, comparing their biceps and admiring Jennifer Aniston's hair on the cover of *Cosmopolitan* while their infants slept and the older boys ran wind sprints throughout the coffee shop. A pack of twentysomethings were expressing their disdain for the suburbs; three teenagers talked about auditioning for *American Idol;* two hipsters discussed the inherent genius in David Sedaris' new book; an old guy at the counter bemoaned the price of a small coffee; and, on the sidewalk in front of Southside, a lesbian couple were having a heated discussion. One woman, dressed all in black, was waving her arms up and down, thrusting them forward and up in the air, while the other woman, arms akimbo, wearing a soiled softball uniform, leaned against a parked car. Teeny said something like "catfight" and meowed. I put my failed poem aside and jotted some notes on the brawling couple.

Notes for a play...

The WOMAN IN BLACK walks away from her girlfriend, FRANCES, but quickly returns. This goes on for only ten minutes but it feels like hours.

Teeny reached into his back pocket, took out his wallet and asked me if I'd like to see nude pictures of the guy he'd been seeing, the hairy barista covered in tattoos who worked the night shift at Southside. I explained that I was "busy working on something" and went back to my notes. Teeny said that he'd always wanted to be a writer but hadn't found the time and asked me what I was working on. I told him "nothing interesting" and started writing.

More notes on the play . . .

After winning the softball championship, FRANCES and her teammates celebrate at Ginger's Bar on Fifth Avenue. They party into the early morning hours. THERESA, the first baseman, has had her eye on FRANCES for some time, but the WOMAN IN BLACK is always in the dugout cheering the girls on and in between innings making out with FRANCES. On this particular night, the WOMAN IN BLACK isn't at the bar, so THERESA seizes the opportunity and makes her move on FRANCES. After several drinks, they go back to

THERESA'S apartment. FRANCES spends the entire evening with THERESA.

The next morning, FRANCES thinks the WOMAN IN BLACK is at work, but she is sitting in front of Southside Coffee, hoping FRANCES might turn up there.

> WOMAN IN BLACK

Where have you been?

> FRANCES

I was out with the girls. I told you that.

> WOMAN IN BLACK

All night?

> FRANCES

We were celebrating.

> WOMAN IN BLACK

All night?

> FRANCES

Yeah. We won the championship.

> WOMAN IN BLACK

That gives you the right to stay out all night?

> FRANCES

Come on, babe. Don't give me grief over this.

> WOMAN IN BLACK

Have you thought about my grief, Frances?

> FRANCES

I was having fun. That's all.

> WOMAN IN BLACK

You don't even have the courtesy to call?

> FRANCES

I'm sorry. I should have called. You're right.

The WOMAN IN BLACK cries. FRANCES takes hold of her, but

she breaks free.

FRANCES

Where are you going?

WOMAN IN BLACK

I can't do this anymore, Frances.

FRANCES

I'm sorry. Don't walk away.

WOMAN IN BLACK

This isn't working for me.

FRANCES

I'm sorry.

WOMAN IN BLACK

Don't patronize me.

FRANCES

Don't go.

WOMAN IN BLACK

Tell me why I shouldn't go.

FRANCES

I love you.

WOMAN IN BLACK

If you loved me, you would have called.

FRANCES

Don't run off like this. Let's talk about it.

WOMAN IN BLACK

Talking has gotten us nowhere.

FRANCES

Please don't run away. Calm down and talk to me.

WOMAN IN BLACK

I should have run away from you a long time ago, Frances.

FRANCES

You're talking crazy. Come here.

WOMAN IN BLACK

Fuck off, Frances.

FRANCES

Babe, please don't go. Come back.

The WOMAN IN BLACK sprints directly into the traffic on Seventh Avenue. An off-duty policeman, late for his shift, is trying to beat the traffic light that has just turned yellow. His car hits her with such force that she is propelled into the windshield of an oncoming automobile.

Even though it was pure shit, I was thrilled that I had written something. Teeny asked to see my notes. At first, I refused, but then he said something about writers needing thick skin. Before I handed Teeny my notebook, I informed him that it was just an exercise and not even a first draft. When he was done reading, he rubbed his bald head and looked off into the distance, not saying anything for a long time. Then he shredded the four and a half pages and handed the pieces to me.

—Why are you writing about lesbians?

—What's wrong with lesbians?

—I'm not into the whole lesbian thing myself . . . but that's not the point. It's just that—I'm no writer, but shouldn't you be writing about the things that trouble you?

—What makes you think that I don't find these two women to be troubling?

—Readers want to read your story. Tell me. What's your story?

—My story? My whole story?

—Yeah. What's going on in your life? You must be going through something. You're always in this dungeon by yourself, looking out the window, scribbling away.

—Well for starters, I blew it with a hot waitress in Seattle. She really wanted me, too.

—Yeah, what happened?

—I started to cry.

—A hot waitress wanted to fuck you and you broke into tears?

—On account of my recent divorce.

—There, that's something. It's pathetic but write about that.

—Really? You'd be interested in that story?

—Not really, but somebody might. Now if you had made it with the waitress, that would have been more my cup of tea.

Teeny was easy to talk to, and though I didn't really know the guy, I opened up to him. I told him that even though I didn't want to get back together with Emma, I'd been calling her from time to time, waiting for her to say that she was having a shit time letting go, like me. She told me that she missed my corny jokes, self-deprecating remarks and silly dances. Even my stupid, ugly red bathrobe. But she never once said that she wanted to come back home. Actually, she sounded like she was doing okay.

Whenever I asked her about Zack the Poet, she'd steer the conversation in a different direction. "What have you been doing with yourself, John?" I wanted to make her jealous, so I told her that I had finished writing the play I had been talking about forever, been traveling around the world and seeing a couple of women, a pediatrician and a dancer. I don't think she bought any of my lies.

—Why does your happiness depend on someone else?

—I don't know, Teeny. You're the shrink. You tell me.

—Hey, I didn't sign up for this. I'm no head doctor.

—Oh, come on. You've been really helpful so far.

—Well, John, don't you think the focus should be on you and not your ex-wife?

—I think she's over me.

—Once you commit to a healthy, productive life, you'll see that anything is possible.

—Man, you're a bag of clichés.

—Okay, you're cured. Now kiss my big, bald head for improving your life.

—I think my real shrink is going to prescribe me an antidepressant.

—Are you going to give it a try?

—Kafka wouldn't have been Kafka if he had taken an antidepressant.

—You're not comparing yourself to that fuckup, are you, big boy?

—The man was a genius.

—That may be, but he was a major head case. All kinds of daddy issues going on there.

—I don't want anything to interfere with my work.

—What do you do for a living?

—I sell textbooks, but I was talking about my writing.

—You're here all the time, big boy. I thought you were unemployed.

—I'm just taking some time for myself.

—Listen, I could really use a hand with my next job. A hand job is all I really need. I bet you do too. It's gonna be a bitch for one guy. What do you say?

—You have a job? I thought you were unemployed.

—Don't sound so surprised.

—It's just that you're here all the time.

—Work's been kind of slow lately.

—I'd like to help you out, but I'm not good with my hands, Teeny.

—Let me be the judge of that, big boy.

When Stephanie died and my life fell apart in 1985, I'd taken Wellbutrin for about a year. Dr. Miller had claimed that it would temper my behavioral highs and lows. Sure, I'd been less suicidal, but I'd paid the price: the drug turned me into a robot. I became less interesting, less passionate, less intelligent. Just less. I stopped playing the guitar and lost my libido. My doubts about antidepressants, however, didn't stop Teeny from offering me a bottle of Zoloft.

—I'm your shrink now, handsome. Besides, I don't need this shit anymore.

—Do you have any more drugs in that bag of yours?

—I'm not a dealer, big boy.

—I'm having trouble sleeping.

—Here. Take these. Zolpidem. They'll make you sleep like a baby. But be careful. Don't take them with the Zoloft.

Now that Teeny was my therapist, I started out for home rather than Dr. Miller's office. On the corner of Seventh Avenue and Twelfth Street, I bumped into Richard Pritchard, the neighborhood homeless guy. I gave him a buck from time to time, which always resulted in a friendly conversation about the ways in which the neighborhood had changed. Richard never smelled, never looked like he needed a shower and, being originally from Virginia, had an undeniable southern charm. Richard was the classiest guy I knew. No matter the time of year, he always wore a beige trench coat and a collared dress shirt underneath a V-neck sweater. He loved to chat with the folks in Park Slope and smiled a lot for someone who had been in and out of shelters for nearly twenty years. The neighborhood looked after Richard. He got free bagels and coffee every morning from Southside. Tony's Pizzeria gave him leftover slices and Lucky Fortune offered him old fried rice and egg rolls. He got his cigarettes from the corner deli, his clothing from Goodwill, rides to OTB from a degenerate gambler who lived up the block from me and free gin and tonics and buffalo wings at Cosby's, the neighborhood dive. In some ways he had it better than me. He took life in stride and always had a cigarette in his mouth, lit or unlit, never taking it out, even when he spoke. Today he was cradling his dog, Pablo, a brown Chihuahua who rested comfortably in his arms and never barked.

—How goes it, Sir John?

—Things could be better.

—Ain't that the truth. Now, back in the eighties, folks in this here neighborhood stopped from time to time to chat with me. These people today, these rich aristocrats are too busy to talk to the neighborhood homeless dude. They're afraid of me. Lock me up, throw away the key. I'm an eyesore, an urban blight, a drunken fool, a menace to society. That shit ain't right. The poor fucked-up folks in the shelter are more pleasant than these here rich motherfuckers.

—Well, some of what you said is true.

—Which part?

—You're a drunken fool.

—Hey, I might be a drunk, but I ain't no fool.

—Just pulling your chain, man.

—Ah, man. I can always count on you for some friendly banter.

—See? Some folks in Park Slope do stop to talk to you. Here.

—Now, why did you have to go and do that?

—What?

—I didn't ask you for no dough, man.

—I just thought that was our arrangement.

—Our arrangement?

—Yeah, you give me good conversation and I repay you with a buck.

—Damn, my insights is worth more than a damn dollar.

—Okay, here.

—Damn it, John. I don't want your damn money.

—Then what can I give you?

—How 'bout a handshake and a rub behind the ear for Pablo?

—That's it?

—What do you think? Everybody wants something from you?

—I just thought—

—You just think that I'm a money-grubbing, drunken fool, taking shit that don't belong to me.

—I don't think that.

—Now, I'm just pulling your chain, brother.

I gave him a buck anyway and made my way home. When I got back to the apartment, I poured a glass of wine and swallowed a handful of Zoloft, called Dr. Miller and apologized for missing my appointment. I was never going back to therapy. Across the alley, my neighbor with the fake tan and tits—TNT had become my pet name for her—was kneeling on the kitchen linoleum. I wondered if she had a job or if she was playing hooky like me. At first, I thought she was doing yoga, but then I realized that she was praying. She must have really been enjoying it; her ass was moving up and down like she was giving a lap dance, which really aroused me, so I opened my robe, pulled down my boxers, leaned back in my chair and pictured myself sticking her from behind. It was heaven!

THERE IS NO END TO THIS SLOPE

When I was finished doing my thing, I sprawled out on the couch, where I buried my head under some pillows and did what I had been doing a lot of lately: I wept. Ever since my pitiful breakdown with the waitress in Seattle, I had been crying all the time, and it was freaking me out. On my way to work, I'd break down. Sitting in the coffee shop, I'd cry over my cappuccino. I was losing control and terrified of spiraling into oblivion. I thought about calling my mother, but I was afraid that she'd detect the desperation in my voice. I didn't want her to know that I was in such bad shape. If she thought that I was in the least bit of trouble, she would have sent my father to bring me home, and the last thing I needed was their pity.

After a few hours of good, wholesome bawling, I figured that smashing Emma's bookcase into a million splintery pieces would make me feel better. It didn't. And it didn't take long before Pete was tapping his cane on my door. He was concerned about the floors.

—John. John. John, is everything all right?

—Yeah, everything's okay. I'm exercising. That's all.

—It sounds like World War III up here.

—I'm doing some push-ups.

—Please open the door.

—I'm busy.

—You'll find someone, John. There are plenty of fish in the sea.

—Yeah, I know, Pete.

—You gotta stop beating yourself up.

—Good fences make good neighbors, Pete.

—Maybe my son Carmine can introduce you to a young lady.

—Uh, no thanks.

—I'm just tryin' to help.

—I know you are, but I'd like to be left alone.

—You made decisions. Some didn't turn out the way you had liked.

—Do you speak only in clichés?

—You've made decisions, not mistakes. Decisions. Ya hear me? Please open the door.

I opened the door and stood there completely naked, having forgotten to put on my robe. Pete examined me, hunched over, perspiring and flushed with embarrassment, clutching a hammer and a piece of splintered wood. He started to pity me.

—You gotta start takin' better care of yourself, John.

—I'm trying to. That's why I took that trip to Seattle.

—You might start by trimmin' your hair and beard.

—Is that what you wanted to talk to me about?

—You know, I could of gotten at least two hundred dollars more for this apartment, but I liked the idea of havin' an attractive young couple livin' above me. Clara would of liked that too. And you admired my

73

hardwood floors. It didn't hurt that you're Italian.

—That's the only time my ethnicity ever got me anything.

—What kind of nonsense are you spewin'?

—Never mind.

—Emma reminded me of my childhood sweetheart.

—Did she?

—Broke my heart, I don't mind tellin' ya.

—Emma hated you.

—I know she did, but she never really knew me. Was she unfaithful?

—Good fences make good neighbors, Pete.

—What the hell does that mean?

—It's a line from . . . it just means mind your own business.

—I don't mean to pry. My childhood sweetheart was unfaithful. Nearly killed me. Me and Clara had our struggles, don't get me wrong, but there was never an issue of infidelity. Couples just didn't get divorced the way they do now. It was a last resort. God, do I miss Clara. Sometimes I don't want to go on without her.

Married couples of Pete's generation worked through a crisis, for better or worse, but my generation, with the fast food we eat, the text messages we send and the trendy electronics we purchase and discard for a newer model, abide by a hollow, disposable ideology, according to Pete. I was so absorbed with my own grief that I never had acknowledged that the old guy had obviously been grieving as well.

—The world has gone crazy. Nobody sticks it out anymore. Just move on to the next thing.

—Do you think I planned this, Pete?

—I don't mean to be heartless. I'm just surprised, that's all.

—You and me both.

—Were you sleepin' with another woman, John?

—Good fences, Pete.

—Again with the fences?

—It's a private matter.

—By the way, you owe me for last month's rent. And put on a robe for God's sake.

I put Pete's mind to rest by promising that I'd give him the rent check next week and that I'd get a roommate. That seemed to satisfy him. For now. I cleaned my apartment for the first time since Emma had moved out. Bending down to pick up a fur ball, I came across a recent pay stub underneath the couch. The mere sight of such mediocre numbers made my blood boil. Hell, my low salary wasn't surprising. I worked on commission and had been missing an awful lot of work lately. Ten-year-old boys with lemonade stands earned more than I did. I threw a fit anyway, punching another hole in the bathroom door and smashing the kitchen window with a broomstick. Now I'd have to leer at TNT through shattered glass. I waited for Pete's knock, but it never came.

I couldn't sleep, so I popped a few Zolpidem and while I waited for them to perform their magic, I gave Teeny a call. He was "entertaining" a guest, but he took the time to talk me.

—I want to be happy, Teeny.

—That waitress in Seattle would have made you happy.

—Why can't I be happy?

—We can't be happy all the time, big boy. Sadness serves a purpose, you know.

—I deserve happiness, don't I? I'm a good person.

—What makes you think that you deserve anything?

—We all deserve happiness. Right?

—You have to earn it, John. Look at me. I'm so happy right now I could shit. I've got this pimply kid straight out of high school in my bedroom willing to let me do anything to him. You've never known such happiness. I'll take pictures for ya.

—I thought you were seeing the hairy barista from Southside.

—I am, big boy, but that doesn't mean I can't explore my options. That's how things work in my league. Why don't you come play on our team, John?

—I'm having enough trouble with my own team right now.

—Think about it, handsome. Have you called you-know-who again?

—I don't think Emma wants me to call her anymore.

—And what do you want?

—I don't know what I want.

Teeny had to get back to his guest, so when he hung up on me I thought I'd give Emma a call. By her "hello," it sounded like she was in the middle of something. I slammed the phone down before she uttered another word. I think I just needed to hear her voice.

LIBRARY
North Central Michigan College
1515 Howard St.
Petoskey, MI 49770

BONG LIZARD GYPSY

By the end of the summer, my one-bedroom apartment was feeling awfully big and empty. I was so goddamn lonely. Colette did her best to keep me company, following me around from room to room and napping with me on the couch, but hell, she was a cat. I really missed being with a woman. I asked Teeny, who had become a good friend, to move in with me, but he was a pig in shit in his rent-stabilized one-bedroom in Cobble Hill. He wasn't going to walk out on a good deal, though he suggested that I move in with him. It was a friendly gesture, and I appreciated it, but I wasn't prepared to leave my home just yet.

Teeny insisted that a genuine commitment to a "healthy, productive life" would unclasp the stranglehold the past had on me and that my mistrust of everything new would eventually become old. Although I wasn't anticipating a miracle, I continued to medicate. It gave me the impression that I was working on myself. I developed a talent for recognizing my fellow drug-induced New Yorkers by their steady, fixed and blank gaze, which made them look like *Night of the Living Dead.*

—I bet she's taking antidepressants. Check her out, Teeny. Pathetic.

—Depression is the least of her worries. Look at her hair.

—And that tall guy over there. He looks medicated too.

—I'd like to medicate him.

—And that fat guy, over there—

—Don't concern yourself with others, big boy. We're human beings. We all have our ups and our downs. More downs than ups. You're beginning to learn how to enjoy your highs and manage your lows. You're discovering ways to keep yourself afloat during this difficult time. You're catching yourself before you hit rock bottom. That's something.

—I've been thinking about writing the play I've been thinking about for years.

—You've been thinking about writing the play you've been thinking about writing? Come on, big boy. That's the lamest thing I ever heard. Shit or get off the bowl. You haven't contacted Emma, have you?

—She's my wife.

—She's your ex-wife. Every time you contact her, you stir the pot.

—I still kind of like calling her *my wife.*

—Again, she's your ex-wife. You know what you're doing, John. I don't have to tell you.

—I can't stand the loneliness.

—Repeat after me, John: *I want to live a healthy, productive life.*

—*I want to live a healthy, productive life.*

—*I will stop calling my fucked-up ex-wife.*

—*I will stop calling my fucked-up ex-wife.*

—So far, so good. *I will stop writing letters to the dead girl.*

—Writing to Stephanie comforts me.

—It's fucking weird, John.

—I think it's been kind of helpful. I've been keeping a journal.

—Is that your journal on your lap?

—Yeah.

—Hand it over. Let me take a look at the bullshit you've been up to.

—I've been writing an awful lot about the final months of high school, just before Stephanie died.

—Oh, brother. What is wrong with you, you sick fuck?

—Hey, you told me to write about things that trouble me.

—Things that are troubling you now not a hundred years ago.

—This shit is still troubling me.

—Is there any sex in here at least?

—Yeah, a little bit.

Before I could warn Teeny that it was sentimental drivel and not erotica, he yanked the marble notebook from my hands, called me a "sick fuck" then started reading about the band me and Joey played in. He didn't get very far before coming to an abrupt stop and slamming the book shut.

—Wait a minute. What time is it?

—I don't know. Noon?

—I got to go paint a house in Brooklyn Heights. I love rich people. They'll pay the price you quote them without any haggling whatsoever.

—Will you be here later?

—I'm afraid not, big boy. I have a date.

—With the hairy, tattooed barista or the kid right out of high school?

—Do you really think he's hairy?

—His beard starts just beneath his eyes. He's a werewolf barista.

—Listen to me, big boy. Do yourself a favor and put down that journal. Pick up your guitar. It's a lot healthier than fixating on a girl who's been dead for twenty years. Hell, put the band back together.

When Teeny went off to work, I ordered another cappuccino, opened my journal and permitted my mind to wander freely.

At the Valentine's Day dance, Joey Santone and I played our first and only gig as Bong Lizard Gypsy, a name we'd come up with the night before the dance, right after we smoked a bunch of weed. We rocked out on three songs: "Rock and Roll All Nite," "Twist and Shout" and "Jumpin' Jack Flash." And even though our electric guitars were out of tune and we sang out of key, we instantly became the coolest kids in school. It was the only time in my life that I felt like I fit in. Overnight, I had become a rock star with all the right moves—like Elvis, like Bowie, like Jagger. We even had our very own groupies lining up to go out with us. Joey was getting pretty serious with Stephanie, so I had the pick of the litter and chose Grace, a short, voluptuous blonde whose breasts were so gigantic that I overlooked her callous heart. Grace was the first girl I ever had sex with. If you could even call it that. It was more like a brief encounter. Very brief.

We were in the backseat of my father's '79 Cadillac Seville, which didn't offer enough room to stretch out. While I was ramming my head against the roof, Grace was sliding off the leather seat. I had to stop my erratic hip thrusts repeatedly in order to pull her back up. For me, the entire fifteen seconds was mired with thoughts of Stephanie. Joey had been giving me the play-by-play of their recent sexual exploits. Every minute detail, right down to the mole on her inner right thigh. He was quite thorough in his accounts. Stephanie, on the other hand, had been giving me the entire overview of their burgeoning love affair and their plan to skip the prom and spend the weekend in a hostel in the West Village. I was getting it from both ends and couldn't wait to start college in the fall so I didn't have to see them together all the time and fake my enthusiasm about their happiness as a couple.

I pulled up my pants and told Grace that I thought we were rushing things. She interpreted my reluctance as rejection, which it was, but at least I was being a gentleman about it. Grace knew I had a thing for Stephanie; Joey and Stephanie did too. Hell, the whole freakin' world knew.

—I don't see what's so great about Stephanie. She's kind of a freaky rocker chick, if you ask me, with her dyed black hair and black nail polish.

I couldn't sit in the beach parking lot another second, listening to a girl I didn't even like trash the girl of my dreams, so I turned on the radio, turned it way up and drove her home. I parked in front of her house and listened to all of Bruce Springsteen's "Thunder Road"—which is one long-ass song—waiting for Grace to get out of the car. She was apparently waiting for an apology—arms folded, staring straight ahead, refusing to look at me, chewing gum, blowing bubbles. The night had been a complete bust, but I thought I'd salvage some of it by at least getting a good-night kiss. As I leaned in, Grace pulled back and slapped me so hard she gave me a nosebleed.

—You've got some fucking nerve, John Lenza.

—What? I was trying to say I'm sorry.

She tore the fuzzy dice from the rearview mirror, stormed out of the car and kicked in the passenger-side taillight.

—Asshole.

—Yeah, Grace, it takes one to know one.

Later that evening, while I was lying in bed with a wad of toilet paper stuffed up my left nostril, my balls began to throb. I started fantasizing about Stephanie and Grace, making out with both of them at the same time. Stephanie pulled off my pants and crawled on top of me while Grace pulled off my shirt and stuck her tongue in my ear. Just when they were both about to slip off their bras and panties, my bedroom window rattled, snapping me back into reality. Stephanie was in my driveway flailing her arms, signaling for me to step outside. I put on my robe and snuck downstairs and out the side door.

—If my father catches me, he's going to kill me. He's already pissed that Grace broke the taillight on his car. Grace didn't call you, did she? It was only this one time. I swear to God.

I was doing my best to make Stephanie jealous, but she was so deep in thought she didn't even acknowledge what I'd just said. I watched her pace the driveway for what felt like three hours. Up and down. Up and down. Up and down. When she finally exhausted herself, she plopped down on the front bumper of my father's Cadillac, her skirt pulled up underneath her. I could see her red panties, but I tried not to stare. Stephanie was in her goth phase: black nail polish, heavy black eyeliner, bright red lipstick and blue eye shadow, both ears were enveloped by an assortment of earrings and her dyed black hair was streaked blonde at the top. She was buried underneath a dungaree jacket that hung on her like a pall. Stephanie had painted a picture of Siouxsie Sioux on the back; the singer's black mane poked out in every direction; she wore black fishnets underneath skimpy black shorts and black leather knee-high boots.

Both of Stephanie's hands pressed the top of her head, digging tiny holes into her scalp. She might have had the weight of the world on her shoulders, but it only made her hotter. After she let out an exaggerated sigh, she walked down the driveway, away from me. I called out to her. When she turned around, her mascara was running down her face and she was holding something that looked like a thermometer.

—I can't believe this happened.

—What's going on, Steph?

—Will you look at this?

—Do you have a fever or something?

—I'm pregnant. Take a look at the stick.

—Pregnant? Come on. Really?

—What do you have up your nose?

—Grace smacked me.

—I don't even want to know what you did to deserve it.

—I was just trying to tell her I was sorry and she hauled off on me.

—For what? What did you do? Forget it, I don't want to know.

—Are you sure you're pregnant?

—The stick doesn't lie.

—It doesn't?

—Nope.

—You should have been more careful, Steph.

—I came over here to talk to you, not to hear you lecture, Gianni.

—I'm sorry. Joey's the father, right?

—Of course he is, John. What the hell is wrong with you?

—Are you sure?

—What the fuck, John? I haven't been with anyone else.

—This is a disaster, Steph.

—Thanks for stating the obvious.

—What are you going to do?

—I don't know. I don't know.

—You're not thinking about keeping it?

—I don't know. I don't know.

—You're too young, Steph. It'll ruin your life.

—You don't know that.

—What are people going to say?

—I don't care what people will say. It's my life, John.

—What did Joey say?

—I haven't told him yet.

—Don't you think you should be telling him all this and not me?

—I care about the guy. I don't want to hurt him.

—What are you going to do?

—I don't know. I don't know.

—Promise me one thing.

—What's that?

—Think about it. Mull it over. This decision will affect the rest of your life.

—I'd be a terrific mom. Better than my mother.

—Your mom has it rough.

—I wish she'd get over my father already and move on with her life. He's been gone for years.

—I hope she gets it together. Promise me, Steph, you'll give it some time. Think about it. And tell Joey, for God's sake.

—Okay, I will.

—If there's anything you need, I'm here.

—You're always there for me. That's why I love you.

—You love me?

—Of course I do. You're the love of my life, Gianni Lenza.

—I don't know what to say.

—You've had a crush on me forever.

—We're best friends.

—We are best friends.

For the next two weeks, Stephanie and I went to the Staten Island Mall every day after school. We observed new mothers, wheeling their toddlers around the food court. We watched them breastfeeding their babies, tossing a ball to their sons, reading *Goodnight Moon* to their daughters. It was a huge waste of time. I think Stephanie had already decided that she was going to have the baby with or without Joey. She was determined to prove to herself and her mother that she was a strong and capable young woman who could raise a child on her own. I'm not sure she really understood how drastically her life would change.

—You used to talk about hitchhiking around the world, when we were kids.

—I guess I'll have to put that dream on hold for a while.

—What are you going to do about Parsons?

—College will always be there.

—But Steph, painting is your life.

—I'll figure something out.

—But what if you don't?

—You make it sound like my life is going to end.

—In some ways it will.

—I'm going to prove you wrong, John Lenza.

—What did your mother say?

—I haven't told her.

—That I can understand, but I still don't know why you haven't told Joey yet.

—I'll tell him as soon as I see him.

—You're avoiding him?

—I don't think he's going to handle the news very well.

—But he's the father. He has a right to know.

—Of course he does, but Joey can't even take care of himself.

—He's a good guy.

—I know he is, but I'm going to have the baby with or without him. And I'm going to need your help.

—Whatever you need. I'm here.

Stephanie might have been ready to be a mother, but Joey, on the other hand, was definitely not prepared to be a father. The poor guy had trouble changing the strings on his guitar.

—Joey, I've got to tell you something. It's about Stephanie.

—What is it? Is she going to break up with me?

—It's big news, and I'm not sure that I should be the one telling you this, but I think you should know.

—She's going to break up with me. I knew it wouldn't last. A girl like that—

—I'm just going to tell you. Okay? Here it goes.

—Oh, God.

—Stephanie's pregnant.

—What did you say?

—Steph's going to have your baby.

—Wow. Wait. What?

—Steph's pregnant.

—Are you sure?

—I saw the pregnancy test.

—Why did she tell you before me?

—I wouldn't take it so hard. We go back a long way.

—And it's mine?

—Of course it is. What kind of a girl do you think Stephanie is?

—Just want to be sure.

—Well, it's not mine.

—It better not be, Lenza. How far along is she?

—A couple of months.

—What am I going to do? I can't be a father.

—You'll be fine.

—She doesn't want to keep it, does she?

—I think she does.

—Shit! What am I going to do now?

—You'll figure it out. We'll all figure it out together.

I closed my notebook and ordered another cappuccino.

TWO BROOKLYNITES

Summer had exhausted itself. There was a time when September breathed new life into me, but I was no longer hopeful. I felt ugly and was in dire need of something beautiful, fearing that whatever lay ahead was not going to be pretty. Teeny had advised me to put music back into my life, so I finished my fourth cappuccino, thanked the shaggy, tattooed barista for getting me wired and made my way to the only music shop left in Park Slope, the Music Den, with the intention of buying Brian Wilson's latest record.

On the corner of Fifth Avenue and Union Street, sat the junkie I had seen a million times before on her stoop, barefoot, cigarette dangling from her mouth, smoke blowing into the slits of her eyes. She always wore the same beige dress, no matter the season. It was something of a prom gown: the sleeves were ornately trimmed in purple and gold and the neckline sank low, exposing the tops of her sunburned breasts. She was trapped in purgatory, somewhere between the stranglehold of sleep and the headlock of consciousness. Whenever I saw her, I felt both envious and sympathetic. To be able to shut yourself off like that and tune out the world. I wondered what it would be like to be that oblivious, yet her talent to power down is what startled me the most about her.

As I approached, her head dropped onto her chest, and she toppled down the concrete steps into a bunch of garbage cans. I stopped dead in my tracks and called out to her.

—Hey, you! Hey, there. Hello? Miss?

Nothing. I really wanted to leave but there was no one else on the street and I felt obligated to do something. I rolled her onto her back and noticed the track marks that ran down both of her legs, beginning just underneath the knees and traveling down to her soiled feet between her toes. Her eyes rolled to the back of her skull. I thought of myself as a lifeguard, checking her pulse, tearing the front of her dress and locating her heart. I pumped a few times before opening her mouth, shoving a couple of fingers inside and clearing a path. At the precise time I pressed my lips to hers, she seized hold of my ass with both hands, thrust her tongue down my throat, and gave me a sloppy, wet kiss. I hated wet kisses!

—Fuck. What the fuck are you doing?

—Don't be like that, baby. Come back here. Gimme some more lovin'.

—I thought you were dead.

—Just dying to kiss you, baby. I've wanted you for so long. Let me taste your honey lips again.

The gash on her forehead above the right eye bled down her cheek and into her mouth, so I handed her my handkerchief and told her to apply pressure, but she stuffed it into her bra.

—Now that that floozy dumped your sorry ass, we can finally be together.

—What floozy? What are you talking about?

—You're Gianni Lenza. Oops, excuse me. John. John Lenza. The guy with the suitcase of textbooks and the mediocre looks.

—Do I know you?

—You were married to that neurotic dipshit. She was pretty, though. Terrific eyes. Great tits. But now you're all alone. Boohoo! You could use a haircut, a shave and a few pounds. Your ass is kind of scrawny, if you ask me.

—All these times I've walked past you, I thought you were wasted.

—I probably was. Am right now. The name's Havannah. Nice to finally meet you. Wanna buy me a drink?

—How do you know so much about me? Have we met before?

—You must know that she cheated on you with that so-called poet. I read some of his work. Not a big fan.

—Are you talking about Emma?

—Oooh, she's got a tasty tongue that one. Like cinnamon. How could she be faithful when she has never been true to herself? If I may, you two were a train wreck. What are you holding on to, anyway? There was nothing there. Let go. Move on. She has. A new beau she has.

—You're fucking crazy.

—Stoned, cold and crazy like a loon. Now what do you say you buy me that drink?

—Havannah, keep out of my business.

—And John, the dead girl. Please. Let her rest in peace.

—This is too fucking weird.

—And do yourself a favor, honey lips. You're about to start something with a new girl. Don't fall in love with her. She's not worth it. Fuck her and leave her. Speaking of fucking. Want to go upstairs?

—Goodbye, Havannah.
—See you soon, John Lenza.
—Oh, I don't think so.
—You can run but you can't hide from your Havannah.
—You're a fucking wacko.
—Ouch! You really know how to hurt a girl's feelings.

The Music Den wasn't much larger than a walk-in closet, but what it lacked in size it made up for in stature. A dozen or so milk crates containing used CDs and vinyl records were near the front door along with two golden retrievers, Dizzy and Bird. Despite the shop's inherent disorder, whenever I rummaged through the haphazard stacks on the crooked shelves, I was bound to discover a gem, such as the time I bought Bob Dylan's *Blonde on Blonde* for a quarter.

Nirvana's *In Utero* was blaring. Kurt Cobain was shredding through "Rape Me" while a gaunt, hipster clerk resembling Buddy Holly was checking in a UPS delivery at the front counter. He was wearing a long-sleeved tee shirt underneath a torn polo, drinking a Starbucks coffee and occasionally glancing at me from behind his colossal vintage black eyeglass frames. Meanwhile, the other clerk futzed around in the jazz section. Her skintight black jeans were tucked into black motorcycle boots. She had one foot on a step stool and the other on a lopsided shelf. She tossed Billie Holiday's *Lady in Satin* next to Thelonius Monk's *Straight, No Chaser*, tiptoed down the step stool and, back on solid ground, touched her toes. Then she lifted her right leg, placed it on a milk crate and leaned forward, rubbing the back of her thigh. She was killing me. I had this image of her stretching with me standing behind her, cupping her perfectly round breasts, sinking my teeth into the back of her neck and giving it to her from behind. When the goddess with the olive skin noticed my lecherous stare, she flashed me a half smile; it was so warm and inviting that I nearly dropped dead right on the spot.

She sauntered behind the register—I could swear I saw her nipples through her white tank top—and perched herself in front of a shrine of posters dedicated to the guitar gods: Jimi Hendrix, Jimmy Page, Chuck Berry, Eddie Van Halen, Jeff Beck, George Harrison, Pete Townshend, Eric Clapton, Dick Dale and Prince. I wondered why Sting had been canonized. He was primarily a bass player and not really deserving of such an honor. Meanwhile, I was holding *Brian Wilson Presents Smile*, the record that took the musical genius nearly forty years to complete, but ever since the goddess had cast a spell over me, I had been unable to feign interest in the fabled album. I was defenseless, and there was nothing I could do but gawk at her. She was sultry as hell, but that quality didn't overpower her refinement. I studied her perfect posture as she handled a hipster customer, who was complaining about the price of a used Death Cab For Cutie CD, with grace and tact.

When the goddess was finished ringing up the dude, she opened a book of French poetry. Did she feel akin to Rimbaud? Did she have the fire of Baudelaire? The despair of Desnos? She said something to Buddy Holly, who glanced at me and snickered. I hated to think that they were talking about me. I shouted over Nirvana.

—Why is Sting up there?

I couldn't make out Buddy Holly's reply over the music and Dizzy and Bird's barking. The goddess turned down the music and called out to me.

—Can I help you with something?

—Yeah, you should replace Sting with someone worthy of being enshrined, like Johnny Ramone or Keith Richards.

—The owner is a big fan of the Police.

—Such a pretentious band.

—I see you're holding *Smile*. I love the Beach Boys.

—I knew that you couldn't have hung the Sting poster.

—And how did you know that?

—Well, I would think a woman of your beauty and intellect has better taste.

Buddy Holly cracked up. "That's funny shit, man." The goddess told him to shut up and stepped down from behind the counter, a parting from the guitar gods and French symbolists and headed toward me. At that moment, I got really dizzy and thought I was going to faint. I hadn't been eating well—frozen dinners, pints of Ben and Jerry's ice cream and far too much caffeine, wine and antidepressants. I had recently lost the bottle of Zolpidem Teeny had given me, so my sleep had been restless and sporadic, three hours at a time, if I was lucky. I took deep breaths, bent over to touch my toes and repeated, "Be cool. Talk like a normal person. Be cool. Talk like a normal person." When I finally gained some semblance of composure, I stood up and muttered something under my breath, like, "Holy shit," or, "Sweet Jesus," or, "You've got to be kidding me." I wasn't trying to be insulting. I was just honoring her beauty, and she chuckled, so she must have been flattered. My eyes worked their way up, and when I settled on her face, I stared directly into her green eyes, saw the back of her skull, my stare was so deep. My mouth was probably hanging wide open.

Buddy Holly was getting a big kick out of the whole damn thing. I tried to look aloof by shoving the *Smile* record into the stacks, my book into my armpit and both hands into my front pockets. Shoulders back. A grin. Not too wide. Not too goofy. "Are you looking for anything special?" She was soft-spoken and her enunciation, like her posture and taste in literature, was impeccable. She emphasized the *ing* in *looking* and *anything*. I was about to say something corny, like, "I've been looking for you. Where have you been all my life?" but I thought better of it and got unsettled, dropping my book. She picked it up, flipped through its pages and rubbed the cover with her long fingers before handing it back to me.

—This is an underrated play. Everyone admires *Waiting for Godot*, and it's a great play, don't get me wrong, but *Endgame*...This one I think is his real masterpiece.

—There is a mutual dependence between Didi and Gogo that Beckett really expands on with Clov and Hamm.

—Are you an actor?

—Me? No, I just...um...I don't act. No.

—Of course you're not. An actor would never say anything half as smart. You must be a playwright.

—Not a playwright either. I'm just a salesman.

—Do you sell vacuum cleaners? Just kidding. Do you? Not that there's anything wrong with that.

—Actually, vacuum cleaners are more appealing to me than textbooks. I mean at least you get to throw dirt onto carpets.

Textbooks. Yes, I sold textbooks for a living. For me, nothing could be more boring and demeaning than working a dead-end job I thoroughly hated, so why did I feel compelled to announce to Aphrodite that I was an underachieving, pathetic depressive? If I wanted the entire world to know, I could have just written LOSER on my forehead in large black letters. In *Endgame*, Samuel Beckett writes, *Nothing is funnier than unhappiness*. If somebody had written a play based on my life, it would have been a laugh riot. Right then and there I wanted to quit EverCover and work at the Music Den, where I could hang out with Aphrodite and play my favorite records all day. Countless hours of *Exile on Main Street* and *Marquee Moon*. Oh, the joy!

—So do you enjoy the theater?

—Yeah, but I don't go nearly as often as I should.

—I should go more often too. It's one of those things about living in New York. There's so much of it available that most people don't really go.

—It's expensive as hell.

—I really despise musicals.

—I hate the corny songs.

—But I love *Cabaret*.

—*West Side Story* is pretty cool too. Hi, I'm John Lenza.

—I'm Dawn Bello.

—Are you new here? Because I've never seen you before.

—It's my brother's shop. I'm just giving him a hand today.

—Your brother is the Police fan?

—Yep. Don't hold it against him. He's a really talented songwriter.

—Buddy Holly over there isn't your brother, is he?

—Oh, you mean Jonathan? I guess he does look a little like Buddy Holly.

—He's not a musician, is he?

—Actually, Jonathan is a drummer, but he's not my brother.

—So are you a musician too?

—No, I'm an actress.

—Oh, have I seen you in anything?

—I doubt it. But maybe you'll come see me in this new play that I'm doing. Previews start next week.

—Off-off-Broadway?

—Broadway, actually.

—Wow! Look at you. What play is it?

—It's called *Edna's Journey*. I'm Edna.

—Well, I'm impressed. That's really something.

—I've been at this thing a long time. I'm not getting any younger.

—Do you get a lot of work in New York?

—I've been getting by, but I've been thinking that I should move to LA. That's where the real work is.

—We should go to a play sometime.

—How about a movie? Tonight. It's my last night off for a while.

—I'll need to move a few appointments around, but it should all work out.

—Tarkovsky's *The Mirror* is playing at Anthology.

—Let me ask you a question. Coppola or Scorsese?

—Scorsese.

—*Raging Bull* or *Goodfellas*?

—Neither. *Mean Streets*.

—You know, I've never seen that movie.

Halfway into *The Mirror*, when I had completely given up on following Tarkovsky's stream of consciousness, I sank into my seat and my shoulder brushed against Dawn's. For somebody who was inching toward middle age, I was surprised that the mere touch of a stranger's shoulder could give me a hard-on. The shoulder isn't even the most erotic body part. It's got nothing on the thigh or breast, but Dawn's shoulder made me feel young and alive, as if I were back in my twelfth grade English class the day Mrs. Simmons had asked me to recite Hamlet's *What a rogue and peasant slave am I* monologue in front of the entire class. I had been gawking at Stephanie's perky breasts and was sporting a major erection, so I refused to come out from behind my desk, preferring the zero to a lifetime of embarrassment.

Dawn must have been turned on too because she didn't move a muscle for the rest of the film. I was poking Dawn in the ribs with my elbow when she took hold of my bicep and started running her fingers up and down the protruding veins in my forearm. I was eager to touch her olive skin, but I let her take the initiative for a while.

As the credits started to roll, Dawn leaned forward and that's when I took my cue, placing my hand on her lower back and caressing it. I slowly made my way around her waist, gracing her thigh and giving her a gentle squeeze. She remained leaning forward, resting her head on the seat in front of her and flashing me a half smile. My smile in return was wide—goofy, I'm sure. She massaged my shoulder. I placed my hand on her belly. The audience left the theatre. The credits ended. The screen went black. And that's when I kissed the back of her neck. It was the single most erotic experience of my life. The film had just ended, but I couldn't remember a damn thing about it.

Dawn Bello was a Brooklynite and, like me, an Italian American born in the summer of 1967 (the Summer of Love) in Brooklyn Hospital on DeKalb Avenue in Fort Greene. We had settled into our middle thirties in the only place we really knew: Brooklyn. We remembered when walking on Smith Street was an adventure, before it became a stretch of trendy, overpriced restaurants. We had witnessed its mass gentrification. We'd never thought that Williamsburg would become the mecca for hipsters. We had seen rents skyrocket, the locals get pushed out, the minorities in Park Slope slide below Fifth Avenue. We were shocked at the construction of a Fairway and an Ikea in Red Hook, a West Elm in Dumbo and a Starbucks in Greenpoint. We had both been raised in a more modest Brooklyn, Manhattan's stepchild, long before it became the fashionable "New Manhattan." Our city and Italian American heritage united us. And we both loved our rock and roll. She also didn't mind playing my little game.

—Mick or Keith?

—Keith.

—John or Paul?

—John.

—Prince or Michael?

—Prince.

—Johnny or Joey?

—Dee Dee.

—Roger or Pete?

—Pete.

—Robert or Jimmy?

—Jimmy.

—Sid or Johnny?

—Johnny.

—Iggy or David?

—Now that's a tough one. Both.

—You can only pick one.

—I can't. Give me another one.

—Stevie or Sly?

—Another tough one.

—Stevie? Sly? Which one would you choose?

—I can't choose. How can you choose just one? Give me another one.

—Velvet Underground or Bong Lizard Gypsy?

—Velvet Underground. I never heard of Bong Lizard…what's its name.

—Gypsy.

—Yeah. Who are they?

—They were great. They could have been huge.

—What happened?

—Like all bands, they broke up.

—Did they record anything?

—Nope.

—Ever play live?

—Yep. Once.

—And you were there at the show?

—Yep.

—What was it like? Was it great?

—It changed my life.

—Where can I get a recording of this legendary Bong Lizard Gypsy show?

—There is no recording. Just one big, beautiful memory.

About a month into our thing, Dawn and I were stretched across my bed, underneath my thick comforter, sweating our asses off. I was pulling lint from my beard; she was tugging the hair on my belly. I felt happy for a change. I wasn't thinking about Emma or my dead-end job, the overdue rent, how I'd blown it with the waitress in Seattle or how I'd been responsible for the death of Stephanie and her baby. I was completely in the moment. Dawn got out of bed, and when I reached for the towel that she was about to wrap around her waist, she stepped back and tied a knot before I could get a good look at her.

—Take off the towel. I want to see you.

—You want to see me? Here I am. Look all you want.

—Come on, take it off. Let me really see you.

—I've put on a little weight.

—We're in our thirties. A little flab here, a slight paunch there. That's what happens.

—Okay, but if I'm going to do this, then I'm going to do it the right way.

—Whatever do you have in mind, Ms. Bello?

—Sit back and enjoy the show, Mr. Lenza.

Dawn slipped into her motorcycle boots then pranced, twirled and gyrated throughout my bedroom as if she were on stage at a strip club. I whistled and hollered and even tucked a dollar bill in her towel. I never saw a woman move like that. And nobody ever moved like that for me. The striptease was topped off by her slowly shedding her towel, placing it between her legs and simulating intercourse. When she was finished grinding the towel, it was my turn. She lowered me on the bed, slithered up and down my body a couple of times before straddling me.

—Wow!

—You like?

—Wow!

—I'll take that as a "yes."

—Now that I have your full attention, there's something I've been meaning to tell you.

—Oh, man. You mean there's more? I don't think I can take it.

—Will you be serious for a minute? It's important.

—Okay, shoot.

—I'm married.

—Come again.

—I said I'm married.

—I'm sorry, I thought you said you were married.

—Are you ever serious?

—Oh, I knew that you were married.

—You did?

—Sure. I'm not blind.

—How did you know?

—For one, we're always hanging out in my dumpy apartment.

—The floors are gorgeous, though.

—Yes, they are, but the rest of the place is a hole.

—That's pretty good, John, but we've only been hanging out for like a month.

—Two, you wear a wedding ring.

—So do you.

—But I'm divorced.

—Then why do you still wear the ring?

—I thought it would help me with the chicks.

—So you don't mind that I'm married?

—Mind? Why would I mind? It's a minor inconvenience.

—Anyway, my marriage is running its course.

—Does that mean you're breaking up?

—I'll probably end up leaving him.

—How long have you been married?

—Is my being married going to be a problem?

—Well, it's certainly an obstacle.

—We'll figure it out.

—We will?

—We won't let it get in the way of what we have together.

—We won't?

—No, we won't. How long have you been divorced?

—Oh, I don't know. Eight months or so. Something like that.

—You're really together.

—I am?

—You are. You're doing great.

—I am?

We were moving quickly, but that's the way I operated: swiftly, impulsively and recklessly, often disregarding the sensible voice inside my head that had warned me about marrying Emma, about playing that dangerous game with Stephanie, about getting involved with married women. Dawn was a wounded warrior, just like me, and let's face it, I told myself wounded people were the only people worth knowing. Happiness was an illusion. Our natural state was one of misery. When I got mixed up with Dawn Bello, I knew that I was only setting myself up for inevitable, insurmountable pain, but maybe I needed to suffer.

The day after Dawn told me she was married, I was lying in the silky grass in Brooklyn Bridge Park, reading Bob Dylan's autobiography, *Chronicles*, on a perfect October afternoon. Shifting my weight on my arms with the turn of every page, I read about Dylan's retreat from the psychosis of the sixties and the labels he felt compelled to shed: "spokesman of a generation," "great American poet," "prophet," "visionary," "the Messiah." Dylan passes over most of the sixties and seventies without any acknowledgment. He never delves into "going electric," skipping out on the Woodstock festival or converting to Christianity. Instead, several chapters are dedicated to his motorcycle accident and retreat from society, trying to live a normal life with his wife and children in Woodstock. It was Bob Dylan's story to tell. He was at the helm, the pilot, navigating his course, rewriting the tragedies for sure, maybe avoiding them altogether, and most likely reimagining the highlights of his life. He was devising his own myth. If I were ever to write an autobiography, would I tell my entire life story? What would I say about my ex-wife? How much would I share about Stephanie's tragedy? How many chapters would be dedicated to Dawn? What events in my life would I leave out?

I couldn't care less about the musical Dylan was attempting to write with the poet Archibald MacLeish, so I put the book down and scanned the Brooklyn Bridge, my favorite bridge. My thoughts drifted in and out, from the ordinary drawbridge in Fremont to the hot waitress I'd blown it with. I wondered what she had told her friends about me. Was I the impotent depressive from New York? Or was I the heartbroken poet so deeply in love with his dead wife that he was incapable of getting over the loss? It was her fiction to devise, the way that I had devised my own about her.

When I shifted my gaze to the vacant warehouse nearby, I spotted Dawn and her husband, Kurt, a tall, clean-cut, blond dude who looked as if he was chiseled out of granite. Dawn hadn't told me that she was married to the Incredible Hulk. Holy shit! After noting the enormous dimensions of my competitor, I prayed to God that he didn't know anything about me. I was no fighter! They were holding hands, meandering along a dirt path, making their way toward me. Dawn was scanning the ground before her and didn't see me, but Kurt caught my scrutinizing stare. He looked me right in the eye and opened his mouth as if he was about to say something, so I opened *Chronicles* and shoved my nose into it, retreating into Dylan's mythological world. I was already uncomfortable knowing that Dawn was still sleeping with her husband, but seeing them together, holding hands, really freaked me out, especially since she'd told me that she was going to leave him.

I wanted to believe that I had something genuine with Dawn. I wanted to believe that Dawn was sitting in the front row at my show, feeding me lines, cheering me on and laughing at all my jokes, yet anyone in his right mind could have seen that she was in love with the Incredible Hulk and was never going to leave him. But it was too late for me: I had become obsessed with Dawn Bello. I was already afraid to go on without her.

The following weekend, while Kurt, who was also an actor, was out of town, shooting a commercial for athletic supporters, Dawn and I were doing all kinds of new and exciting things in his bed. Oh, the joy! Unfortunately, I didn't get a good peek at Dawn's perfectly round breasts, but at least we were at her place for a change, a swanky loft in Gowanus, the top floor of a converted warehouse on the corner of Union and Bond. She had a good view of the Expressway snaking around the outskirts of the city and the F and G trains rumbling into the Smith-Ninth Street station. We toasted Dawn's ten years of sobriety with nonalcoholic beer, but the guest of honor wasn't in the mood to celebrate. Dawn Bello was still trying to put her self-destructive inclinations to rest. Like me, she had spent most of her life flirting with masochism. Her fixation on securing the next acting gig had a way of keeping her locked in a perpetual vacuum of anxiety.

As a veteran New York actor, Dawn finally landed the role of a lifetime—the lead in a Broadway play—but she was eager to complete the run of *Edna's Journey* and move to Los Angeles where she said the "real work" was. I guess her obsession with landing the next job was the result of the unfavorable reviews the play had been receiving. Critics were particularly harsh on Dawn. They wrote scathing things like "a mediocre actor gives a mediocre performance in a mediocre drama" and "Dawn Bello is pretty to look at but not pretty to watch." Dawn was not only deeply hurt by the reviews, she agreed wholeheartedly with them. She was unsatisfied with her performance and expected either to be fired or for the show to close prematurely. Perhaps the character she was playing was a little too close to home.

Edna is the alcoholic wife of an abusive alcoholic, and like most alcoholics, this couple is unable to love completely. The bottle is their one true love. Edna's husband steals from her and has countless affairs. Eventually, she finds a lover of her own, but she refuses to leave her husband and two children. Meanwhile, her lover, a music producer who drives a 1966 Corvette convertible, never stops pursuing her. He makes Edna feel like a teenager, the star of her own narcissistic, erotic dream. Every waking moment. Every time she touches herself. Such fantasies are made for the big stage.

Dawn hoped that *Edna's Journey* would give her the financial freedom to complete the documentary she and her husband had shelved about orphans living on the streets of urban America. Dawn and Kurt had already interviewed several homeless urchins in New Orleans, Portland and Los Angeles as well as the Brooklyn orphanage where Dawn had lived for three years until her aunt gained custody of her and her brother.

I was kind of bored listening to Dawn babble on about the play, the critics and the film role she might be up for, so I turned on the television, surfed the channels and eventually settled on *The Sopranos*. Tony Soprano is strangling a little guy in khakis, bringing him to his knees and pistol-whipping him until he was a bloody pulp. Tony lights a cigar, kneels down, pulls out a handkerchief and wipes the blood off the poor schmuck's shoes. "I took it easy on ya 'cause you're like a brother to me. Next time I'm not gonna be so nice. Ya have till Tuesday to come up with the dough." Soprano looks at his watch, gives the little guy a friendly wink, hops into his Lexus and drives away.

—He's such a stereotype.
—What are you talking about? Tony Soprano's an iconic character.
—How come every ethnicity but ours has made strides on television?
—People love *The Sopranos*. It's a groundbreaking show.
—We're either the Neanderthal thug or the bumbling fool.
—I don't find it insulting.
—You should. You're an actor.
—You're so uptight. It's only a television show.
—Not all of us are in the mob.
—No kidding, John.

Recently, I had been at a high school in Crown Heights, waiting for the chairperson, when I struck up a conversation with a group of juniors. A short, dark-haired girl with bright red lipstick asked me what I was. I told her I was a textbook salesman, but she was more interested in my ethnicity. "What *are* you? Puerto Rican?" When I told her I was Italian American, the entire group took a step back. Their reaction confused me. Then the same girl asked, "What are you doing selling textbooks?" and I naively replied, "I really want to be a writer, so I'm doing this until that ship comes in." The girl laughed. "You're in the Mafia. You don't need to sell textbooks unless it's a front or something like that."

—That's hysterical, John.

—You have a warped sense of humor, Dawn.

—Some of the stereotypes are true. You have to admit that.

—The media makes caricatures of us.

—Oh, I get it now—Gianni Lenza, of course. That's it.

—Get what? What are you talking about?

—Why don't you want to be called Gianni?

—It's one of my things. I'm working on it.

—Well, I like your name. Can I call you Gianni?

—Please just call me John.

—You're trying to detach yourself from your heritage.

—That's what my ex-wife said.

—What are you worried about? Look at you. You're breaking the stereotypes. You went to college; you're not in the Mafia; you don't dress like a guido. I don't see a pinky ring.

—My father wears one.

—Does he have a gold rope chain too?

—First of all, I never finished college. I used to drive a Cadillac Seville. And I own a gold cross that my mother bought for me one Christmas.

—Oh, so the stereotypes are true.

—Not funny, Dawn.

—Lighten up, Gianni.

—Don't call me that.

—Oh, come on.

—Only my mother and Stephanie ever called me that.

—Stephanie? Who's Stephanie?

—My best friend.

—She gets to call you Gianni but I can't?

—That's right.

—Is she more important to you than I am?

—You're both important to me.

—So when do I get to meet this best friend Stephanie.

—She's dead so—

—Oh, I'm sorry.

—That's okay. It happened a long time ago.

—Sounds to me like you're still mourning.

—Yeah, well it's my fault she's dead.

—What happened? Let me guess. You pushed her in front of a moving train.

—Not funny, Dawn.

—I'm just kidding around. Seriously, what really happened?

—Can we talk about something else?

—Okay, but don't you think it's kind of unhealthy, holding on to the guilt like that?

—Don't you think having an extramarital affair is kind of unhealthy?

—Touché!

Dawn answered her cell phone, opened an O'Doul's and stepped onto the fire escape. I went back to channel surfing. There were far too many channels and nothing worth watching. Just sitting next to a television—it didn't even have to be on—I felt as if I'd lost a couple of hundred brain cells. On channel 465—the shitty sitcom network—I came across *Everybody Loves Raymond*. My parents loved the show, so I decided to give it a shot and see what they professed to be "the most hilarious sitcom of all time." I suffered through almost the entire episode before Dawn came back inside.

—Another fucking stereotype.

—It's a funny show, John.

—Who was that on the phone?

—Nobody.

—It was him, wasn't it?

—Kurt?

—I saw you with your husband last weekend.

—That wasn't me.

—You were holding hands in Brooklyn Bridge Park.

—I told him all about you.

—He knows about me? Why did you do that? He's the Incredible Hulk. He's going to kill me.

—Don't call him that.

—Have you seen the guy? He's a fucking monster.

—He's not a monster, John. He wants us to work things out.

—You're not going to do that, are you?

—He's my husband.

—But you don't love him. You love me. Right?

—We've been together for fifteen years.

—But your marriage isn't working. You said so yourself.

—I love you, John. I really do, but Kurt's my husband.

—If you really love me, you'd leave the guy already.

—I need to reexamine what Kurt gives me and what I need in a relationship.

—You're never going to leave him.

—Please understand that I can't leave my husband for another man. I'd have to leave for me. You know what I mean?

—You deserve to be happy, Dawn.

—Why do people always say that? Maybe I don't deserve happiness. Has everyone on this planet earned the right to be happy?

—So you don't think you deserve happiness?

—Good people deserve it. I'm not sure that I do.

—Are you saying that you're not good?

—I could be better. Would you like another O'Doul's?

—I don't want to hang out in your place anymore. In your bed. In his bed.

—Okay. We'll stay at your place from now on.

I'd been irritable lately and figured it had something to do with my insomnia, my poor diet and the antidepressants. Teeny told me that sleeping with a married woman wasn't helping matters. Anyway, the combination was killing me. Something had to go, so I handed Dawn the bottle of Zoloft and asked her to dispose of it for me. She emptied the contents into the toilet, flushed and tossed me the bottle. I flung it in the trash can. Funny thing, as soon as the antidepressant was gone, I started to regret my decision.

—Now we're both clean and sober.

—I'm not sure that I really want to be.

—Today is the first day of the rest of your life.

—I really hate that saying. And I really hate that you told your husband about me. He's going to kill me.

—I just wanted to prove to you that I love you more than anything else in this world.

—Leave him. That would be all the proof I need.

—You're the love of my life. That should be all you need.

—How did he react to the news?

—He took it very hard, but I owe it to him. I owe him the truth.

—So you were looking out for him?

—I was looking out for you. Me. Him. All of us.

—You were looking out for yourself mostly.

—I never loved him the way I love you, John.

Dawn was playing with my head, and I really wished that I hadn't dumped the Zoloft. It was only later, in hindsight, that I was able to decipher her circuitous way with words, her never-ending story of bullshit. I wish I had known when we first met that I'd end up being a detective. I might not have applied for the job. I'm no Columbo.

Who am I kidding? I would have followed Dawn to the end of the earth.

97

The train ride along the Hudson River can be a bucolic jaunt. A mere twenty minutes north of Manhattan you can escape the confines of the concrete metropolis. However, a true urbanite can never entirely purge the city. Not even the smell of pine, the open space, and the river can cleanse a New Yorker; his soul has been permanently contaminated. Nevertheless, somehow the world looks more appealing when you're looking at it from a moving train. Even bleak places, Peekskill for instance, appear downright idyllic when viewed from a grimy window on the Metro-North. Dawn and I sat in a crowded car, behaving like oversexed teenagers, flirting and giggling, making out while the other passengers looked on. She bit my tongue. I licked her face. We were happy. I was happy. And it was still autumn, so I was feeling somewhat confident.

A German tourist snapped a picture of us standing on a hill in Beacon above the Hudson River. Dawn had her arm around my waist, squeezing me tightly. She was glowing, looking up at me with her half-smile. Grinning with optimism, I stared directly into the lens. I had never felt so present and full of life. It's the only photograph of us together.

The Dia Museum had once been a Nabisco factory. The building itself was a work of art. We strolled arm in arm past some of the most significant art of the contemporary era, pausing before Robert Smithson's *Map of Broken Glass*. Both of us appreciated its symmetry, closing one eye and tracing its oblong shapes with our fingers. Looking deeply into the prisms, I was propelled into another dimension, inside Alice's looking glass, and my imagination ran amuck. The first thing I did was stuff Dawn's husband down a rabbit hole, and then she and I ran off into a field of lotus. After we sipped tea with the March Hare, the Hatter posed the riddle: *Why is Dawn like a writing desk?* When we couldn't solve the riddle, we were swept away by the Queen of Hearts, who married us—though we escaped before she chopped off our heads. Later, we ate raspberry tarts with the Knave of Hearts. A splendid time was had by both of us.

When I popped back into reality, Dawn was sporting a paradoxical look, grinning like the Cheshire Cat but wearing her melancholy like the Mock Turtle.

—Let's pretend that we're in Italy at the premiere of my documentary. Oh, never mind. Forget it.

—I'm game. Let's pretend. Who should I be?

—It's a stupid fantasy.

—Fantasies are supposed to be far-fetched. I was just pretending—

—I'm not interested in your fantasies right now, John.

—What's eating at you?

—Nothing. It's just that I'm enjoying this day so much.

—Me too. We should do stuff like this more often.

—But it's going to end soon.

—What is? The day?

—Well, at least we can enjoy it while it lasts.

Dawn grabbed my hand and dragged me to Joseph Beuys's *News from the Coyote*, but I couldn't concentrate on the art. Whatever was gnawing at Dawn was beginning to gnaw at me. She let go of my hand and sauntered over to the other side of Beuys's piece. *It's going to end soon.* Was she going to break things off with me? I looked at the coyote, then at Dawn, the coyote, then Dawn, the coyote, then Dawn. I eventually settled on Dawn, who rolled up her program, crossed her arms behind her back and stared at the ceiling, looking like she'd rather be anywhere but there with me. Her indifference made her even more appealing.

While I was standing inside Richard Serra's *Torqued Ellipses*, the enormity of the curved steel plates created a disorienting visual illusion. Dawn grew unexpectedly playful, skipping away from me. I was feeling lightheaded but trailed behind her, trying to maintain my focus and balance. Serra had said that he was interested in "the opportunity for all of us to become something different from what we are." At that moment, Dawn Bello was a coquettish Little Red Riding Hood. "Come and get me. Catch me if you can." And I was the Big Bad Wolf, looking to shred her to pieces with my grisly claws and jagged teeth. "I'm going to get you, Little Red Riding Hood. I'm going to eat you up." I chased after Dawn but was overcome with dizziness, tripped and fell into a steel plate. When Dawn skipped over to me, I threw my arms around her and pretended to bite her neck. She shrieked like a damsel in distress and tried to squirm free, but I had hold of her waist and pulled her into me to steady myself.

—Stop, you're going to make me want to do something to you right here.

—That's the point, my dear.

—Ooh, you feel so good.

—The art arouses me.

—You're beautiful, John.

—You make me feel beautiful.

—I want a life with you. You make me want everything. A career, a house in the country, a dog, children.

—I had no idea you were thinking about such things. What do you say we get a little place in Beacon?

—We could have had a beautiful life together.

—We still can, Dawn. Leave Kurt. Give us a shot. Let's get a dog. A dachshund.

—John, are you okay? You're as white as a ghost.

—I don't feel so great.

I had killed the moment, and then I almost blacked out on the museum stairs and nearly killed myself.

—I need to sit down.

—The café is right over there. Can you make it?

—Give me your arm.

I put my head down on the table in a corner booth in the museum's cozy café. The late afternoon sun pierced the trees; long splashes of orange and yellow light penetrated the café's windows, covering us in both light and shadow. I was a little woozy and struggling to regain my equilibrium while Dawn pulled out her cell phone and listened to her messages but paused to thank the debonair waiter who brought us a couple of cappuccinos and a slice of chocolate cake.

—Hey, John. How are you feeling?

—Like a million bucks.

—Have something to eat and drink. Can I get you a glass of water?

—I'd rather have a Valium.

—I better get you home.

—Thanks for taking care of me. Who was that on the phone?

—That was the director of this film I was up for. I got it.

—What film?

—This is really big. It shoots in California.

—That's amazing, Dawn. Congratulations.

—It's so overwhelming. I can't even wrap my brain around it.

The debonair waiter came over to see if everything was all right and then paid us a compliment.

—Please allow me to tell you that you are a beautiful couple, the most beautiful couple that has ever eaten here.

—Thank you. That's awfully kind of you.

—No, thank you for visiting our humble café. Thank you. Thank you, beautiful people.

The waiter bowed a hundred times, clicked his heels and took us in one last time before exiting to the kitchen. I figured he must have recognized Dawn and was just buttering us up so we'd leave a generous tip. Dawn, on the other hand, was quite flattered. Sometimes she could be so naïve.

—That was such a nice thing to say.

—Don't you know he's just being nice so we'll leave him a big tip?

—Not everyone has an ulterior motive, John.

—I wish I could believe that.

—What is wrong with you?

—Other than almost blacking out and feeling like total shit, there's nothing wrong.

—Have something to eat and drink. It'll make you feel better.

—I'd feel a hell of a lot better if you spent the weekend taking care of me.

—I already told you I couldn't.

—You're never going to leave him are you?

—I'm not going to say this again: I will not leave my husband for another man.

Maybe Teeny had been right all along: it's impossible for me to live a "healthy, productive life" while I'm seeing a married woman.

—I'm barely staying afloat, John.

—I'll help you in any way I can.

—I need to help myself first. I have to be able to take care of myself. I want to be self-reliant. This cake is delicious. Why don't you have a bite?

—I'm not really hungry.

—It's the best cake I've ever tasted. Try some. Open up. Here comes the plane.

—Really, I'm not hungry. I don't want to lose you.

—You'll never lose me, John Lenza.

—You said earlier, "It's going to end soon." What did you mean by that?

—Not now, John. Isn't my love enough for you?

As the train pulled into Grand Central Station, Dawn woke up from her nap, turned to me and pleaded, "Please let me go, John. I'm no good for anyone. Please. Let me go. Please. I'm sorry." She kissed my forehead and leaped off the train before I could grab her. I jumped out of my seat, sprinted out of the car and down the platform, dodging the rush hour commuters. I spotted her in the main concourse, dashing for the exit. I raced out the door onto Park Avenue, but I was too late. Dawn had disappeared into the rising night.

In hindsight, I realized that Dawn always came off as more theatrical than genuine. I never really trusted her, never could distinguish between when she was telling the truth and when she was just acting. She was always on stage, playing a role. Her masterful performance as the recovering alcoholic trapped in a loveless marriage tricked me into believing that we were soul mates. I knew that Dawn and her husband were serious about moving to Los Angeles. They were trying to save their marriage, start a new life together and kick-start their careers, but I pursued her anyway. What does that say about me? Dawn might have exited stage left, but did that mean the curtain had finally dropped on our melodrama?

The night *Edna's Journey* was to close, I paced the lobby of the Ethel Barrymore Theatre, wondering if I should spring for the $85 ticket in the nosebleeds. Around ten minutes into the show, while I was still pacing the lobby, there was a round of electrifying applause. I pictured Kurt, in the front row, beaming with pride, leaping out of his seat to lead the standing ovation. I snuck past the usher and opened the theater doors to get a look for myself. A security guard asked for my ticket but when I told him I lost it, he escorted me back to the lobby. I repeated this pathological cycle a few hundred times until security finally kicked me to the curb. I stopped in the bodega next door, bought a forty-ounce Budweiser and made the rash decision to storm back into the theater, shouting "Fire!" with ushers and security at my heels and then sprint back outside, down Forty-Seventh Street to Eighth Avenue where I'd get lost in a crowd of pedestrians. When I approached the theater, two policemen were standing out front, twirling their batons, so I slipped the beer inside my jacket, gave the officers a friendly smile and salute and moped all the way to the subway, back to my shithole.

EVERYTHING AND NOTHING

In the weeks that followed our breakup, I must have dialed Dawn's number a hundred times only to hang up in that thought-provoking, split-second silence right before the phone actually rings. I compulsively checked my voice mail and email. Even though Dawn didn't work at the Music Den, I spent a lot of time hanging around the store, buying a shitload of records, chatting with Buddy Holly, hoping she'd stop in to see her brother. I was staring at every woman in Southside, on the subway, on the street and in Cosby's, the dive bar where I had been hanging out with Teeny, who had fallen off the wagon. (I'm afraid I might have pushed him off.) I was longing for Dawn to pursue me, maybe even plead with me to get back together.

Physically, I was a wreck. Teeny was really concerned about the black circles around my eyes and how freakishly frail I had become. My stomach was also killing me, but I kept that bit of information to myself.

—When are you going to see a doctor, big boy?

—Hey, I got *Physical Graffiti* for a dollar at the Music Den.

—Stop hanging around there. It's creepy. She doesn't even work there.

—You're the one who told me to put music back into my life.

—Have you taken a good look at yourself lately? You're a walking disaster.

—I feel like a million bucks.

—Bullshit. Take care of yourself, big boy.

—I have you to take care of me, Teeny.

—I'm doing my best, but you're only giving me so much to work with.

—I'm listening. Tell me what I should do now that the only woman I've loved since Stephanie broke up with me.

—You've stopped calling your ex-wife, right?

—I haven't done that in a long time.

—Stop writing letters to your dead girlfriend.

—I'm working on that.

—Just stop it. You've punished yourself for too long.

—Apparently, not long enough.

—John, listen to me. Stop pursuing the married chick.

—But I think we were meant to be together.

—John, she's more fucked up than you are. At least there's some hope for you.

—You think so?

—Come work for me. It'll take your mind off her.

—I already have a job.

—Yeah, some job. They should have fired your ass a long time ago.

—Hey, I'm a valuable asset at EverCover. Been there a long time.

—You're just afraid to quit. You're waiting to be fired. What are you going to do when they kick your ass into the gutter?

—I'll get by.

—You can't even pay your rent now.

—I just gave my landlord some money. That should hold him off for a while.

—Do you hear what you're saying? You're falling apart. Are you taking the Zoloft?

—That shit was killing me.

I wasn't in the mood to discuss any of the shit that was weighing me down. I was more interested in the novel Teeny had on his lap, J.M. Coetzee's *Waiting for the Barbarians*, but he changed the subject altogether. He shoved a bunch of photographs into my hands and urged me to peruse the compromising positions of the college guys he had been sleeping with. Teeny had been meeting young men, who were not much older than boys, on Craigslist; it had become something of a hobby. He'd experiment with them and then construct an elaborate photo shoot of his conquests in provocative poses.

—Do you want to see Teeny's beefcakes for the month of November?

—No, that's all right, Teeny. I got to get going.

—Where are you going? I know it can't be work.

—I have things to do.

—Things to do? Oh, don't tell me you're going to the Music Den.

—I'm going to do some work on the play I've been writing. I think I really got a bead on it.

—You're not working on a play. You're going to look for her.

—I thought I'd see what she's been up to.

—She's no good for you. Stay away from her, you sick fuck.

—I'll meet you at Cosby's tonight.

—Drinks are on me. Lord knows you're going to need a few hundred when you get back.

So I disregarded Teeny's advice and went looking for Dawn. I figured I'd just show up at her door. Surprise her. See if she missed me. Make one final plea for us to be together. When I left Southside, the Velvet Underground's "Pale Blue Eyes" popped into my head. Lou Reed's heavy New York accent complemented the awkward rhythm of my pace, while the desire to see Dawn propelled me forward. I was a robot, placing one foot in front of the other down the slope. For the moment, just having a purpose satisfied me.

I stopped in front of a poster for *Edna's Journey* at the bus stop on the corner of Seventh Avenue and Ninth Street. Dawn's costume consisted of the same clothes she'd been wearing the day we met at the Music Den: a tight, white tank top—I could just make out her nipples in the picture—and skintight black jeans tucked inside motorcycle boots. Eyeliner ran down her face. She looked like she had been out all night drinking and hadn't cleaned herself up. She was on all fours, staring straight ahead, looking sultry as hell. Behind her on the left was a tall, tan man in a black pinstripe suit, cradling an infant in one arm while a young boy clutched his leg. On her right, a shirtless man wearing a white cowboy hat and jeans was sitting on the hood of a red Corvette convertible, looking like Paul Newman in *Hud*. He was the threatening, bad boy with chiseled but predictable good looks. Large orange letters spelled out DAWN BELLO. To me, Dawn was the embodiment of Hollywood rather than an Italian girl from Bensonhurst. She was no longer an ordinary person; she was a celebrity. I was kind of glad that the critics panned her and that the play had closed. I hated to think of Dawn as a successful actress, that she had surpassed me in any way, so I pretended that I was looking at an established Broadway actress instead. A Tony Award winner. Cate Blanchett. Patti LuPone. Bebe Neuwirth. Someone had written "slut" above Dawn's head. I thought about the thousands of people who must have seen that poster. I spat in my hand and tried to rub off the slur, but it had been written in permanent black marker and nothing came of my hard work.

I strolled past Vito, the old barber who had been a mainstay in the neighborhood for more than forty years. He was sitting in a chair, smoking a cigar, reading the *New York Post*, waiting to clip someone's head as talk radio droned on. Last summer, I'd stopped in for a trim. His air conditioner had been broken, and when he stripped down to his boxers and wife beater, I fled the shop before the degenerate even laid a finger on my head. On this particular day, he was wearing a plaid shirt and khakis, and though I really could have used a shave and a haircut, I wasn't going to let that perverted old man touch a single hair on my noodle, so I kept moving.

The Vietnam veteran who everyone called Tank was armed with a broom and dustpan as he methodically swept the corner of Seventh Avenue and Third Street. When I accidentally kicked his pile of debris, Tank turned his broom into a rifle and gunned me down. I went along with his pantomime and played dead, but he told me to fuck off, so I kept moving.

My least favorite character in the neighborhood was the belligerent Puerto Rican gentleman who sat on an empty milk crate, drinking a forty-ounce in front of the laundromat, shouting at unsuspecting passersby. When he spotted me approaching, he jumped up and shouted in my face; his drunken words were surprisingly decipherable.

—Go back to where you came from, whitey.

—This is where I'm from.

—Rich white people like you are ruining my neighborhood.

—Do I look rich to you? Here's a buck. Now leave me alone.

—So that's all I'm worth to you?

—Do I look like a bank? Here's another buck.

—Thanks, cracker. You ain't half bad.

The drunk gathered his things inside the milk crate and raced off to the deli for more beer. I kept moving.

I paused in front of a house on Garfield Place that had a twenty-five-foot flagpole in the front yard. An American flag the size of Texas was waving from it. The PROUD TO BE AMERICAN placards that were plastered in the front windows of the house blocked the sunlight from streaming into the living room. I saluted the flag and belted out a few bars of "God Bless America" before moving on to a seven-foot statue of Jesus in the front yard of a house on Carroll Street. I made the sign of the cross and said a Hail Mary, then continued onward.

On the corner of Sixth Avenue and Union Street, I bumped into Richard Pritchard, who was cradling Pablo in his arms and singing "Papa Was a Rollin' Stone" with an unlit cigarette in his mouth.

—Hey there, Sir John. Can you believe those motherfuckers stole my shopping cart? That shit would not have happened back in the eighties. Folks knew me back then. Nowadays they could give two shits about the hobo on the street.

—I thought you slept in front of the police station when you weren't in the shelter.

—I did, but I hit the bottle real good last night.

—Sounds like you were comatose.

—Just about. *Papa was a rollin' stone. Wherever he laid his hat was his home—*

—Is there anything I can get you, Richard?

—Well, since you asked. I could use a pack of Marlboros.

—I mean is there anything you really need?

—Yeah. Cigarettes. I really need a smoke.

—I can do better than a pack of Marlboros.

—You ain't got a bottle of Gordon's for me, do you?

—I was thinking you could come stay with me for a while.

—I wouldn't want to intrude, Sir John.

—It'll be a break from the shelter and the street, and I could use the company. We'll be helping each other out.

—And what about Pablo?

—Bring him along. My cat could use a friend. But there's no smoking. My landlord would have a conniption.

—And he won't mind there being a homeless man on his property?

—What homeless man? You're my friend.

—I don't know, Sir John. I've gotten pretty used to the streets.

—You can stay as long as you like. Leave when you want.

—I can always count on you. My man. Sir John, the noble knight. You don't look too good, brother. Looks like you got your balls in a knot.

—I haven't been feeling well.

—You gotta lay off the booze, son.

—You should heed your own advice, Richard.

I tossed Richard the keys to my place, gave him my address and continued east on Union Street, where I encountered a pack of preteen girls who had commandeered the entire sidewalk. Two were sitting on a brick wall, one was on a fire hydrant, two were on the curb, and at least three were sitting in the middle of the sidewalk. As I got closer to them, they each put on a blank, stoic expression and stared me down. They were probably playing one of their little games—stare down the old guy and make him feel self-conscious—so I stared back. That's when they started in with their inane cackling that made me feel uneasy. I tried to save face, since I didn't want to look like a total putz. I couldn't let a group of pubescent girls think they'd defeated a weak, pathetic fool like me, so I glared at one of the older girls and spoke softly. "You're all a bunch of stinky little cunts." They began shouting things like, "You're a nasty old man," "Fuck you, Grandpa," and "My dad is going to kick your ass." Somebody pegged me in the back of the head with a tennis ball. I turned around, took an exaggerated bow and then continued on my way to Fifth Avenue.

On the corner of Fifth Avenue and Union Street, Havannah the Junkie was sitting on her stoop, looking like she always did, cigarette dangling from her mouth, smoke blowing into the slits of her eyes. Even though it was unusually warm for the last day of November, she was barefoot and wearing the beige prom gown with the low neckline that now exposed an enormous tattoo of what appeared to be two mating snakes. She sort of lit up when she saw me.

—Well, if it isn't the one and only Gianni Lenza. Sorry. John Lenza.

—I don't have anything to say to you.

—Boy, don't sound so happy to see me. Come here for a sec.

—I'm in a hurry, Havannah.

—Oh, so you do remember my name. I must have made quite the first impression.

—You sure did. Nice tattoo.

—Thanks. Did it myself. I told you that you couldn't run away from me.

—Watch me, Havannah.

—Wait a second. Hold on. You're going to see that bitch, aren't you?

—I don't know what you're talking about.

—You couldn't just fuck her and leave her. You had to go and fall in love with the bitch.

—If you're referring to Dawn, she fell in love with me too.

—You're a walking disaster. Do you know that?

—It takes one to know one.

—You're juvenile too. Listen, you deserve better than her. Wanna buy me that drink you owe me?

—Havannah, you scare the hell out of me, but you're the most clairvoyant junkie I've ever met.

—I don't know what you just said but thanks. So tell me. How does it feel to see her fail? I didn't think the play was so great, but she was downright abysmal. Wouldn't you say? I bet you're a little happy that she failed. Makes you feel better about yourself. I remember the time you two fought about how she was going to give her husband another chance. Lucky for you that she's moving to California. You'll never see her ass again. Goodbye and good riddance is what I say.

—Havannah, I won't tell you again. Stay the hell out of my business.

—What about that drink you owe me?

—You're already shitfaced. You don't need alcohol.

—Listen now. Don't fall for the lie she's going to tell you. Don't believe her. But you will. I know you will.

I moved on.

As soon as I rang Dawn's bell, I wanted to turn back. I began to doubt my purpose, if I even had one. I mean, what was I doing? What if the Incredible Hulk was home? I was taking my life into my own hands. But then Dawn came on the intercom, and there was something about the lilt in her voice that made me somewhat optimistic about my mission.

—Hi, it's me.

—John?

—The one and only.

—How are you?

—Like a million bucks.

—It's good to hear your voice.

—It's good to hear yours.

—No more fainting spells, I hope.

—Not since the museum. Listen Dawn, I think we're supposed to be together. Me and you. That's how this story should end.

—I'm glad you're here. I was going to call you.

—I was going to call you too, but I figured you needed some time alone. To think.

—Come on up.

—Is the Hulk there?

—That's not nice, John. Come on up.

Dawn was wearing her infamous tight white tank top and a pair of very short denim shorts. I looked for her nipples, but I couldn't see them. At least I had her legs to ogle. She had a pen behind her ear and was holding a manuscript. The television droned on in the background. *Sex and the City*. Dawn enjoyed the glamorous show, the way it mythologized New York. She believed she had a kinship with Carrie Bradshaw, a sympathetic thirtysomething trying to maintain her writing career and find love in the big city. I hated the show.

—John, what happened to you?

—What?

—You look like death.

—I'm trying something new with my hair. You don't like it?

—You don't look well. Is everything okay?

—I feel like a million bucks but enough about me. What do you have there? A script?

—Yep. We start shooting in a couple of days. I'm scared to death.

—What about *Edna's Journey*?

—The show closed.

—Oh, I'm sorry to hear that.

—You never got to see it, did you?

—Oh, no, I saw it. You were great. Really great.

The coffee table was covered with dirty plates, glasses and empty bottles. The apartment was cluttered with cardboard boxes. Some were labeled. Some were numbered. Brown packing tape. Bubble wrap. Scissors. Rope. A hand truck. Piles of books, records and CDs. Bags of clothes.

—Where are you going? Are you moving?

—I'm moving to LA. I thought you knew.

—How would I know that?

—I don't know, I just thought—

—Is Kurt going with you?

—John, are you feeling okay? You're as white as a ghost.

—When are you leaving?

—Tomorrow. Are you still having trouble sleeping?

—Tomorrow? You weren't going to tell me?

—I was going to call you.

—When? When you got to LA?

—I don't know, John. This isn't easy for me.

—Dawn, do you know a junkie? Havannah? She lives over on Fifth and Union. It's the oddest thing—

—Who? No. Why? Who is she?

—She told me you're moving. Are you sure you don't know her? She's a junkie with the gift of prophecy. She knows all sorts of things about me and you and—

—You're not making any sense, John.

—She said that you're going to lie to me today.

—John, are you okay? You look like you're going to pass out.

I wasn't going to pass out, I was going to puke, so I sprinted for the bathroom, knocking over a couple of boxes and tripping over the hand truck in the process. I got down on my knees, lifted the toilet seat, stuck my head in and while I waited for the inevitable purge I thought about the lie Dawn was going to tell me. When I was done puking my guts up, Dawn walked in, kneeled beside me and held my hand.

—I want us to be together, Dawn.

—I think you need to see a doctor.

—I'm feeling better. Don't go to LA.

—You're the love of my life, Gianni Lenza.

—Then stay. Let's try again.

—Listen, there's something I have to tell you.

—Tell me you're leaving him.

—Let's get out of here before Kurt gets back. He only went out to get more boxes.

Dawn threw on a pair of jeans and boots, grabbed her leather jacket and a picnic blanket and scribbled a note to her husband. *Be back soon, baby. Love, Lil' Thrills.* I plucked a bottle of Cabernet, a bag of breadsticks and a couple of plastic cups from an open box and snatched goat cheese and grapes from the refrigerator before she whisked me out the door, up the slope all the way to Prospect Park. We sat on a hill above the dog beach where an old woman tossed a tennis ball to a Jack Russell terrier. While Dawn carried on about unfair theater critics, the new film that she believed was going to catapult her to riches and fame and starting her new life in California with the Incredible Hulk, I enjoyed the wine and splattered ants that had gathered on a piece of goat cheese I had dropped in the grass. I waited impatiently for the lie she was going to tell me.

—This wine is delicious. Did Kurt pick this specific bottle out?

—I don't know, John.

—It's full-bodied. Would you like some?

—You know that I don't drink.

—Yeah, but it's a special occasion.

—It is?

—Yeah, it's a new start for the both of us.

—Well, maybe just a sip. A sip won't hurt. It's been so long.

—Here's to your new life in Los Angeles.

—And to the new phase in your life.

I poured her a full cup of Cabernet, hoping that she would clam up, but now she went on and on about how things were going to get better for me, and how I was going to turn my life around by writing the play I had been thinking about writing and quitting my job at EverCover Books. When it started to drizzle, Dawn draped the picnic blanket over our heads. I wrapped my arms around her and started thinking that if this was going to be our last time together then maybe I could take her back to my place for one final roll in the hay.

—What does Lil' Thrills mean?

—Oh, it's a pet name Kurt gave me before we were married.

—Yeah, I gathered that much, but why does he call you that?

—That's not important, John. I have something I need to tell you.

—Leave him, Dawn. You're supposed to be with me.

—Not now, John. I'm trying to tell you something.

—Okay, shoot.

—I've always accepted you for who you are and not for who you might become. You're the man of my dreams, John, the love of my life. You're the only man who has ever listened to me, really listened to me, rant about my career, complain about my age, express my fears of growing old alone…

Then Dawn blindsided me just as she'd done the day at the Dia when she ended things between us. Nothing could have prepared me for what she said next. Absolutely nothing.

—I'm pregnant.

She blurted it out just like that, and then smeared goat cheese on a breadstick as if she'd thrown down a full house in a game of poker, confident in her hand. I downed my wine, crushed the plastic cup and watched the little dog play fetch with the tennis ball, which was nearly as big as his head.

—John? John? Say something.

—I'm really happy for you and your husband.

—You're the father, John.

—Oh, no, no, no, I don't think so.

—Yes, you're the father.

—I'm not a gambling man, but if I were, I'd bet the house on the Incredible Hulk.

—What the fuck is the matter with you, John?

—I just don't believe you, that's all.

—You're the father, John. Why do you think I'm telling you this?

—Why are you telling me this?

—'Cause it's your baby. I thought you should know.

Having grown up an orphan, Dawn might have been looking forward to being a mother, the kind of mother she never had, the kind of mother she had always dreamed she'd be one day—one who'd make grilled cheese sandwiches; talk openly about sex, drugs, fears and doubts; and hold her daughter by the elbow when they walked in the park. I thought for a moment about my father, who dropped me off at my Little League games on his way to OTB. The prospect of being a father frightened the hell out of me. Would I turn out like my old man? Fatherhood was far too much responsibility for me. I had trouble changing the strings on my guitar, so I went on believing it was a lie, just as Havannah had warned, even though I didn't think Dawn had anything to gain from spinning such a tale.

—I mean you're still sleeping with the fucking Incredible Hulk, aren't you? It's got to be his baby. You'll see after you give birth. Baby Hulk is going to come out one gigantic green muscle.

—Stop behaving like a child, John, and take responsibility.

—This is a disaster, Dawn.

—That's a cruel thing to say.

—What are you going to do?

—What do you mean? I'm going to keep the baby, of course.

—Don't be ridiculous. That's what Stephanie was going to do. What about Joey? Have you thought about him?

—Who? What are you talking about? Who's Joey?

—So, let me get this straight. You're keeping the baby. Am I right?

—That's right.

—You're moving to California with the green superhero.

—Right again. And stop calling him that.

—And you're going to raise my child with him?

—Yes. I'm sorry, John, but that's what I think is best for me and the baby.

—You're just trying to hurt me. Who's being cruel now, Dawn?

—I thought you'd want to know. We should be honest with each other.

—You want honesty? I'll give you honesty. I hope you and the baby and Joey have a miserable life together.

—Who the hell is Joey?

—Well, thank you for your honesty. Thanks for ruining my life, Steph.

—What are you talking about, John? Are you drunk?

—Not yet.

—I don't want you to hate me.

—I could never hate you, Steph.

—Oh, my God. You're mixing me up with that girl, your friend who died.

—Don't worry. I'm not going to fight for custody.

—I think it's for the best, John. Maybe you should sit down. You seem disoriented.

—Joey's a good guy. He's going to be a good father.

—Kurt. Kurt is a good guy. John, are you okay? Do you know who I am?

—I don't want your baby, Dawn.

—I'm so sorry about all of this.

—Please say anything. Anything but you're sorry. It's condescending. The last thing I want is your pity.

—I never wanted to hurt you.

—You should have thought of that before you told me that you're going to raise my child with the Incredible Hulk.

—What would you have me do? Abort the baby?

—You're going to do what you're going to do, Dawn. It's been that way ever since we met.

—Goodbye, John. I'm sorry. I'll send you pictures of the baby.

—Dawn. Wait a minute.

—Yes?

I got on my knees, placed both hands and my ear on her belly and sobbed like a baby. Dawn tried to run her fingers through my hair, but they got stuck. When she yanked her fingers out, she pulled some of my hair along with them and I cried even more.

—Rock or disco?

—I don't want to play your silly game, John.

—Just answer the question, Dawn. Indulge me one last time.

—Okay. Rock.

—Italian or Thai?

—Italian.

—Los Angeles or Rome?

—Rome.

—Beckett or Pinter?

—Beckett.

—*Bonnie and Clyde* or *Butch Cassidy and the Sundance Kid?*

—*Butch and Sundance.*

—Boots or heels?

—Boots.

—Baseball or football?

—Baseball.

—See?

—See what? I don't get it.

—You have a perfect score. We're a perfect match.

—We are a perfect match, John. By the way, I think it's a girl.

Dawn kissed the top of my head, stepped out from underneath the blanket and walked down the hill, passing the Jack Russell, who ran up to me and dropped his slimy tennis ball at my feet. The old woman called to her dog. "Jack. Jack. Come here, boy. Leave the poor man alone. I'm sorry. He's very friendly." It made sense for Dawn to stay with her husband. Kurt had been the only real family she had ever known. But did it make sense for them to raise *my* daughter? Anyway, Dawn's pregnancy was the end of the line for me. I didn't know very much about Kurt, but I figured he'd be a better dad than I ever could be. I was too afraid of turning out like my old man. It was the first time in my life I had ever been that honest with myself, but this particular insight didn't comfort me at all. In fact, my guilt had begun gnawing at me from the moment I said goodbye to Dawn Bello and my daughter. Should I have fought harder for Dawn? Should I have put up a fight for my daughter?

With the picnic blanket still draped over my head, I tossed the tennis ball into the water. Jack sprinted down the hill and leaped in, swimming to the far reaches of the pond, and retrieved the ball. The owner, who was twirling Jack's leash, thanked me, coaxed the dog out of the water, snatched the ball and rubbed him behind both ears. "Good boy. What a good boy you are."

I met up with Teeny at Cosby's where he bought all three hundred rounds. The gay Hugh Hefner had spent the day with one of his Craigslist conquests and was utterly giddy as he showed me the photographs.

—I don't want to see this shit, Teeny. Not today.

—Come on, big boy. He's a thing of beauty.

—Should you be drinking so much?

—I'm a big boy, big boy.

—Yeah, but you were sober for a long time.

—Sobriety is overrated.

—I feel bad about pulling you off the wagon.

—Actually, I could use another drink.

—So could I.

—John, you did the right thing. Let her go.

—But she's taking my baby with her.

—You don't know that it's yours. You don't even know that she's pregnant. The woman is fucked up. You can't believe a word she says.

—I love her, Teeny.

—I know you do, but she wasn't good for you, big boy.

—I haven't loved anyone since—

—Since the dead girl. I know, John. I've heard it all before. It's time to move on with your life. Listen to me. Teeny won't steer you wrong.

—Why do you care so much about what happens to me?

—I think because your suffering helps me understand my own.

—What do you mean you're suffering?

—When are you going to figure out that everybody is suffering? Phew, I haven't been this shitfaced since I wrapped my father's car around a telephone pole.

I walked beside Teeny while he tottered up the slope on his ten-speed. We stopped at an all-night bodega where I bought a bottle of Fantastik and a sponge. I dragged him to the corner of Seventh Avenue and Ninth Street, to the poster of *Edna's Journey*, and sprayed the entire bottle of Fantastik on the graffiti above Dawn's head and started scrubbing.

—John, what the fuck are you doing?

—Some vandal defaced this poster.

—Don't you think "slut" is kind of fitting? Stop fucking around. Let's go. It's late and I'm drunk.

—Why do people do such fucking things?

—John, she was no good for you.

When we got to my apartment, Colette was sitting in the window, looking down at us on the sidewalk—two drunken fools babbling on about break-ups, loneliness and suffering. Teeny spotted Colette, clawing the screen.

—At least you got a cat in the window waiting for you. Who do I have?

—You got me.

—Yeah, I got you. Hey, this is the shit you should be writing about, John.

—I don't think I can go there right now.

—You've got to face your fears dead on, big boy. Actually, I started writing something the other day.

—I didn't know you wrote.

—Neither did I. It's not a big deal, but I like it so far. I might steal some of your story. You okay with that?

—Yeah, just change my name. Can I read it?

—When I'm finished with the first draft, big boy, you'll be the first person I give it to.

—I wonder if Richard's home. He's got my keys.

—And John, the homeless dude…what were you thinking?

—You told me to put music back into my life. Richard's a singer.

—You don't know anything about this guy.

—I know he's a drunk and a degenerate gambler.

—Now there's a winning combination.

—He seems like a good guy. You'd like him.

—Fuck, if you're that lonely, come stay with me.

—I'm not ready to leave my home just yet.

—Here, take this, big boy. You really need it. You're a sick fuck.

Teeny tossed me a bottle of Zoloft, slapped me on the ass and then rode off into the dark underbelly of the evening. Richard wasn't home, so I plopped down on the stoop, swallowed a handful of blue pills and glared at the boutique apartment building that by now had been completely rented. I took Stephanie's graduation picture out of my pocket. I'd been carrying it around ever since Dawn and I split up. There was something about Stephanie's grave expression that consoled me. Then I fell asleep without the aid of any sleeping pill.

At some point, Richard came home, pushing his new shopping cart and singing: *We are amazed but not amused by all the things you say that you'll do. Though much concerned but not involved with decisions that are made by you.* Richard had fronted a funk-rock group that recorded a couple of records and then went on tour in the early seventies with Marvin Gaye. He had a pretty cool voice, and I liked his repertoire of songs, but at that moment, I just wanted to be left alone so I could sleep the entire day away.

—Look at you, Sir John. Thin as a rail. And drunk as a funky skunk. What are you doing out here?

—Fuck, Richard. I was sleeping. And keep it down. My landlord might be awake.

—Well, why ain't you in bed?

—You have my keys.

—Shit. Sorry 'bout that, man. Can you hold Pablo a sec? They're in my shopping cart somewhere. What do you think of my new wheels?

—You can't leave that thing out here. You better bring it inside.

—Got 'em. I got a couple slices for me and you from Tony's. I paid for them with my winnings at OTB.

—Thanks, but I'm not hungry.

—You need to eat something, brother. You gotta put some meat on them bones.

Once we were upstairs, Richard fixed us a couple of gin and tonics. I slid the cheese off my slice, folded the crust in half, took a couple of bites then dropped it onto the bag. The pizza was antagonizing my stomach. Richard lit a cigarette, but I didn't try to stop him. I was preoccupied with TNT, waiting for her kitchen light to go on and for the star of my fantasies to make her grand entrance.

—What's with all the salad dressing in the refrigerator?

—They were a joke gift from my wife. Funny, isn't it?

—I guess you had to be there. You're married? Where's your wife at?

—The East Village with her boyfriend.

—Oh, one of those. You look like shit, brother.

—This coming from a homeless man.

—Yeah sure, have a laugh at my expense, but when was the last time you took a good look at yourself? You've got dark circles under your eyes. Your hair is a mess; your beard is out of control; your clothes are hanging off your body. Not exactly the picture of perfect health.

—I'm fine, Richard. Really. Thanks.

—Then eat and stop telling me you ain't hungry.

—I'll eat later.

—You're gonna force me to force-feed you. Let's not go there, John. It won't be pleasant. I can assure you of that.

I looked at myself in the mirror that was hanging above the kitchen sink. My sunken brown eyes were bloodshot. There were thick, dark circles around them too. I licked sauce off my beard and gazed out the window, anxiously waiting for TNT, but much to my dismay she never came on stage that night. Richard rolled his eyes and took a shot of gin.

—Man, you don't know what real hunger is.

—You don't know shit about my hunger, Richard.

—What you got in your hand, Sir John?

—A photograph.

—Let me take a look at that.

—Why?

—Just fork it over.

—I don't know why you want to see it.

—Pretty girl. Is this your wife?

—Nah, just the love of my life. She's dead.

—You wanna see the love of my life? She's dead too.

Richard dug into his front pocket and handed me a photograph of him, his wife, Laverne, and Richard Jr. Father stood in the background wearing a white shirt with a big collar and a fat burgundy necktie while mother, in a minidress, held her son in her arms. Late 1960s fashion. Polyester. Velour. Afros. Holiday smiles. Richard and Laverne couldn't have been more than twenty years old. Richard told me how Laverne had pleaded with their son to sit still and look at the camera. Baby Richard had been restless, though;

he'd pinched his mother's forearm, forcing her to stifle a scream, resulting in her uncomfortable appearance. Richard said that he hadn't heard from his son in years. Then he tugged the photograph from my grasp, tore it to pieces, tossed them into the trash can and poured another drink. "Good night, brother." Richard staggered into my bedroom and collapsed on the bed. I retrieved the pieces of the photograph and tried to tape them back together, but his work was so diligent that I quickly gave up, scooped the pieces into an envelope and brought them to him.

—I think when you wake up, you might want this.

—Fuck, John. I was sleeping.

—Here's your picture.

—If I was you, I'd get rid of that picture you got of that dead girl.

—That picture is all I have left of her.

—Okay, Sir John. Whatever. Good night.

—Hey, this is my bed. You get the couch.

—Yeah, right. Thanks for giving me a place to sleep. I appreciate it, brother. Throw that shit away for me, will ya?

I pulled some photographs out of my nightstand. Me and Dawn, standing in front of the Hudson River. Emma getting her portrait in Florence. I tore both of them to shreds, tucked them in the envelope with the remains of Richard's family photograph, tossed the envelope in the trash can and burned it. I stayed up all night, drinking gin and staring at Stephanie's picture and the watermark on the bedroom ceiling.

WHITE HEAD

I was sitting on my suitcase full of textbooks in the Bergen Street subway station, which reeked of urine, thinking about why I'd ever taken the job at EverCover Books in the first place. Back in '86, I'd needed the cash. But I also really needed something to keep me occupied. Stephanie had died, and I was so consumed with guilt that I tried to off myself by doing a belly flop off the Brooklyn Bridge into the East River. An off-duty policeman talked me down and that's when I started seeing Dr. Miller, dropped out of Brooklyn College and took the sales gig to occupy my time and take my mind off the tragedy that had befallen me. So you could say that EverCover saved my life. It was just a job, not a career that would interfere with my dreams of writing. I'd figured that being a salesman would give me the flexibility to flex my writing chops. It was a nine-to-five, in-and-out kind of job. No overtime, take-home work or weekends. In a sense, I was my own boss. But I'd quickly learned that I had neither the time nor the financial freedom I had been seeking, and nineteen years later I was in the same predicament, still starving and still unable to write.

It was one of those rare mornings when Brooklyn felt oddly still. I stepped away from the squalor of the green pillar, edged closer to the platform's edge, toes on the orange line, and searched the gaping black hole for the F train. When I pulled my hand out of my front pocket, my wedding band slipped off my finger and landed in a puddle of piss and rainwater in between the two main rails. Without hesitation, I jumped onto the tracks but fell on my arm, slicing it open on a rusty nail. I lingered in the stagnant water for a bit as I tried to regain my composure. It didn't take long before a police officer called out to me, "Hey, what are ya doing? You're gonna get hurt down there." He probably thought that I was scrawling my tag on the wall or something sinister like that. I told him that I had lost something valuable and continued searching for the ring. "Your arm's cut. Wait a minute, I'm comin' down." The cop removed the baton from his belt and took off his jacket, placing them on the platform, and hopped onto the tracks. "I'm okay, officer, really." He was a fairly young guy, in his twenties, but he was husky and this movement had rendered him out of breath. When he doubled over, his cap fell into a puddle. "Fuck. I just cleaned that damn thing. Let me take a look at your arm." The gash on my forearm was long and deep. He took out his handkerchief and tied it around the wound. Then he took off his shirt and fashioned some kind of sling from the sleeve. The fucking guy was Supercop. "Are ya in pain? It looks like ya might need stitches. It might be broken too." I got to my feet and thanked him. "Your head's cut. You okay? Are ya ready to move?" Blood trickled down my forehead. I started to shiver. "I'm looking for something that's important to me, officer." I had never seen anybody sweat as much as this guy. He rubbed his forehead with the back of his large paw. A hot gust of air from the approaching train slapped us in the face. "You're gonna get us both killed." We both caught a glimpse of the headlights, bearing down on us. "Fuck. Ya gotta stop. Please." The train operator blew the horn, and that's when I spotted the ring next to a rusted Coke can. "Got it." Metal scraped against metal. With one tremendous heave, Supercop tossed me onto the platform then struggled to lift himself from the trench. The train rumbled forward; the operator covered his eyes; the police officer collapsed onto the platform, gasping for air.

The train came to an abrupt stop halfway into the station. The doors opened and several passengers, unaware of the close call, stepped out of the cars and went about their business, whereas a few other perplexed passengers approached Supercop with caution. The conductor jumped off the train, shouting into his walkie-talkie. A bunch of concerned commuters propped Supercop against the green pillar. An old woman dialed 911 on the payphone. I must have been mistaken for a homeless man because nobody paid any attention to me, lying on the platform next to my suitcase, bleeding to death. Somebody offered Supercop a bottle of water, while a woman wiped his forehead. I got to my feet, brushed off my pants and stuck the ring in my front pocket. The damn thing was too big so there was no point in putting it back on. It hadn't gotten me any chicks either. "Thanks a lot, officer. For everything. You deserve the Purple Heart or whatever it is they give you for helping out a knucklehead like me." I lugged my suitcase up the stairs and hailed a taxi. When I slid into the backseat, the driver got a good look at me, looking like death, in his rear-view mirror, rolled his eyes and let out a tremendous sigh.

—You want me to stop at Long Island College Hospital?

—No, thanks. Just take me home. Please.

—You know your head's bleeding?

—Yeah, I know.

—Looks like your arm's broke.

—Yeah, I know.

—You sure you don't want me to stop at the hospital?

—Yeah, I'm sure.

—But you're bleeding all over my backseat.

—You're a real compassionate guy. You know that?

—Hey, this car is my livelihood.

—I know. I know. Just fucking drive me home. Now!

The driver pulled over and ordered me to get out of the car. When I refused, he came around back and physically threw me into the curb. Then he tried to hit me with my suitcase, but I ducked and it slid down the street, bursting open on top of a grated sewer, where a bunch of textbooks fell in. I called him an asshole as he sped off. I gathered my things and walked up the slope back to my apartment.

On my way home, I decided that the best thing for me to do would be to take some time off from EverCover Books, an unofficial leave of absence. Pretending to be Dr. Ford, my gastroenterologist, Richard informed my boss that I had been hospitalized with colon cancer. My boss wasn't too pleased to be losing his "Brooklyn man," but Richard assured him that the cancerous tumor had been removed and that I would return to work as soon as I was able to lug my hefty suitcase of textbooks. After all of the shenanigans I had pulled, I was kind of shocked that I wasn't fired right then and there.

I stayed in bed for all of December and planned on sleeping through the

New Year and the fireworks over Grand Army Plaza until Pete woke me up, banging on a pot with his cane from the sidewalk below. It had been a month of discontent. I wished it had been a meaningless month like March. (If it had been wiped off the calendar nobody would miss it.) Aside from napping, staring at the watermark on the bedroom ceiling and occasionally picking at the meals Richard prepared, the only semi-constructive thing I'd done was scribble random thoughts in my notebook. Eventually just about everything had become monotonous and tedious, and when I was finally ready to exit my lair for good and reenter society, broken arm and all, Richard was waiting with a plate of scrambled eggs, bacon and toast.

—Good morning, Sir John. Happy New Year.

—Why are you so happy? You're homeless.

—What have you got to be so miserable about? You're white.

—What makes you think 2005 will be any different from 2004?

—You got a lousy attitude, brother. Anybody ever tell you that? Anyway, I fixed you some breakfast, the most important meal of the day. I hope you don't mind, but I helped myself to the bread that was in the kitchen drawer.

—There was money in the drawer?

—A few bucks, not much.

—You didn't have to do this, Richard.

—The hell I didn't. I'm trying to repay you for helping me and Pablo out. Don't forget to take your multivitamin now.

—It's like you really care about me.

—I'm just trying to be a friend to a brother who could use a little help.

—Not even my mother cares about me the way you do.

—Is that what you think? Is that why you ain't taking her calls?

—What did she have to say? She isn't sending my father to get me, is she?

—Well, let me put it to you this way: she knows that a black man is taking care of her pasty-ass son, and let's just say she ain't happy. Now eat them eggs before they get cold and I have to feed them to Pablo. Oh, and this dude, goes by the name Teeny, called a couple times.

—What did he want?

—To see you if you're okay. He wasn't too happy with me either. Does he have a thing for you?

—He's my drinking buddy.

—Said he was going to call the cops on me. You sure he ain't interested in you in a romantic sort of way?

—He's a good friend. That's all.

—What you got there?

—My journal.

—Let's see what you've been up to, locked inside your laboratory.

—It's shit, really. Just random thoughts. I didn't finish a damn thing.

—Let me be the judge, Sir John, let me be the judge. Somehow I doubt that it's shit. But sometimes even shit don't stink.

Richard poured me a cup of coffee and mixed a gin and tonic for himself. I took a seat at the kitchen table and doused my eggs with black pepper and hot sauce while he opened the marble notebook, turned to the first page and read aloud.

—Tough to read, John.

—Tough to write with my left hand.

—You better get that arm checked out, brother.

I pretended to be involved with my breakfast and indifferent to what Richard thought about my writing, but deep down I was really hoping that he'd like it.

Day 2 of my retreat

This is all that I choose to remember about Emma and Dawn…

I can't remember what they look like, what they smell like, if their laughs were contagious or annoying. I used to have pictures of them in my head that I could recall anytime; these pictures were taken when we first met, but they have since been reconstructed and re-imagined so that now they are no longer honest portrayals. These convoluted pictures float through my foggy head: Emma in Florence and Dawn by the Hudson River.

My relationship to women is like my relationship to books. If it's a really good novel such as *The Catcher in the Rye*, it will stay with me forever. I have read Salinger's masterpiece dozens of times; I have studied it, even committed some of the more extraordinary lines to memory. *What really knocks me out is a book that, when you're all done reading it, you wish the author that wrote it was a terrific friend of yours and you could call him up on the phone whenever you felt like it. That doesn't happen much, though.* I would love to give Salinger a call, but I don't think he's listed in the phone book. He's been hiding away from the world in a cabin somewhere in New Hampshire for the past thirty-five years. On the other hand, if it's a really awful book, I'll put it down long before I grow tired of it, not remembering a single word. I'll even stick it on the curb for someone else to share my misery.

I've shredded the pages of both works of fiction, the Emma saga and my love triangle with Dawn and the Incredible Hulk, into a million tiny pieces, tossed them in the air and taped them back together. One enormous Dadaist collage in which I've integrated memories, fantasies, high points, low points, facts and fiction from both stories. I've thought about placing both books on the curb, but I don't want to dispose of my history altogether, even if it is a miserable history. If I'm going to become the person I would like to become then I must at least try to look back on my most formidable antagonists and learn from them.

There is a sliver of a memory burned into the synapses of my brain, and if my brain is capable of holding but one grain of these memories, if it is able to contain a fragment of only one grain, it would be neither massive nor biblical in stature. This would be it: I've been married, I've been divorced, I've fallen in love with a married woman, she got pregnant with my child, she walked out of my life, and I walked away from my daughter.

Day 3

We may have experienced things together, but do we share the same memories? What do you remember about our time together? What story have you written in your journal? What story will I write? What will I leave in? What will I leave out? I wonder how compatible our stories would be.

I know one thing…my story will never end.

Day 4 of this mess

I don't have much to say today. I just read what I wrote yesterday, and I'd like to elaborate. Memories give birth to nostalgia. Nostalgia suggests disappointment. A nostalgic person idealizes an illusion of a more meaningful time. I'm both nostalgic and idealistic, so my story will never end.

Richard closed the notebook, closed his eyes and pinched the bridge of his nose. I waited for him to say something like, "This is the most incredible thing I've ever read. You're the next Faulkner." When he finally opened his eyes, he looked off in the distance as if he were out to sea, searching for land. I kept waiting for him to say something, but then I figured he was doing what I'd often done: gawking at TNT across the way. She was in her kitchen, prancing around in just a red bra and panties. Richard mixed another gin and tonic and continued to stare off into the distance, deep in thought. When my neighbor put on her pink robe, I lost interest and turned back to Richard, who was still lost in thought, still pinching the bridge of his nose so tightly that it looked like he was cutting off circulation to his brain. I had grown impatient, so I slapped the kitchen table with an open hand to get his attention.

—Well?

—That girl's really got it going on.

—Not my neighbor, the writing.

—That's the shit, my brother.

—I told you it's shit, Richard.

—No, that's what I'm talking about. Don't forget to take your vitamin now.

—What are you talking about, Richard?

—This is the shit you should be writing about in your plays.

—This? Everything in here is bullshit, fucking nonsense.

—You know what your problem is, man?

—I got plenty of them. Pick one.

—You gotta love yourself a little more, man. You're so fucking down on yourself. You think you're no good. You gotta love yourself a little more. That's the title of a song I wrote for my baby, Laverne, back in the day: "You Gotta Love Yourself a Little More."

Richard was straightforward, truthful and completely accurate: I had to love myself a little more, but how was I supposed to do that? Colette and Pablo followed me back to my bedroom, making themselves comfortable across my chest and lap. Richard knocked on my door, urging me to come out, take my vitamin and talk about what was on my mind, but I told him that I wanted to be alone. Richard said that he'd be there for me when I was ready to talk. Then he went back to the kitchen and read more of my journal. I think he read it out loud as a way to coax me out of the bedroom.

Day 5, around 1:00 p.m.
I think I remember the white lilies that I had pulled from the ground. Their appearance paled in comparison to the actual labor that had been required to secure them. I think the ground was frozen. Nature was performing its duty, and I was there to interfere with progress, to put an end to the blossoming.

I hope that I have recalled the event correctly. This is how I think I remember it. I remember it to be this way. I think. This is the way it was. I think.

Day 5, evening
It takes courage to conjure pain. Why do I remember only the tragedies, the disasters? Does this mean I'm a hero?

Day 6 of isolation
Will I find redemption? Why should I think that anything could change now? My story goes on and on and on and it won't stop, not even till the break of dawn. I hope that I'm wrong.

Day 7
The blood flows under the bridge, and I am floating upstream without a paddle. The futility has exhausted me, drained me of anything remotely promising.

Later…
Did we lie in bed on a Sunday morning and read? Was there an earthquake in India that reached the depths of the West and shook both of us in our queen-size bed in Brooklyn? Did we

shimmy with the aftershock?

Even later…
Dawn left me for her husband. A dagger in the back of my neck. What story will Dawn tell our daughter? Will there even be a story? Will my daughter know that I exist?

Day 8
Cotton mouth. I have been drinking Richard's gin and popping Zoloft and Zolpidem. All three are brutal on my stomach. I wish there was another way to mollify the pain.

Things end only to end again. Alone and tempted to follow through with the promise I made to myself. Does an end bring finality? I'm going to write another ending to my story that never ends.

At that point, Richard put down my notebook and answered the door. I knew by the five aggressive taps that it could only be Pete, and for a brief moment, I thought about coming out of my bedroom and directing him back downstairs, but then I heard his raspy voice and that was enough of reality to send me back to bed, pulling the covers over my head and clutching Pablo and Colette to my chest.

Pete told Richard that he was concerned about me, but he was probably more worried about the rent that was long overdue. Richard covered for me by telling Pete that I was recuperating from an operation on my colon.

—Oh, I had no idea he was seriously ill.

—Yeah, he's cleaned up now.

—Is he okay? Is it life-threatenin'?

—All the men in his family croaked from it, so the doctors aren't taking anything for granted. You know what I mean?

—Is there anything I can do?

—You could give him a little more time on the rent. That'd be a friendly gesture.

—That boy's gotta take better care of himself.

—He's going through a rough patch, for sure.

—Excuse me, who are you?

—The name's Richard Pritchard. I'm John's close friend. I'm taking care of him.

—I'm Pete Marzo. Has somebody been smokin' in here? 'Cause smokin' is prohibited on the premises.

—It's a pleasure to meet you Mr. Marzo. I've heard so much about you. You have a lovely home. Such beautiful floors.

—They are beautiful, ain't they?

—Can I get you something to drink?

—A little early in the day for booze, Mr. Pritchard.

—Nonsense. Never too early to smile.

Richard poured on the charm along with a couple of shots of Gordon's. He toasted my good health and Pete followed with an enthusiastic "Salute!" There was the clinking of glasses and some laughter for now, but I had a feeling it was only a matter of time before Pete made a racist comment or figured out that Richard was homeless and then I'd be forced to separate the two of them.

—I prefer Beefeater. The licorice is a little overpowerin', but that's the way I like it.

—It all goes down the same to me.

—Can you believe that some people put carpet over these gorgeous parquet floors?

—That's some stupid shit, man. Here's to your beautiful home, Mr. Marzo.

—Please call me Pete. So, our friend John has had some troubles.

—He's got worse troubles than the cancer. I'm reading all about them in here.

—What's that?

—His journal.

—I didn't know he was a writer.

—Neither does he.

—How could he not know that he's a writer?

—He don't have the confidence a writer really needs to put himself out there. Here, listen to this.

—Should we be readin' his journal, Mr. Pritchard?

—Please call me Richard. It's okay, man. Get this.

I listened to Richard read to Pete.

Day 8, again
The country air. The mountains. Everywhere but here. You and me. Alone. Evergreens in my eternal desert. The skirmish between the depression and the mediocrity. I think that I remember it all. The loss of time. The loss of friends. The loss of family. The loss of a daughter. I am lost in the evergreens. Their scent has lured me into darkness.

Day 9
Who has laughed at Gianni Lenza's sorrow? Who laughed when he puked his integrity down the toilet? They watched him fall. Mess that he was. They didn't pick him up. And he just stayed face down in the gutter.

Dawn's face. Close to mine. Warm breath on my neck. I loved to listen to her breathe while she slept. I rubbed my finger across her chapped lips. I wanted her lips to be mine. Such ecstasy in suffering. We participated in the torture. Our relentless ignorance. Cruelty and deceit. We were cruel to each other. We deceived ourselves with our deception. The pretense. The fiction.

Day 9, later but not feeling any better
Gian means God's gift, but I'm a motherless child, son of the devil.

Still Day 9
Dawn's masturbatory promises. Her unbelievable lies. She never wrote a poem for me but words spilled from her loins. You desired me? You wanted to fuck *me*? I thought we had something beautiful between us. I felt beautiful for the first time in my life.

An unmoved participant wandering in a circle in the darkness. Feeling detached but connected to the chaos around me. My hands plunged deep into my back pockets. Your tongue on the back of my neck. I have stopped seeking knowledge. My brain has thrown in the towel. I can only take so much.

At that point, Pete asked to see the notebook, but Richard was reluctant to hand it over. He called out to me, checking to see if it was all right for Pete to take a look, but I ignored him. There was a moment of silence and then I heard the turning of pages, the clinking of glasses and Pete's distinctive voice.

—This boy's a poet. He has awful penmanship, but he's a poet.

—He's hurtin'. He's hurtin' real good right now, Pete. I know what he's feelin' too.

—I lost my wife of fifty four years. I know what hurt is.

—Sorry to hear that, man. My wife died when she was just twenty-three.

—Clara was a good woman. There ain't too many of them out there.

—You said it, brother. Here's to good women.

There was more clinking and another enthusiastic "Salute!" from Pete. Then there was a moment of silence that was finally shattered by their whistling and catcalls. I figured they were probably checking out TNT, so I opened the shade to get a look at her, but I couldn't see anything, not even her orange glow.

—That girl across the way's a real looker. Hey, what happened to that window?

—Yeah, she's got it going on, for sure. Except for that weird-ass complexion.

—She's a good woman despite all of the—how shall I put it— enhancements. I've got to talk to John about that window.

—Maybe you should introduce her to John.

—That boy had a nice girl.

—Dawn? She was a bitch, man.

—Who is Dawn?

—The chick with his baby. Weren't you listening?

—I was talkin' about Emma, his wife.

—That one? He didn't love her, man. Dawn broke the guy's heart.

—Emma was a beautiful girl. She had some loose screws, but boy was she a looker.

—Good-lookin' women are some fucked-up, evil women.

—She reminded me of a girl I once knew.

—I didn't know John's real name is Gianni. What's that, Spanish?

—It's Italian. Gianni Lenza. It's a good strong name. He don't eat like no Italian, though. I'll tell you that. Listen to this.

Pete read my notebook aloud.

Day 10

I just ate a slice of stale Wonder bread with margarine.

—Can you imagine that? Not even a piece of Italian bread? And margarine, not butter?

—Go on, man, get to the good stuff.

Pete continued to read.

In bed on a Sunday morning. The world will wait. We worked together under the covers. It was cold. Amber days, months after May. You were with me. We knew what we had. Nobody knew we existed, together. Only Kurt, your husband. You didn't tell anyone about me. Only your fucking husband. I did not exist. I was an abstraction swimming in your imagination. I surrender. The white flag is raised. I wave it high. With my good arm. Above my bushy head. So my daughter can see it. It's not easy to retreat.

Day 11

It was all too much, so I retreated. Back to bed. You are not here. Under the covers. In my robe. My pas seul. A violent offensive. I am defensive. My troops and their coup d'état. I was never courageous in battle. Never the lionhearted. Frightened of silence. Stillness unnerves me. You haven't heard from me. The cacophony of the whisper turned me out of sorts. Lonely with the madness I have grown so accustomed to. My books have betrayed me. I read the great works, but I got lost in the fiction. I have too many stories inside my head. I remember only what I care to remember. First-rate predicaments in a third-rate mind. C'est la vie.

—Why is he writin' in French?

—What you talkin' 'bout? Sounds like English to me.

—He's usin' French phrases.

—Yeah, so what?

—The French are cowards. We bailed their asses out of World War II.

—That was a long time ago, man.

—I was there. I know.

—I'm sorry, Mr. Marzo. I didn't mean no disrespect.

—You young people don't have no respect for the wars we fought for your sake.

—Young people? Shit! I'm fifty-six years old. And with all due respect, Mr. Marzo, I fight a war every day.

—I imagine things must be difficult for colored people.

—"Colored people"? Mr. Marzo, my name is Richard Pritchard. I was born in Richmond, Virginia, in 1949. Dropped out of high school at seventeen to play music. I lost my band 'cause I lost myself. I've been addicted to everything: cocaine, amphetamines, heroin, alcohol, laziness. You name it. I lost my beautiful Laverne to the same junk I was addicted to. The government took away my son seeing as I was unfit to raise him. I moved to New York where I lost my job as a janitor. I lost my home. Hell, I lost everything but my self-respect. I've been in and out of shelters. And here I am still fighting the fight. You fight yours and I fight mine. But I ain't no "colored person." I'm just Richard Pritchard. Hear me?

—I'm sorry, Mr. Pritchard. No offense. I guess your people have it a lot harder in some ways.

—Forget it, man. Another drink?

Richard poured another couple of shots and made another toast.

—Here's to fightin' the fight.

—Salute.

Pete continued to read aloud.

Day 12

I was unable to distinguish a fuck from love. I designed the movements. I choreographed the foreplay, even with my two left feet. I'm holding on to those memories. Recalling pictures. Hoping that you're doing the same.

Day 14

There is a prick in the side of my neck. And I no longer dream of playing center field for the Mets. To end it all. Is *all* an accurate word? I need to focus on *it*, not *all*. I should end *it* and that will change *all*. I cannot begin again. When I rot away, only then will I flourish. Will you be there waiting for me? Will your husband be there too? Where will my daughter be? Will she curse me and the ground I have walked on?

Death will be life. I've been waiting for my crutch to give way. To go splat on the pavement. I've been waiting for my cup to fall. For scalding coffee to drip down my leg. The vase to shatter. The white lilies to wilt and waste away. The salad dressing to sour. The door to close. The ball to drop.

It was a new year, but I was still the *old me*. A cliché. There must have been a time when I mattered. You stood by me as I made this discovery. I reflected during the television commercials. I thought of what was, what will be, what is, what will become. I am tired of feeling.

Day 15

I need changes. Serious changes have to be made. Move to Paris? Wine and dine some ingénue and have primitive sex? I need. Something has to be done. Some thing. I want more Sunday mornings. Did I ever laugh? How could I ready myself? There is a plague in my house. I am sick, sick to the bones, sick to the core, sick. The puking has given way to diarrhea. Bile and piss. I want to destroy. Tear down. Smash and break. Punch and stab. Prick and kick.

Day 16

I used to begin my day with you. Watch you sleep. So still. A smile. A kiss. I used to end my day with you. A few words before we fell asleep. There was warmth. There was?

Day 17

Paint is dripping from the bedroom ceiling. It's early in the evening and I am still in bed. My thick comforter will not shield me against the white paint that is falling all around me, striking my head. Maybe I should surrender, go to the kitchen, make a cup of tea, read the daily paper, feed Colette and Pablo and hang out with Richard.

I am not a pugilist. I have taken too many blows to the head, been down for the count and walked away stripped of the title belt. I have nothing to prove. Nothing to gain. I have nothing. No things. My bedroom has collapsed around me. Brian Wilson understands. I want to understand. I am vermin. My head cannot take the torment. Gregor Samsa has eight legs and a thorax. I have a white head from the drip, drip, drip of the paint, pain, paint.

Pete stopped reading.

—I should do somethin' about the leak in his bedroom.

—There ain't no leak, Pete. He's speaking in metaphors.

—'Cause if that leak gets worse then you got a big money job on your hands.

—This kid's really in trouble. We gotta help him.

—Sounds like my home is in trouble too. First the window, now the leak—

—Ah, man. He's speaking figuratively, you know what I mean?

—I'll be right back.

—Let the poor boy be, man.

Pete got up from the table and limped over to my bedroom door and rapped five times with his cane. I ignored him. His irritating knock again. I ignored him again.

—John, if you can hear me, I'd like to take a look at the ceilin'. I need to repair that leak before it gets any worse. You know how much it will cost to call a roofer in?

Pete kept talking to me through the door, while Richard called out to me from the kitchen.

—Why are you writing letters to a dead girl? That's some serious fucked-up shit, bro.

—Things will get better, Gianni. I promise you. They will. Remember, you've made decisions, not mistakes. Are you sure I can't poke my head in there and take a quick look at the ceilin'?

—Give me that picture, John, so I can tear it up. Pete, you got to hear this shit.

—By the way, you owe me a lot of money, so when you're feelin' better just drop it off. Take care of yourself, Gianni. What happened to this door? It looks like somebody punched a hole in it.

Pete limped back to the kitchen.

—It sounds like he may do harm to himself. Should we have one of those interventions?

—This is the shit right here, Pete, listen to this.

Richard poured some more gin and read one of my letters to Stephanie aloud. This felt like an intrusion, a violation, but I did nothing to stop them.

Day 19

Dear Stephanie,

Lately, I've been thinking about us.

We played all day, turning your mother's couch into a castle. You were my queen, and as your valiant king I protected you from the alligators that swam in the moat.

Remember the first day of kindergarten? While the other children were crying and vomiting, we sat across from one another, staring into each other's innocent and frightened eyes, scared of the chaos that surrounded us and thankful that we had each other.

In the seventh grade, even though we were in the same class, I pretended that we weren't friends. I tried to act cool in front of the other boys. That's a strange age. Boys and girls who are genuinely fond of one another have the propensity to treat each other with unpredictable and uncertain cruelty.

You are the only friend I have left in this world.

Miss you,
Gianni

After Richard read the letter, he and Pete were silent for so long, I thought that maybe they had left. I cracked the door open, thinking it was safe to move to the couch, but then I heard Pete. "Sounds like neither Emma nor that Dawn character were his true love." I stopped just outside the door. Pablo and Colette raced into the kitchen. Meanwhile, Richard started reading about me and Stephanie, but I was tired of him digging up my skeletons. He was sharing my darkest secrets with my landlord. That was the last straw.

—All right, stop. Stop right there.

—John, you look like a disaster.

—Thanks, Pete.

—What happened to your arm?

—He's been on a drinking binge—

—What happened to your head?

—Give me the book, Richard.

—Have a seat, brother. Looks like you could use a drink.

—You're not goin' to kill yourself, are you, Gianni?

—Please call me John.

—Are you going to harm yourself?

—That's it. I've had enough. Everyone out of my house.

—You got to rip that picture up. That girl is haunting you, brother.

—What picture?

—He's carrying around a picture of the dead girl, Stephanie.

—Sit down, Gianni. Get it off your chest. You'll feel better.

—My name is John.

—It may do you some good, brother. Let it all out.

—I think you've heard enough of my sad story for today. Now, everybody, get out!

—Are you sure, man? 'Cause I think you really need to work this out. You know?

—There isn't enough time in the world to work all this shit out.

—Well, I'm gonna go downstairs and have lunch. We'll talk about the rent when you're feelin' better.

—It was a pleasure meeting you, Pete.

—Would you care to join me, Richard? I'm always eatin' alone. I'd love some company for a change.

—For lunch? No shit?

—I made lasagna and braciole.

—You made your own lasagna?

—Well, of course I did. My Clara used to make the most delicious lasagna. She was a wonderful cook.

—I usually get by on a couple of beef jerky.

—I'm afraid I don't have any wine.

—Leave that to me, Pete. I've been striking gold at OTB lately. I'll run to the liquor store and get a nice bottle of Chardonnay.

—Make it red, Richard.

—You got it.

—Gianni, you're welcome to join us.

—Thanks, Pete, but my name is John.

—I like Gianni.

—Me too.

—It's John.

—I'll make you a dish and bring it to you later, Gianni. We can talk about the rent then.

—Thanks, but I'd like to be alone, Pete.

—I'll bring it up later. Somebody will eat it.

Pete hobbled downstairs. Richard dropped the multivitamin into my hands and then headed over to Park Slope Liquors. I picked up my notebook, took a seat at the kitchen table and read the final entries of my month-long seclusion.

Day 26

I've never been good with silence. Too many interpretations. I crave sound. Moans. Groans. Whimpers. Whispers. Words. Even facial expressions. Gestures. I have never been good with distance either. Silence and distance. Not a winning combination.

Day 27

We had the experience but missed the meaning—T.S. Eliot

Day 28

Stephanie and I had meaning. I thought Dawn and I had meaning. I don't know what Emma and I meant to each other. Who do I want to be? Who was I? I'm a father who has abandoned his daughter. She's a fatherless child.

Day 29

A long time ago, I made a conscious decision to groan my way through life. It wasn't the most reasonable decision, I grant you. Now, I long for the groaning to stop. I long for something beautiful. I'm reminded of a song me and Joey were writing back in high school. We called it "Happy World."

> It's a beautiful world, but it's passing me by.
> When I'm through sleeping, I'll awake to close my
> eyes.
> There's a heavy hand, and it's pushing me down.
> Saw some green grass yesterday now there ain't
> none around.

Stephanie died, her baby died, the band broke up, and I tried to finish the song but I never could.

I took a pen from the junk drawer and started scribbling in my notebook. One more entry, and then I'd put my journal writing to rest, at least for a while.

January 1, 2005

I got to love myself a little more.

SUBWAY RIDE

When I was ready to crawl out of my apartment, I decided to return to what I knew best, the only thing that I really knew at all: selling textbooks. I wanted to believe that my life had a purpose, some meaning that would present itself in time, but I was growing tired of waiting and I was losing faith. Had selling textbooks become my sole purpose in life? What a tragedy that would be; I wasn't even a good salesman. The Willy Loman of the textbook world.

I wheeled my bulky suitcase over to Southside to get sufficiently wired and to see what Teeny was up to, but he wasn't there. The hairy tattooed barista told me he hadn't seen much of Teeny lately. I sat in the lumpy couch by the window, sipping a cappuccino and watching a couple of teenagers make out on the bench in front of the shop. By the time I finished my third cappuccino, the teenagers were still at it, locked in a lip embrace while their hands remained still on each other's thighs. It was time for me to go to work, so I gave the shaggy tattooed barista a salute, rolled up a dollar bill, dropped it on the teenagers' backpacks and proceeded to the subway.

Commuters contorted their necks for a clear view of the F train rumbling through the tunnel, rounding the bend and eventually shimmying into the station. Some welcomed its arrival while others expressed contempt for its delay with deep, frustrated sighs and pointed curses. I boarded the train with benign indifference, though my arm was still in the sling Supercop constructed for me and lugging a suitcase that was overloaded with textbooks wasn't easy. Establishing your own space on the F train during the morning rush hour is an accomplishment. The middle seat is not kind to people, regardless of their shape or size, but on this day it was all mine. On my left sat an elderly, overweight woman who was deeply engrossed in the Old Testament. Her lips moved, but she didn't say anything discernible, although I did hear her mutter an *amen* or a *hallelujah* on occasion. On my right was a middle-aged man who smelled as if he had been drinking Jack Daniels, smoking Camels and eating garlic for months on end. You could tell that he had tried his best to stave off his stale scent by bathing in Old Spice, which was so powerful it forced me to breathe through my mouth. His legs were spread as if the Empire State Building were jutting from his groin, asserting his manhood as he engulfed his seat.

With my suitcase in front of me, resting against my legs, which were braced together, I attempted to read Nabokov's *Bend Sinister*, gripping it with my functioning hand and turning the page with my nose. A good novel has a way of making a subway ride less insufferable. I was in the chapter where Paduk the tyrannical dictator and his Party of the Average Man are in the process of arresting dissenters, but I was having trouble concentrating. A passive-aggressive little pixie who was suffering from a case of "seat envy" was practically standing on my feet. She rested her brown Bloomingdale's bag on my suitcase, and every time the train came to a stop her inertia sent her anorexic frame into my suitcase and nearly onto my lap. "Pardon me." I thought about offering her my seat, but I was getting a real kick out of watching her struggle to maintain her balance. It was an unusually warm winter's day and the subway's air conditioning wasn't on. I was perspiring; my shirt was clinging to me. I loosened my tie but was in such a claustrophobic space that I was unable to maneuver my good arm to take off my coat.

In the mid-eighties, long before the trains were air conditioned, subway riders tossed open the narrow windows in a futile effort to invite a breeze from the tunnel into the stifling cars. The lights occasionally flickered or shut off entirely, leaving the passengers in complete darkness. You'd frequently encounter teenagers break dancing to rap music beating from their boom boxes. Back then, the trains, which were plastered with graffiti, had a frenetic energy about them. They were dangerous. There was a lack of police presence, and you were fortunate when a Guardian Angel boarded your car. In 2005, the subways were more sedate and aseptic, although every now and then you'd see some horrendous things that evoked an earlier time. For instance, before my self-imposed exile, I witnessed a depraved old man urinating in the doorway of the G train. He slid his trench coat to the side, opened his fly, yanked out Little Willy and released. Then he suspended the flow and moved to the next doorway and the next, marking his territory like a cat, throughout the car. Subway etiquette is tacit, but one should abide by it nevertheless. Urinating in the car is an obvious faux pas, but there are so many others: boarding the train before passengers exit; leaning against the pole on a crowded train when somebody needs to hold on; occupying an empty seat on a busy train with either your bag or your feet; molesting the female passengers; eating sashimi.

I tried to get back into my book but was distracted by a guy wearing a white fedora and long white leather coat and sunglasses, standing by the doors at the far end of the car, bopping his head to a cacophony of horns blasting from his iPod. Was he listening to Miles Davis?

At Smith and Ninth Street, I became preoccupied with a brown-haired, olive-skinned woman who bore an uncanny resemblance to Dawn. She was standing as straight as an arrow in the doorway — another subway faux pas — staring directly into her cell phone, oblivious to the passengers boarding the train who had to maneuver around her. When I looked away from Dawn, I noticed, sitting across from me, a delicate brunette with striking pale blue eyes who looked just like Emma. She was engrossed in her *Us Weekly*, but when she felt my stare, she glanced in my direction. I buried my head in my book to avoid looking like the "lecherous subway guy" that women of New York City are so intimately familiar with. I was surrounded by my foes, and that's when I started feeling sorry for myself. I was already anxious about going back to work. The last thing I needed was to be haunted by my exes.

I was beginning to feel lightheaded and didn't want to pass out on the F train in front of Dawn, Emma, the guy in the white fedora and all these other characters. I took a deep breath, nearly choking on the scent of Old Spice, and closed my book. I needed something to calm me down, so I swallowed three or four of the little yellow and blue pills, mixing the Zoloft and Zolpidem. I closed my eyes, hummed "Mother's Little Helper" and eventually began to settle down. That's when an unusual thing happened: Stephanie appeared, looking the way she did just before she died.

STEPHANIE

Take me with you, Gianni.

JOHN

Where the hell have you been for the last twenty years?

STEPHANIE

I've been busy being dead, but now I'm poised for my resurrection. Take me away from all of this.

JOHN

Your wish is my command.

From a nearby cliff, the Sirens, accompanied by melancholy violin strings, enticed me to dive into the vast turquoise ocean, swim to the end of the earth and retrieve Stephanie, who was now floating on her back. I tossed my coat and tie onto the sand, unbuttoned my shirt, closed my eyes, took a deep breath and thanked Zeus and the mighty gods of Olympus for bringing Stephanie back to me. This was her second coming, her revival, and my second chance at happiness and a decent life. I wasn't going to miss my opportunity. I was Orpheus, standing at the threshold of the underworld, prepared to retrieve my wife, Eurydice. Stephanie urged me on, but by the time I leaped into the ocean she'd disappeared. "Don't leave," I pleaded, but she had vanished as swiftly as she had arrived. I got down on my knees and wept. "Don't leave me. Don't leave. Me. Again." Then I realized I was on the F train and not in the Mediterranean. Everyone was staring at me, so I blew kisses and took a theatrical bow. "Thank you for your time. I hope that you enjoyed the show." I stumbled around the car with my hand held out, begging for change. While most of the passengers refused to give me the time of day, a bratty little girl spit her gum into my hand. I thanked her and went back to my seat, opened my suitcase and stuck my head inside, pretending to be looking for something.

The fantasy about Stephanie's return had given me false hope, and I feared that the further I moved away from reality, the closer I got to the truth: I was to blame for Stephanie's death, her baby's death too. They died a long time ago and would never return.

At Bergen Street, the elderly overweight woman's glorious exodus coincided with the arrival of a beautiful, leggy blonde. I must have said "holy shit" too loud because a few passengers, as well as the leggy blonde, glared at me. I rifled back. "Hell, it was a compliment." That only prompted more glares. The conductor announced that there was a sick passenger on board and that the train would be moving shortly. I was going to be late for my appointment with Dr. Hicks at Cobble Hill High School, but I didn't mind the delay. I was sitting next to a gorgeous woman who happened to be reading one of my favorite books—*Revolutionary Road*—and every time she flipped her hair to the side, I was thankful that I was downwind of her delicious scent. I wanted to ask her what she thought of April Wheeler's attempts to combat the conformity of suburban Connecticut in the 1950s, but all I could do was nod and give her a goofy smile. She got up and moved to the end of the car.

"Next stop, Jay Street/Borough Hall." I had been so consumed with the leggy blonde that I hadn't realized I had been at my stop all along. When the bells rang, I sprang to my feet and wedged my suitcase between the doors to keep them from closing. I leaped onto the platform but couldn't tug my bag free. "Open the fucking doors." Passengers were growing restless. "Open the fucking doors already!" Passengers were now huffing and puffing and shouting obscenities at me. The doors finally opened, and the guy in the white fedora gave me a hand with my suitcase. "There you go, chief." When I realized that I had left my coat and tie on the floor of the car, I motioned to jump back onboard, but White Fedora stepped in front of me and pushed me back onto the platform. "Some people got to get to work, chief."

I didn't have an umbrella, so I was caught in a downpour, hauling my books through the chaotic streets of downtown Brooklyn. By the time I arrived at Cobble Hill High School, I was drenched. I had crawled out of bed and escaped my apartment; now I was going to die of pneumonia. Wouldn't that just be my luck?

I sat at the colossal oak table in the center of the English department, waiting for Dr. Hicks, who had gone to assist one of her colleagues deal with a fight between two tenth grade girls. Piles of books—*Jane Eyre*, *The Scarlet Letter*, *Beowulf* —were scattered on the table, sprinkled with mouse droppings, which I thought fitting for three books that I'd really hated in high school. My head was spinning, and I felt apprehensive, so I attempted to make myself more comfortable by removing my belt and unbuttoning my pants. I took off my shoes and placed my socks on the radiator to dry. I was about to pull the shade on one of the large oval windows so I could check out the view of downtown Manhattan when Pamela Flaherty tapped me on the shoulder.

—Going for a swim?

—Pamela! How are you? Long time.

I hadn't seen Pamela Flaherty since that infamous summer of the blackout when Emma had invited her over for pizza and beer. She drank about a million Rolling Rocks and bitched about her job, ex-husband and school loans. When she finished bitching and drinking the last beer in our refrigerator, she passed out on the couch right next to Emma, who had already been sleeping for some time.

Pamela Flaherty, who had entered the profession directly out of college, was a mousy schoolmarm. She looked forty-eight rather than thirty-eight (her actual age) and even less put together than I remembered. A red hairclip was stuck in the middle of her head; a tuft of gray hair ran amuck down the side of her face. She had ink stains on her wrinkled beige top and chalk marks on her black skirt. Teaching was her life, but it looked like the profession had beaten the life out of her.

—You might want to put your clothes on before the queen comes back.

—A little minx like Dr. Hicks…I'm sure that she has seen many a naked man before.

—I see you haven't lost your sense of humor. How have you been, John?

—Just grinding away, trying to pay the bills. You know how it is.

—All too well. Sometimes I wonder if it's all worth it.

—The work you do is important, Pamela.

—I used to think it was.

—I think that if I were to do it all over again, I would teach English.

—A lot of people say that. It's such a condescending remark.

—But I'm serious. I don't mean any disrespect.

—It's a grueling job. I never thought I'd be a lifer. Thought I'd do five, maybe ten years and move into what I really wanted to be doing.

—What do you really want to be doing?

—I would love to paint all day, every day, for the rest of my life.

—I didn't know you were a painter.

—In my previous life.

—I would write all day if I could.

—I always thought Emma was the writer. I didn't know you were a writer too.

—Well, I haven't written anything yet, but I have an idea for a play.

—I envy Emma for just walking away from teaching and going for it.

—Is she dancing again?

—She's been writing travel essays. Publishing them, too.

I had only ever seen Emma scribbling in her journal, taking notes, jotting down ideas for essays. Like me, she was horrified by the possibility of rejection. We both preferred something less painful, like a stake through the heart. I was kind of surprised to learn that Emma had been putting herself out there like that, and the news didn't make me feel any better about myself.

—I haven't heard from Emma in a while. How's she doing?

—She's the same. Same old Emma, you know? She has her good days and bad. Like the rest of us.

—Is she seeing anyone?

The bell rang. Pamela packed up her things and grabbed a box of chalk from the supply closet. "Take care of yourself, John. It was great to see you." She scampered away, but I followed her into the hallway and called out, "Is she still with Zack?" Pamela didn't respond. I was glad in a way; I didn't really want to know if Emma had been seeing anyone. Just knowing that she had been writing essays and publishing them was already a bitter pill to swallow. Considering how impetuous Emma was, she was probably living with someone. Hell, she was probably married with four children by now.

—Why are you shouting in the hallway, Mr. Lenza?

—Hi, Dr. Hicks. I was talking to Ms. Flaherty—

—This is a public high school, Mr. Lenza. Do you have no sense of decorum?

—Well, I'm still wearing my pants, but if you had come a few minutes later, who knows? I might have—

—Mr. Lenza, you are aware that this is not a beach or a public pool?

—I was just joking, Dr. Hicks—

—Would you like to tell me what you are doing?

—I wasn't feeling well, ma'am. I almost passed out on the subway ride over here.

—Are you feeling better now?

—Yes, ma'am. I think the wooziness has passed.

—Good. Now, I suggest that you put on your clothes, pack your bag and leave the building.

—What about those books you ordered?

—You're through, Mr. Lenza. I no longer wish to do business with you.

—You're going to let this little misunderstanding get in the way of your students' education?

—Goodbye, Mr. Lenza. I'll be sure to notify your supervisor about this little incident. Give my regards to your wife.

—Actually, we're not together anymore.

—Oh, I'm sorry to hear that.

—We got divorced.

—I can't say that I'm surprised.

—What is that supposed to mean?

—Ms. Rue…your wife…was rather…now, how should I put it?

—A flake?

—Yes, I suppose that's being delicate.

—I'm better off without her.

—Well, that's your business, Mr. Lenza.

—Don't you think I am?

—I wouldn't know, but I could tell you that Ms. Rue's students are better off without her.

Dr. Hicks and Emma had had their differences, but I thought that they at least had respected each other professionally. As far as I knew, Emma showed up every day, prepared to teach. She might not have loved her job—she wasn't as dedicated as Pamela Flaherty—but she knew her literature and cared about her students somewhat.

—Are you saying that she wasn't a good teacher?

—Do you mean, you don't know?

—What? Know what? What happened?

—There was an incident involving Ms. Rue.

—An incident?

—At one of the school dances.

—She never told me anything about that.

—Far be it from me to interfere, Mr. Lenza.

—What happened?

—It's in the past. It shouldn't be a concern to you now, Mr. Lenza.

—But it does concern me. I'd like to know. Tell me.

—Good luck to you.

Having opened Pandora's box, Dr. Hicks strolled into her office.

After I put my clothes back on, packed my suitcase and left the building, I wandered aimlessly in the rain, thinking about Dr. Hicks's insinuation. Was Emma too drunk to chaperone? That's what I had surmised. I was so damn intrigued that I returned to Cobble Hill High School to ask Pamela what had happened at the dance, but the security guards wouldn't let me back in. As it turned out, I never did learn what Dr. Hicks was implying, and that was last thing I ever heard about Emma Rue.

When I finally got to Southside, Teeny was in his usual spot by the window, boots off, holes in his white socks, scribbling in a marble notebook. I hadn't seen him since my self-imposed exile, and I kind of missed the big lug.

—Where's your coat, big boy? And umbrella?

—It's a long story.

—And what the fuck happened to your arm?

—Another long story.

—Everything with you is a long story, a never-ending one. You know that, you sick fuck?

—I haven't seen you in a while and this is the greeting I get?

—You're right. Come here and give Teeny a big ole kiss.

After Teeny put me in a bear hug and planted two sloppy kisses on both of my cheeks, he handed me the first scene of a one-act play he had been writing, based on my life. I was coming down from the pills I'd taken on the subway and couldn't focus on the Teeny's play. If it was based on my life, it was most likely a comedy. My neighbor, TNT, was sitting directly across from us, working on her laptop and talking on her cell phone. I pointed her out to Teeny. I wanted to know if he thought she was attractive.

—So that brick shithouse is the star of your little pornographic fantasies?

—Yeah, that's TNT.

—Do you think she ever saw you? You know…doing your thing?

—I don't think so. God, I hope not. I don't know.

—That would be pretty freakin' kinky if she knew you were choking your chicken and went along with it anyway. Wouldn't you say?

I had spied on TNT at least a hundred times from my kitchen window, but I had never seen her in public. It was a little unsettling. Teeny urged me to introduce myself. He said that if I wasn't going to write the play I had been talking about writing then I should have indiscriminate sexual encounters because they would be a nice distraction from my everyday miserable existence.

—I've already tried the dating thing.

—I'm not talking about dating married women, big boy. I'm talking about fucking your brains out.

—I tried that too.

—Bullshit. The only thing you've fucked is yourself.

—And it hasn't been enjoyable. Let me tell you.

—Are you taking the Zoloft I gave you?

—Yep, but I don't think it's working. I think I've become immune to it.

—Watch it with that stuff and don't take it with the sleeping pills. It could be dangerous.

—Don't worry, Teeny. I'm committed to a "healthy, productive lifestyle."

—I don't believe you. You're taking steps backward, John. That leech, Richard, told me you were in bed for a month. You wouldn't take my calls.

—I was going through something.

—I can see that. You're a walking disaster.

—I'm doing all right now.

—I think you need to see a doctor.

—I feel like a million bucks.

—How are things working out with the hobo?

—Pretty good. Richard makes me dinner.

—Big deal. Come stay with me. I'll make you dinner.

—I'm not ready to leave my home just yet.

—Are you still writing letters to the dead girl?

—I don't want to talk about it. Hey, I went back to work today.

—Yeah? How did that go?

—I don't want to talk about it.

—Why don't you go over there and talk to your neighbor? She looks nice despite her reptilian skin.

—I don't know. I don't think I can get past the orange glow.

—It is a little unsettling. But the quicker you get back in the saddle—

—The quicker I'll fall off.

—And then you'll get back on that old horse and ride into the sunset, cowboy. That's how life works.

You didn't have to be a shrink to figure out that Teeny was trying his best to fend off loneliness. He had spent countless evenings with younger men, some he didn't find attractive or even like, occasionally arranging two dates in one evening. He didn't want to admit that these vapid encounters made him even lonelier. Maybe that's why he'd started doing something more productive with his time, like writing a play. Charles Bukowski said, "Poetry is what happens when nothing else can." I didn't have the heart to tell Teeny that the life of a writer is a lonely existence.

I glanced down at the title of Teeny's play: *The Never-Ending Story of Bullshit* by Rutherford B. Duncan. He claimed that he'd stolen the line from me, but I don't remember ever saying such a thing. Maybe I had been bitching about how stories, particularly tragedies, have no ending: you may think the catastrophe is over, but once you step ashore, thinking that you have sure footing, the undertow has a way of yanking you back into the turbulent sea.

—I like your pseudonym.

—What pseudonym? That's me, dumb ass.

—That's your name?

—What's so funny, big boy? I'm from Ohio. So was he.

—What does the *B* stand for?

—Bad motherfucker. Now, if you're not going to talk to TNT, then I will.

Teeny gave TNT a limp, two-finger salute, but she was so engrossed in her phone conversation that she didn't notice the three-hundred-pound bald man trying to get her attention. That didn't deter Rutherford B. Duncan though. He started calling out to her. "Hey, Tan and Tits! TNT! Over here, baby." And when that tactful approach didn't work, he stood on the couch and began waving both arms over his head. "Hey, sweet tits. TNT. I'm talking to you. Where did you get that tan? Were you in the Caribbean?" By some miracle, we weren't thrown out of Southside. And not only did he have everyone's attention in the coffee shop but he had my neighbor's as well.

—I'm sorry, what was that?

—What are you working on, baby cakes?

—Nothing exciting. Believe me.

—I doubt that, gorgeous. I don't think it's possible for you to be dull. I'm sure of it.

—What's that you're holding?

—My friend and I are collaborating on a play.

—Really? That's far more exciting than what I'm doing over here. I guess you win.

—My name's Rutherford, but my friends call me Teeny. I can assure you that I'm nothing of the sort.

—Oh, is that so? Let me be the judge of that.

—Ooh, I like the way your mind operates. This walking disaster over here says that you two are neighbors.

—Oh, hey. Have we met before?

—Not really.

—You two live right next door to each other.

—Is that right? I thought you looked familiar.

—His name is John. John Lenza.

—Nice to meet you, John and Teeny. I'm Heather.

I gave her a goofy smile. Teeny hissed at me to quit looking like a "sick fuck." My mouth was probably hanging open. I was pretty sure by Heather's greeting that she had never seen me before. That was a relief. At least one awkward moment had been avoided, but I was sure there was more awkwardness to come.

Teeny picked up his notebook and scribbled my name next to his. "Would you rather be Gianni Lenza?" I didn't have time to answer before he proposed that the three of us have an impromptu reading of the first scene. I was shocked when Heather agreed to read the part of Dawn. I had to hand it to Teeny. For a gay man, he had pretty good game with the ladies.

—I've always wanted to play a bitch like Alexis Carrington, so I'll be Emma. And of course, John, you'll be John.

—I don't know about this, Teeny. This is really personal.

—Come on, cowboy. Be a team player.

—I don't know if I want my life out there like this.

—Consider this reading a catharsis. Think of it as a way to put these demon women to rest.

—I thought you'd at least change my name.

—Oh, but *John* really fits the character. I could change his name to *Gianni* if you'd like.

—No, John is fine.

—Oh, I like Gianni.

—Thanks, Heather, but John is just fine.

—This is going to be fun.

—If you say so, Heather.

Teeny gave TNT a thirty-second synopsis of the last two and a half years of my life. After the two of them had had a good laugh at my expense, Heather told us that she'd moved from Topeka to pursue a career in journalism. She seemed to be an ambitious type A, constantly checking her Blackberry for messages. Teeny bought three cappuccinos and we huddled around the notebook. Heather was sitting on my left, while Teeny was on my right, practically on my lap. Heather smelled really good, a lot better than Teeny, who stunk of turpentine. She was wearing the same fragrance as the leggy blonde on the subway, and for a moment I flashed back to my morning daydream about Stephanie. Teeny grabbed my elbow and asked if I was all right.

—You look like you're going to pass out, big boy.

—I'm just a little nervous, putting myself out there like this.

—Settle in, John. You have the starring role.

—Maybe we should do this another time when John is feeling better.

—Bullshit. Now's the perfect time. I've been working my ass off on this play and I'd like to hear it. Besides, I think it'll do ole Johnny boy some good.

Heather took off her boots and socks and crossed her legs underneath her. Her toenails were polished red to match her fingernails. Her long, curly blonde hair brushed against my shoulder. Our legs were touching. It felt strange being so close to her and not separated by glass, brick and fifteen feet of concrete. Despite the orange glow and leather skin, Heather was pretty in person. Teeny read the opening stage directions and off we went.

The Never-Ending Story of Bullshit
By Rutherford B. Duncan and John Lenza

Scene One. Lights up on EMMA, DAWN and JOHN, three goldfish inside an aquarium. They move from side to side, sometimes rise to the top for a breather or something to eat, and occasionally they swim to the bottom to feast on algae.

I pulled away from the huddle, sat back on the couch and drank my cappuccino. It wasn't easy being a team player.

—What's the matter, big boy?

—Goldfish? We're fucking goldfish?

—We're not "fucking goldfish," John. We are goldfish.

—Hey, I thought the both of you were writing this play.

—Teeny wrote the first scene, Heather. I haven't written a damn word.

—Oh. Well it's an avant-garde piece. Right?

—That's right, baby. Sexy over here's got it. Why can't you get with it, big boy?

—It's a metaphor, right, Teeny?

—You got a good brain to complement those good looks, baby. Let me tell you.

—You flatter me, Mr. Duncan.

—You haven't heard anything yet, baby doll.

Heather suggested that we change the characters' names so that I'd feel more comfortable, but Teeny argued that keeping the real names was essential to maintaining the play's authenticity. What the hell did he know about writing plays anyway? He was a housepainter for God's sake. Teeny began reading and Heather followed suit. Eventually, I settled into playing the role of John. It was a role I was intimately familiar with. And I did want to be a member of the team, after all.

EMMA

It can't be done.

DAWN

It can't be done.

EMMA

But you said it could be done.

DAWN

I never said such a thing. You said it could be done.

JOHN

I never said a thing about doing anything.

DAWN

Not a moan.

EMMA

Not even a grunt.

JOHN

But I groaned.

EMMA and DAWN (*overlapping*)

You said it. You said it.

EMMA

Somebody said "yes."

JOHN

And I trembled at the word.

EMMA

It can't be done.

DAWN

It can't be done.

JOHN

Somebody do something.

                    EMMA

You didn't want me.

                    DAWN

I should have been so lucky.

                    JOHN

Lucky? Fuck luck. Fate. Now that's the way, baby.

                    EMMA

The way to San Jose?

                    JOHN

Is there a reason you two called me here today?

                    DAWN

Is there a reason you're here?

                    EMMA

We're all stuck in this miserable tank.

                    DAWN

Together.

                    JOHN

On display for everyone to see.

            DAWN and EMMA (*overlapping*)

We want answers. We want answers.

                    JOHN

I can supply the questions. Answers, however, are not my
strong suit.

                    EMMA

Question #1. No, question #18.

DAWN

Why did you love me?

EMMA

That's your question?

JOHN

I can answer that.

DAWN

Why did you walk out on your daughter?

JOHN

I can't answer that.

EMMA

There's a child involved?

DAWN

Wrong answer.

JOHN

But I didn't say anything.

DAWN

Wrong answer again.

EMMA

Question #34: Why didn't you fight for me?

JOHN

I can't answer that one.

DAWN

I can answer that one.

EMMA

Please do.

JOHN

I didn't have any fight in me.

DAWN

When you left, he saw things clearly for the first time in his miserable existence.

JOHN

That sounds about right, but I didn't really see anything clearly.

EMMA

Wrong answer.

JOHN

Wrong answer?

DAWN

Question #54: Did you love the two of us simultaneously?

EMMA

Is that even possible?

JOHN

Too many questions. Overload. Overload. Breakdown.

EMMA

One at a time?

JOHN

One at a time.

DAWN

What's your answer?

JOHN

I loved you both. Still do? I must have.

DAWN

You have now answered three wrong.

JOHN

Two wrong.

EMMA

And there's the issue of the dead chick.

JOHN

Oh, right. Stephanie.

DAWN

Oh, her.

EMMA

The love of your miserable existence.

JOHN

That she was. Is.

DAWN

One more wrong answer and you've failed the test.

JOHN

I thought I was telling you what you wanted to hear.

DAWN

Question #76.

JOHN

Please, let me ask the questions.

LIBRARY
North Central Michigan College
1515 Howard St.
Petoskey, MI 49770

DAWN

You're going to run the show? You can't do that. Don't be ridiculous.

JOHN

I can swim on my own.

EMMA

You'll never be able to swim without us. Without Stephanie.

JOHN

Question #125.

EMMA

True.

DAWN

False.

EMMA

A.

DAWN

B.

EMMA

All of the above.

DAWN

17.

JOHN

You always gave your answers before I asked the questions, and that is why I loved you both.

DAWN

I used you.

JOHN

I know you did.

DAWN

Why did you let me abuse you like that?

JOHN

I loved you.

EMMA

You caught him at a low point in his miserable existence.

JOHN

Will you stop saying "miserable existence"?

DAWN

He was even lower than I was?

JOHN

I need a breather. Time out.

JOHN swims to the top of the tank. A green net plunges into the water. It skims the surface and captures JOHN.

EMMA

Terribly fastidious, that one up there.

DAWN

My husband likes a clean tank.

EMMA

Can't blame him. My boyfriend keeps a very clean tank himself.

JOHN (*from offstage*)

I knew you had a boyfriend.

DAWN

Do you think John is in trouble?

EMMA

John is always in trouble.

DAWN

He killed that girl, you know.

EMMA

He did?

JOHN (*from offstage*)

And don't forget that I killed her baby too.

DAWN

And her baby. He killed her baby too.

EMMA

And her baby?

DAWN

John, would you like a hand?

EMMA

Let him work it out for himself.

JOHN (*from offstage*)

I got it. I think.

JOHN breaks free and swims back to the others.

JOHN

Shit. That was a close one.

EMMA

My love.

DAWN

My baby.

JOHN (*turning first to Emma, then to Dawn*)
My love? My baby?

DAWN

The tank is pristine. What more does my husband want?

JOHN

Your husband is just like you. Demanding.

DAWN

He demands everything and more.

EMMA

My brother went to war.

JOHN

I liked your brother. I didn't know him.

DAWN

I have a brother too.

JOHN

I hate my sister.

EMMA

Into the jungle he roamed with the mosquitoes, the leeches, the snipers.

JOHN

He never made it home.

DAWN

My husband went to war.

JOHN

I liked your husband. I didn't know him.

EMMA

You must really love your husband.

JOHN

I find their love to be intoxicating.

DAWN

He made it to the bridge. Made it across. Almost blown to pieces.

JOHN

Nearly came home in a body bag.

DAWN

He's my family.

EMMA

He's your brother.

JOHN

He's your sister. A friend and not just a sister.

DAWN

He's my husband, the love of my life.

JOHN

I'm the love of your life.

EMMA

You're the love of my life, John.

                    JOHN
Let me ask the questions now.

                    DAWN
Shoot.

                    EMMA
Don't say that.

                    DAWN
Say what?

                    EMMA
Shoot.

                    DAWN
Don't say that.

                    JOHN
Question #247.

                    DAWN
I refuse to answer that.

                    EMMA
Let him ask the question first.

                    JOHN
Why did I love the two of you?

                    EMMA
Good question.

                    DAWN
We're both cute.

EMMA

True. We are cute.

JOHN

You were both unavailable. You were both cruel. Deceitful. Manipulative. Wounded. And I loved you anyway.

DAWN

You're lying. The truth was never your strong suit.

EMMA

You are deeply flawed, John.

JOHN

Dawn is deeply flawed too.

DAWN

Emma is deeply flawed too.

EMMA

Leave me out of this. Let's talk about John's flaws. They're so much more entertaining.

DAWN

Did you know about Stephanie?

EMMA

I was jealous of her.

DAWN

Because she was John's one true love?

EMMA

Because she's no longer here.

DAWN

Who am I?

EMMA

You're Dawn.

DAWN

You don't even know me.

EMMA

Yes, I do. You're Dawn.

JOHN

I've been swimming for so long. Immersed in water, stuck with the both of you in this God forsaken aquarium.

DAWN

There was a museum. We dreamed of Italy. There were children and wine. Friends and cappuccino. I loved you.

EMMA

We went to Prague. Florence too. The sheep and cows and a little dog that followed us over the cliff. I loved you.

JOHN

Is that what you call love? Cappuccino and a little dog?

Lights fade to black. End of Scene One.

When the reading was over, I stretched out on the couch behind Teeny and Heather and buried my head under a pillow. I felt like I had just been run over by a bulldozer. My entire life had flashed before me in a measly five-minute scene. I'd always figured that if somebody were to write a play based on my life, it would be a laugh riot, but this one wasn't funny at all. It was kind of amusing in a bleak way. Heather pulled me up, put her arm around my shoulder, looked deeply into my eyes and whispered, "It sounds like you've been through a lot, John. You poor guy." It was a nice moment, but then I thought, "How does she know what I've been through?" Maybe she knew Emma. Maybe they used to talk on the street or at yoga class or on the subway, but she doesn't know me, what I've been through, how much I've been through, how "poor" I really am.

In the meantime, Teeny was strutting around the coffee shop like a beefy peacock, chanting, "Ain't too bad for a high school dropout. Ain't too bad for a high school dropout." He grabbed Heather by the waist, gave her a bear hug and kissed his way down from her head to her neck, arms and hands. She made a high-pitched squeal, then twirled back into Teeny's massive arms, planted a big, sloppy wet one right on his big bald head and the two of them danced the tango. Teeny was proud of his work, and I had to hand it to the guy: for his first time writing, he'd really nailed it.

When Teeny professed that this had been his most memorable ménage à trois, Heather roared so loudly that the entire coffee shop came to a halt. The two of them didn't care that they were making a spectacle of themselves. In fact, they were relishing every bit of the attention they were getting. Heather suggested that we have another "threesome" right after me and Teeny finished writing the play. Teeny, thinking it was a fabulous idea, told her that we shouldn't wait so long, that we should all go out for sushi long before the play was even finished, next weekend, and asked for her phone number. Heather thought it might be fun to bring a friend along, but Teeny vetoed her suggestion.

—Why ruin a good thing, baby doll? Let's keep it a threesome. A really good one is so hard to come by. We'll be like the modern-day David and Catherine Bourne.

—And don't forget Marita.

—Look at this little bookworm over here, big boy. She knows Hemingway.

—Is that *A Moveable Feast*?

—*Garden of Eden*, baby doll.

—Oh, right. I had to read it in some English course I took a million years ago.

—You hear this over here, John? "A million years ago." You can't be any older than twenty-five, twenty-six tops.

—Oh, you do flatter me, Mr. Duncan.

It took them a hundred years to say goodbye, and when they were finally through with all of the hugging and kissing and flirting, Teeny started packing up, while Heather gave me a big, sloppy wet kiss on the cheek. "Things will get better, John. I'll see you in the neighborhood. Hang in there."

Teeny offered to buy me a couple of drinks at Cosby's. It was still raining when we stepped out of Southside, so the budding playwright handed his umbrella to me, draped his long wool coat over my shoulders and walked alongside his ten-speed. He was so excited at the prospect of his play that on our way to the bar, he blurted out the name of every actor he'd ever heard of, trying to cast the piece before he even completed the damn thing. Mr. Playwright promised to submit his latest work to every theater, festival and contest in the country and wouldn't shut his trap about movie rights and sequels. I was tired of listening to Edward Albee babble on, tired of his naive enthusiasm, tired of dragging my suitcase, tired of everything.

—Will you shut the fuck up about your fucking play? You're not even done writing the fucking thing.

—Hey, it's not my fault you're not getting laid. Don't take your sexual frustrations out on me.

It was pretty early for us to be at Cosby's, and we were the only customers in the dive. For the first few hundred drinks, we sat there and didn't say a word to each other. I was checking out the basketball scores on ESPN, while he was twirling the straw in his glass, staring out the window, watching people wrestle with their umbrellas. Teeny eventually broke the awkward silence with a direct order for me to complete the play.

—You're right. The play's not done. I think it's important that you exorcise these demon women, big boy, and writing may be the only way of doing so. Maybe it's not, I don't know, but it's worth a shot. What do you have to lose? It's your story. You know it better than me. Besides, your name is already on the script, and you don't want to disappoint Teeny now, do you?

Honestly, I was afraid of fucking up his hard work. The play was pretty good. I liked it and I was proud of the guy. I should have told him so. He would have liked that. At that moment, I realized I might not be a writer at all. I might be a fraud. That prospect frightened me more than the possibility of fucking up Teeny's play. I didn't want to disappoint my friend, but I was more worried about disappointing myself. Writing is not for the faint of heart. Writing is not for the weak, the well intentioned. Writing is not for the lazy or the ambivalent. Writing is not for those who talk about writing. Writing is for social pariahs with something to say, those who are able to cope with the discord of their own isolation. You should not take up writing as a hobby. Trust me. Play with trains. Play guitar. Collect baseball cards. Sell textbooks. Do anything else but write. In the end, it's not very rewarding. There is a ton of rejection and no promise that anyone will ever read your work. It's not like studying medicine and becoming a dermatologist, for which there is a guaranteed, captive audience eagerly waiting for you to pop their zits.

Teeny slid the script across the bar to me. On top of it was a wrinkled napkin with Heather's number scrawled in pink ink. "You better call her now. She's cute. She's smart. She's cool. She's convenient. Don't fuck this one up. It's a slam dunk. Know what I mean?" I ordered another round and stuffed Heather's number into my pocket. I started thinking about how I would say hello if I ever called her.

Hi there, Heather, it's me, the walking disaster.

Yo, Heather baby. What's up?

Hello TNT, it's John the Stalker from across the way. You know. The guy who whacks off to you.

Hello, I'm not sure if you remember me. It's John, John Lenza, the guy from the ménage à trois the other night.

Hi, it's Teeny Duncan's friend John Lenza calling.

Hi.

Then Ornette Coleman came on the jukebox.

—Ornette Coleman doesn't get the respect he deserves. Don't you think?

—You got a couple bucks? I'm going to put Cher and Barbra Streisand on.

—Tell me you're kidding, Teeny.

—Actually, I wouldn't mind listening to something with a melody.

—He's incredible. Listen to him.

—Jazz isn't really my thing, John.

—I don't have patience for someone who only listens to dance music.

—What makes you think that I haven't tried listening to Ornette Coleman before?

—Well, I don't know for sure. I'm making an assumption.

—And you're making an ass of yourself in the process.

—Well, you didn't want to go to the Village Gate with me that time—

—That's because my ex hangs out there, you asshole, not because I don't like jazz! Well, I don't like jazz, but that's beside the point.

—I'm sorry.

—You can be a real asshole sometimes.

—I know. I'm sorry.

I had never seen Teeny so angry. He was drinking like a fiend, and I was feeling pretty guilty about pulling him off the wagon. After a bit, he told me that he had been thinking about going cold turkey, and when that day came he wanted me to lock him inside his apartment for at least a week. Drinking was second nature to Rutherford B. Duncan. He'd started when he was only eleven years old. In Cuyahoga Falls, Ohio, drinking was an organized sport.

—If I forgot to turn off the light, my father, who I affectionately called Godzilla, whacked me. If I used my own fork instead of the serving fork, he slapped me. If I tried to speak to him when he walked in the door, he punched me. When I came out of the closet, he never stopped beating me. Godzilla was a real monster. My mother just gave up after a while. Sometimes she tried to fight back with humor, but most of the time she just drank to forget. She was a lightweight really, and couldn't keep up with my old man. She would have a couple of whiskey sours, puke and black out. There were so many mornings when I was getting ready for school and instead of having a bowl of cereal or scrambled eggs waiting for me, I'd find my mother passed out. It was a good morning when she was on the couch and not on the kitchen floor.

One night, Godzilla came home smashed and started thrashing Teeny's mother. Even though Teeny was a scrawny seventeen-year-old and no match for his hulking father, he came to his mother's defense. He pushed Godzilla with all of his might, causing him to trip into the fireplace and crack his skull open. His mother refused to take her husband to the hospital, so Teeny had to drive him.

While they were in the waiting room, Godzilla told him that his mother had deserved the beating. Allegedly, she had been cheating on him with his best friend. Teeny didn't know whether his father was telling the truth or not. It was the only time he ever saw his father weep, but he didn't console him. He didn't put his arm around his shoulder and tell him everything would be okay. While the doctor stitched Godzilla up, Teeny sat in the car, listening to the radio.

—When I dropped Godzilla off at home, I didn't say goodbye. I just kept driving until I got to New York. I've been here ever since. I used to hear from my mother from time to time. I never asked her if she had been unfaithful. She might have been. Can't say that I blame her. But after a while, I got tired of the way she enabled my father, so I stopped calling her. We haven't spoken in some time. I haven't spoken to Godzilla in almost thirty years.

It was still raining and pretty late when we stumbled out of the bar. I asked Teeny if he wanted to join me for scrambled eggs at the diner, but he just wanted to go home and get some sleep. He claimed that all that writing, drinking and reminiscing had sucked the life out of him. "Make sure TNT doesn't catch you spanking the monkey. You won't have any chance then. And do your best with the play. That's all you can do. Make me proud." He hopped on his bicycle and rode down the slope to Cobble Hill.

My good arm was sore and beginning to throb from hauling my suitcase around, so I dropped the shabby thing, which I'd had since I'd started working at EverCover, on the curb next to a garbage can on the corner of Seventh Avenue and Ninth Street, underneath Dawn's poster. Someone had drawn a penis in Dawn's mouth and written SUCK IT above her head. I laughed my head off. The day had really worn me out, and I didn't think I could manage walking the few blocks home, so I hopped on the F train.

Except for a very made up, dark-haired woman who had on black hip huggers, red lipstick and toxic perfume, the subway car was empty. When I flopped down next to her, underneath the advertisement DON'T LET IMPOTENCE RUIN YOUR LIFE, she rolled her eyes and cracked her gum. Another subway rule: if there are seats available elsewhere, never sit directly next to a passenger. R & B was pouring from her iPod, and she was mouthing the lyrics to a song that I couldn't make out. I popped a couple of Zolpidem and Zoloft and started fantasizing about her. There was no end to my fantasies. We were set to embark on a subway tryst, and this was how my pipe dream played out in my head: we would engage in meaningless conversation about the weather before discussing our jobs, never once exchanging our names. We'd flirt and reminisce about all the public places we'd had sex. We'd get off at Second Avenue, wander around the East Village, stroll down Bond Street, and step inside a trendy vintage clothing store, where we'd both be horrified at the price of a pair of ripped jeans. Then, after we ate in a crowded, expensive café on Ludlow Street, Hip Huggers would lead me to a park off East Houston, where we'd have the best sex of our lives underneath the monkey bars.

The subway car rattled me back to reality. Hip Huggers stood up at the Church Avenue stop; the back of her thighs brushed against my knees as she made her way past me to the doors. I thanked her for starring in my three-minute daydream, but she couldn't hear me, so she took off her headphones, and I thanked her again. "Thanks for an incredible three minutes. Was it as good for you as it was for me?" She looked at me as if I were a pathetic, lecherous old man, which I was, then made a strange movement with her mouth and gave me the finger. "Fuck off!" If Hip Huggers only knew that three-minute fantasies were all I had left, then maybe she would have been more sympathetic.

I had already missed my stop and it was really late, but I got a second wind and thought I'd ride all the way to Coney Island just for the hell of it. I was skimming through *The Never-Ending Story of Bullshit* when the train stopped at Kings Highway. I was hoping a beautiful woman would board and be the star of a new three-minute fantasy. That's when Stephanie got on, looking the way she did just before she died.

JOHN

You're back.

STEPHANIE

I never left.

JOHN

What are you talking about? You've been dead for like twenty years.

STEPHANIE

Well, I'm here now. Take me and the baby with you, Gianni.

JOHN

What about your boyfriend Joey Santone?

STEPHANIE

He's not half the man you are.

JOHN

Well I know that. Who is? But we should at least tell him.

STEPHANIE

My old man ran out on me. My baby deserves a real father. And Joey would not be half the father you'd be.

JOHN

Well I know that. It's not fair to compare Joey to me. But what should we do? Where should we go?

STEPHANIE

Take us to a remote island somewhere in the Mediterranean where we could live the rest of our days together.

JOHN

The Mediterranean is pretty far away. Would you settle for Coney Island?

Stephanie and I got off at Coney Island. She grabbed my hand, and we sprinted to Nathan's. We poured mustard and relish on our hot dogs and drenched our fries in ketchup. When we were finished eating, we strolled the boardwalk, arm in arm. I pointed out the building where Harpo Marx played his first gig. She caught a glimpse of the Cyclone and started squealing. "I wanna ride. I wanna ride. I wanna ride." She let go of my arm and ran recklessly through the crowds to the legendary roller coaster. I hate roller coasters almost as much as I hate dance music, so I chose not to ride. I watched her buy a ticket, climb the stairs and step into the first car. She raised both arms above her head and waved to me. The roller coaster scaled the first hill. When it reached the top, as it paused for a moment, Stephanie placed her hands over her eyes. And then the roller coaster descended. I watched her take the first drop. I heard her scream. Then she disappeared. And I was alone. Again.

By the time I got home, the rain had stopped and the sun was coming up. I wasn't surprised to learn that my boss had called to fire me. Richard had left a note on the kitchen table: *He wants you to drop off your samples Monday morning. Pete's son Carmine came looking for you. Said something about owing months of rent. Your mother called again. Help yourself to the fried rice in the fridge.* My home life had become precarious. It was only a matter of time before Pete, Carmine or my mother caught up with me.

I had worked my entire adult life at a job I hated, towing a massive suitcase around the busy streets of Brooklyn, playing the flunky to intellectual types like Dr. Hicks, and I had nothing to show for my hard work. I was Willy Loman, a "dime a dozen," a salesman who couldn't sell anything, living in "a nuthouse of a city." So there I was, face to face with the truth: I was unemployed, broke and alone, with a broken arm to boot. It was an equation that I dared not compute, but for the moment it felt pretty good to be rid of EverCover Books.

THERE IS NO END TO MY FICTION

I never had any intention of working on Teeny's play, partly because I didn't feel like revisiting my past and partly because I didn't want to ruin his work. But even if I wanted to screw it up I couldn't because I'd left the manuscript on the subway the night I went to Coney Island. Since I didn't have much going on at the moment, I thought that I'd get back in the saddle and try my hand at the whole dating thing—or, as Teeny liked to put it, the "fucking my brains out" thing. It was kind of crazy not to give Heather a call, but I had what I referred to as a severe case of "impotence due to proximity," and since Teeny was having so much success on Craigslist, I decided to give Match.com a try.

I played on the dating site for hours at a time, entering my requirements and refining my searches until I was presented with hundreds of female playthings from all five boroughs. The elaborate fairy tales that most women had written about themselves seduced me to the point that I created one of my very own, omitting a few minor details such as being divorced, unemployed, unable to pay the rent, having a homeless man as a roommate, drinking too much, popping too many pills, impregnating married women and killing my best friend and her baby.

I transformed John Lenza into the Six Million Dollar Man: Anton Chekhov (my alias) was the youngest of three sons in a prosperous midwestern family. He had traveled the world, working with the Peace Corps and volunteering with Doctors Without Borders before graduating from Princeton, where he had played basketball, and becoming the world's most prominent gastroenterologist, who also wrote short stories and plays in his spare time. He was a gourmet chef and wine connoisseur, fluent in five languages including Mandarin, and one weekend per month he whisked underprivileged, inner-city children from their tenements and into the country, where they fished, rode horses and toasted marshmallows around a campfire while he played guitar and sang "There's a Hole in the Bucket." Hocus pocus! Presto chango! Alakazam! I was a different man. Anton Chekhov was every woman's wet dream.

Even though I could tell more about a woman in five minutes face to face than I could in fifteen thousand emails, I stayed on my laptop in Southside for weeks on end, flirting with dozens of lovely ladies at a time. *She thinks I'm witty? She thinks I'm funny? I'm the most interesting guy she's ever spoken to? She wants to have a picnic with me in Prospect Park?* The Internet bred a kind of detached foreplay, and these provocative exchanges never failed to excite me as well as boost my severely damaged ego. I could see why Teeny was drawn to such games, tennis matches that continued as long as you were willing to volley, and for once in my life I thought I was winning and in complete control of my serve.

All that changed when I got a risqué email from Charlene: *I'm in NYC for 1 nite I saw ur profile & pic would like 2 spend it with u can promise u 1 super fun time (lol).* Charlene was a fair-skinned brunette who enjoyed black-and-white movies, jazz, theater, yoga, taking long walks in the park, Pinot Noir and photographing bridges. (This last hobby really intrigued me.) She claimed to be thirty years old, but if she was desperate like I was and had fabricated her profile like I had then she was most likely closer to forty, like I was. Her photograph was of her head and torso. Her bare arm was strategically draped across her bare breasts, gripping her bare shoulder. Charlene was drop-dead gorgeous, but her picture might have been taken years ago, as mine had been, or she could have been really crafty and used a photograph of somebody else, as I had been inclined to do, though I didn't think Teeny's headshot would be an improvement over my own.

I had never been a promiscuous guy. I was no Teeny Duncan—although at the time, I wanted to sleep with every woman in New York. All this Internet browsing was making me horny as hell, but I made one date and Charlene was the lucky girl. She was beautiful, desperate, available, admired bridges and really wanted me. What more could I ask? If Heather was a slam dunk, then Charlene was a hole in one, a touchdown, a grand slam and a slam dunk all rolled into one erotic ball of sex.

We arranged to meet in Manhattan at the fleabag hotel where she was staying, the Howard Johnson on Eighth Avenue in the Theater District. I ironed my black pinstripe suit and threw on my red tie for the occasion. When I arrived, the disheveled old guy behind the front desk, who had a splotch of mustard on his worn black sweater, handed me a perplexing note with a curious yellow stain plastered across it: *Come up Anthony I'm in rm. 802.* Had the old guy used the note as a napkin? Who the hell was Anthony? Was this note for somebody else?

The elevator car reeked of urine and the button was sticky. I wiped my finger on my blazer and waited a hundred years for the doors to close. As the elevator rose, so did my inhibitions. I sprayed half of Richard's Old Spice on my neck, smacked my cheeks and shoved a few hundred Mentos into my mouth. With the exception of the book I was holding, I was empty-handed and regretted not having brought a bottle of wine or flowers, something, but I'd been in such a hurry to get laid that doing anything remotely romantic had completely slipped my mind.

I bought a package of peanut M&M's from a vending machine and meandered until I stumbled upon room 802. As soon as I knocked on the door, I wanted to turn back. I began to doubt my objective. I mean, what was I doing there? Was I that desperate? I decided that I couldn't go through with it, but when I turned to walk away the door swung open and Charlene was standing in the doorway wearing a white flowing negligee.

—Hi, there. You must be Anthony.

—Please call me Anton. And you must be Charlene.

—The one and only. But please call me Charlie. You smell great.

—Masculine, I hope.

—Very macho and very handsome in your suit.

—And you in your negligee. Wow! Simply stunning.

—I have planned a very special evening for you, Anthony.

—The name's Anton. I hope that you didn't go through too much trouble.

—It was no trouble at all. Is that for me?

—Uh, yes. I hope you're not allergic to peanuts.

—How thoughtful.

The hotel room was exactly what I had expected. Two single beds. Bad lighting. Cheap, dark furniture. An olive-green, shabby carpet with matching curtains and bedding. Paintings of the Empire State Building and the Flatiron Building hung over their respective single beds. Chintzy. The bathroom door was closed, but the light and the fan were left on.

Charlie looked nothing like her picture. She was at least ten years older and fifty pounds heavier. Her hair was shorter, dyed blonde and unkempt, and I could not tell the color of her eyes behind her unfashionable, large eyeglass frames. Pockets of fat were seeping out from her negligee. Her unsightly appearance made me even more uncomfortable than I'd been before the door opened. I wondered if she were as disappointed with me as I was with her.

—Make yourself comfortable. Can I get you a drink?

—Sure.

—Scotch? Gin? What's your poison?

—Sure.

—Which one?

—I'll have whatever you're having.

The desk functioned as a bar. Bottles. Plastic cups. Olives. Lemon. Lime. Straws. Although her email had stated that she was in New York for a single night, room 802 looked as if she had been partying there since the eighties. Yet there wasn't a single suitcase in the closet. Nothing was hanging either. No dress. No skirt. No coat. Nothing. The closet was empty. Charlie dipped her hands into the ice bucket and dropped a few cubes into two red cups. She held her cup between her crooked teeth while she fished around in my drink for something, maybe a hair, before letting out a big sigh and handing it to me.

—So Antonio. You're even more handsome in person.

—Please, call me Anton. You're not so bad yourself.

—What happened to your arm? You look pale. Are you okay?

—On the way over here, I got into a bit of a fracas with some thug.

—Oh, my. Are you all right? Can I get you a Band-Aid?

—I'm fine, thank you. You should have seen what the other guy looked like.

—Oh boy, it sounds frightening.

—It was nothing. Really. It happens all the time in my homeland.

—So where are you originally from? California or someplace like that?

—Russia, actually.

—Really? The farthest south I have ever been was Virginia Beach. What brings you to New York?

—My work brought me to this great city.

—Do you work at one of the hospitals?

—I'm on a book tour.

—It said in your profile that you're a doctor.

—That's true, I am, but I'm also a writer.

—That's right. Your profile said that you wrote several books. I was never any good at writing in school. I hated school, actually, so I dropped out.

—In fact, this is one of my books.

—Wow! How exciting! *The Cherry Orchard*. I never heard of it. I don't like to read, myself.

—Here. I'd like for you to have my copy. I'll personally autograph it for you. Have you got a pen?

Charlie fetched a pen from the desk drawer and fixed herself another drink.

—*Medicine is my lawful wife and literature is my mistress*. I don't know what it means, Anton, but it sounds nice.

—Well, it's another way of saying...never mind. It doesn't matter.

Was Charlie that ignorant? Maybe she was playing coy. Either way, she was getting pretty bombed, and I figured if she didn't detect my Brooklyn accent and call me out on my lies I might as well have a little fun. I'm a pathetic man, I know. She sat close to me, practically in my lap, and planted sloppy wet kisses on my neck. I followed her lead, but when I tried to place the book and pen on the nightstand, I spilled my drink all over myself. I started toward the bathroom when Charlie leaped in front of me and blocked the door. "I'll take care of it, Anton. You just make yourself comfortable on the bed. Charlie will be right back, and then we'll pick up where we left off." I thought about making a getaway, but she was quick to return, reaching into the bathroom and grabbing a towel as if somebody were in there assisting her. While Charlie was patting down my crotch with the towel, there was a crash in the bathroom.

—Is there somebody in your bathroom?

—My bathroom? Oh, no, that's the noisy couple next door. M&M?

She tore into the bag of M&M's and poured a couple of scotches although they might have been gin, I don't remember. We toasted our good health and tossed them back. Charlie returned to slobbering all over my neck, and that's when I started to feel queasy. It couldn't have been the alcohol. I wasn't a heavyweight like Teeny or Richard, by any means, but it took more than two shots to make me sick. Could it have been the combination of nerves, alcohol, antidepressants and sleeping pills? Maybe it was the painful conversation, but whatever it was, I had to excuse myself before I vomited all over Charlie and her white negligee.

—You look like you've had one too many.

—I'm not feeling well, Charlie. I need to use the loo.

—Don't you think you should go to the bathroom?

—I don't know what's wrong with me. I'll be right back.

—I hope you'll be of some use to me when you return. Charlie's got a big surprise for you.

I stripped off my blazer, stumbled into the bathroom and flipped the switch, but the light had already been on, so I mistakenly turned it off. When I found the switch and turned the light back on, I paused underneath the harsh yellow fluorescent bulb to inspect my face in the mirror. I looked pale and old. My bloodshot eyes had dark circles around them. A deep dark line shot across my forehead. While I was tracing it with my finger, I noticed that my hand was shaking, and I could not steady it.

I dropped to my knees and lifted the toilet seat. While I waited for the inevitable purge, it crossed my mind that maybe good ole Charlie had slipped something into my drink. I closed my eyes, swore to God that I'd never go on a blind date again and recited the Act of Contrition. When I finished spewing my guts, I lifted my head from the toilet at the same time a large, ominous figure emerged from behind the shower curtain. Before I could shield myself, he thumped me across the side of my head with a blunt object, knocking me backward into the sink and to the floor. I thought that if the gorilla knew I was still conscious he would kill me, so I played dead.

While the gorilla fumbled through my pockets, his face was so close to mine that I caught a whiff of his coffee breath. Then he sneezed in my face, but I didn't budge. I wanted to wrap my hands around his neck and squeeze the last coffee breath out of him, but I had only one good arm and didn't think that I stood much of a chance against a gorilla. He might have had a gun for all I knew. Charlie came into the bathroom, announced that she was packed and ready to go, and urged the big oaf to hurry.

—I feel a little sorry for him.

—You should feel sorry for us. He doesn't have much on him. You told me this chump was rich.

—His profile said that he's a doctor and comes from a wealthy midwestern family.

—Well, his work ID says his name is John Lenza. We got a few bucks. Let's get out of here before he wakes up.

—He's a fucking liar. He's not a doctor. I bet he's not even a writer.

—You can't believe everything you read.

Charlie picked up my blazer, then flicked off the light and gave me a nice swift kick in the stomach before fleeing the scene. I played dead until I was sure that they were gone. Then I turned over, pressed my face to the cold tiles and started to cry. Charlie and the gorilla had snatched my wallet. I had just cashed my last check from EverCover. It wasn't much money, but it was all I had left. They'd even run off with my copy of *The Cherry Orchard*.

The pounding of my head made me dizzy, the dizziness made me nauseated and the nausea made me incapacitated. It took me a hundred years to get to my feet, peel off my clothes and feel around for blood. I took a cold shower, trying to settle my throbbing head and get the blood circulating. When I stepped out of the shower, I slipped and nearly cracked my skull open on the tile. I needed a drink, but the entire bar had been cleared away.

With no money to get back to Brooklyn, I wandered around Times Square, asking tourists for a handout. Most of them just ignored me while a few women gave me sympathetic looks. A guy in a three-piece business suit told me to get a job. A teenage girl reached into her backpack and handed me an apple. I imagined how vulnerable Richard must feel on the street. Was this what real hunger felt like? At least Richard could sing. He had the gift of gab. And he was charming too. What did I have to offer?

I sat on the curb at Forty-Second Street and Seventh Avenue and watched people go in and out of the Hard Rock Cafe and the ESPN Zone. Times Square had officially become Disney Square. Gone were the seedy adult theaters, go-go bars, sex shops, hustlers, prostitutes and runaways that I remembered from my youth. Once, when I'd been a little boy walking down Forty-Second Street, sandwiched between my parents, clutching their hands, frightened by all of the unfamiliar sights and sounds of the city, I'd seen a scruffy blond teenager with puke all over his plaid shirt jogging in a circle with his eyes closed, mumbling the lyrics to Elton John's "Rocket Man." *I miss the earth so much, I miss my wife. It's lonely out in space.* He stumbled

THERE IS NO END TO THIS SLOPE

into a garbage can, then collapsed onto the curb, his head in the gutter, blood on the pavement. Nobody helped him. Except for me, I didn't think anybody had even noticed him. One man, rushing to catch a bus, stepped right over the boy. He was just a messed up kid who needed a little help. My mother said, "You're lucky that you have two parents who love you. Otherwise that could be you in the gutter." She had a way of scaring the hell out of me.

I was unable to panhandle the two-dollar subway fare, so I hopped the turnstile and rode the number 2 train to Grand Army Plaza, which was a pretty fair distance from my apartment, but after the evening I had just had, I thought a walk in Prospect Park might do me some good. When I got to the top of the hill, I was surprised by how bright the stars were shining. I continued along the paved road that circles the park, admiring the stars, when I accidentally stepped between two runners. One of them tripped and nearly fell. "Watch it, dipshit." That's when I decided to go for a little run of my own, so I took a deep breath and started stretching. I'd never gone jogging in my life, but there I was bending at the waist to touch my toes. I could barely touch my knees let alone my toes. Through my legs, I saw an orange glow light up the road, and emerging from it was good ole TNT, heading right for me, except she didn't see me and tripped over my big foot and fell pretty hard. I wasn't in the mood to talk to her, so I continued stretching, staring at my feet, hoping that she'd dust herself off and keep going, but I had no such luck. TNT bounced right back up, headed straight toward me and placed her hand on my back. She seemed more concerned about my welfare than her own.

—Sorry about that. You all right?
—Yeah, I'm okay. Are you?
—Hey, how's it going? You're Teeny's friend.
—That's me.
—I didn't know it was you. What a coincidence.
—I didn't see you coming around the turn there.
—I practically ran you over. I'm sorry. Are you okay?
—I'm fine. I'll see you around. You take care now.
—Wait. Wait. Are you going for a run?
—Right after I stretch the ole hammies.
—It's good to see you. How is your arm feeling?
—Feels like a million bucks.

—Are you able to run with it in a sling like that?

—Oh, sure. I've run with it like this many times.

—Where's your sweatshirt? It's pretty cold out here for March.

—I find the cold air to be invigorating.

—Would you like mine? I'm wearing enough layers.

—Thanks, but pink isn't exactly my color.

—Are you going to run in those shoes?

—Enough about me. What are you listening to?

—Madonna, mostly.

—Oh, do you like dance music?

—Yeah, I do. Especially when I'm running.

—I didn't know you were a runner.

—There's a lot that you don't know about me, Jim.

—John.

—Oh, I'm so sorry. John. Right. Teeny—Rutherford B. Duncan—and John, John, John—

—Lenza.

—That's right. Lenza. How silly of me.

—Please, don't let me take you away from your run.

—Would you like to run with me?

—Sure, why not.

—Not too many people wear a tie to go running.

—I thought I'd class up the joint.

Heather's taste in music was unsettling, but her penchant for the color pink was even more so. To augment her pink sweatshirt, she wore pink lipstick, pink earrings, a pink headband, pink shorts over pink Lycra tights, and pink running sneakers. She looked like she had stepped out of a Madonna music video. TNT, all the way. Still, despite Heather's questionable taste in music and clothing and her bright orange glow and leather skin, there was something about her that I really liked. She didn't remember details like my name, but she was easy to talk to, kind of like Stephanie. Heather must have thought that I was easy to talk to as well because on our run she told me some really personal things about the year she had dropped out of college and moved to London to be a poet. I was out of breath, so I let her talk away.

She had lived in a one-room flat with her boyfriend, Ian, another aspiring poet, who turned their place into an office where he held editorial meetings with the staff of the literary magazine that he helped edit. Ian hosted a poetry reading in the basement of the Lion's Head where Heather waited on tables. She'd loved his accent. He'd loved her American naiveté. They'd rolled their own cigarettes, drunk red wine as if it was water, read poetry and stayed up all night with friends, talking about art, literature, music, pop culture, politics, their future plans and goals. Heather had spent more time lecturing about the merits of literature than actually producing any whereas Ian had dedicated every waking minute to completing a book of his sonnets. While Ian had pursued his writing with a recklessness that only a nineteen-year-old could possess, it had become evident that Heather lacked the patience and determination to be a poet, which put a strain on their relationship. It all came to a head one night when Ian never came home.

—He didn't have the decency to call?

—We didn't have a telephone. It was so annoying being cut off from the world. I wasn't used to living that way.

—Still, he left without saying anything to you.

—Are you okay? You seem really fatigued.

—Don't worry about me. I'm fine. You were telling me about Ian.

—Ian was a writer. I was a fraud. The starving artist thing wasn't for me. Deep down, we both knew it. It just took me a while to admit it to myself.

—But you are a writer. You're a journalist.

—Yeah, a writer. I'm a glorified fact checker. Ian was a poet. He wrote such beautiful things. He said that I was too much of a coward to ever be a poet.

—He sounds like an arrogant jerk.

—No, no, no, he was right. I was an overindulged, entitled American girl. I had everything handed to me and never had to really work for anything. It all became clear to me the night I was going to read at Ian's poetry reading.

Heather's pink shoelace had come undone, so she cut her story short to tie it. When she noticed that my shoelace had also come undone, she didn't think twice about tying it for me. I watched her delicate hands pull and tug and double knot.

—You should always double knot.

—Thanks. Having one arm makes it kind of difficult.

—You should really get that checked out.

—Yeah. I will. I definitely will.

—How did you break it?

—It's a long story. Hey, would you mind walking for a bit?

—Sure, you seem kind of winded. Which way are you headed?

—The same way you are. We're neighbors, remember?

—Oh, right. Funny, I've never seen you in the neighborhood. This way then?

—Yep. I like to keep a low profile. Anyway, you were telling me about the poetry reading.

—I couldn't go up there and read in front of all those people. I just froze. I couldn't do it.

—I can't blame you. It has to be scary to bare your soul in front of an audience.

I'd always fooled myself into thinking that I could write something, create something worthwhile, something that might live on when I was long gone, but no matter how much I dreamed of being a writer, it just didn't seem possible. My father had a saying: "If it ain't in your hands, then it's nowhere." My hands were empty and I was nowhere. Heather was honest about her fears, doubts, needs and desires. I could use more honesty like that in my life.

—I don't like to fail. What if I had written something that wasn't any good? The fear of actually completing something was scary to me. You need thick skin to be an artist. But I don't need to tell you that. That's why I'm so impressed with the play you and Teeny are working on. You're really putting yourself out there, and I think it's great.

—Yeah, it's been a challenge. Teeny's doing most of the work.

—He seems like a brave guy.

—He's been submitting it to theaters and contests. It's not even finished.

—So he's stupid too. Sometimes that's a winning combination.

—I admire him. He's got a huge brass set of balls.

—He's a great guy too.

—He's one of a kind. What did you do after London?

—I came back home, enrolled at Kansas State, studied journalism, and the rest is history. Ancient history.

—You seem to be doing okay for yourself.

—I manage. I'll feel better when my daughter gets here.

—Daughter? I didn't know you had a daughter.

—There's a lot that you don't know about me, Jim.

—John.

—I know. It was a joke.

—Funny.

—She's in Topeka with my mom, who's taking care of her until I get settled.

—How long have you been in Brooklyn?

—Two years. It's taken me some time to get my act together. I was kind of in a bad place for a while. I came to New York to get cleaned up and find work.

—I wasn't prying or anything.

—Have you been stalking me, John Lenza?

—No. No. Don't be crazy. What's your daughter's name?

—Theresa.

—How old is she?

—She's almost two and a half.

—So she was pretty young when you left.

—Yeah, it killed me to leave but I had to get out of Topeka. I was running with a bad crowd. I'm in a much better place now. I miss her so much.

Me and Heather had come from similar backgrounds, except she got out, had the courage to live elsewhere and experience something different. I had remained in Brooklyn, just rotting away.

—This is so crazy that we live right next door to each other, and I've never seen you.

—It's a very New York thing. Not knowing your neighbors and all.

—Is Pete your father?

—Pete? No. Hell no. Pete's son, Carmine, never even visits the old guy.

—Pete's a sweet old man. He's always giving me vegetables from his garden, and he tells me more than I will ever need to know about the neighborhood.

—You don't think he's a blowhard?

—That little old man? He's adorable.

—I think you mean abominable.

—He's a real sweetie. He really loved his wife, you know.

—Yeah, I guess he really did.

—I think he's dying of a broken heart.

—Can somebody die of such a thing?

—It's pretty obvious that he can't go on without her.

—Do you think he's a danger to himself?

—I hope not.

—Me too. Uhm, Heather…

—Yeah?

—Uhm.

—What is it?

—What is it?

—I don't know what it is. You have to tell me.

—Oh, yeah. I wanted to ask you something.

—We've already established that.

—I guess we have.

—It's getting cold. I should get inside.

—Heather?

—Yes, Jim? Only kidding.

—Good one. What's it like being a mother?

—It's great.

—Yeah, everyone says that, but what's so great about it?

—It's exciting and scary at the same time. It's the ultimate adrenaline rush.

—Does being scared out of your mind make it great?

—It makes it interesting, that's for sure. Do you have any children?

—Me? No, no, no. I was just wondering what it was like. I bet you miss her a lot.

—I call her every chance I get. Good night, John. I'll see you around.

—Good night, Heather.

—Hey, John?

—Yeah?

—You want to get coffee some time?

—Sure, you know where to find me.

—Maybe tomorrow night?

—Sounds great. Hey, which do you prefer, cappuccino or espresso?

—Latte.

—Oh.

—Is this a quiz?

—Sort of.

—Well, did I pass?

—With flying colors.

—Cool.

Heather answered her cell phone, opened her front door, picked up Buffy, kissed her head and gave me a friendly wave before entering her apartment. I returned her wave with a salute and opened my front door as quietly as I could without disturbing Pete. I hobbled up the stairs and into my kitchen, searching for the bottle of Zolpidem, but I couldn't find it anywhere. I threw down a couple of shots of Gordon's and took a long, hot bath. The tiles in the bathroom needed plastering; several of them had already fallen out. The shower curtain needed to be replaced. The tub needed to be scrubbed. The place was a disaster.

Just as I settled in, the telephone rang. The answering machine picked up.

—Hello Gianni. It's me, Pete. You've been avoidin' me, Gianni. I thought we were friends. You haven't paid your rent in a long time. I have a mortgage to pay, you know. And you never told me that your colored friend is homeless. And he's livin' with you? I don't even care about that. I like Richard. He's a decent guy. But you should have told me, Gianni. Richard told me that you lost your job. You don't have a job, Gianni? What are ya goin' to do? Maybe Carmine can get you somethin' at the plant. Please call me when you get this message. We'll figure somethin' out. Call me. Ciao.

I put on some music that didn't quite match my mood, the Rolling Stones' *Beggars Banquet*. Threatening, raunchy, filthy Stones at their peak, before they became a corporation—when Mick was threatening, Keith was writing incredible guitar licks and Brian Jones was poised to do himself in. I felt inspired to play along to "Stray Cat Blues," but couldn't find my guitar, so I stretched out on the couch with Pablo and Colette. Despite my raging headache and that I didn't pop a sleeping pill, Mick's pedophiliac lyrics somehow lulled me to sleep, but shortly after, Richard came home drunk and woke me up.

—What up, man? I'm sorry. Did I wake you?

—You have a habit of doing that.

—Sorry, man. Go on back to sleep.

—I can't now.

—Ain't you taking those pills?

—Hey, have you seen my guitar?

—Don't be angry, Sir John.

—What happened, Richard?

—I took it to the corner where I sing for change, Sixth Avenue and Union Street. I busted out some Sam Cooke and Jackie Wilson tunes I hadn't played in a while—

—That's great. What happened?

—I must have turned my back for a moment and—

—Fucking great. I've had that guitar a long time.

—I'll get you a new one, man. I promise.

—That guitar meant a lot to me.

—I never heard you play it.

—Just get me my guitar back.

—I'll get you a new one just like it.

—Yeah, how? You don't have any money.

—Don't you worry. Richard Pritchard has his ways.

—And did you see my bottle of sleeping pills?

—No, man. Haven't seen those. What do they look like?

—They're little yellow pills in a brown bottle that says Zolpidem on it. What do they look like!

—No need to get nasty. I was just asking.

Richard followed me into the kitchen, where I took a seat at the table. He held up the bottle of Gordon's to the light and shook it. "We're running a little low." He poured two shots. Across the way, Heather's kitchen light went on. She was on the phone, dressed for bed, neatly tucked inside her pink bathrobe, her blonde hair pulled back into a long ponytail. Buffy was by her side. She opened the refrigerator, pulled out a carton of orange juice, shook it and poured a big glass. It was as if Heather and Richard were mimicking each other.

—I don't have any more money for booze, Richard. You're on your own from now on.

—Why don't you go work for your buddy Teeny? I don't understand you.

—I'll figure something out.

—Is there something wrong with painting houses?

—Richard, how much do you make a day on the street?

—Whoa, whoa, whoa, Sir John. The street ain't for you, man. You'd better put that idea to sleep. It ain't for me either, truth be told.

—I was just curious.

—It takes a certain personality and you ain't got it.

—What do I need?

—For one thing, a decent robe.

—What's wrong with this one?

—That one there is from the year of the flood, brother.

He poured two more shots and started rummaging through my mail, which blanketed the entire kitchen table. "Nothing here for me?" I'm not sure what he was looking for, but he kept hunting around until he uncovered Stephanie's picture. He held it up to the light to get a good look at it. Meanwhile, Heather, who was still on the phone, started rummaging through a drawer. She pulled out something that looked like a photograph and propped herself up on the counter and sobbed.

—She sure was a pretty girl.

—Yeah, Heather's not bad. She's cool too.

—I thought you said the dead chick's name was Stephanie.

—Oh, you meant Stephanie. Yeah, she was gorgeous.

—What happened, John?

—I told you, she died a long time ago.

—Man, you've been carrying this shit around with you. You got to let it go and find some love for yourself.

—I'm trying to get over her. I just can't seem to do it.

—Just say the word, and I'll rip this photograph to shreds.

—What is it with you, man? Why are you so bent on destroying her picture?

—I'm just saying that I'll do your dirty work for you if you can't.

—Just replace my guitar. I need my guitar.

—But you never play the damn thing.

—Just get me a guitar.

Ever since Richard had moved in, he'd been telling me to tear up Stephanie's picture and open up about the day she died. Across the way, Heather hung up her phone. Buffy leaped into her lap. She was still sobbing and tore up the photograph or whatever it was she had in her hand, then tossed the pieces in the trash and turned out the light. For some reason, at that moment I suddenly felt like telling Richard all about the day Stephanie died.

—Do you really want to hear about how she died, Richard?

—Sure, brother. Tell me all about it.

—Me and Stephanie played a dangerous game when we were in high school. It was something I came up with.

—All kids do stupid shit, man.

—We'd stand on the corner of a busy intersection, waiting for the DON'T WALK sign to stop blinking—when you clearly weren't supposed to walk—and then we'd sprint across the street. Stephanie couldn't run fast enough, the last time.

—What did you play such a stupid-ass game for?

—I don't know. We were bored. It was the suburbs. There was nothing to do. The game was an adrenaline rush. It was like a drug.

—Just stupid. That's what it was.

So there I was with my drunken homeless roommate, somebody I hardly knew, spilling my guts about the most crucial event in my life. I looked over at Heather's, but her kitchen was still covered in darkness.

—So tell me what happened on that particular day?

—We were on our way to school. She was wearing her long black coat even though it was May. We were running across Hylan Boulevard. She was normally faster than me, but at the time she had put on a few pounds due to the pregnancy and the coat got in the way too. An off-duty cop, rushing to get to work, pulled into the right lane, trying to get a jump on the green light. He never saw her.

—She was pregnant?

—Yeah. It was the day before her eighteenth birthday too.

—Man, that's heavy shit.

—Now you see why I can't forgive myself.

—We both lost women we loved, John.

—She was the most important person in the world to me.

—You were young. Young people do crazy-ass shit. Pete joined the army. I started shooting junk. Laverne started 'cause I got hooked on the shit. I was lost for so many years, I even lost my son.

—I'm sorry, man.

—Not a day goes by that I don't regret it. But life goes on.

—Do you know where your son is?

—He's in Richmond, Virginia. I'm trying my damnedest to make amends with the boy. He's stubborn. Like his old man. I was hoping that he'd wrote back to me, but I can't find nothing in this here mess on the table.

Heather was back in her kitchen, back on the phone. Richard mumbled something about the size of her breasts. I told him that I thought they might be real. He laughed his head off. He thought it was the funniest thing he'd ever heard. "Yeah, and I'm a natural redhead. I just dye my hair black." Richard grabbed the bottle of gin and staggered into the living room.

I had been saving a bottle of Montepulciano for a special occasion. I didn't see anything special on the horizon, so I figured I'd open the bottle, but I couldn't find the damn corkscrew. It could have been buried underneath the mountain of junk mail, credit card bills, and overdue telephone, electric and gas bills for all I knew. I couldn't find anything that night.

I opened the window and called out to Heather, thinking she might join me for a glass of wine. She was so involved in her conversation that she didn't hear me, so I opened a drawer, took out a tennis ball and tossed it at her window, but I missed. I couldn't throw with my left hand. Hell, I couldn't throw with my right either. As I called out again, her light went out. I closed the window, broke off the top of the wine bottle on the counter, and poured a glass. I gave Stephanie's photograph one more glance before tucking it in the front pocket of my bathrobe. Then I turned off the light, sat down at the table and listened to Richard sing. *One day I got to pay for my mistakes. It's gonna carry me straight to my grave.*

THE OTHER SIDE OF THE ATLANTIC

The following night, instead of having coffee with Heather, I was wandering aimlessly around the Slope. At some point, I decided to drop into Holy Name Church to see if there was any room for God in my life. I was feeling anxious, so I reached into my pocket for the Zoloft, but I must have left it at home. The last time I'd set foot inside a church was right after Stephanie died, but there I was, making the sign of the cross, praying to the Lamb of God, reciting the Apostles' Creed and dropping a few coins—all I had left to my name—in the offering basket. It was like old times. Not that it felt good or anything. It was just something familiar.

When it was time to receive communion, I didn't get up. I remained kneeling in the last pew, thinking back to when I was seven years old and excited about receiving the holy sacrament for the first time. Me and my classmates, decked out in white, did as the nuns instructed: pressed our palms together, held our hands below our chins as if we were praying, formed the straightest lines we possibly could and tried our best to look like innocent little angels.

I was in the first seat of the first pew, so I was the first in line, first to receive. When it was time, I jumped up and walked briskly down the aisle. Father Flynn placed the stale wafer on my tongue and, being so eager, I closed my mouth, nearly biting off his hand. He glared at me as smoke poured from his ears, and I raced back to the pew. I put my head down, swallowed the Eucharist and started praying. I was disappointed that the wafer didn't satisfy my sweet tooth. It was the size of a Nilla wafer, and I thought it would be sweet and sugary but instead it tasted like cardboard.

When I finished my second Hail Mary, I looked above Father Flynn's bald head at the enormous crucifix on the back wall behind the altar and started thinking about the sacrifice Jesus had made for me and how he was now inside of me—not only in spirit but also how his body was somewhere in the pit of my belly, an anchor, clawing the sand of a great big ocean. I felt like a new boy. Sacred. Valued. Loved. Safe. Worthy of the name Gianni: God's gift.

In the years that followed, I became very serious about the very serious business of Catholicism. I was a devout crusader, and with more enthusiasm than all twelve apostles, I sort of obeyed the Ten Commandments, occasionally breaking the third and fifth ones. Whenever I cursed my parents, I broke them simultaneously, but I didn't think God really gave two shits. He was busy with bigger things like numbers six and seven. All of my religious fervor came to an abrupt end after Stephanie's death. That's when I grew skeptical, bitter, fed up with the church. I questioned Christ's relationship with Mary Magdalene and doubted the Immaculate Conception. I couldn't wrap my brain around original sin. I thought that giving up meat on Fridays during Lent was a bad prank, and I didn't understand why women weren't allowed to become priests.

A couple of weeks after Stephanie's death, I walked into the confessional to spill my guts to Father Flynn, not really knowing that it would be my last time.

—Forgive me Father, for I have sinned. It has been two months since my last confession.

—Okay my son, you may begin.

—My friend was killed. She was hit by a car. And I've been thinking long and hard, but I can't come up with one good reason why God would want to take her away like that.

—Is there something you'd like to confess, my son?

—There are a lot of bad things happening all the time. War. Drugs. Poverty. Murder. There's so much more bad than good. Don't you think?

—Without suffering we would never know the true meaning of joy.

— I have a tough time believing that God wants us to experience so much pain and suffering in order to appreciate the occasional good time. And what about the hypocrisy?

—What about it?

—The hypocrisy of the church is too much for me to overlook, Father.

—What are you referring to?

—The gold cups you drink from. The large amounts of money that this parish makes. There's a priest who drives around in a Cadillac. I know a few who wear gold rings, drink and gamble. So I'm leaving the church.

—Not every priest is a saint.

—I understand that, Father, but there are too many corrupt ones. I'm sorry. I don't mean any disrespect, Father.

—None taken. So, am I to understand that you no longer believe Christ to be your Lord and Savior?

—He couldn't save my friend or her baby. What could he possibly want with an unborn child?

—I didn't know the young woman was expecting. Such a tragedy.

—Why should I believe that he could save me?

—I suppose you don't want absolution, then.

—I don't want to be a hypocrite. What's the sense in praying, anyway? Nothing changes. Nothing at all.

—Well, you can think of prayer as a form of meditation.

—Do you mean like what the Tibetan monks do?

—Something like that.

—No more praying for me. I'm through with it, but thanks for listening, Father. I appreciate it.

—Can you do me one favor, John?

—How did you know it was me, Father?

—You've been confessing your sins to me since you were a little boy. Just do me this one favor.

—What is it?

—Think about it, give it some time and come and talk to me, face to face, before you make your final decision.

After I had made my confession, I wandered the empty streets of Staten Island, walking all the way to the end of the island, which in 1985 was still so rural it felt like I had strolled into the backwoods of Arkansas. By the time I got home, my father, who had been drinking martinis all day, slapped me for having missed dinner while my mother watched him take out his frustrations with his boss on me and did nothing about it. My best friend had just died, but the only thing they cared about was that my pork chop had gotten cold.

I pushed my father out of the way and ran out of the house, into town and up the rectory's steps. I was prepared to confess my sin to Father Flynn, the one that I hadn't confessed earlier, and it wasn't taking the Lord's name in vain or disgracing my parents. It was one of the big ones— number six: murder. It had been my idea to play that insane game that killed Stephanie and her baby and it was eating me up. I rang the bell and waited. And waited. And waited. I rang the bell again, and then I remembered how much I hated those people who ran to God whenever life got difficult, or asked him for something like a good grade on a math test, a new guitar or a base hit with a runner in scoring position. I had been guilty of asking for all three, but this time I thought I was acting like a real hypocrite, so I ran down the steps and all the way to the keg party that was in full swing at Great Kills Beach.

National Geographic had just declared Great Kills Beach one of the most contaminated in the world, but for suburban teenagers the polluted shoreline was our retreat from the harsh realities of life, a relief from the pressures of adolescence, a refuge from adult scrutiny where we were free to screw up all we wanted. Hanging out and partying on the beach was our own version of *Lord of the Flies*, and we had only four rules: (1) maintain the bonfire, (2) make sure it's extinguished before leaving, (3) return the keg to the distributor and (4) collect the deposit. Whenever a keg party started to wind down, Stephanie and I liked to climb into the lifeguard's chair and catch up.

Now it was just me and Joey, so we climbed into the chair and stared into the Atlantic Ocean. Below, Anthony DiMarco argued with the others about the number of beers he'd drunk while couples slipped away from the rest of the gang, looking for a quiet place to make out, and some boys and girls who couldn't hold their liquor were lying on the hood of Joey's Monte Carlo.

The Atlantic Ocean was deep, dark and vast. Looking into it was like peeking into the future. At one time, I might have had an idea of what I wanted my future to look like, but when Stephanie died everything began to look deep, dark and vast.

A full moon was suspended in the infinite magenta sky. It was so bright it illuminated the entire beach. We couldn't look at it without squinting. Joey had completely broken down when Stephanie died. He had always been an uncomplicated kid, but his grief was overwhelming, so I listened to him go on and on about Stephanie and the baby. Joey was my friend, and I wanted to be there for him though I think I was only listening to him as a way to repent for my own sins. When he was done baring his soul to me, I put my arm around his shoulder and we both had a good cry. I thought about the millions of full moons that lay ahead.

—Hey Joe, what do you say we swim out to the sandbar?

—Do you know how many people have died trying to swim out to that thing?

—Stephanie and I did it last summer. Shit. I'm sorry, Joe.

—That was during the day, and you weren't drunk. Andrew Fuller died a couple years ago. The undertow took him out. He was only twelve years old. He's gone forever, John. Like Stephanie and my baby. Gone.

—I don't like who I am, Joe. And what I've done.

—Why were you playing such a dumb fucking game?

—I don't know. I'm an asshole.

—You're telling me.

—I said I was sorry a million times. What do you want from me?

—I wish you had been hit by the car.

—That's fucked up, Joe.

—I hate what you've done. I hate you.

—I'm sorry, Joe. I'm fucking sorry. I wish that it had been me too. Believe me. I don't know how I'm going to live with myself.

Joey jumped off the chair and headed back to the party. I should have let him go, but I followed him, tugging at the bottom of his dungaree jacket, which had Stephanie's painting of Ozzy Osbourne on the back, dressed as a werewolf, barking at the moon. Joey made it clear that he wanted to get away from me, but I needed for him to stop blaming me. I needed Joey's forgiveness, but he wasn't offering any.

Joey's first punch landed right on my jaw, sending me onto my back. He pounced on top of me and wouldn't let me up, pinning my arms down with his knees. His punches had real rage behind them. I think he was trying to kill me, but I didn't even try to defend myself. It was my penance of sorts. Eventually, Anthony DiMarco pulled Joey off me. Joey busted my nose that night, and ever since then, it has slanted slightly to the left. I begged him to stop blaming me for Stephanie's death and to forgive me. He spit in my face. "Stay the fuck away from me. I don't want to see you ever again. You and me. The band. It's over."

I stood alone on the shoreline, skimming rocks and holding the makeshift icepack to my nose, one that DiMarco made from one of the several red bandanas he had wrapped around his legs. An empty red Doritos bag blew across the sand. I watched the mouth of the black water swallow it whole. I stepped into the frigid water, thinking about the other side of the ocean and the darkness that I'd have to navigate alone, without Stephanie or Joey. I thought about swimming to the sandbar, but my legs gave way. I dropped to my knees, raised my hands to the sky and asked God why he was doing this to me. Why was he punishing me?

Joey sat next to me in calculus senior year and while I kept busy reading some of my favorite books—*The Count of Monte Cristo*, *Oliver Twist* and *The Three Musketeers*—he would take notes and participate in the class discussions. I was passing the class only because he let me copy his homework and gave me the answers to the tests. With less than a month to graduation, Joey dropped out of school and went to work at his father's auto shop. After I made up calculus in summer school, I moved to Brooklyn, started college in the fall and never saw Joey Santone again.

I never told Father Flynn that I thought Jesus was a pretty cool dude and that I respected his morals and teachings. I think he would have liked that. What I failed to understand was why Jesus had to be God. Wasn't it cool enough to be a total badass? Whatever Catholicism was selling, I was no longer buying—like the concept of heaven. I thought that it was a pleasant enough idea, but if there was so much unhappiness in this world, there was no telling what the next one might have in store for all of us sinners. I was consumed with guilt, and I really wanted to believe that Stephanie was enjoying her second life in paradise, but I just couldn't fool myself into falling for such never-ending bullshit.

So there I was, twenty years later, in Holy Name Church, listening to a young priest's sermon about the temptations of Satan and how we all have the power to choose where we'd like to end up, heaven or hell. He was no Father Flynn, who delivered some of the most passionate sermons I'd ever heard. While the young priest continued to extol God's virtues, I was looking forward to wishing "peace" to the smelly old man sitting next to me. The Catholic Mass is robotic and devoid of any passion, humor or spirituality. For the most part, the congregation is indifferent; however, toward the end of the service, after the perfunctory recitation of the Our Father, when the congregation shakes hands and offers each other peace, there is a brief interval of grace. For a few minutes, everyone within the church walls is seemingly united. That solidarity had always given me hope. I shook hands with the smelly old man. "Peace be with you." I even hugged him and kissed his cheek. Granting peace to a stranger and thinking about his welfare rather than my own for a change, even if it was only for a few seconds, made me feel a little better.

When Mass ended, the young priest stood by the front doors, shaking hands with the congregation while I remained kneeling in the back pew. I craved the silence. I had wanted the Mass to make me feel something, make me feel like I belonged somewhere. I wanted to believe in something bigger than myself, but I guess that I no longer had room for God. At that moment I would have done anything to exchange that pew for the lifeguard chair, either sitting with Stephanie and talking about music, painting and plays or putting things right with Joey.

I finally left the church and started making my way back home, but I had difficulty walking up Third Street. My arm was throbbing, my head was aching and I was feeling woozy, so I sat on the curb to catch my breath and stared at the gasoline rainbow in the puddle by my feet. I watched it tremble whenever a car passed by. When I pulled Stephanie's graduation photograph out of my pocket, my wedding ring plopped into the puddle and nearly rolled down the sewer. I slipped the ring back on my finger and thought about how Richard wanted me to tear up Stephanie's picture, but I stuffed it back in my front pocket before I did anything drastic. I wasn't ready to give up her picture.

Meanwhile, the 67 local bus was barreling right for me. The driver blew his horn, but I took my time getting to my feet. The bus went through the puddle, soaking me from head to toe. I stepped aboard but then remembered that Charlie and her gorilla had stolen my wallet along with my MetroCard, so I hopped off before the driver closed the doors.

I went into Cosby's looking for Teeny, but the bartender reminded me he was having dinner with a Guess model. He had been looking forward to this date for weeks and was so excited about having the opportunity to photograph a model, someone with real experience. He had promised to show me the pictures afterward.

I sat at the bar, running up Teeny's tab, watching ESPN—the Mets had lost a doubleheader—while John Coltrane's saxophone poured out of the jukebox. *A Love Supreme*. I wasn't really sitting at the bar. I was in Staten

Island with Stephanie, so I did what I normally did whenever I felt this way: I wrote her a note on a cocktail napkin, which wasn't easy to do with my left hand.

Dear Stephanie,

The world doesn't take to me. I've been trying to find my way, but I don't know where to turn. I need to love myself a little more. The way I love you.

I will always love you for having loved me a little more than I ever loved myself.

Gianni

When I got home, Richard was sitting on the stoop. He trembled when he saw me then flicked his cigarette into the gutter. He picked up Pablo, kissed his head and told me that Pete had died.

—What happened? I didn't know he was sick.

—Ain't it obvious? He died of a broken heart.

—C'mon, Richard. You don't believe that shit. Do you?

—The old brother couldn't go on living without his wife.

—I don't understand. His heart just gave out?

—The Zolpidem had something to do with that, I'm sure.

—What was he doing with Zolpidem?

—I gave him your bottle. I didn't think he was gonna kill himself. He told me he had trouble sleeping.

—That was fucking stupid, Richard.

—I didn't know he was going to swallow the whole bottle.

—I had a feeling he was going to harm himself.

—He's in a better place now.

—Don't tell me you really believe that.

—Hey, I gotta believe in something. This world is a pretty depressing place. I hope I'm going to a better one when I die.

Pete had told me that when he came home from the war he was never able to sleep through the night. He had become a teeth grinder, a sleep talker, a blanket grabber. His legs shimmied all night long, but since his wife's death, his insomnia had worsened. I hoped that his suffering had finally come to an end and that he had joined Clara in heaven, but I couldn't fool myself into believing such never-ending bullshit. Like Stephanie, the poor bastard was just food for worms.

NOTHING TO BE DONE

A couple of days after Pete's funeral, good ole Carmine moved into his father's apartment and evicted me and Richard. He confiscated everything I owned, which included my computer, couch, record collection, stereo, even Emma's desk, for the back rent. Before I moved out, I took a screwdriver to Pete's precious hardwood floors throughout the apartment; then I threw some clothes and my notebook into a duffel bag that was the size of Manhattan and handed Colette over to Richard.

—Take good care of her, man.

—Sure thing, Sir John. Hey, where you heading?

—I'm going to stay with Teeny until I get back on my feet.

—Then why ain't you taking your pussy with you?

—I'll be back to get her once I get settled.

—I still don't understand why you ain't holdin' on to her.

—You hold on to things better than me, Richard.

—I'll take real good care of her. Don't you worry 'bout a thing.

—Hey Richard, do you believe in second acts?

—What do you mean?

—You know…like a comeback.

—Hell, yeah.

—Are you hoping to make a comeback, Mr. Pritchard?

—All I got left in this world is hope, Sir John.

—But what if you have nothing to come back to?

—Hey, John, put an end to this kind of bleak philosophy. Everybody got something or someone to come back to. Even you. Here, take this.

—I don't need your gin, Richard.

—You need it more than I do.

—Thanks. I'll see you soon.

—You know where to find me. And John, try to find some love for yourself. Dig deep, brother.

Richard wrapped his trench coat around Colette's carrier case and placed it in his shopping cart. Then he took hold of Pablo's leash and meandered up the slope. I figured Colette would be all right. The streets were in Richard's veins, and if he'd taken care of his dog all these years then he'd take good care of my cat too. Since I hadn't attended Pete's funeral, I thought I should visit Green-Wood Cemetery and pay my respects to the old guy.

I began my trek across the Slope, but I didn't have a song in my head. No lyrics. Not even a melody. Just static. I didn't get far before my stomach started acting up, and since the gorilla slammed me in the head, my noodle had been killing me, so I stopped for a breather in an elementary school playground where I observed a little boy and girl on a seesaw. Up and down. Up and down. Up and down they went. It was a pleasure watching them get along the way they did, laughing their heads off as if they were the only two kids in the world. That is, until the messy girl, who looked as if she had taken a bath in chocolate ice cream, leaped off the seesaw and chuckled when her little boyfriend crashed to the ground. When the boy started to cry, both mothers, who were sitting at a picnic table, drinking coffee and smoking cigarettes, charged the playground. The girl's mother reprimanded her daughter, then kissed her dirty forehead and wiped some chocolate from her cheek. The boy's mother pulled her son's dirty-blond hair out of his eyes, straightened his shirt and tied his shoes. The girl's mother apologized for her daughter's behavior while the little girl hugged her mother's leg, refusing to say she was sorry. The boy's mother graciously accepted the apology, and then the little boy smacked the little girl in the head. So the little girl retaliated by punching the boy in the nose. There was more bawling, a bit of blood and plenty of reprimanding. I'd had enough drama for one day, so I stepped inside a bodega, slipped a forty-ounce Budweiser and a bouquet of lilies into my duffel bag and headed for the cemetery.

Havannah the Junkie was sitting on a headstone near the cemetery's Fourth Avenue entrance, looking like she always did, cigarette dangling from her mouth, smoke blowing into the slits of her eyes, wearing the same beige dress that exposed the tops of her sunburned breasts and snake tattoo. I had only ever seen her on that stoop on Union Street, so coming across her in the cemetery kind of unsettled me—although when Havannah spotted me, she shot right up, leaped off the stone and clicked her heels with unbridled enthusiasm. I put my head down and kept walking, hoping that she wouldn't say anything to me, but I wasn't so lucky.

—Well if it isn't Gianni Lenza. We're old friends. I can call you Gianni now, can't I? Look at you. You're a walking disaster.

—I have nothing to say to you, Havannah.

—I guess I should congratulate you.

—For what?

—Getting your ass evicted. Nice going. You're a sick fuck. You know that? Come here and let Havannah console you.

—I lost my job. I couldn't pay the rent.

—And that bitch stole your wallet. You really are a desperate motherfucker. What were you thinking?

—I was lonely.

—And pathetic. You should have come to see me. Havannah would have shown you a good time. I'd have made you breakfast too.

—Your idea of a good time isn't exactly my idea of a good time, Havannah.

—And what do you mean by that?

—You know what I mean. The junk.

—The junk? What are you, Gianni Lenza? A saint? What about your booze and pills? Hypocrite.

—You got me there.

—And that other bitch. I told you not to believe her lies. She's an actor. Lying is her livelihood. She lies like a rug. But you fell for it, hook, line and sinker. Knew you would.

—I let them go, didn't I?

—Yeah, but you're beating yourself up over it, staying in bed for a month, feeling sorry for yourself.

—I'm out and about now, aren't I?

—Come over here and give ole Havannah a kiss. I missed you.

—I got to get going.

—When are you going to take care of that arm?

—It's in a sling.

—You look like shit, man. You need a haircut and a shave. You're not taking me out looking like that. No way, Jose.

—You don't look so great yourself.

—Hey, I shaved this morning. Did you know that there are over six hundred thousand stiffs buried here? Leonard Bernstein, Peter Cooper, Charles Ebbets, Jean Michel Basquiat and the guy who played the wizard in *The Wizard of Oz*, to name a few.

—Is this where you want to be laid to rest?

—They're going to sprinkle my ashes in the Hudson River. Did you know there's a memorial in here dedicated to the Delaware Regiment that fought in the Battle of Long Island? They retreated across the Gowanus Canal.

—They're being honored for their cowardice?

—I guess sometimes it's better to retreat than to attack.

—You're a wise person, Havannah.

—And I'll tell you this, Gianni Lenza: that chick with the fake tan and tits? She's a keeper. So far, I'd say she's my only real competition. I mean nobody can really compete with the dead bitch.

—Once and for all, how do you know so much about me?

—I'm Havannah. I know everything. Those are pretty flowers. Are they for me?

—They're for my friend.

—Oh, great. Don't tell me. Another dead person you're hung up on. He chose to die. You had nothing to do with it. So, it was your bottle of sleeping pills. He was going to find a way to end things with or without your damn pills.

—Hey, you want a sip?

—If it's one of those fancy craft beers, then you can forget about it.

—It's Budweiser.

—Okay.

—Here. You can keep the bottle.

—I see you're still wearing that ring that never fit you and never got you any chicks either. I bet you're still writing letters to the dead bitch too.

—For your information, I stopped writing to her a long time ago.

—Yeah, right. You probably have a letter in your pocket right now.

—No, I don't. Really. I don't.

—C'mon, hand it over.

I reached into my pocket and gave Havannah the letter that I had written to Stephanie before I'd vacated the apartment.

—You got pretty crappy handwriting. You know that?

—It's not easy writing with my left hand.

She read it out loud.

Dear Stephanie,

I have been so passive, so weak, so indecisive. My self-destruction has destroyed us, but I don't know any other way. I was not born a coward, and I'd like to think that I could be heroic when the time calls for heroics—

Havannah stopped reading and tore the letter to shreds.

—This fatalist bullshit is so unsexy. If you want to get down my pants, you better try another approach 'cause this shit does nothing for me.

—I'll be seeing you around, Havannah.

—Hey, what are you going to do when your gay fat friend moves back to Ohio?

—There's no way Teeny's going back to Cuyahoga Falls.

—Who else is going to take care of his ailing father? His elderly mother can't.

—He hasn't spoken to his parents in years.

—Poor Gianni Lenza won't have anyone to take care of him then.

—Believe me, there's no way Teeny is going back home.

—He is. And you will too.

—That's a laugh. There's no way I'm going back to Staten Island.

—You're both going back to the womb, so to speak.

—You ought to lay off the drugs, Havannah. I'll be seeing you around.

—Actually, that's it for me. I'm getting off the Gianni Lenza express to nowhere.

—So that's it?

—Yep, that's it.

—I'm never going to see you again?

—Never again. Will you miss me?

—Yeah, I think I will.

—What do you say to a little farewell screw behind that gaudy headstone over there?

With outstretched arms, Havannah took a few steps toward me. I put my head down and ran away, causing an oncoming hearse to swerve and nearly go off the road. I stopped to catch my breath underneath the white birch trees that lined the pond. A middle-aged woman was sitting on a bench not far from Leonard Bernstein's grave, reading a book whose cover was neon pink. I assumed it was either a chick-lit novel or self-help book, but for all I knew it could have been *Ulysses*. Still, I couldn't help myself from blurting out, "That book changed my life." She frowned. I saluted her, then trotted past the Delaware Regiment Memorial and hundreds of American and Puerto Rican flags jutting out from the swampy ground before stopping in front of a gray headstone the size of a Cadillac: *Pete Marzo 1925–2005: Devoted husband and father. Decorated veteran.* Pete's wife, Clara, was buried with her husband. The Marzo grave wasn't in the most pastoral location (I could see the traffic on Fourth Avenue), but it was situated underneath a magnificent weeping willow that hung so low its leaves graced the top of the headstone. Underneath Pete's name was a Winston Churchill quotation: *Courage is what it takes to stand up and speak; courage is also what it takes to sit down and listen.* If telling a never-ending story of bullshit was all it took to be courageous, then Pete was the bravest man I had ever known.

Churchill's quote reminded me of something I read in my Introduction to Philosophy course during my brief stint in college. I thought it was Jean-Paul Sartre who'd said a coward has made himself a coward by his actions. Would Sartre have considered Pete's suicide a cowardly act? Life was about making decisions and taking action, and the old guy had made a decision and taken consequential action. Wasn't it better to give up rather than participate in life's never-ending bullshit? Alas, poor Pete, an infinite pest. I dug a hole and planted the stolen lilies.

On the other side of the cemetery's rolling knolls, an inconsolable woman was lying in the fetal position above a newly dug grave. It was an eerie sight. The hair on my good arm stood up, and yet I couldn't take my eyes from her. I imagined her grief was so insufferable that she wished she could switch places with the recently deceased, who might have been her husband or, worse, her child.

Coming from the same direction, a blinding orange glow appeared on the narrow dirt path, and emerging from it was Heather, who was heading directly toward me (bumping into each other in unexpected places had become a pattern of ours). She was pushing a sleeping baby in a stroller and carrying a hideous bouquet of blue tulips in her hands. I wasn't in the mood for chitchat, but it was too late to escape. Heather waved and called out to me.

—Hey, John. How are you?

—Feel like a million bucks.

—That's quite the duffle bag. Is everything you own in there?

—Yep. I'm moving in with Teeny.

—Oh, that's awesome. So now you two can really focus on the play.

—Yeah, well, something like that. I just got evicted.

—Oh, I'm sorry to hear that.

—I thought Pete was a pain in the ass, but his son Carmine really takes the cake. Did you go to Pete's funeral?

—It was a nice affair. There weren't many people there.

—I didn't want to run into his son.

—Carmine delivered a moving eulogy.

—Really? Carmine?

—He told a very touching story about how Pete coached all of his Little League teams.

—I didn't know the guy was capable of sincerity.

—It's a shame. Pete was such a sweetie. He just couldn't go on without Clara.

—I couldn't bear to see the old guy lying in a box.

—He's in a better place now.

—You don't really believe that, do you?

—I'd like to think that something more beautiful awaits us in death.

—This life is a living hell, and unfortunately I think it's the only life we'll ever know.

—Having some kind of faith works for me.

—If there is a God, he's playing a cruel joke on us all.

—Enough about religion. It's a messy topic. Aren't these tulips awesome? The guy spray-painted them for me, free of charge.

I planted Heather's blue tulips next to my lilies and told her that Pete would be fertilizing them. Heather was convinced that Pete died of a broken heart because suicide was a mortal sin for a Catholic, and he would never have put himself in a position to be denied permission into heaven. Even though I didn't agree with Heather's views, it was nice to talk to someone who actually believed in something bigger than us.

—So is this your daughter?

—This is Theresa. It feels so good to have her with me. My mother surprised me with her a couple of days ago. I've been so busy, as you can imagine. Otherwise, I would have taken you out for that coffee I owe you.

—She looks like you.

—Thanks, but she's all her father.

—Is he still in the picture?

—He sends us a check once in a while. Her birthday. Her christening. Things like that. Although he forgot to send her something for Christmas.

—Why did you have her christened?

—Well, I'm Catholic. It's what we do.

—Do you really believe in original sin?

—Not really, but it's nice to think that Theresa has been cleansed, so to speak. Though I don't think children are capable of sinning.

—Yeah? You should have seen the little girl I saw on the playground a few minutes ago. Pure evil.

—A little girl? Pure evil? Come on, John.

—You should have seen her. Satan's daughter. I swear to God.

I never could come to terms with the concept of original sin. What did Adam and Eve do that was so wrong anyway? Could you really blame them for seeking knowledge? What's wrong with wanting to be well informed? When Theresa woke up, Heather took her out of the stroller and tickled her belly with a dandelion she had pulled from the grass near Pete's grave. She lifted Theresa to the sky, and the baby giggled her head off.

—Would you like to hold her?

—I better not.

—Oh, come on. You don't think she's pure evil, do you?

—It's not that. I'm just not good with babies.

—It's nothing. Just cradle her bottom like this.

—I don't want to drop her.

—You won't.

—She's not going to puke all over me, is she?

—She won't. Go ahead.

—It's just that it's the first time I've ever held a baby.

—You'll be great.

I cradled the baby, who then rested her head on my shoulder, and imagined myself as her father: holding her by the waist while she rode the carousel in Prospect Park, holding her hand as we stood in line at the ice cream shop, teaching her to play "Yellow Submarine" on guitar, coaching her Little League teams, reading Dr. Seuss's *Oh, the Places You'll Go!* before she goes to bed.

Had I done the right thing by letting my daughter go to LA? I plunged my face into Theresa's belly and made fart sounds. She started to cry, so I handed her back to her mother. Then I felt like I was going to be sick and dropped to my knees.

—John, are you okay?

—I haven't been feeling well lately.

—You should really get your arm checked out.

—My arm is the least of my problems. I think I might have a brain tumor.

—What?

—Forget about it. It's nothing.

—Is there something I can do?

—I'm fine. Can I ask you something?

—Yeah, sure. What is it?

—Rock or disco?

—Oh, the quiz again, huh?

—I like to think of it as a game. Well?

—Disco. Why?

—Oh, boy.

—What's wrong?

—The Verrazano Bridge or the Brooklyn Bridge?

—I don't understand these questions, John.

—Humor me.

—The Verrazano?

—Why? Why? Why the Verrazano?

—I don't know. It's long? I'm not from here. I don't know.

—New York or Paris?

—I haven't been to Paris.

—Mets or Yankees?

—Well, I'm from Kansas. So the Royals.

—The Royals?

—I don't really like baseball.

—I should really get going.

—Wait. Wait. Did I pass?

—We'll see. The jury is still out. Bye, Heather.

—Wait. Wait. Wait. What are you doing later? I'm going to take Theresa to that new ice cream shop on Sixth Avenue. Want to join us? My treat.

—Maybe some other time.

—Oh, okay. Have a good day, John.

—It's been a hell of a day so far.

—The day is still young. You have plenty of time to turn things around.

—That only means it could get worse.

—Forever the pessimist.

—That's me.

—Let me give you my number. Put it in your cell phone. Call me sometime.

—I don't have a cell phone.

—Oh, okay. I'll give you my number the old-fashioned way. I think I have a pen here somewhere.

—You have nice penmanship.

—Thanks. Give me a call. I still owe you that coffee.

—And I'm holding you to it.

When I got to the road, I glanced at the distraught woman lying on the grave in the fetal position then I looked back at Heather, who was kneeling in front of Pete's grave, saying a prayer or something. It must be nice to think that somebody is actually listening to you.

I spent the next two months in Cobble Hill on Teeny's couch. A slab of concrete would have been more comfortable, but I couldn't complain, despite the soreness in my lower back. The entire time I was there, I felt like that mouse in the English department at Cobble Hill High School, stuck to a glue trap, unable to break free from the couch. But at least I had a roof over my head, and most nights Teeny cooked for us and for his new boyfriend, Carmen the Guess Model, whose career had peaked in the late eighties and had been living off the money he earned during that lucrative period in his life. I knew that Teeny was serious about Carmen because he never showed me any compromising photographs of the guy. Teeny wasn't a gourmet chef; about all he was capable of making were burgers and Caesar salads, but I didn't have the heart to tell him that I didn't care for either one, particularly salads. He might have been an awful cook, but he was a good friend who went out of his way for me. For the first time in a long time, I felt at home and somewhat at ease.

I watched television and browsed the Internet on Teeny's computer. The Internet was so accessible and comprehensive that you never had to leave the confines of your home. The World Wide Web was my oyster. Need driving directions to Cuyahoga Falls, Ohio? Want to know the year *When Harry Met Sally* was released? Want to see early photographs of the Hudson River? Need tickets to the Wilco concert? Want to learn the chords to Marvin Gaye's "What's Going On"? Want to know who the Mets got in the Tom Seaver trade with the Reds? Looking for a lovely escort on a lonely evening? The Internet was there to oblige and serve its master.

I scribbled in my notebook from time to time. One afternoon, after watching three hours of daytime soap operas, I jotted this down:

this thing
that never
was
this
was never
this thing
that
was
was never
meant to
be
this
thing that
never was

I never finished the poem, but Teeny suggested that I submit it to magazines as he had been submitting the incomplete *The Never-Ending Story of Bullshit* to theaters, festivals and contests around the country. Rejection letters were pouring in, and rather than perforating them, putting them on a roll and wiping his ass with them as I would have done, Teeny decided to turn them into a motivational tool by wallpapering his entire bathroom with them. He never took any of the rejections personally. He went so far as to embrace them. They were evidence that he was doing something productive, which was better than receiving no letters at all, as some theater companies ignored submissions. For someone like me, whose entire life was a series of rejections, I could not have dealt with reminders that I was a failure every time I took a shit. Most of the letters read like this:

Dear Mr. Duncan,

Thank you for your interest in [insert theater company, festival or contest name here].

We have received an overwhelming number of submissions. Unfortunately, we will not be able to use your play in this upcoming season. We cannot comment on each submission, for our staff is relatively small.

We hope that you will consider sending us something in the future. Good luck in your creative endeavors.

> *Sincerely,*
> *[Insert artistic director's name here]*

Blood, sweat and tears in exchange for an impersonal, dismissive form letter. It was an unfair exchange. Nevertheless, Rutherford B. Duncan, a possessed man, someone who refused to take no for an answer, persevered. One theater company returned his manuscript with a pink Post-it attached that read, *Pass.* After a while, he stopped calling them rejection letters altogether; he was partial to euphemisms, something more positive such as "unacceptance letters." Teeny claimed that he didn't care if the play was ever produced. It was more important for him to finish what he started and just write the best play he possibly could.

Whenever Teeny needed inspiration, he went looking for it in the bathroom, surrounded by four walls of rejection that somehow spurred him on. He wrote, sitting on the bowl, in longhand with a no. 2 pencil and a good eraser.

—Teeny, you've been in there for three hours. I have to take a piss.

—I'm feeling it, big boy, and I gotta say it's feeling pretty damn good.

—Open the door, man. I need to use the bathroom.

—John, please. Not now. I'm in the groove.

—This freaky artistic behavior is really freaking me out, Teeny.

—I'll be out soon. I want to get your opinion on something.

—But I got to piss.

—Piss in the kitchen sink. The words are surging through me, big boy. I don't want to interrupt the creative flow.

—Teeny, this letter came for you in the mail.

—Slide it under the door.

—It's from your mother.

—Who?

—Your mother.

—Oh. Really? Slide it under the door.

While I was standing on a chair, peeing into the kitchen sink, aiming for the hole in the soggy donut in my coffee mug, Teeny popped up behind me. He was wearing only a towel, holding the envelope in one hand, the letter in the other, looking like he had just been evicted from his home.

—Judging by your face you're not holding another unacceptance letter.

—I'm afraid it's something more serious than that, big boy. It's a family matter.

—What did your mother have to say? Tell me about it.

—I think you should get ready 'cause Heather and Carmen are coming by to read the second scene, and you don't want to be caught dead looking like that.

—What's wrong with the way I look?

—It's not so much your look, although you could use a shave and a haircut, but you really need a shower.

—You know I've sworn off bathing until I meet someone.

—Why don't you go out with Heather? The chick obviously digs you.

—What's the point, Teeny? I know how it's going to end.

—You're a hopeless cause. You know that? I used to think that you were just going through a rough patch and that you'd work your way out of it, but there's nothing to be done with you. I give up. I wash my hands of you.

—Oh, is that your analysis, Dr. Freud?

—Sometimes the way up is down, the way forward is backward. With you, John, you seem to have fallen downward into a bottomless pit. You're still falling. I don't think you're ever going to climb out of the hole. What's worse is I don't think you want to climb out.

—Thanks for having such faith in me. I thought you were my friend.

—I am your friend, your only friend.

—Then how could you spew such bullshit?

—Just being honest, big boy. You could use more of that in your life.

—You don't need to express every single thought that enters your bald head.

—The truth is I'm still pissed that you left the first scene that I slaved over on the subway.

—I said I was sorry. What do you want from me?

—Is that the way you take care of things? My things?

—I made a mistake. Crucify me.

—I've been working my ass off, John, and I think I really have something here.

—I can't write like you, but you keep forcing me to.

—Let me take a look at what you've been working on.

—I've been meaning to tell you this for a while now…I didn't do it.

—You haven't written anything?

—Not a goddamn word.

—We were supposed to collaborate on this play.

—You've got a handle on it. You don't need me.

—That's not the point, John.

—There is no point, Teeny. It's your play.

—That's not the point, John.

—What is the point?

—It's in the doing. Write something. Anything. And finish the fucking thing. You've been trying to sabotage the play from the beginning.

—I was afraid of letting you down.

—Boy, did your parents do a number on you.

—I've let myself down.

—You sure did. Take off that ratty robe. Our guests will be here soon.

It was bad enough that I had failed myself—I was accustomed to that. In fact, I was used to failing others too, but letting down my best friend, my only friend, someone who'd gone out of his way to look out for me, really knocked the shit out of me. Still, in a strange kind of way, I was relieved. I wasn't exactly thrilled about putting my life on display for everyone to see and Teeny knew that going in. Why did he think that I'd collaborate on the play in the first place? Why did he have so much faith in me?

Ever since I had known Teeny he had been a voracious reader, but once he figured out that he had been thinking about writing all wrong, he had become a prolific writer too. Teeny thought in shapes and sizes. He was convinced that writing prose was horizontal like the keys of a piano while poetry was vertical like a guitar fret board. Plays could be horizontal and vertical, even perpendicular and adjacent at times. Well, those were his theories anyway. Take them or leave them. They were pretty interesting for a guy who'd stopped playing piano in seventh grade to take up modern dance. Somehow, they worked for him. Nothing seemed to work for me.

I returned to the couch, turned on *Judge Judy*, opened my notebook and tried to finish the poem I had started, but I didn't get far. There was nothing I could do. Nothing to be done. Meanwhile, Teeny stepped outside, wearing only a towel and holding the letter from his mother, and paced the sidewalk in front of the apartment, deaf to our neighbor's barking dog, a German shepherd who was dying to be rubbed behind his ears.

Heather, bearing two bottles of white Zinfandel, was the first to arrive. Teeny, who had decided to wear only a towel for the entire evening, poured a couple of glasses for the both of them and made me a gin and tonic. Teeny grabbed Heather by the wrist and twirled her around. "Let me inspect the goods." She was wearing black tights underneath the shortest denim skirt imaginable. She had on knee-high blue suede boots. Her tight pink belly shirt that nestled her fake tits presented a dragon tattoo with splayed tongue around her pierced belly button.

—You're one sexy piece of ass, baby. I could eat you up.

—You flatter me, Mr. Duncan.

—Doesn't she look gorgeous, big boy?

—Very beautiful.

While Teeny brought Heather up to speed about the love of his life, Carmen the Guess Model, I occupied myself with pornographic fantasies of Heather. I wondered what she would be like in the sack. Would she be selfless? Would she be reckless? Would she let me see her naked? Would she put on a striptease for me? Teeny had been telling me all along that we'd be a good match, but I didn't have much to offer Heather even if she were interested in me. I wasn't exactly a "catch." I was the fish you throw back because it's too scrawny to eat. From what I knew about Heather, aside from being cool and easy to talk to, she was gentle, generous and kind—three qualities that I admired—but I had real trouble getting past her bad taste in music and clothing, her daughter and, most of all, her religious beliefs. I was curious to see if at some point she was going to ask me why I hadn't called her.

Carmen showed up late. He was tall, tan, blond and at least fifty pounds overweight. He was wearing a white V-necked mesh shirt and tight black jeans. His hair was greased back and pulled behind his pierced ears. I didn't care for the white leather loafers he was wearing. When I'd first met Carmen, I was surprised that Teeny had fallen in love with a washed-up pretty boy, but when I got to know him I discovered he really wasn't a bad guy at all.

By the time Teeny finished introducing Carmen to Heather and we settled down to read the second scene of the play, we were all pretty lubricated. Teeny handed each of us a copy of the script. He'd even gone so far as to highlight our lines for us. Heather was going to read Dawn, Carmen was going to read Emma and I was going to read the part that was tailor-made for me. For some reason, Teeny had left my name as the co-author on the script. He told Carmen and Heather that I had written most of the second scene. Was he trying to make me feel guilty? I went along with his lie anyway. I figured if they ended up liking the play, maybe they'd end up liking me. When I caught a whiff of my rancid self, I moved to the empty chair on the other side of the living room. I should have listened to Teeny and taken a shower. The playwright gave us a few instructions, read the stage directions, and got ready to take notes while we read.

The Never-Ending Story of Bullshit
By Rutherford B. Duncan and John Lenza

Scene Two. Lights up on three goldfish, EMMA, DAWN and JOHN, convening at the bottom of the tank.

EMMA
It looks like your husband is cleaning the tank again.

DAWN
He must be cleaning it for me.

JOHN
Well, he's not cleaning it for me.

EMMA and DAWN (*overlapping*)
I miss my boyfriend.

JOHN

I'm right here.

EMMA and DAWN (*overlapping*)

I miss my husband.

JOHN

I'm right here.

DAWN

And now I'm pregnant.

EMMA

I wish I were pregnant.

JOHN

Swim right this way, baby, and we'll just see what we can do about that.

DAWN

You'd have been an awful father.

EMMA

She's right. You can't even take care of yourself.

JOHN

Must you insult me?

EMMA

I want to hurt you.

DAWN

I never told you the truth. Not for one minute.

EMMA and DAWN (*overlapping*)

I want to carve you up like a dirty piece of catfish.

JOHN

Carve elsewhere. The two of you.

EMMA

I never loved you.

DAWN

I never loved myself.

EMMA

I never loved myself.

DAWN

I never loved you.

JOHN and EMMA and DAWN (*overlapping*)

Have I hurt you?

DAWN

It's what cannot be undone that hurts the most.

JOHN

It's what hurts that hurts the most.

EMMA

Let's carry on with the proceedings, shall we?

DAWN

Let's do what we came here to do.

EMMA

Let's put an end to words.

DAWN

And let the carving begin.

JOHN

I'm waiting. Been to the top of the tank and back. Through the fake plastic trees, around the silver scuba diver. Let's get on with the proceedings.

EMMA and DAWN (*overlapping*)

Cut the dramatics. Cut the shit.

EMMA

Do you have the knife?

DAWN

I thought you were going to bring the knife.

EMMA

I thought you were going to bring the knife.

JOHN

Any sharp object will do.

DAWN

I bet my husband has one.

EMMA

I bet my boyfriend has one.

JOHN

Someone must carve me. Cleanly this time.

EMMA

Remember the time you held me while I puked in the gutter?

DAWN

Remember when I told you that you were my daughter's father?

EMMA

The vows you wrote?

DAWN

The game we played?

EMMA

The cat in the window?

DAWN

The Dia Museum?

JOHN

I miss the cat in the window.

EMMA

She was never yours.

JOHN

She licked my nose.

DAWN

I read your poem.

EMMA

I read nothing.

JOHN

She licked my balls.

EMMA

I hated your poem.

JOHN

I wasn't finished writing it.

                    DAWN

I hated you.

                    JOHN

I never let on to be somebody else. I am Gianni Lenza.

                    DAWN

You fooled me.

                    EMMA

You fooled yourself.

                    JOHN

I rubbed the cat's belly.

                    DAWN

I loved you.

          EMMA and DAWN (*overlapping*)

I left you.

                    EMMA

I loved you.

                    JOHN

I rubbed behind her ears.

                    DAWN

I never left you.

                    EMMA

I never loved you.

                    JOHN

What was that cat's name?

                    DAWN

You were.

                    EMMA

The love.

                    JOHN

She was black and white.

              DAWN and EMMA (*overlapping*)

Of my life.

                    EMMA

Let's talk.

                    JOHN

Of winter.

                    DAWN

Of snow and nonalcoholic beer.

                    EMMA

Let's surrender.

                    JOHN

To the disaster.

                    DAWN

Of love left to rot.

                    EMMA

Everything has been said.

                    JOHN

I haven't said anything.

DAWN

Some words need to be unspoken.

EMMA

Live with it.

JOHN

I have no choice.

EMMA

Go forward.

DAWN

Just go. Somewhere.

JOHN

Let's start the proceedings. Let's get on with it already.

EMMA

I gave you the best that I had. Knotted up like a lace on a child's shoe.

DAWN

I needed you then. You were there. It could have been anyone. But it was you. Thank you.

JOHN

I heard every word. I believed in you. I believed in the inevitable. I've become an enemy. But I'm not vicious. I'm not like either of you.

EMMA

That's it. Let it all out.

JOHN

Some attention—

DAWN

Let it all out.

JOHN

—must be paid.

EMMA

I want to remember those days we had together but I can't seem to remember when that was.

DAWN

I want peace of mind.

EMMA

I wasn't coming home at night.

DAWN

I couldn't move in with you.

EMMA

I had an affair.

DAWN

I was having an affair with my husband.

EMMA

I didn't want to talk.

DAWN

I didn't want to act.

EMMA

I didn't want to work.

DAWN

I didn't have to work.

EMMA

You drove me to drink.

DAWN

You drove me to drive across the country.

JOHN

I've hated you both for so long. I want to murder you both. A sensible slaughter.

DAWN

Be kind, John.

EMMA

No, I deserve it.

DAWN

I deserve it too.

JOHN

Who's going to carve me up? Let's go already.

EMMA

I want to remember. I want to remember that I once loved you.

DAWN

I no longer. I no longer love you. I'll carve. Where's the knife?

JOHN

I wanted to be your husband but I was already married.

EMMA & DAWN (*overlapping*)

Married to that dead bitch Stephanie.

EMMA

You were my husband.

JOHN

I wanted to be a father.

DAWN

My husband will be a good father.

JOHN

Your best friend.

DAWN

I got everything I needed from you. And now I'm over it.

JOHN

We taught each other so much. But I was so sick of school.

EMMA

I feel a peace that I have never known. Never thought I could own. Let me own it.

DAWN

Let me.

JOHN

Let me.

EMMA

Go.

JOHN

Go.

DAWN

There is a place.

EMMA

I have dreams.

JOHN

We will find something?

EMMA

When we decide to dream.

DAWN

I will find a place.

EMMA

He's here?

JOHN

Your husband?

DAWN

My husband.

EMMA

He's here.

JOHN

Your husband?

DAWN

That's my hubby.

EMMA

Believe me, that's not your hubby.

DAWN

That's my husband?

JOHN

Emma will have to do the carving then.

EMMA

My pleasure.

JOHN

Quickly so I don't feel any pain.

EMMA

I don't have the knife.

JOHN

Dawn, help us.

EMMA

You should do things on your own.

DAWN

I'm out of here. My husband and I are going to the movies tonight.

JOHN

What's playing?

DAWN

Jaws. Bye, you two.

JOHN

We are not through here.

DAWN

I am finished. You are the love of my life, John.

Dawn swims off. John reaches into his blazer and pulls out a knife.

JOHN

Will you look at that? I've had one all this time.

                    EMMA

You know how to use it.

                    JOHN

Can you do it for me?

                    EMMA

This one is all on you, John.

                    JOHN

Stay with me. Don't go.

                    EMMA

Dawn's husband is taking me to see *Jaws* tonight. I have to get
ready.

                    JOHN

You're going out with her hubby?

                    EMMA

I love you, John.

                    JOHN

Please stay. Please carve.

                    EMMA

It will get better.

                    JOHN

Please carve. Please stay.

                    EMMA

You are the love of my life, John.

                    JOHN

Who's going to do the carving now?

Emma swims off. John remains holding the knife. Lights fade to black.
End of play.

When the reading was over, Carmen and Heather jumped up and applauded. They did a few tequila shots and danced the tango before bombarding Teeny and me with overblown praise, wet kisses and bear hugs. I was embarrassed by the spectacle of it all. Somebody needed to put the event into perspective. I liked the play, don't get me wrong; I even thought that Teeny had some talent, but by the way they raved on and on about *The Never-Ending Story of Bullshit*, you would have thought we had just finished reading *A Streetcar Named Desire*.

When Carmen and Heather were through gushing about the play, they started to critique it. I kept to myself, sipping the cheap champagne Carmen brought. Heather wanted to know why I was so quiet. Teeny told her that I was a humble artist. Carmen interrupted Heather's discourse on absurdist theater by making a harmless yet naive toast that really rubbed me the wrong way.

—Here's to my brilliant boyfriend. Broadway, look out 'cause here comes Rutherford B. Duncan and he won't take any prisoners. Trust me. Cheers. I love you, baby.

—And here's to my collaborator, John Lenza, the greatest writer of our time.

—Fuck off, Teeny.

—What's wrong with him?

—What's wrong, John?

—Look at him, Heather. He's the epitome of humility.

—I didn't write the fucking play so stop with the charade.

—But your name's on the play.

—Teeny put it there. It was his way of motivating me. I guess.

—So you didn't write the play?

—No, I didn't write a single word of it.

After my confession, Carmen began to psychoanalyze John. He was somehow unaware that it was based on me. Hell, it was my life. Carmen carried on and on about how John will never find happiness because he has too many earthly attachments. I respectfully told him that I thought his Buddhist beliefs were nothing more than a bunch of never-ending bullshit.

—Don't you think that when John frees himself from these women, the past, all of his earthly attachments, he will then find the freedom he is seeking?

—Can you imagine a hunk of man like that with a brain to boot? I could just—

—Pardon me, Teeny.

—Of course, John.

—That's all well and good, Carmen, but letting go can be a tricky thing.

—What John fails to realize is that his suffering doesn't belong to him.

—Who does it belong to then? Heather? Teeny? Theresa?

—Who's Theresa?

—She's my daughter.

—I'd love to meet her sometime.

—I'll bring her around. My mother's watching her tonight.

—Bring your mother around too. If she looks anything like you...Wow, what an orgy that would be!

—Oh, Teeny you are too funny.

—I'm not joking, Heather.

—Suffering is a phantom of his mind.

—"Phantom of his mind"? Nice one, Carmen.

—It's a figment of his imagination then.

—Are you saying that I've never suffered? I've only imagined it?

—I'm not talking about you, John. I'm talking about the character.

—Honey, John is John.

—What are you talking about, Teeny?

—The play is based on John's life. It is John's life.

—Oh, I had no idea. Forgive me, John.

—It's all right. I find your theories fascinating, Carmen. Please. Go on.

—Okay. I'm trying to say that you've become attached to transitory things.

—Don't you think everything is transitory?

—Yes, I think you're right, Heather. Everything is transitory. Including this world and this life.

I didn't agree with anything Carmen had said, and though I might have come across as a little crotchety, I really enjoyed talking to him (Teeny and Heather too). They made me feel something. They stirred something in me. I liked all of them, and I was pretty sure that they liked me too, even if I didn't write the play. I reclined in my chair, finished the bottle of champagne and felt content for a change. The funny thing was—and I didn't tell Carmen this—that at that moment I felt attached to everyone in that room, connected in a very real way.

—Okay, I've had enough of this cerebral crap. Let's move on to my favorite part of the evening: the lovefest.

—I'm going to bed, Teeny. I'm exhausted.

—Carmen, don't poop out on me. We've taken all of the skeletons out of Gianni Boy's closet. Look at him. He looks as if he'd seen the devil. Now it's time to have a little fun.

—Some other time. I'll see you in bed. Good night, everyone.

—Okay, Carmen. I won't be long. Love you.

When Carmen went to bed, Teeny took the opportunity to get to know Heather better. He poured a couple of glasses of Zinfandel and sat down on the couch while Heather sat on his lap. He rubbed her thighs; she touched his chest when she spoke. I was feeling like a third wheel, so I looked over the second scene. I really loved Dawn's line, "Of love left to rot." I should have told Teeny that. He would have liked it, but I kept it to myself, wishing I had written the play and not him.

—What are you looking for now, sexy? Sex or commitment?

—I'm not sure, Teeny.

—How was the sex with your husband?

—We were never married.

—Just shacking up?

—I was in a bad way a couple of years ago. A lot of booze and a lot of men.

—We're all in the trenches, Heather.

—He was no good for me, so I relocated to New York. I think I've got my shit together now.

—Are you ready to get back in the saddle?

—You have to be happy with who you are first. Right?

—And so are you happy with who you are?

—Yeah. I can honestly say that I am.

—Sounds like you're ready for Mr. Right.

—I'm just worried that Mr. Wrong is going to show up again.

—If Mr. Wrong knocks on your door, you kick him to the curb. You hear me?

—I'm sorry, Teeny. I just don't have any faith right now. I'm alone in a big city that I still don't really know.

—Right now, you just take care of yourself and your daughter. Look at that sick fuck over there. He's been in this city his whole life and he's still alone.

—John is not a sick fuck. How can you say that about him?

—You've read the play. How can you say that he's not?

—John is…well, he's just limited.

—Limited? What the hell does that mean, Heather?

—Don't get angry, John. I was just saying—

—John needs a little tenderness that's all. That's why I'm here.

—You're a good friend, Teeny.

—You two should go out for coffee sometime. You're both lonely.

—Well, if John would call me—

—Why haven't you called this gorgeous woman, John?

—Well…I…uhm—

—It's okay. You don't have to call me if you don't want to. I was just kidding.

—The hell he doesn't. Wouldn't it be nice to have a cup of coffee with Heather?

—Yes, it would be nice.

—Then make it happen, big boy. Make it happen.

Heather was right: I was severely limited. I had so much desire but lacked passion of any kind. I couldn't free myself from the restrictions I had constructed. I wanted something more but didn't know what it was, where I could find it, how I could get it. At the moment, I really desired silence and to be left alone on Teeny's couch, so while Heather and Teeny went on and on about love, dating in New York and raising a baby as a single mother, I couldn't keep my eyes open any longer and fell asleep.

A PHANTOM AMONG PHANTOMS

Shortly after the reading, Havannah the Junkie's prediction came true: Teeny moved back to Cuyahoga Falls to help his elderly mother nurse his dying father. And he even brought Carmen along. Meanwhile, I made my new home, which consisted of a bunch of cardboard air conditioner boxes that I had fitted into a hut, in Brooklyn Bridge Park. I would have set up camp on the bench in front of Southside, but after the landlord tripled the rent, the coffee shop had to close its doors, and a Brooklyn Properties opened. Just what Park Slope needed—another real estate company. Anyway, it kind of made sense for me to live in this park, underneath my favorite bridge. Years before Dumbo's redefining as a swanky neighborhood, I walked the deserted cobblestone streets, a blend of natural and industrial much like Fremont in Seattle. I hung out in the only bar on Front Street long before Starbucks could even locate it on a map. I walked aimlessly up and down Water Street years before the chocolatier Jacques Torres moved into the neighborhood. In the eighties, Gleason's Gym represented Dumbo's moxie and edge, but by 2005 it had become a relic, out of place with the organic markets, bookstores, antique shops, condos, art galleries and hip cafés. Even the term *gym* was antiquated; *fitness club* had become the euphemism. Dumbo had once been a neighborhood on the fringe of a decaying city, but that gritty New York, my New York, had vanished in the great recession of 1987.

On the second day in my new digs, in early June, I was caught in a massive thunderstorm. The fierce wind tore the roof off my hut as I clutched a wrought-iron fence with both hands, looking deeply into the dark, vast sky. The Manhattan skyline stood somewhere behind the thick gray curtains of rain and fog. I tried to picture the Twin Towers above the black clouds, looking invincible as they once had. The Statue of Liberty was a specter battling the harsh elements, and while the Staten Island Ferry crawled past it, I imagined the Argo, with Jason at the helm, striking the clashing rocks, evading Scylla, but ultimately sinking in the whirlpool Charybdis. A gust of wind blew my Mets cap off my head. It sailed across the rocks at the shoreline and drifted into the turbulent East River. Watching my hat sink reminded me of the poet Paul Celan's fatal dip into the Seine. You'd think at fifty years old, the poet would have figured things out. Maybe he was lonely like me and Pete. At that moment, I decided that I needed my cat Colette, so I went looking for Richard.

On my trudge to the Promenade, the Brooklyn Heights brownstones resembled giant yeti. Even on a clear day, their beauty was daunting, but now the wind, fog and rain had magnified their monolithic, menacing stature. The streets were lonely, dark and deep, and though I couldn't locate a single steeple in the storm, I followed the ringing of a church bell, thinking that it might possibly guide me to shelter. By now, there was too much distance between me and my faith to trust that the God I once believed in could offer me a shot at redemption, but I no longer wanted to crawl through this unexceptional life. When the church bell stopped ringing, I gave up my search for shelter in a place of worship, and made a feeble attempt to shield myself with the umbrella Teeny had given me the night of our impromptu reading at Southside, which wasn't an easy feat with one arm. The wind wrestled it from my grip before I got the damn thing open. I chased it down Atlantic Avenue until it blew underneath the tires of an oncoming Fresh Direct truck. That's when I stepped inside a liquor store for refuge as well as much needed spirits.

The shop was something of a relic, built in the seventies, decades before Brooklyn's gentrification, when the borough was Manhattan's neglected stepchild. A disheveled clerk as gray as his wrinkled Yankees jersey, scrutinized me as he stood hunched over the cash register inside his Plexiglas cage, listening to the Bronx Bombers battle my lowly Mets. He breathed heavily, waiting impatiently for me to make my choice, which wasn't easy. There were hundreds of bottles of wine, vodka, gin, rum, and scotch to choose from.

—Hi. Hello? Can I help ya with something? Sir? Hello?

—Ah yes, I would like that bottle of white Zinfandel above your head. Not that one. No. That one. To the right. Up. Down. Yes. No. Sorry. Over. A little more. Nope. That one. Not that one. Not that one either. Almost. Not yet. Yes, that's the one. You got it.

—Are you sure now?

—I think so. Can I have a look? I'm sorry, but that's not the one—

—I'm not going to climb the ladder again.

—Okay, I'll take whatever you're holding then.

I handed over the last of the money Teeny had loaned me, while the clerk let out a great huff before passing the dusty bottle, a couple of dollars and some change through a square cutout in the Plexiglas. I felt like I was at the McDonald's drive-thru.

—I was wondering if I could try it before I buy it.

—What do ya mean? Ya just bought it.

—Do you have a corkscrew?

—I have one, but ya already bought that bottle. Once it's open there are no returns.

—I'd like to sample the bottle please.

—I'll open it for ya, but ya already bought the bottle. This is no wine tasting. Ya want something fancy like that ya can go to that yuppie wine store over on Smith Street.

I passed the bottle through the cutout. The clerk opened it, put the cork back in and returned it to me.

—Aren't you going to give me a glass?

—A glass? What do ya think this is?

—Look, I'm not asking for the world. Just a plastic cup.

—Here. Here's your chalice, sir.

—You see? Now was that difficult?

—Is there anything else I can get ya? Some cheese? Olives perhaps?

—No, the wine will be all. Thank you.

—No kidding.

—Who's winning?

—You see what it's like outside? There's a rain delay.

—Well, who was winning?

—It wasn't the Mets.

—No kidding.

Zinfandel dripped from a crack in the cup, spilling down the front of my robe. After a few more sloppy gulps, I crushed the cup, tossed it over my shoulder, placed the cork back in the bottle and got reacquainted with the relentless storm.

My sneakers made a squishing sound as I walked down Court Street. *Squish. Squish. Squish.* The wind had intensified, and I was no match for the formidable gust, so I stepped inside the lobby of a snazzy apartment building. I took a few swigs of Zinfandel to warm up. It didn't take long before the doorman, who must have been a hundred years old, confronted me. I offered him some wine, but he pushed the bottle away then pushed me out the door, back into the storm. I was cold, drenched, a bit buzzed and hungry, so I followed the scent of dough and sugar that permeated the block to Enzo's Bakery.

The *B* in the blinking red neon sign was out. The cavernous bakery was dark, dingy and grim. An elderly woman—maybe she was Mrs. Enzo—wearing a white apron over a black dress, black stockings and black shoes was fastidiously sweeping the front of the store when I stumbled in. She looked at me as if she had seen a ghost, lifting the broom over her head, prepared to swat me away.

—Easy there, sister. I'm a paying customer.

—Forgive me. You gave me a fright.

—I seem to have that effect on women.

—Sweetie, what would bring you out on such a vile day?

—I'm looking for a good cannoli, actually. Got any?

—You must really like our cannoli. You didn't even take the time to get dressed.

—I hear that they're the best in Brooklyn.

—You're going to catch pneumonia. Take off your robe. Make yourself comfortable. I'll bring you a cup of coffee.

—Do you have cappuccino?

—No cappuccino. Just caffè. How do you take it?

—Black thanks. And don't forget the cannoli. And not the chocolate kind either.

—What's your name, sweetie?

—Gianni.

—*Giovanni è un forte nome.*

—Actually it's Gianni. G-I-A-N-N-I.

—*Oh, sei Italiani?*

—*Sì.* Gianni Lenza.

—*Un molto solido nome.* Sit down, please.

—*Grazie, signora.*

Mrs. Enzo poured me a cup of coffee while I sank into the chair by the front window underneath the blinking red neon sign, put my feet up on a milk crate and closed my eyes. I didn't feel like making small talk, so I pretended to fall asleep. The old woman set the cup of coffee and cannoli on the table, took the empty wine bottle from my hands and threw it in the trash can behind the display case.

—*Enzo, uscire di qui!*

—*Che cosa? Che cosa e esso, Carmella?*

—Some guy. He wandered in. He said he's looking for cannoli.

—He looks terrible. *Che cosa è il suo nome?*

—Gianni Lenza.

—*Un molto solido nome.* He's sleeping?

—Poor boy. He could use a bowl of soup.

—It looks like he can use more than a bowl of soup, Carmella.

—Get him a bowl of the leftover minestrone, Enzo, won't you?

—I'm going to throw him out. That's what I'm going to do.

—Just get the boy some *zuppa,* will you, Enzo?

It didn't take long before I nodded off. I dreamed that I was riding the F train during rush hour, reading something by Camus. Maybe it was *The Stranger.* Maybe it was *The Fall.* By some subway miracle, I had enough room to make myself comfortable, so I stretched across three seats. An obese man in tight bicycle shorts and a white tee shirt with Charles Manson's face plastered on it was sitting across from me. His eye patch made him look like a cyclops, and his manic gaze matched Manson's as he randomly surveyed the car. He rested his bloated, bare feet on his white leather sneakers while he picked the bleeding sores on his swollen ankles. He was repulsive, but I could not turn away from him and his offensive legs. At West Fourth Street, a seventeen-year-old Stephanie, looking just as she did the day she was killed, boarded the train. She skipped right over to me, dropped to her knees and kissed my hand. That's precisely when the cyclops sprang to his feet—"Fuck You, Lenza, she belongs to me"—and attempted to devour Stephanie. Still lying down, I unsheathed my elongated sword and plunged it into his one functioning eye. The cyclops crumpled to the floor, writhing in pain. I tore open a bag of Pop Rocks and shoved them into his mouth. Then Stephanie poured a gallon of milk down his throat and we waited for him to explode. 3-2-1. Boom! Pieces of swollen and bruised flesh splattered everywhere. We reveled in our victory. I wiped a bloody piece of skin off Stephanie's face and she embraced me.

STEPHANIE

Don't go home to your wife, Gianni. Stay with me. We'll ride this train forever.

JOHN

My wife has been fighting off her suitors for twenty years, and I must get home to my kingdom before my enemies plunder my city.

STEPHANIE

This F train can be ours, away from the rest of the world. Stay with me, Gianni. I will love you forever.

JOHN

I must get home, Stephanie. Staten Island needs me.

Stephanie slipped out of her long black coat, slid her hands up my thighs, leaned into me and kissed my neck. When I shirked her advances, she pulled back. I condemned her for having slept with my archrival, Joey Santone, and I was just short of shouting *Get thee to a nunnery*, but I was not Prince Hamlet, and as much as I would have enjoyed being the savage for once, I didn't really have it in me. It was all just a dream, and no matter how determined I was to remain asleep and avoid reality a little longer, I could not defeat the inevitable. Eventually, I would wake up in Enzo's Bakery.

STEPHANIE

I want you, Gianni. I need you, Gianni.

JOHN

What do you want with me? I'm no Odysseus.

STEPHANIE

I don't need the great hero of western civilization. I need a friend, a lover, someone who'll take me to the movies.

JOHN

What kind of a king would I be if I didn't look after my kingdom? My people need me. My wife and daughter need me.

STEPHANIE

Will you ever forgive me?

JOHN

It is not for me to forgive. Look to the gods. I must go home now.

STEPHANIE

Don't leave me. Don't leave me. Don't leave me.

When I woke up, Enzo was setting a bowl of soup on the table, so I pretended to still be sleeping. I was curious to hear what he and Mrs. Enzo would say about me.

—He must be tired.

—It doesn't look like he's getting up anytime soon.

—*Egli non puo stare qui.*

—Let the boy sleep a little. He's obviously distraught.

—Why's he wearing a robe? *Che cosa è lui pazzo?*

—He can catch his death out there.

—This is a place of business. We have our customers to think about. *Non sembra buon, Carmella.*

—Nobody's coming in today. Don't get your blood pressure up.

—Should we call the police?

—*Non essere uno sciocco*, Enzo. It's obvious that the boy is not a threat.

—Remember that other harmless guy? Back in '85.

—This is different. Let him sleep. A half hour.

—Need I remind you, Carmella, that he held us up at gunpoint?

—Enzo, this boy is in trouble. He's not going to cause us any.

—I'm calling the police.

—Enzo! No!

—I don't like the look of him.

Enzo's pronouncement was my cue to exit and look for Richard. When I stood up, I stubbed my big toe on the milk crate.

—Where are my sneakers?

—I put them in the oven. They'll be nice and toasty when you put them on.

—I have to get home. What am I saying? I don't have a home.

—You're a little disoriented. Sit down for a minute. Have some minestrone soup.

—Thank you, but I must be going.

—I hope you don't mind, but I took the liberty of calling your wife. She's coming to pick you up.

—My wife?

—Her number was on a piece of paper in your robe. Here it is. I didn't take anything.

—You spoke to Stephanie?

—Stephanie?

—I can't believe you called Stephanie.

—I didn't speak to Stephanie. I spoke to Heather. She sounds like a lovely girl.

—Heather? Heather's coming to get me?

—She's worried about you.

—I can't let her see me this way.

I put on my sneakers without tying the laces, tossed my socks into the trash can and paused in front of the glass display case. The pastries made my mouth water. This must have been what Richard meant by real hunger.

—What's wrong, sweetie?

—I haven't eaten in a long time.

—Would you like something?

—I don't think I have enough money.

—It's on the house. Take some home to your wife.

—This is all I have.

—Don't worry about it, dear.

—*Grazie, signora.*

—What should I tell your *moglie?*

—M*i dispiace.*

I dropped two crumpled dollars and some change on the counter and went back into the storm, bag of cannoli in hand. Just a few steps into my journey, the bag slipped out of my hand and the cannoli splattered onto the curb. I scraped whatever I could out of the gutter and into my grimy hands, kissed it up to God and while I was busy devouring my first meal in a long time, a curious yet enchanting chorus serenaded me: "This way, lonely wanderer. Take joy voyaging onward. No life on earth can be hid from our dreaming." I was mesmerized by the voices of the Sirens, as I had been on the F train the morning I was returning to work. I followed their dulcet sounds, hoping that they were leading me to Richard so I could reunite with Colette. Instead they guided me to a vacant carriage house that was layered in graffiti. I dropped to my knees, stuck my fingers in my ears and instructed my crew to tie me to the ship's mast. By then, the temptresses had concluded their seductive song; however, there was a lone voice, calling out to me. "John, are you all right?" It was good ole Heather, standing over me, resembling the virgin huntress Atalanta with a fake tan and tits and orange glow, prepared to join Jason and the Argonauts on their quest for the Golden Fleece. She placed her hand on my head then rubbed my cheek with the back of her delicate hand.

—I've been following you for blocks. Didn't you hear me calling you?

—I'm looking for my cat.

—Did she run away?

—My friend is watching her for me.

—Is everything okay? I've been worried about you. Teeny told me that he moved back to Ohio and that he didn't know where you were.

—I've been staying with my friend Richard.

—Oh, so you've got a place to stay. I was under the impression—

—Yeah, yeah. Everything's just fine. No need to worry.

—'Cause I got a call from Carmella at the bakery. She said that you were in trouble.

—Nothing's wrong. Does it look like there's anything wrong?

—I'm concerned about you, John. That's all.

—Don't touch me.

—I want to help you. My car is parked just up the block—

—Thanks, but I can take care of myself.

—You're in trouble, and I want to help you.

—I'm okay, Stephanie. Really. Thanks.

—I want to take you home with me. Who's Stephanie?

—I'm looking for Richard. He has my cat.

—Stand up, John. Let's go back to my place and get warmed up.

—My name is Gianni.

—That's a nice name.

—Nobody calls me that though.

—Why's that?

—You can call me Gianni if you'd like.

—Okay. Thank you. Come with me, Gianni.

Heather helped me to my feet. She brushed the mud from my knees, tied my robe, put her arm around my waist, ushered me underneath her umbrella and escorted me to her car.

—I'm feeling much better now. Thank you. I'd better find Richard. I need my cat.

—I'm taking you home with me, sweetie. You'll get your cat later.

—I used to live next door to you. I could see right in your kitchen.

—I think you should stay with me for a few days until you feel better.

—How's your baby?

—She's good.

—Stephanie's baby died.

—I'm sorry to hear that. Who's Stephanie?

—An old friend. And you're my new friend.

—That's right. I am. Get in the car, John.

—I don't know where my baby is.

—I didn't know you had a baby. Let's get you home and fed.

—How's your dog?

—Buffy's fine.

—I bet she likes to be rubbed behind his ears.

—Sure. All dogs like that.

—You really take good care of her.

—Sure, I care about her.

—And you care about me too.

—I do care about you, Gianni. Get in. Come out of the rain.

—It's nice to know that somebody cares about me.

—Well you care about me too. Right? We both care about each other.

—I thought I was alone. But I'm not, am I?

—No, you're not, Gianni. I'm your friend. I'm here for you.

—I know you are. And it's nice to know that somebody is listening to me.

—I'm listening to you, but now I need for you to listen to me. Please get in the car.

I kissed her cheek and walked away. Heather called out to me, but I never looked back. She probably had a sympathetic look on her face, and I couldn't bear to see her pity me. Heather continued to call me then followed me in her car a few blocks before I slipped down an alleyway and lost her. I didn't want Heather to think that I was in trouble. It's rare to find such compassion in a person, but I wasn't capable of receiving Heather's kindness just then.

The wind had finally eased up and the rain had slowed to a drizzle. I walked through the deserted streets of Boerum Hill, past the projects, crying out for Richard and Colette. The shelter Richard stayed in from time to time was tucked away between Popeye's Chicken and an empty lot. The haggard woman at the front desk told me that she hadn't seen Richard in a hundred years, so I made my way up the slope to his favorite corner, Sixth and Union, but he wasn't there. Richard wasn't on the bench in front of the police station either. I stopped in at all his haunts—Cosby's, Lucky Fortune and OTB—but he was nowhere to be found.

Finally, I walked into Tony's Pizzeria on Seventh Avenue and begged for a slice of pizza. Tony gave me a cold slice and poured me a beer too. He was a decent guy.

—Hey Tony, have you seen Richard around?

—You mean the motherfucker who stole my delivery boy's bicycle?

—I'm talking about Richard Pritchard, the homeless guy.

—Yeah, that's the fuckhead. He's been mooching off me for years. And this is how he repays me?

—Do you know where I can find him?

—Yeah, he went back home, and it's a good thing too, 'cause if I found him I'd break both of his legs.

—Home? Do you mean Virginia?

—That's right. He went home to be with his son. Imagine that fuckin' guy has a kid.

—Good for him.

—Good for him? Fuck him and his kid. I want my bike back.

After all these years, Richard had finally made up with his son. Maybe he'd given up the booze and gambling, come clean, even gotten a job delivering pizza on the bike he'd stolen. On one hand, I was happy for Richard; on the other, I was pissed that he took Colette with him. She belonged to me. Then I started to think that maybe he'd sold her or let her go in Prospect Park. Fuck that guy. What did he do with my fucking cat? If he were here, I'd break both of his legs.

BROOKLYN BRIDGE PARK

Just behind the rocks at the shoreline, I sat in the new shack that I built out of the two-by-fours I had stolen from the construction site on York Street. Above me, the Q train rattled across the Manhattan Bridge while an endless stream of cars, trucks and buses crawled across the Brooklyn Bridge. The Circle Line and water taxis harassed the otherwise still East River. A procession of black Mercedes limousines pulled into the River Café's crowded parking lot. Tourists waited in long lines at Grimaldi's Pizzeria and the Ice Cream Factory. On Fulton Ferry Landing, a photographer took pictures of a wedding party that was the size of a football team. I called out to the groom, "Get out while you can."

I wanted to belong to something bigger than my measly shack, but I just couldn't seem to abandon my small existence. It had been a drawn out, agonizing life and no matter how much I wriggled and wailed I feared that I had finally caught up to my past. At this point in my life, I was looking for any sort of movement. Even reverse would have been a welcome change. Teeny's voice was in my head, "Sometimes the way up is down. The way forward is backward." I heard Richard's voice too: "You gotta love yourself a little more." Even Pete made an appearance: "You made decisions not mistakes." I was tired of waiting for something to happen to me while I tried to figure out how to love myself a little more. I just wanted somebody to crush the life out of me with a trash can. End it.

I popped open a warm can of Budweiser and wrote Stephanie a letter.

Dear Stephanie,

It's my birthday and since there won't be any party or cake or even a Barry Manilow cassette, I'll state my wish right now, right here on this page. I wish you were here. But you already know that. I wish I wasn't here. But you already know that too.

That was as far as I got before I tore the note into as many pieces as possible then sprinkled them onto my sweaty face. A few cockamamie theories about my current predicament entered my head, so I turned to a clean page in my notebook and jotted them down before I forgot them.

July 8, 2005

Theory #1

I have been programmed to fail. My parents taught me that I *should not* dream because I *could never* achieve my dream. I wish that, instead of declaring that I *should not* dream, they had instructed that I *could not* dream because then I *would not* have dared to dream. To me *could not* is the same thing as *would not* while *should not* is synonymous with *must never* and for me there has been nothing more intimidating than defying the odds. I *should not* have made any attempts at dreaming because I *should have* known that these attempts *would never* amount to anything. My parents were right all along: dreams don't come true, so now I've stopped dreaming altogether, just hoping for the inevitable to arrive.

Theory #2

I'm stuck in purgatory. It's worse than hell. All my life I've been waiting for something to happen. I've been pretending to be everything I've ever wanted to be: writer, baseball player, musician, salesman, doctor, husband, lover, friend, even father. My fanciful thinking about what might become of me is what has kept me idle. I've been in a continuous state of becoming. I can't seem to

That's as far as I got when I put down my notebook and watched four teenage boys toss empty bottles into the East River. Some skimmed them,

248

some hurled them. One of the smaller boys lost his grip on a bottle, slipping through his fingers, falling behind his head and shattering onto the rocks directly in front of my hut. His clumsiness sent them all into hysterics. Why must teenagers be so loud?

I'd always fancied myself something of a rock-skimming champion. In Staten Island, at the bulkhead where Stephanie and I skimmed rocks in Great Kills Harbor, five, six, seven skips were the norm. After years of practice, I was finally lucky enough to reach eight, a personal best.

For some reason, I felt obligated to pass down my talent to the four rowdy boys, so I put on my robe, crawled out from my humble abode, and began searching for a flat stone. I found the perfect rock—no blemishes, smooth and flat—next to a garbage can just behind the boys. I picked it up, sauntered over to them, and shouted instructions as if I were their head coach.

—First, your rock has to be flat. You'll never be able to skim properly with an oval rock. You must hold it like this. Notice my index finger is high on the rock. Once you do these two things, you'll need to work on your form. You must throw it sideways, skimming the water's surface. You need to get some distance. Too little and the rock will sink. Too much and you'll never even get it to glide. This takes lots and lots of practice and discipline. You'll need to practice just like you would with anything else. It's like hitting a baseball, playing the guitar or writing a play. Practice hard, practice long and practice often.

The boys looked me up and down as if I had just landed from another planet. In my attempt to give the flat stone to the biggest kid, he pulled his hand away and it fell in between the crevices of the boulders we were standing on. I got to my knees and pointed to the place it had fallen. "That was the consummate stone. You didn't have the opportunity to see its flatness. It was a thing of beauty. Never will we find such a flawless stone again, but have no fear, we must not give up our search."

While the boys mocked me, I searched for another ideal stone, stuffing the rejects into the front pockets of my robe and scouring nearly the entire park before finding an adequate stone in the playground underneath the slide. The boys were dismayed by my return. They thought that they had gotten rid of me, but I was feeling vigorous, so I tossed a couple of stones at the feet of the biggest kid and challenged him to a competition.

—Consider this a challenge, my dear boy.

—Mister, this is some lame-ass shit you're talkin' 'bout here.

—That may be so, but let's see what you're made of.

With my throwing arm still in a sling, I could reach neither the proper speed nor the necessary distance, and rather than skim the surface, the rock struck the water and sank. It was nothing like my tosses as a boy. My very limited athletic skills had the boys doubled over in hysterics. They started taunting me, so I pulled out a random rock from my pocket and tossed it. Again, it hit the water's surface and sank. Again, they thought it was the funniest thing they had ever seen.

—Terrible form. It's all in the form. You can toss a flawless rock, but if you don't follow through…well, you see the result: failure. Let's see what you got.

—What are you gonna give me if I win?

—If you can skim that rock just once, I'll give you twenty bucks.

—Twenty bucks?

—Twenty bucks.

—You got it.

The big kid picked up a rock, turned his Yankees cap around, and tossed it. It was a thing of beauty. One, two, three, four, five, six, seven, eight skips. The rock sank. There was applause for the boy, some heckling for me.

—Not bad. Not bad, if I might say so myself. You know, I was once the rock-skimming champion of Staten Island.

—Where's my twenty bucks? Hand it over.

—I don't have it, but here, have my beer.

—It's warm as shit, man. I want my twenty bucks.

—When I was rock-skimming champion—

—There ain't no such thing. You buggin', mister.

—I was once a champ. I have the trophy to prove it.

—Hey, what's with the robe, man?

—I'll tell you. Did you ever wake up and feel like—what's your name?

—Antoine.

—Did you ever wake up, Antoine, and feel like you weren't yourself? You were someone else?

—This shit is wack, yo.

—So I'm not me, and I'm not sure who I am, but whoever I am, it's better than the person I was yesterday because that guy—that guy—

couldn't skim a rock for shit.

—You're trippin', man.

—Yeah, that's right. I'm trippin'.

I picked up a random stone, approached the shoreline, took my stance, concentrated and tossed it into the East River. Again, it hit the water's surface and sank. I was no longer a champion; Antoine held that title now.

—Now give me my trophy.

—Will a handshake do?

—Nah man, I want my trophy and my twenty bucks.

—How about this?

I handed him Stephanie's graduation picture.

—Who's this?

—That's Stephanie.

—Why would I want this shit for?

—She's a goddess.

—You're wack, mister.

—Stephanie can be your good luck charm, your guiding light.

—I never heard of the bitch.

—She'll watch over you, light your way.

—This picture is old.

—It was taken in the eighties.

—What's up with her nose?

—She's beautiful, isn't she? Take her. Please.

—I don't want this shit, old man. I want my twenty bucks and a trophy.

—Will you at least do me a favor?

—What?

—Teach the others how to skim rocks.

—Are you on crack, man?

—It sure feels that way. My name's Gianni.

—We gonna be going, John.

—Gianni.

—Right. Whatever.

As the boys fled the park, they discussed their plans for the evening. A couple wanted to drink beer and watch pornos, while another one just wanted to smoke pot in the park. Antoine suggested they go into Manhattan for blowjobs.

My interaction with the boys had been the only human contact I'd had since Heather tried to take me back to her place about a month ago. I can't say that I enjoyed talking to them. In fact, I was kind of glad they were gone. I had better things to do, like searching the shoreline for rocks.

I filled my pockets with every stone I could find, flat or not. I tied the belt of my robe the best I could with one arm, picked up a brick and stepped into the water. As I moved forward, I looked across the East River at the white lights of the South Street Seaport. A party boat whooped by. People were dancing to swing music on the top and front decks. I took eight steps forward—one, two, three, four, five, six, seven, eight—heard rousing applause and Stephanie's gruff snort. And then I sank. I was finally a brave man.

IN STATEN ISLAND

Well, that's my story. I guess I needed to share it with someone, so it might as well have been you. I've been carrying an enormous weight around for so long, you'd think I'd feel some kind of lightness after spilling my guts to you like I just did. But I don't. I feel kind of violated. Deep down, I'm really a private guy, and for the life of me I don't know why I went ahead and told you my entire history.

The French poet Charles Baudelaire said, "Genius is nothing more or less than childhood recovered at will." I'm pretty sure that I didn't get all the stories straight, and I probably omitted a few events here and there and left out some minor details. I'm no genius but maybe I'm better than third-rate after all. I can live with second-rate.

I've been told that Antoine and his friends fished me out of the East River. Those poor delinquents weren't acknowledged for their bravery. Not even the local rag the *Brooklyn Eagle* covered the story. It's not much of a story, really. PATHETIC DRIFTER RESCUED BY FOUR HOOLIGANS. What if Baudelaire had been a journalist? Then maybe my shenanigans would have made front-page news. SECOND-RATE HOMELESS MAN SAVED BY FOUR BRAVE LADS!

As Havannah the Junkie predicted, I'm recuperating at my childhood home in Staten Island. After voluntarily placing myself in the psych ward at Brooklyn Hospital, I attended group therapy, regurgitating just about everything you heard me blather on about. Six days later, my psychiatrist released me into the custody of my father who picked me up in his Cadillac and brought me here to get better.

Recovery is an ambiguous thing. Honestly, I don't think such a thing really exists, at least not for me. My way of life is somewhat abnormal, so there's no hope that I'll ever return to a normal state. I wouldn't know normality if it struck me across the side of my head. The notion of normalcy is a relative thing, anyway. Addiction, alcoholism, depression, loneliness, alienation, oppression and repression—we take these gifts for granted. They comfort us in a very normal way. When life goes unimpeded, when things function properly and life is routine, healthy and productive— that's when we are at our most dysfunctional. The funny thing about being sick is that I don't remember a time when I wasn't sick.

My mother has been trying to take care of me. "You never could look after yourself, Gianni. That's why I'm here." We revealed a lot of things to each other and that has brought us closer together. She wants me to speak to a professional. I was a babbling fool in the hospital, confiding in doctors and opening up to those other lunatics in the psych ward so I told her that I'd think about it. Get this: my mother is willing to pay for me to go back to college. It's a very generous gesture, but what would a college degree do for me now? And why would I freely choose to sit in a classroom with twenty-year-olds? I'm too old for that kind of shit.

Other than reprimanding me for refusing to get a colonoscopy, my father hasn't said very much to me, though I can tell by the look on his face that he's disappointed. He thinks I'm a weak man. I wonder if he sees himself in me. Maybe he's come face to face with that awful truth, which is my presence makes him uneasy. It's not like I see him all that much anyway. He spends most of his time in the basement, watching horse racing and wrestling on a fifty-two-inch flat-screen television.

My sister, Gina, lives in New Jersey, only an hour away. You'd think she would take time out of her precious life to visit her poor brother, but she said that she's too busy renovating her basement. Gina never liked me, so I guess, in a way I should be grateful that she hasn't stopped by.

Some of my relatives have come by to give me flowers and share the boring details of their boring lives. Never-ending stories of bullshit: the fertilizer has saved our front lawn; our new truck gets twenty-three miles to the gallon; an investment in a new mutual fund has yielded great dividends; we scalped tickets to the Giants game; our favorite television sitcom has been cancelled; we are thrilled to death that a new supermarket is opening on Amboy Road—inane subject matter that offers evidence of my ordinary existence. These visits are painful reminders that I come from the same place they do and that I'm even more pathetic than they are because I still think that I have the potential to become more than mediocre.

I've been spending most of my time in my old bedroom, staring at what used to be Stephanie's bedroom window. I hung up my old Beatles posters and Mets pennants, and now the room looks pretty much the way it did when I was seventeen. It's kind of a relief to know that some things don't have to change. In a strange way, I feel as if I haven't really changed, that I'm still seventeen. I've been scribbling in my notebook, but I don't have anything to say. And I'm okay with that.

Teeny, on the other hand, hasn't stopped writing. He called just the other day to tell me that he has written two full-length plays and that *The Never-Ending Story of Bullshit* is going to be produced in a small theater in Ohio. I'll never see it. I should have told Teeny that I was proud of him. He would have liked that. After Teeny's father passed away, he decided to stay home and care for his frail mother. And he got sober again. Carmen locked Teeny in the bathroom for a week, and when he walked out, he was a new man. Teeny wants me to visit, but I have no desire to see Ohio; it's too flat. I'm partial to hills, peaks, valleys, mountains and slopes.

I gave good ole Heather a call the other night. We shot the breeze for a while about this and that before I got up enough nerve to thank her for trying to help me the day I went looking for Colette in a thunderstorm. Anyway, I promised to take Heather to see Madonna at Madison Square Garden. I know I'm going to hate it, but she'll have fun. At least I'll be surrounded by thousands of good-looking women. And it will be nice to hang out with Heather, of course.

I told my mother that I was going for a walk. It took a bit of cajoling and my promise to be home for lunch before she let me go off by myself. She forced me take her cell phone, but as soon as I got out the door, I turned the damn thing off.

It's a clear morning, the fourth anniversary of September 11, and I'm heading over to Great Kills Harbor. I have a tune in my head. It's something that I've been singing a great deal since I moved back home. But a Mister Softee truck blasting "Pop Goes the Weasel" rolls past me, and I can't recapture the melody to "Can't Find My Way Home."

Most of the folks who settled in this neighborhood in the late sixties as part of "white flight" are either dead now or living in accessible, obvious and unimaginative places like New Jersey, Arizona, Florida and Colorado. I don't recognize the men who wash their automobiles, mow their lawns and paint their houses, but I smile and wave as I pass them.

I stop by my old elementary school and stand in the middle of the courtyard amid bent basketball rims, graffiti, the scent of urine and broken glass. When I was a kid, Alfonse Marino broke into the school on a regular basis, vandalized the classrooms and stole whatever was valuable. Police cars periodically raced into the playground, lights flashing, sirens blaring, kids scattering into the midnight streets. Anthony DiMarco was taken away in handcuffs a few times. This was my idyllic suburban upbringing, a piece of paradise that my parents thought Brooklyn couldn't offer. In the early eighties, there were plenty of crime and drugs in New York, and the suburbs were certainly not exempt. I can't blame my parents for trying to grab their slice of the American Dream, but little did they know Alfonse Marino and Anthony DiMarco were lurking on just about every corner in Staten Island.

The beach hasn't changed much, though it looks as if somebody has taken a rake to the sand, which really isn't sand; it's still just dirt. Some old men are drinking Budweiser from a can while they keep an eye on their fishing lines. Joggers and power walkers appear from various park entrances, making their way up the main road to the beach, where a few older women, slathered in suntan lotion sit on lounge chairs, reading tabloid magazines and worshipping the sun. A park employee is picking up debris.

The lifeguard, a blond boy in a red Speedo, probably no more than seventeen years old, is hiding behind his Ray-Bans, staring off into the Atlantic. Even though it's been a hundred years since medical waste was dumped offshore, another hundred years are needed before the ocean will be clean enough for swimming. This kid has the cushiest job in the world. Maybe when I'm feeling better I'll get a job as lifeguard. I am intimately familiar with the chair and the ocean. I'd like to kick the pretty boy out of the chair and reclaim my throne, but he could probably beat the shit out of me. Besides, my arm is now in a cast, and I don't want to go back to the hospital.

I try to skim a rock, but it just sinks. My wedding ring falls off my finger and plops into the shallow water. I no longer have the toss of a champion. I'm not sure that I ever did, but it was nice to think that I was good at something. I pick up the ring and slip it on and off my finger. To think that I once went looking for it on the subway tracks. Here I am, standing before the Atlantic Ocean with the Verrazano Bridge in the distance, clutching a relic of my past. Skimming the ring will not suffice, so I throw it as far as I can. It sinks. I applaud my accomplishment, and the lifeguard gives me a funny look. "Some toss. Did you see that? Not bad for an old man."

I wonder how my memories of these past three years will evolve. I like to think that I'll eventually forget the details of such an unfortunate stretch in my life, but I don't think I ever will. I'm damned, for sure.

Before I go home, I stop next door at Stephanie's old house and shamelessly peer inside the front window. Nobody is home. The living room is filled with baby toys, but I can picture Stephanie sitting at the dining room table between her mother and Joey, who has his arm around her shoulder, a birthday cake set down before her. After Stephanie died, her mother moved away. I heard she bought a cabin in the woods somewhere in Pennsylvania. I reach into my pocket for Stephanie's graduation picture, which is kind of creased and wrinkled now, but there she is, looking the way she always has, the way I'll always remember her. I slip the photograph inside a copy of J.D. Salinger's *Franny and Zooey*—the present I had got for her eighteenth birthday—and drop it in the mailbox. I start thinking about Emma, Dawn, Teeny, Heather, Richard, Pete, Havannah even Colette. Everybody I have loved over the past three years. Just because they are no longer in my life doesn't mean that the love is no longer there. Stephanie believed such nonsense and tried to brainwash me with her never-ending bullshit. Maybe it's not nonsense after all. To tell the truth, it looks like some of it has rubbed off on me.

I have to get home now. My mother probably made lunch—a Cobb salad or something good for me like that. She knows I hate salads.

ABOUT THE AUTHOR

Richard Fulco received an MFA in Playwriting from Brooklyn College. His plays have been either presented or developed at The New York International Fringe Festival, The Playwrights' Center, The Flea, Here Arts Center, Chicago Dramatists and the Dramatists Guild. His stories, reviews and interviews have appeared in *The Brooklyn Rail, Failbetter, Front Porch, Bound Off, The Rusty Toque, Full of Crow, Nth Position, The Daily Vault* and *American Songwriter*. He is the founder of the online music magazine Riffraf. *There Is No End to This Slope* is his first novel.

NORTH CENTRAL MICHIGAN COLLEGE

3 8624 01726 7690

33622184R00153

Made in the USA
Lexington, KY
02 July 2014